The Mistletoe Express

Mistletoe Falls Series, Book #3

TARA BAISDEN

STERLING RIDGE PRESS LLC

Copyright

The Mistletoe Express © 2025 by Tara Baisden

All rights reserved. No part of this book may be reproduced, distributed, or transmitted in any form or by any means, including photocopying, recording, or other electronic or mechanical methods, without the prior written permission of the author, except in the case of brief quotations embodied in critical reviews and certain other noncommercial uses permitted by copyright law.

This is a work of fiction. Names, characters, places, and incidents either are the product of the author's imagination or are used fictitiously. Any resemblance to actual persons, living or dead, events, or locales is entirely coincidental.

Cover designed by Sterling Ridge Press LLC

Published by: Sterling Ridge Press, LLC www.sterling ridgepress.com

ISBN: 978-1-966093-38-1 Printed in the United States of America

First Edition: October 2025

For permissions, contact: tara@tarabaisden.com or visit www.tarabaisden.com

Dedication

For everyone who's ever felt like they were wandering—
may you find your Mistletoe Falls.
For those still grieving what was—
may you find the courage to build what could be.
For anyone who's been told their dreams are too small
or their heart too big—
may you discover that the best journeys
lead you home to yourself.
And for my own found family—
you taught me that belonging isn't earned,
it's simply recognized.
This one's for all of us still learning
that staying can be braver than leaving,
that growth honors the past instead of erasing it,
and that love—real love—
is always worth the risk.

With mistletoe and magic,
Tara

P.S. To anyone who's ever ugly-cried,
talked to their dog like a therapist,
or eaten an entire pizza while making life-changing decisions—
I see you. This book is also for you.

Contents

Chapter 1

Sadie Baker eased her foot off the accelerator as her SUV climbed higher into the Smoky Mountains, the late October afternoon sun slanting through clouds that hadn't quite committed to winter yet, even though a few snowflakes were falling gently. Below, in the valleys she'd left behind, a few trees still blazed with autumn color. Up here, though, frost had already kissed the evergreens, and the mountain air carried the sharp promise of colder days ahead.

Sadie had driven this route before—exactly one year ago, when she'd spent three days in Mistletoe Falls documenting the town's Christmas traditions for a travel magazine feature. She'd arrived in November, stayed just long enough to conduct interviews and take photographs, and left with a hefty paycheck and one small souvenir she hadn't been able to resist.

This time, everything she owned was packed in the back of her SUV.

The GPS announced her approach to Mistletoe Falls with its usual bland efficiency, but Sadie didn't need the reminder. She knew the moment she crossed into the town's territory because the road changed—from standard mountain highway to something that felt deliberately enchanted. Scenic Route 265 had been christened Hollyberry Lane somewhere in the last mile, and the road began to narrow a bit.

The road curved slightly, and there it was.

The Snowbell Covered Bridge stretched across Mistletoe Creek like something out of a storybook that had decided to become three-dimensional just for her. The weathered wood glowed in the afternoon light, but it was the decorations that made Sadie's breath catch—evergreen garland draped along the entrance arch, twinkling lights woven through the greenery, and a hand-painted sign that read "Welcome Home to Mistletoe Falls."

Not "Welcome to Mistletoe Falls." Welcome home.

Sadie's hands tightened on the steering wheel as the SUV's tires rumbled onto the bridge's wooden planks. Through the openwork sides, she caught glimpses of the creek below, its water dark and swift as it tumbled over smooth stones worn round by decades of mountain runoff. The covered bridge filtered the afternoon light into stripes of gold and shadow that played across her dashboard, and for just a moment Sadie let herself believe the signs' promise.

Maybe this time, she actually was coming home.

Mistletoe Falls spread out before her exactly as she remembered, only somehow more—more charming, more magical, more impossibly perfect than any place had a right to be. The Welcome Pavilion appeared first on her right, its candy cane striping bright against the mountain backdrop. The hand-carved wooden sign 'Welcome to Mistletoe Falls—Home of the Christmas Spirit' stood beneath an archway of lights that would blaze to life come evening.

Hollyberry Lane became Mistletoe Lane as she entered the town proper, and suddenly Sadie was driving through a Christmas card that didn't care it was still October. The maple trees lining the street had turned brilliant shades of orange and gold, their few remaining leaves catching the late afternoon sun. Shop windows displayed tasteful combinations of fall harvest themes and Christmas decor. Pumpkins nestled beside miniature evergreen trees. Cornucopias shared window space with wreaths tied with burgundy velvet bows.

The buildings themselves looked like they'd been designed by someone who understood that architecture could tell stories. Two-and three-story brick structures lined Mistletoe Lane, their facades preserved from another era but clearly well-maintained. Hand-carved details decorated doorways and window frames. Striped awnings in hunter green, burgundy, and cream stretched over wide brick sidewalks that invited leisurely strolls.

Gas lampposts stood at regular intervals. Sadie could picture how they'd look in full darkness—warm pools of light creating the kind of atmosphere that made people slow down, look around, and actually see each other.

The town square opened up on her left as Mistletoe Lane curved gently around it. The Victorian gazebo at its center stood exactly as she remembered—white paint gleaming, its ornate trim work preserved with obvious care. Ancient oak trees framed the square, their branches reaching overhead like natural architecture. Wooden benches positioned beneath the trees each bore small brass plaques, though Sadie was too far away to read what they said.

She remembered from her previous visit that each bench was dedicated to a beloved community member who'd helped shape Mistletoe Falls into what it was today. The town didn't just remember its history—it wove that history into daily life, making the past a living presence rather than something preserved behind glass.

Sadie guided her SUV around the square, following Mistletoe Lane until it intersected with another street marked by a hand-painted sign: Icicle Lane. She turned right, her heart beating faster as she recognized the corner building ahead.

Holly House Bed & Breakfast rose three stories on the corner of Icicle Lane and Mistletoe Lane, its Victorian gables and wraparound porch exactly as inviting as the website photos had promised. The lovely B&B was already decorated for the Christmas season, as was every other place in this Christmas tourist town. Evergreen wreaths hung on every window, each tied with the same burgundy velvet bows she'd seen throughout town. White lights traced the porch railings and wrapped around the columns supporting the second-story overhang.

A small parking area sat to the side of the building, currently empty except for one older sedan. Sadie pulled into a spot, cut the engine, and sat for a long moment with her hands still gripping the wheel.

This was it. The beginning of her twelve-week trial period as Tourism Development Coordinator for Mistletoe Falls. Twelve weeks to prove to Martha Caldwell, the mayor, and the town council that she deserved the permanent position. Twelve weeks to show everyone—including herself—that she could be more than a freelance journalist chasing stories in other people's hometowns.

Twelve weeks to finally stop traveling and moving constantly and call some place home.

The notification email had arrived three weeks ago, buried between spam with credit card offers and a pitch from a magazine editor looking for holiday content. Sadie had almost deleted it without reading. "RE: Tourism Coordinator Position—Application Status" could have meant anything, and she'd learned not to hope too hard.

But something had coursed through her just before opening the email—a slight tingling of excitement. Maybe it was the fact that she'd applied to Mistletoe Falls specifically, after her visit last year had left her thinking about the town long after she'd filed her article and moved on to the next assignment. Maybe it was the timing, coming just as her lease in Nashville was up for renewal and she'd been trying to decide if she wanted to sign another six-month contract or finally admit she didn't care for the city.

"The Mistletoe Falls Tourism Board is pleased to offer you a twelve-week trial contract as Tourism Development Coordinator, beginning November 1st. Permanent employment will be contingent upon successful completion of the trial period and town council approval."

She'd read it five times before her hands started shaking.

Now, sitting in the parking lot of Holly House with everything she owned packed in her SUV, Sadie wondered if she'd made a terrible mistake.

What did she know about staying in one place? She'd spent seven years perfecting the art of temporary—temporary assignments, temporary sublets, temporary connections that never demanded more than she could give before packing her bags. She knew how to arrive in a new town, charm her interview subjects, write compelling stories about their lives, and leave.

She was twenty-nine years old, and she'd lived out of suitcases more often than she'd unpacked into drawers.

A rap on her window made her jump hard enough to hit her elbow on the center console.

A woman stood beside her SUV, bundled in a puffy jacket the color of cranberries, with auburn curls escaping from beneath a knit hat decorated with snowflakes.

Her smile was wide and slightly crooked, the kind that scrunched up her whole face with genuine delight.

Sadie opened the door and climbed out, her legs stiff from three hours of driving.

"You must be Sadie Baker!" The woman didn't wait for confirmation before stepping forward with outstretched arms. "I'm Abby Miller. Welcome to Holly House!"

Before Sadie could prepare herself, she was wrapped in a hug that smelled like vanilla and cinnamon. The embrace was brief but surprisingly comfortable, as if Abby had decided they were going to be friends and saw no point in wasting time on formality.

"I hope the drive wasn't too difficult," Abby said as she stepped back, though she kept one hand on Sadie's arm. "The mountain roads can be tricky sometimes to newcomers."

"The drive was fine. Beautiful, actually. I'd forgotten how stunning the fall colors could be in this area."

"Oh, you've been to Mistletoe Falls before?" Abby's eyes—a warm brown that matched her general aura of coziness—lit up with interest.

"Last year, for a magazine piece." Sadie pulled her jacket tighter against the October chill that felt sharper up here than it had in Nashville. "I spent a few days interviewing residents about Christmas traditions for a travel feature."

"That's right! I remember Martha mentioning something about that when she signed the lease on the apartment for you." Abby gestured toward the B&B with obvious pride. "I would have remembered if you'd stayed here during your last visit, though. I never forget a guest."

"I stayed at the Christmas Inn on the other side of town."

"Oh, Margaret's place. Lovely woman, makes the best pumpkin bread you'll ever taste." Abby linked her arm through Sadie's with the same casual affection she'd shown with the hug, as if they'd known each other for years instead of three minutes. "Well, you're staying at Holly House now, which means you get my pumpkin bread, and I'm not saying it's better than Margaret's, but I'm not saying it's worse either. Come on, let's get you inside and settled. You must be exhausted from driving."

Sadie found herself being gently guided toward the front porch, too surprised by Abby's warmth and friendliness to protest. This was exactly the kind of immediate, uncomplicated welcome she'd never quite known how to handle—the assumption of friendship before she'd done anything to earn it, the casual touch from someone who didn't know her well enough to know if she liked being touched, the invitation into spaces both physical and emotional before she'd proven she deserved access.

Her father would have been horrified by such informality.

The thought made Sadie relax slightly into Abby's companionable grip.

The interior of Holly House was even lovelier in person than the photographs had suggested. Gleaming hardwood floors reflected the soft lamplight, their shine broken only by braided rugs in cheerful holiday colors. A graceful staircase curved upward, its polished banister strung with evergreen garland and tiny gold bows. Everywhere, the house seemed to hum with quiet warmth—the subtle scent of baking bread drifted from the kitchen, mingling with a hint of cinnamon that clung to the air. In the front parlor, a tall Christmas tree stood proudly near the fireplace, its branches dressed in glass ornaments and delicate ribbons, twinkling lights casting patterns across the walls like stars brought indoors. A quilt draped across the back of a sofa suggested the house was not only beautiful but also lived in and loved.

They climbed the stairs to the second floor, where Sadie glimpsed a hallway with several doors—guest rooms, she assumed—and continued up a narrower staircase to the third floor.

"Your apartment's just through here," Abby said, producing a key from her jacket pocket and unlocking a door at the end of the hallway. "There's another apartment at the other end of this hallway. It's empty right now, so you'll have the floor to yourself. Each apartment has its own entrance from the back porch too, with stairs going down to the parking area, so you can come and go as you please without going through the B&B."

She pushed open the door and stepped aside to let Sadie enter first.

The apartment was small—Sadie had known that from the listing—but it was the kind of small that felt cozy rather than cramped. Slanted ceilings followed the roofline, with exposed beams that had been painted white. A dormer window looked out over the town square, its cushioned window seat perfect for reading or simply watching life unfold below.

The main room held a loveseat upholstered in soft gray, a small dining table with two chairs, and a bookshelf built into one wall. An open doorway revealed a compact kitchenette—a small fridge, two-burner stove, small oven, and a window with a small pot of herbs on the sill. Another door led to what Sadie assumed was the bedroom.

"It's perfect," Sadie said, and meant it.

She'd stayed in enough generic hotel rooms and hastily sublet apartments to recognize something special when she saw it. This space had been furnished with care by someone who understood the difference between a place to sleep and a place to live. The loveseat looked comfortable enough for long evenings. The dining table was positioned to catch light from the dormer window. Small touches—a soft throw blanket draped over the loveseat's arm, a basket of pinecones on the bookshelf, watercolor paintings of mountain landscapes on the walls—suggested someone had thought about what would make a temporary resident feel at home.

"I'm so glad you think so." Abby's smile softened into something more genuine than her earlier exuberance. "I know it's not huge, but I tried to make it feel welcoming. The bedroom's through that door—double bed, dresser, and a closet. I put fresh towels on the rack in the bathroom this morning."

She walked to the kitchenette and opened the refrigerator. "I stocked some basics—milk, eggs, bread, butter, and a few other things to get you started. There's coffee in the cupboard above the stove, and I left my grandmother's recipe for pumpkin bread on the counter if you want to try making it yourself. Fair warning, though—it's addictive."

"You didn't have to do all that."

"I know I didn't have to." Abby closed the fridge and turned to face her, and for just a moment, her warm expression carried a hint of something more serious. "But I wanted to. You're new in town, starting a job that I'm guessing feels pretty high-pressure, and you probably don't know anyone here yet. The least I can do is make sure you have coffee and eggs for your first morning."

Abby crossed to the dining table and picked up a small card. "My number's on here if you need anything. And I mean anything—questions about the apartment, recommendations for where to get the best breakfast in town, someone to talk to if you're feeling homesick or overwhelmed or just want company. I'm usually around, and I'm a good listener."

Sadie took the card, her throat tight. "Thank you."

"You're welcome." Abby headed for the door, then paused with her hand on the frame. "Oh, and just so you know—on Thursday nights there's usually a group of us who get together at The Cozy Cup for coffee and conversation. Nothing formal, just friends catching up. You'd be welcome to join if you want. Caroline—she owns the cafe—makes this incredible caramel apple cider this time of year."

"I'll think about it," Sadie said.

But Abby just smiled like she'd heard the real answer underneath the polite deflection. "The invitation stands whenever you're ready. See you later, Sadie. Welcome home."

She closed the door softly behind her, and Sadie stood alone in her new apartment, listening to Abby's footsteps fade down the staircase.

Welcome home.

Sadie pushed the thought away and headed back down to her SUV. It took three trips to haul up the essentials: her laptop bag and work materials, her largest suitcase with clothes and toiletries, and the carefully wrapped box she'd placed in the back seat rather than trusting to the cargo area.

By the time she'd made the final trip, dusk had settled over Mistletoe Falls. Through the dormer window, she could see the gas lamps had come to life along Mistletoe Lane, creating those warm pools of light she'd imagined earlier. The Victorian gazebo in the town square glowed softly, and the shops along the street sparkled with twinkling lights that seemed to be woven into every available surface in the town.

Sadie carefully unwrapped the packing tape on the box. Inside, nested in layers of bubble wrap and tissue paper, were her Christmas ornaments.

She'd started collecting them without really meaning to. Seven years ago, fresh out of college and desperate to build a portfolio that would lead to steady work, she'd taken an assignment covering a small-town Christmas festival in Vermont. The piece had paid terribly, but it had run in a regional magazine with decent circulation, and the town's gift shop had sold hand-blown glass ornaments that caught the light like captured snowflakes.

Sadie had bought one even though she'd had no tree to hang it on, no permanent address to ship it to, and no reason to carry extra things in her already over-stuffed backpack except that it was beautiful, and she'd wanted to remember the way the festival had made her feel—like she was witnessing something precious that other people took for granted.

Over the years, the collection had grown. A carved wooden reindeer from a craftsman in Montana she'd interviewed for a holiday market story. A painted tin star from a Texas town where she'd spent Thanksgiving documenting small-town celebrations. A ceramic snowman from Wisconsin. A beaded icicle from a craft fair in Maine. Each ornament represented a story, a place, or a moment of connection before she'd packed her bags and driven away.

They'd traveled with her through seven years and a dozen cities, each one wrapped in tissue paper and tucked into dividers she'd fashioned from cardboard. She'd never had a tree to hang them on, never stayed anywhere long enough to justify the space and effort of holiday decorations. But she'd kept them anyway—these fragments of other people's Christmas traditions, these small pieces of belonging she'd collected without ever claiming any belonging of her own.

Now, in the fading light of her new apartment, Sadie unwrapped them one by one and lined them up on the windowsill, where they caught the last rays of sunset.

The Vermont angel with its delicate glass wings. The Montana reindeer, his carved antlers surprisingly detailed. The Texas star with its folk art charm. The Wisconsin snowman with his jaunty carrot nose. The Maine icicle sparkled like real ice in the right light.

And finally, wrapped in its own small box within the larger one, was the ornament she'd bought last year from a shop on Mistletoe Lane during her three-day visit here.

Sadie lifted it carefully, holding it up to catch the light from the window.

The glass snowflake was no bigger than her palm, but the artisan who'd created it had somehow managed to capture the delicate, impossible geometry of actual snow crystals. Each arm of the snowflake branched into smaller arms, those into smaller still, creating patterns that looked random but weren't. Light caught in the glass and fractured into tiny rainbows that danced across her hands.

She'd found it in a shop called "The Christmas Shop," run by a brother and sister duo who'd told her the snowflakes were made by a local artisan. He'd learned glassblowing from his grandfather and sold his work in galleries and gift shops across the Southeast. "But he always makes sure we have the biggest selection here in our store," the woman had said. "Because Mistletoe Falls is home."

Sadie had bought the snowflake even though she'd had no tree for it, even though her budget was already stretched thin, and even though carrying around a fragile glass ornament while traveling for work made no practical sense. She'd wrapped it carefully, and it had made the journey from Mistletoe Falls to Nashville.

It had seemed like a promise at the time—a whisper of possibility that maybe, someday, she'd find a place that felt like more than just another assignment.

Now she set it on the windowsill in the center of the other ornaments, creating a small gallery of places she'd documented but never claimed as home. The irony wasn't lost on her—a collection of other people's Christmas traditions, preserved in glass and wood and ceramic, belonging to no tree, no tradition, no home of her own.

But maybe that could change. Maybe this time, in this town that had already welcomed her twice with those two simple words, she could finally start building one of her own.

Her phone buzzed in her pocket, making her jump.

She pulled it out to find a text from Martha Caldwell.

Looking forward to Monday morning and meeting you in person. Be prepared to hit the ground running. See you at 9 AM sharp.

Sadie read the message twice, her thumb hovering over the keyboard as she considered her response. Professional but warm? Confident but not overeager? She'd spent so many years crafting the perfect professional persona that sometimes she forgot what her actual personality felt like underneath all the careful presentation.

She typed, *"Looking forward to it. Thank you for this opportunity."*

Short. Professional. Safe.

The message showed as delivered, and Sadie set her phone on the windowsill beside the ornaments. Through the glass, she watched the town square settle into evening. A few people strolled along the brick sidewalks, bundled against the October chill. Lights glowed in shop windows. Somewhere in the distance, church bells chimed the hour.

The Mistletoe Falls snowflake caught the light from the gas lamps, throwing tiny rainbows across the growing darkness.

Twelve weeks, she thought, pressing her palm against the cool glass. *Twelve weeks to prove I deserve this job. Twelve weeks to show I can be more than just someone passing through, collecting stories and ornaments, and moving on before anyone expects me to stay.*

Twelve weeks to figure out what home was supposed to feel like.

Chapter 2

T he brass fitting gleamed in the fading October light, but Cole Bennett ran his cloth over it one more time anyway, the way he'd done every Saturday evening for the past four years—the way his father had done for thirty years before that.

"Good enough, boss?" Charlie Dawson called from the passenger car doorway, broom in hand and hope in his voice that suggested he'd been ready to leave twenty minutes ago.

Cole straightened, feeling the familiar protest in his lower back from hours spent bent over machinery and track. "Did you check the floor under the seats?"

"Twice."

"And the brass handrails?"

"Polished until I could see my face in them." Charlie grinned, unbothered by Cole's thoroughness. The kid had been volunteering at the depot since he was fourteen, long enough to understand that Cole Bennett didn't do anything halfway. "It's almost dark, Mr. Bennett. Even you have to eat sometime."

Cole glanced toward the mountains, where the sun was sliding behind the peaks and painting the sky in shades of amber and rose. The temperature was dropping fast. It would probably hit freezing tonight. He should check the heating system in the museum one more time and make sure the thermostats were set properly.

"Go home, Charlie," Cole said. "Your mom's most likely holding dinner."

"You sure? I can stay and help with whatever you're—"

"I'm done here. Just need to lock up."

The lie came easily. He wouldn't be done for another hour at least, not with the safety inspection checklist still waiting in his office and the maintenance log that needed updating. But Charlie had a calculus test on Monday and a life that shouldn't revolve around a train depot the way Cole's did.

After the teenager left with a cheerful wave, Cole stood alone on the platform as twilight deepened around him. The depot behind him glowed with warm light from the lanterns mounted on the building, gas lamps converted to electricity but maintaining their original character, making the building look like something from a Christmas card.

The Mistletoe Express sat silent on its track, the dark green paint nearly black in the fading light. She was a beauty—an 1880s steam locomotive rescued from abandonment in a rail yard outside of town. Thirty-five years ago, Cole's father had taken on the painstaking restoration, first hired to bring her back to life and later entrusted with turning her into the heart of Mistletoe Falls' holiday magic.

Cole walked the length of the train, his boots echoing on the wooden platform. He trailed his fingers along her side, feeling the smooth paint over cold metal, checking for any imperfections his eyes might have missed. The passenger cars were immaculate, with their windows gleaming, their brass fixtures reflecting the depot lights. The observation car at the rear sat ready for tomorrow's afternoon scenic ride, its glass panels spotless.

Everything was exactly as it should be. Exactly as his father would have expected.

Cole pulled his pocket watch from his vest. The cover was warm from his body heat; the brass was worn smooth in places from decades of handling. He flipped it open, the familiar weight settling in his palm like a handshake from a ghost.

Six forty-five. Later than he'd thought.

He stared at the inscription inside the cover, the words his father had engraved there when he'd given the watch to Cole on his eighteenth birthday shortly after he began working beside him at the train station: *Time moves forward - M.B. to C.B.*

Michael Bennett to Cole Bennett. A message that had seemed profound then, though Cole had been too young to understand what his father had really meant. Now, standing alone on a depot platform at thirty years old with nothing but a dog waiting at home, he wondered if his father would be proud or disappointed to see how thoroughly Cole had stopped time from moving forward at all.

He closed the watch with a soft click and tucked it back into his vest pocket before heading inside.

His office occupied a small room off the main ticketing hall, its walls lined with filing cabinets and shelves crammed with maintenance manuals, historical documents, and three decades' worth of operational logs. His father's old desk dominated the space—solid oak scarred by years of use, its surface organized with the precision of someone who believed chaos was just unacceptable.

Cole sank into the leather chair and pulled out the maintenance log, flipping to the current week's entry. He recorded the day's work in his neat, precise handwriting: brake inspection completed, all systems nominal. Boiler pressure tested, within acceptable range. Passenger car cleaning finished; seats and floors spotless. Brass polished, wood treated, glass cleaned.

The same entries he'd made last Saturday. And the Saturday before that. And the one before that.

He should feel satisfied. The Express was in perfect condition, ready for another week of scenic rides and school tours. The depot was immaculate, the museum displays were properly maintained, and every safety protocol had been followed to the letter.

Instead, he felt hollow.

Cole pushed away from the desk and walked through the depot's main hall, his footsteps echoing in the empty space. The ticketing counter stretched along one wall, its oak surface polished to a shine. Behind it, shelves held ledgers dating back to the depot's founding in 1892. Historical photographs lined the walls—images of the original station, of trains long since scrapped, and of men in conductor's uniforms who'd been dead for generations.

And there, in the place of honor above the restored ticket window, hung the photograph that mattered most: his father standing beside the newly restored Express on the day they'd first fired her up after years of restoration work. Michael Bennett's smile was enormous, his arm around Cole's young shoulders, both of them covered in grease and grinning like they'd won the lottery.

Cole stopped beneath the photograph, tilting his head back to study his father's face. How many times had he stood in this exact spot, looking for guidance or approval or just the comfort of a familiar image? Too many to count.

Cole locked up the depot with his usual systematic efficiency, checking each door twice, setting the security system, and making sure the exterior lights were on their timers. The walk to his cabin followed a narrow path that wound through the woods behind the depot, just visible in the moonlight filtering through the bare branches overhead.

The cabin appeared after a quarter mile, its outline familiar enough that Cole could have navigated there blind. He'd had it built five years ago, shortly after Sarah had left, choosing the location specifically for its proximity to the depot and its distance from everything else. Close enough to walk to work in a few minutes. Far enough that he could live a life of peace and quiet.

Cash met him at the door, the three-year-old rescue dog's entire body wiggling with enthusiasm. The golden-brown fur was warm under Cole's hand as he scratched behind the dog's ears.

"Yeah, I missed you too," Cole muttered, stepping inside and letting the door close behind him.

The cabin's interior was exactly as he'd left it that morning—bed made with military precision, kitchen counter clear of clutter, boots lined up beside the door. The main room held a leather sofa that Cash had claimed as his own, a coffee table stacked with railroad history books, and a stone fireplace where Cole had already laid kindling for tonight's fire.

Cole hung his jacket on the hook by the door and moved through his evening routine with the same methodical efficiency he brought to everything else. He lit the fire, fed Cash, and started dinner—chicken breast and vegetables because it was Saturday and that's what he always made on Saturdays.

While the chicken cooked, he stood at the kitchen window and looked out toward the dark woods. Somewhere beyond the trees, the depot's lights would still be glowing. He'd left them on timers, the way he always did, so the building would never sit in complete darkness. So it would look welcoming even when it was empty.

Cash nudged his hand, and Cole realized he'd been standing motionless for several minutes, staring at nothing. He finished cooking, plated the food, and settled on the sofa with Cash sprawled across his feet and a documentary about the transcontinental railroad playing on the television.

He'd seen this one before. Watched it at least a dozen times. But the familiarity was the point—no surprises, no challenges, no reminders that the rest of the world kept changing while he stood still.

His phone buzzed halfway through dinner. A text from Martha Caldwell:

Don't forget Monday's meeting at 9. Looking forward to introducing you to our new Tourism Development Coordinator.

Cole stared at the message longer than necessary, the knot of tension he'd been ignoring all week tightening in his shoulders. He'd almost forgotten about the new hire. He'd almost convinced himself that Martha's brief mention last week had been theoretical rather than imminent.

New coordinator, he typed back. *Didn't realize you'd made a final decision.*

The response came quickly:

The trial period starts on Monday. Twelve weeks to prove herself. A very talented young woman with excellent credentials and a fresh perspective. You'll work closely with her on all Express-related initiatives.

Fresh perspective. The words sat in his stomach like stones.

Cole set his phone aside and tried to focus on the documentary, but his mind kept returning to Martha's text. A trial period meant they weren't sure about her yet, which was something. Twelve weeks wasn't permanent. And if this new coordinator had "fresh ideas" that threatened what his father had built, Cole would simply make sure those ideas went nowhere.

He'd done it before. Last year, when the previous tourism coordinator had suggested modernizing the depot's signage. Two years ago, a consultant had proposed changing the Express's routes to include "more dramatic" scenery. And again six months ago, when someone had floated the idea of themed rides beyond the traditional Christmas programming.

Every time, Cole had stood firm. Explained patiently why the current system worked. Demonstrated through meticulous record-keeping that innovation wasn't necessary when tradition was already successful. The Express didn't need fixing because it wasn't broken.

His father's vision didn't need improving because it was already perfect.

Cash shifted position, draping himself more completely across Cole's feet as if to pin him in place. On the television, the documentary narrator discussed the challenges of maintaining historical railways in modern times—the balance between preservation and progress, and the tension between honoring the past and building for the future. Cole reached for the remote and changed the channel.

By ten o'clock, he'd completed his evening routine—dishes washed and put away, fire banked for the night, teeth brushed, and tomorrow's clothes laid out. He stood in his bedroom doorway for a moment, looking at the space that had become his refuge. The bed was perfectly made. The dresser held his father's old pocket watch stand, empty now because Cole kept the watch with him always. A single photograph sat on the nightstand: the Bennett family at Christmas, taken the year before his father died. Everyone smiling, everyone together, everyone unaware that the following year, everything would shatter.

Cole climbed into bed with Cash settling on the rug beside him, the dog's breathing evening out almost immediately. But Cole lay awake, staring at the ceiling and trying to ignore the knot of tension that had been building all week—ever since Martha had mentioned the new coordinator would be starting Monday, someone young and enthusiastic with "fresh ideas for increasing tourism for the entire town."

Fresh ideas. In Cole's experience, that was code for someone who didn't understand the first thing about what really mattered. Someone who would look at the Mistletoe Express and see a project to fix rather than a legacy to protect. Someone who would want to change things that had worked perfectly well for decades, who would dismiss tradition as outdated, and who would push for innovation that would strip away everything that mattered.

Probably someone who would leave after a few months when they realized small-town Tennessee wasn't exciting enough.

Cole closed his eyes and tried to empty his mind, to find the blank quietness that usually came easily. But tonight, sleep felt impossible. Tomorrow he'd conduct two scenic rides, each one running with the precision that had become his trademark. On Monday morning, he'd sit through a meeting where some eager newcomer would probably pitch ideas about social media marketing and interactive exhibits and other ways to complicate what should remain beautifully, necessarily simple.

And somehow, he'd have to maintain his patience. Protect his father's vision. Keep everything exactly as it should be.

The pocket watch sat on his nightstand, its ticking barely audible but present enough that Cole could track it if he concentrated. Time moves forward.

Outside, the wind picked up, rattling the nearly bare branches against the cabin's exterior. Cash twitched in his sleep, chasing some dream-rabbit through dream-woods. And Cole lay awake in the darkness, his jaw tight and his shoulders tense, already preparing for a battle he suspected would start in less than thirty-six hours.

Twelve weeks. He could manage twelve weeks. The trial period would expose whatever weaknesses this new coordinator had, and by January, everything would return to normal. The Express would continue running exactly as it should, the depot would maintain its historical integrity, and Cole would still be here, keeping his father's promise.

Some people might call that being stuck. Cole called it loyalty.

Chapter 3

Sadie arrived at Town Hall seven minutes early, which felt like exactly the right amount of time—punctual without seeming overeager, professional without being rigid.

The building occupied a prominent corner on Pine Cone Pass and Icicle Lane, a short walk from the B&B. A three-story brick structure that managed to look both official and welcoming—harder to pull off than it sounded. The words "Mistletoe Falls Town Hall - Est. 1892" were carved into the stone archway above the entrance, and two fresh evergreen wreaths hung on the front doors.

She'd spent yesterday settling into her apartment and exploring the town on foot, mapping out the businesses along Mistletoe Lane and familiarizing herself with the layout of the town. She'd even ventured down to the train depot and stood on the platform for a few minutes, studying the Mistletoe Express, its dark green paint gleaming in the afternoon sun.

Now, smoothing down the front of her wool coat, Sadie pushed through the door into Town Hall.

The interior was precisely what she'd expected from a small-town municipal building: polished wood floors, high ceilings with exposed beams, and walls lined with historical photographs and community announcements. A grand staircase curved upward to the second floor, its banister decorated with what looked like hand-carved acorns and oak leaves.

"Sadie!"

Martha Caldwell emerged from a hallway to the right, moving with the brisk efficiency of someone who had places to be and very little patience for people who wasted time. She was exactly as Sadie remembered from their video call—petite but commanding, with silver hair pinned in an elegant twist and stylish glasses perched on her nose. She wore a burgundy wool skirt and cream sweater, with a holiday brooch shaped like a Christmas tree pinned to her lapel.

"Good morning, Martha." Sadie managed what she hoped was a confident smile rather than a nervous one. "I hope I'm not too early."

"Early is exactly on time." Martha's expression softened into something that might have been approval. "Mayor Hayes is waiting upstairs. He's eager to officially welcome you to the team." She paused, then added in a tone that suggested this information was important: "Cole Bennett is already here as well."

Sadie's stomach did something complicated. She'd studied the organizational chart Martha had sent last week, so she knew Cole Bennett was the lead conductor and operations manager of the Mistletoe Express—which meant he'd be her primary collaborator on all the tourism initiatives centered around the train. But she hadn't expected to meet him on her first day, and certainly not in the mayor's office.

"I thought we'd do introductions right away," Martha said, already heading toward the staircase. "Get everyone on the same page from the start. The Express will be central to your work here during your twelve-week trial period, and Cole runs that operation with more dedication than anyone I've ever known."

The way she said it didn't quite sound like a compliment.

Sadie followed Martha up the stairs, her boots clicking on the polished wood. The second-floor hallway stretched in both directions, with doors bearing brass nameplates: Town Clerk, Building & Zoning, and Parks & Recreation. Martha led her to the end of the hall, where a door stood open, revealing a spacious office with windows overlooking the town square.

Mayor Roger Hayes rose from behind his desk as they entered, his smile enormous and genuine. He was exactly what Sadie would have cast in a movie about a small-town mayor—broad-shouldered, balding, with a white mustache and the kind of face that suggested he smiled more often than not.

"Sadie Baker!" He came around the desk with his hand extended. "Welcome, welcome! We're so pleased to have you here in Mistletoe Falls."

"Thank you, Mayor Hayes." Sadie shook his hand, grateful for the warmth in his greeting. "I'm excited to get started."

"Please call me Roger. We're not very formal around here." He gestured to the seating area near the windows, where two leather chairs faced a small sofa. "Come, sit. We've got a lot to discuss, but let's start with introductions."

That's when Sadie noticed the man standing by the window.

He'd been so still she'd almost missed him. As he turned to face her, Sadie felt her breath catch in a way that had nothing to do with professional courtesy.

Cole Bennett was tall—easily over six feet—with the kind of build that came from actual physical work rather than a gym membership. Broad shoulders filled out a flannel shirt in dark green, and he wore dark blue denim jeans. His hair was dark brown and slightly tousled, falling across his forehead in a way that made her fingers itch to smooth it back—which was an absolutely inappropriate thought to have about a colleague she'd known for approximately three seconds.

But it was his eyes that held her. Steel blue, intense, observant—the kind of eyes that noticed everything and gave away nothing.

"Cole," Martha said, her tone carrying a note of warning that Sadie couldn't quite interpret. "This is Sadie

Baker, our new Tourism Development Coordinator. Sadie Cole Bennett—he's the Lead Conductor and Operations Manager of the Mistletoe Express."

Cole stepped forward, and Sadie found herself shaking his hand before she'd fully processed the movement. His palm was rough with calluses, his grip firm but not aggressive, and he held her hand perhaps a beat longer than strictly professional before releasing it.

"Miss Baker." His voice was deep and measured, with the kind of careful control that suggested he was used to choosing his words precisely.

"Mr. Bennett," Sadie said. "It's a pleasure to meet you. I'm looking forward to working with you on the Mistletoe Express initiatives."

Something flickered in his eyes—surprise, maybe, or suspicion—but his expression remained neutral.

"Let's sit, let's sit," Roger said, gesturing them toward the seating area. "Coffee? Hot chocolate? I've got both."

"I'm fine, thank you," Sadie said, settling into one of the leather chairs. Cole took the other chair, positioning himself so he could see both the mayor's desk and the door.

Martha claimed the sofa, crossing her legs and pulling out a tablet. "Let's get started. Sadie, I know we've discussed this over email, but I want to make sure everyone's on the same page about your role and responsibilities during this trial period."

Sadie nodded, hyperaware of Cole's silent presence beside her.

"Your primary focus," Martha continued, "will be increasing tourism visibility for Mistletoe Falls, with particular emphasis on the Mistletoe Express, the depot, and the railway museum. We've got a good thing going here—our Christmas season brings in solid numbers—but we're not reaching our full potential. We need fresh marketing strategies, a stronger social media presence, and innovative programming that attracts more visitors year-round, not just during the holidays."

"The Express is already successful," Cole said quietly. "We run near capacity during peak season."

"Near capacity isn't full capacity," Martha replied, her tone gentle but firm. "And peak season is only a few months a year. We want to expand that window, increase off-season ridership, and make the Express a destination rather than just an attraction."

Sadie could feel the tension rolling off Cole like heat from a radiator. She kept her expression neutral, her hands folded in her lap, while her mind raced through the preliminary ideas she'd been developing since accepting the position.

"I've been reviewing the current programming," she said, choosing her words carefully. "And I think there's a tremendous opportunity to build on the strong foundation that already exists. The Express has a wonderful reputation, and the historical preservation work is exceptional—that's clear from everything I've read."

Cole's posture shifted slightly, and Sadie wondered if she'd just said something right.

"But," she continued, "I think we could expand the storytelling around the train's history, create more interactive experiences for visitors, and develop signature events that give people reasons to plan trips specifically to Mistletoe Falls."

"What kind of events?" Cole's question came out more like a challenge than an inquiry.

Sadie met his gaze directly. "That's something I'd want to develop in collaboration with you. You know the Express better than anyone—what it can handle operationally, what would honor its history, and what the community would support. I'm thinking about ways to enhance the existing Christmas programming, maybe add some themed experiences that showcase the train's heritage while creating memorable moments for families."

"The Christmas programming doesn't need enhancing." Cole's voice remained carefully controlled, but Sadie heard the edge underneath. "We've run the same seasonal schedule for years. People come back year after year because they know what to expect."

"And that's wonderful," Sadie said, meaning it. "Consistency is valuable. But we could also create some new traditions alongside the existing ones. Give people reasons to visit multiple times per season instead of just once."

"My father designed the current programming." Each word came out precisely, measured. "Every event, every ride, every tradition—he built it all with specific purpose and meaning."

The air in the room shifted, growing heavier.

"Cole," Martha said quietly. "Your father would want the Express to thrive, not just survive."

"It is thriving." Cole turned to look at Martha, and Sadie saw something flash in his eyes. "Revenue is stable, ridership is strong, and the community supports everything we do. Why risk changing what works?"

Roger cleared his throat. "Because the world changes whether we want it to or not, son. Tourism patterns shift. Marketing needs to evolve. If we don't adapt, we'll get left behind."

"The Express has been here for years," Cole said. "I think we'll manage."

"The Express was also abandoned and rusting in a rail yard in 1975," Martha pointed out. "Your father brought it back to life because he understood that preservation sometimes requires evolution."

Sadie watched the exchange with growing understanding. This wasn't about marketing strategies or event programming. Cole Bennett saw any change to the Express as a betrayal of his father's memory—which made her job exponentially more complicated.

"I don't want to change what your father built," she said, pulling Cole's attention back to her. "I want to honor it by helping it reach new audiences. Everything I've read about the restoration work suggests your father cared deeply about sharing this piece of history with people. I want to help continue that mission."

Cole studied her for a long moment, those steel-blue eyes searching her face for something—sincerity, maybe, or evidence that she was just saying what he wanted to hear.

"What do you know about trains?" he asked finally.

"Not much," Sadie admitted. "But I know how to tell stories. And the Mistletoe Express has an incredible story—the restoration, the community coming together to save it, the way it's become the heart of this town. That's what I want to share with people."

"We already share it. The museum has all the history; the depot has photographs and exhibits—"

"Which most visitors never see because they're only here for a two-hour ride." Sadie leaned forward slightly, warming to her subject. "What if we created ways to deepen that engagement? Historical tours that showcase the restoration process? Behind-the-scenes experiences that let people see how the train operates? Story-based programming that connects the Express to the broader history of Appalachia?"

"That's not what people come here for," Cole said. "They come for Christmas magic and family memories."

"They come for that because that's what we offer them," Sadie countered. "But what if we could offer them more? What if families came back three times a season instead of once? What if history enthusiasts added Mistletoe Falls to their must-visit lists? What if we became known not just as a Christmas town, but as the place that kept an important piece of American history alive?"

Cole's jaw tightened. "The Express isn't a theme park attraction."

"I never said it was—"

"All right," Martha cut in, her voice carrying enough authority to silence them both. "This is exactly why we're having this meeting. You two are going to have to find a way to work together, whether you like it or not."

She looked directly at Cole. "Sadie has been hired to increase tourism visibility and revenue. That's not optional. Her ideas will be implemented, with appropriate input and collaboration from you to ensure they respect the Express's history and operational requirements."

Then she turned to Sadie. "And you need to understand that the Express isn't just a business asset. It's part of this community's identity. Every decision you make about programming or marketing will affect real people who've been caring for this train for decades. That includes Cole, whose family has sacrificed more than you probably realize to keep it running."

Sadie felt heat rise in her cheeks, though she wasn't sure if it was embarrassment or frustration. "I understand that. I'm not trying to turn this into something commercial or artificial. I want to preserve what makes it special while helping more people discover it."

"By changing everything my father built," Cole said flatly.

"By building on what your father created," Sadie shot back. "There's a difference."

"Is there?" Cole stood abruptly, his chair scraping against the floor. "Because from where I'm sitting, it sounds like you're here to fix something that isn't broken, and I'm supposed to smile and cooperate while you dismantle everything that matters."

"Cole—" Roger started.

"I'll work with Miss Baker because you're asking me to," Cole said, his voice tight. "But let's be clear about what this is. She's here on a trial basis for twelve weeks. The Express has been here for one hundred and forty-five years. I know which one I'm betting on."

The silence that followed felt like the moment after lightning strikes, when you're waiting to see if anything caught fire.

Martha stood, her expression unreadable. "You'll both report to me weekly on collaboration progress. I expect professional behavior from both of you, which means open communication, mutual respect, and a genuine effort to find common ground."

She looked at Roger, who nodded in agreement.

"Sadie, you'll work with Cole to develop a comprehensive proposal for the next twelve weeks of programming, including any new initiatives you want to pilot. Cole, you'll provide honest feedback about operational feasibility and historical appropriateness. Together, you'll present a joint recommendation to me in two days."

"Two days?" Sadie's voice came out higher than she intended.

"Is that a problem?" Martha's eyebrow arched.

"No." Sadie straightened her spine. "Two days is fine."

"Good." Martha gathered her tablet. "Cole, please give Sadie a complete tour of the depot, the Express, and the museum this afternoon. She needs to understand what she's working with before she can make informed recommendations."

"Fine," he said. "One o'clock. Don't be late."

Then he strode toward the door without looking back, and Sadie sat very still in her leather chair, trying to process what had just happened.

Roger let out a long breath. "Well. That could have gone worse."

"Could it?" Sadie asked faintly.

Martha actually smiled. "Cole's protective of the Express. He'll come around once he realizes you're not here to destroy his father's legacy."

"And if I can't convince him of that?"

"Then you'll fail your trial period." Martha's bluntness was almost refreshing. "The Express is central to everything we do here. If you can't work with Cole, you can't do this job. It's that simple."

Martha headed for the door, then paused. "For what it's worth, I think you can. You asked the right questions and showed respect for the history while making the case for growth. Cole heard that, even if he wasn't ready to admit it. Now, let me show you to your new office and give you a quick orientation of the layout of the building as well."

Sadie nodded. She'd known this job wouldn't be easy. She'd prepared herself for the challenge of proving her worth in twelve weeks and for the pressure of creating results in an unfamiliar town.

What she hadn't prepared for was Cole Bennett's steel-blue eyes looking at her like she was the enemy. Or the way her heart had stuttered when he'd shaken her hand. Or the uncomfortable realization that the greatest obstacle to her success wasn't going to be the work itself—it was going to be convincing a man that change didn't have to mean loss.

Sadie stood, smoothed her coat, and followed Martha to her new office. Cole's last words ringing in her ears.

One o'clock. The depot. Don't be late.

Chapter 4

C ole checked his pocket watch for the third time in ten minutes. Twelve fifty-eight. She wasn't late yet, but she would be. People like Sadie Baker—people who talked about "fresh perspectives" and "innovative pro-gramming"—were always late, too busy checking their phones or answering emails to respect other people's time.

He snapped the watch closed and tucked it back into his vest pocket, then bent to scratch behind Cash's ears. The dog had been restless all morning, picking up on Cole's tension the way he always did. Having Cash at the depot on Mondays wasn't typical, but after the disaster of this morning's meeting, Cole had needed the comfort of something uncomplicated. Cash didn't care about tourism initiatives or trial periods or women with stunning hazel eyes.

"Mr. Bennett?"

Cole straightened so fast his lower back protested. Sadie Baker stood at the depot entrance, silhouetted against the afternoon light streaming through the doorway. She'd changed since this morning—traded the wool coat for a more practical jacket in deep red, and she carried a leather messenger bag slung across her body. Her chestnut hair was pulled back in a ponytail now, revealing the clean line of her jaw.

One o'clock exactly. Not late.

Cole felt unreasonably irritated that she'd denied him even that small justification for his mood.

"Miss Baker." He kept his voice professionally neutral, the same tone he used with difficult tourists who complained about the seating or the sluggish air conditioning in a hundred-year-old train car. "Right on time."

"I try not to waste people's time." She stepped fully into the depot, and Cash immediately trotted over to investigate, tail wagging.

"Cash, heel." Cole's command came out sharper than he'd intended.

But Sadie was already crouching down, letting Cash sniff her hand before she stroked his head. "Hey there, handsome. Aren't you friendly?"

Cash leaned into her touch, his entire rear end wiggling with pleasure, and Cole felt a flicker of betrayal. Traitor dog.

"He's usually more reserved with strangers," Cole said.

"Animals tend to like me." Sadie glanced up at him, and there was something in her expression—not smugness, exactly, but maybe a hint of amusement at catching Cole off guard. "I had a cat growing up. Before..."

She didn't finish the sentence, just stood and adjusted her bag. The momentary softness in her face vanished behind professional pleasantness.

"So." She looked around the depot's main hall with obvious interest. "Where do we start?"

Cole had a plan. He'd spent the hours since this morning's meeting developing it while he'd worked through his maintenance checklist and convinced Hank to come in and cover the afternoon scenic ride. The plan was simple: overwhelm her with technical details, use terminology she wouldn't understand, and make it clear that the Express was far more complicated than her marketing degree had prepared her for. By the time he finished the tour, she'd understand that Cole Bennett knew this operation inside and out, and any "fresh ideas" she had would be built on a foundation of ignorance.

"We'll start with the history," he said, gesturing toward the museum entrance at the back of the main hall. "Follow me."

He set off without checking to see if she followed, Cash falling into step beside him. His boots echoed on the polished wood floors as he led her past the ticketing counter and through the doorway marked "Mistletoe Falls Railway Museum—Admission Free."

The museum occupied what had once been a warehouse attached to the original depot building. Cole's father had overseen the conversion years ago, working with local carpenters and craftsmen to create a space that honored the depot's history while serving as an educational resource. The high ceiling still showed the original exposed beams, and the brick walls had been carefully cleaned and restored rather than covered.

Cole stopped in front of the first display—a timeline of the depot's construction and early years, complete with photographs and artifacts under glass.

"The depot was built in 1892," he began, his voice taking on the cadence of a lecture he'd given hundreds of times. "It served as a critical junction point for logging operations in the Smoky Mountains. Timber from the high elevations would come down by spur line to here, then get loaded onto cars heading to mills in Knoxville and Asheville."

He pointed to a photograph of the original depot, a simple wooden structure that looked nothing like the grand building they stood in now.

"That burned down in 1904. The current building was constructed in 1905 with brick and stone, designed to last. The addition of the warehouse came in 1912, when the logging operations expanded."

"What ended the logging operations?" Sadie asked.

Cole glanced at her, surprised by the question. Most people just nodded along, waiting for him to move on.

"National forest protections in the 1920s," he said. "By 1935, the depot's primary use had shifted to passenger service, bringing tourists up from the lowlands to enjoy the mountain air. But passenger rail was already dying by then. By 1950, the depot was barely operating, and in 1967, the line shut down completely."

He moved to the next display, which showed photographs of the abandoned depot—windows broken, roof sagging, weeds growing through the platform.

"It sat empty for years. The town council talked about tearing it down, using the land for parking or maybe a park. Then, my father and a group of other residents formed a historical preservation society and convinced the council to let them restore it instead."

Cole felt his throat tighten the way it always did when he talked about his father's work. He cleared it roughly and continued.

"The restoration took years. My father was the project lead—he'd worked for the railroad for a length of time and knew every inch of this place. He was fascinated by everything to do with trains. They rebuilt the roof, replaced the floors, and restored all the original woodwork and plaster. Then they added the museum wing in the back, converting the old warehouse space."

"It's beautiful," Sadie said quietly. "The craftsmanship is extraordinary."

"My father didn't believe in cutting corners." Cole moved toward the center of the museum, where the main exhibit dominated the space. "But restoring the building was only the first part. He wanted to bring a train back to life."

The exhibit told the story of the Mistletoe Express's resurrection—photographs of the locomotive rusting in a rail yard, detailed drawings of the restoration process, and artifacts from the decade-long project. A glass case held tools his father had used, each one labeled and preserved.

"The Express was built in 1887," Cole said, and despite his determination to keep this clinical and overwhelming, he felt the familiar pull of the story, the way it lived in his bones. "She ran passenger service out of Virginia for forty years, then got converted to freight. By the 1960s, she was obsolete—diesel had taken over. The railroad company was going to scrap her."

He stopped in front of the photograph that always made his chest ache. His father, a young man at the time, stood beside the locomotive in the rail yard. The Express looked like a corpse—paint peeling, brass fittings missing, the smokestack bent at an angle.

"My father was deeply involved in this city and managed to interest the town officials in restoring the Express. My father was given a modest budget by the city, and he also received a grant and bought her for eight hundred dollars in 1990 and spent the next fifteen years bringing her back to life."

"Fifteen years," Sadie repeated, her voice soft with something that sounded like awe.

"Steam locomotives are complex machines. Every part had to be either restored or fabricated from scratch. The boiler alone took three years. He taught himself metalworking, studied engineering manuals from the 1800s, and consulted with every expert he could find. He did a lot of the work himself and worked long hours."

He gestured toward a display case containing one of his father's old work jackets, its canvas stained with grease and scorched in places from welding sparks.

"He worked eight-hour days at his regular job with the town, then came here every night and weekend. My mother used to bring him dinner because he'd forget to eat. Luke, my younger brother, and I grew up running around this depot, handing him tools, learning how engines work by watching him put one back together bolt by bolt."

Cole moved to the final display in this section—the Legacy Wall. Photographs covered the entire wall, documenting the Express's first run after restoration. His father stood in his conductor's uniform, his hand on the engine, his smile enormous. Younger versions of Cole and Luke flanked him, both grinning.

Below the photographs, a brass plaque read, "In memory of Michael Bennett (1965-2021), who believed that preserving the past gives meaning to the future."

Cole stood silent in front of the wall, his jaw tight. He'd walked through this museum thousands of times, given this tour hundreds of times, but he'd never quite figured out how to talk about his father without feeling like someone had reached into his chest and squeezed.

"He must have been an incredible man," Sadie said.

Something in her voice made Cole turn to look at her. She was staring at the Legacy Wall with an expression he couldn't quite read—not the polite interest tourists usually showed, but something deeper. Her eyes were bright, and were those—were those tears?

"He was," Cole managed. "He was the best man I've ever known."

Sadie reached out as if to touch the photographs, then seemed to catch herself and dropped her hand. "The love is evident in every detail. You can see it in the way he's looking at the train in these pictures. And in the way you talk about him."

Cole felt something shift uncomfortably in his chest. He'd expected professional interest, maybe some questions about historical preservation for her marketing materials. He hadn't expected this—genuine emotion, authentic recognition of what his father's work had meant.

"The museum documents the entire restoration," he said, his voice rougher than he'd intended. "Every phase, every challenge, every solution. If you want to understand the Express, this is where you start."

"May I?" Sadie gestured toward the display cases.

"That's what they're here for."

She moved slowly through the exhibits, and Cole watched her instead of looking at the artifacts he'd memorized years ago. She didn't just glance and move on the way most visitors did. She stopped to read every placard, studied every photograph, and occasionally pulled out her phone to take pictures—not selfies or casual snapshots, but carefully framed shots of specific details.

At the case containing his father's tools, she crouched down for a better angle, her fingers hovering near the glass as if she wanted to touch but knew better.

"These are beautiful," she said. "The patina on the handles, the way they're worn smooth in places from years of use. They tell a story all by themselves."

"My father used those exact tools right up until..." Cole stopped, the sentence catching in his throat.

Sadie looked up at him, and her expression was so openly compassionate that Cole had to look away.

"The depot tour is next," he said abruptly. "We should keep moving if we're going to get through everything today."

He didn't wait for her response, just headed back toward the main hall with Cash padding beside him. But he heard her following, her footsteps quick on the polished floor as she caught up.

The depot's main hall opened up before them, and Cole forced himself back into tour-guide mode. He could do this. He could show her the operational side, explain the systems, make it clear that running the Express required expertise she didn't have. That was the plan.

"The ticketing counter dates to 1905," he began, gesturing toward the oak structure that stretched along the west wall. "Original wood, restored and sealed. We still use handwritten tickets for traditional rides, though we've added a computer system for reservations and record-keeping."

"Do people appreciate the handwritten tickets?" Sadie asked.

"Families love them. Kids especially—they get to keep them as souvenirs." Cole moved toward the office door behind the counter. "My office is back here. It was originally the stationmaster's office, and we've maintained that function."

He pushed open the door, revealing the small room with its filing cabinets and shelves. His father's desk dominated the space, its surface organized exactly the way Michael Bennett had left it—Cole had never been able to bring himself to change the arrangement.

Sadie stepped inside, her gaze traveling over the space with the same careful attention she'd shown in the museum.

"You keep your operational logs by hand," she observed, nodding toward the leather-bound ledgers on the shelf.

"My father did. I've continued the tradition. There's something about writing things down—it makes you pay attention to details you might miss if you're just typing into a computer."

"May I?" She gestured toward one of the ledgers.

Cole hesitated, then pulled down the current year's log and handed it to her. She opened it carefully, running her finger down the neat columns of Cole's handwriting.

"Your entries are incredibly detailed," she said. "Temperature readings, pressure tests, timing logs, passenger counts, even notes about weather conditions during each run."

"Operating a steam locomotive isn't like driving a car. Everything affects everything else. Temperature, humidity, and altitude—they all matter. Keeping detailed records means we can predict problems before they become dangerous."

"Your father taught you this?"

"Every bit of it." Cole took the ledger back and returned it to the shelf. "He believed that maintaining this engine wasn't just about keeping it running. It was about honoring the work of everyone who'd ever operated her. The engineers and conductors who ran her a hundred years ago—they kept logs just like this. We're continuing that tradition."

Sadie was quiet for a moment, and when Cole glanced at her, she was looking at his father's desk with an expression he couldn't quite read.

"You said earlier today that I'm here to fix something that isn't broken," she said finally. "But I don't think that's what I'm trying to do. I'm trying to help more people understand what you just showed me—the love and the history and the tradition. Because if people understood all of this the way you do, they'd care about it the way you do. And that would ensure the Express keeps running for another hundred years."

Cole opened his mouth to respond, then closed it again. He wanted to argue, to point out that she was still talking about change, about doing things differently. But the sincerity in her voice made it difficult to summon his usual defenses.

Cash, who'd been lying in his bed beside the desk, chose that moment to stand and trot over to Sadie, pressing his head against her leg.

"Traitor," Cole muttered.

Sadie laughed—a genuine, surprised sound that made something warm flicker in Cole's chest before he could stop it.

"Come on," he said, more gruffly than necessary. "You need to see the train itself."

They walked out onto the platform, and the afternoon sun caught the Express's dark green paint, making the brass fittings gleam like gold. Cole felt the familiar swell of pride and grief that always hit him when he saw the locomotive like this—fully restored, maintained to perfection, exactly as his father had envisioned.

"She's beautiful," Sadie breathed.

"One hundred and thirty-eight years old and still running like she did in 1887." Cole walked toward the engine, reaching his hand out to touch the smooth metal. "The boiler's original, relined twice. The drive wheels are the same ones she was built with. Even the whistle is authentic—my father found it in a salvage yard in Pennsylvania."

He spent the next thirty minutes walking Sadie through every detail of the locomotive—the firebox, the water systems, the steam distribution, and the braking mechanisms. He explained how they'd converted her to burn cleaner fuel while maintaining historical authenticity, how they'd upgraded safety systems without compromising the original design, how every repair was documented, and how every replacement part was fabricated to match the 1880s specifications.

And Sadie listened. She asked questions that showed she was actually processing what he was saying—not

just nodding politely, but genuinely trying to understand. When he explained the complexity of maintaining
proper steam pressure, she wanted to know how his
father had learned those skills. When he showed her
the brass fittings, they'd hand-polished to restore the
original shine, she asked about the techniques they'd
used.

By the time they moved to the passenger cars,
Cole was volunteering information he hadn't planned
to share—stories about specific restoration challenges,
anecdotes about his father's problem-solving methods,
and small details about the care that went into every
decision.

"The seats are reproductions," he explained as they
entered the main passenger car. "The originals were
long gone by the time my father recovered the train.
He worked with a furniture maker to recreate them
based on photographs and catalog descriptions from
the 1880s. The fabric pattern is historically accurate."

Sadie ran her hand over the back of one of the seats,
her touch gentle. "The tartan plaid—that's traditional for
mountain railways, isn't it?"

"You did your research."

"I told you, I'm good at telling stories. But I can't tell
this one if I don't understand it first." She looked at him
directly, and her hazel eyes caught the light streaming
through the windows. "This isn't just a train to you. It's
your father's legacy, your family's history, and the heart
of this community all rolled into one. I get that. I really
do."

Cole felt his carefully constructed defenses waver. He'd spent four hours preparing to intimidate her, to make her understand that she was out of her depth. Instead, she'd listened with genuine interest, asked thoughtful questions, and shown respect for everything his father had built.

It was deeply unsettling.

"You may want to take a ride during one of the tours," he said, changing the subject before she could see how much her words had affected him.

"Yes. I need to experience it the way visitors do—see what captures their attention, where their questions naturally go, and what moments feel special. I can't enhance the rider experience if I don't understand what that experience actually is."

"We have scenic rides on Tuesday, Thursday, and Saturday afternoons. There's also a school group coming Wednesday morning."

"Could I observe the school group ride? That might give me different insights than the tourist runs."

Cole nodded slowly. "I'll add you to the manifest."

They finished the tour in the observation car, where large glass panels gave clear views of the mountain scenery the Express passed through. Sadie stood at one of the windows, looking out toward the peaks visible in the distance.

"I understand why people fall in love with this," she said quietly. "It's not just about a train ride. It's about connection—to history, to place, and to something bigger than our everyday lives. Your father understood that."

"He did."

"I'd like to stay for the rest of the afternoon, if that's all right." Sadie turned to face him. "Work on some initial ideas while everything's fresh in my mind. Then maybe we could meet tomorrow morning at nine to start developing the proposal for Martha?"

Cole wanted to say no. He wanted to tell her that the depot was his space, that he didn't need her sitting in his office or the main hall, and that her presence would be a distraction he didn't need.

But he'd agreed to work with her. And Martha had made it clear that cooperation wasn't optional.

"Fine," he said. "You can set up in the main hall. There's a table by the windows that gets good light. The Wi-Fi password is posted behind the ticket counter."

"Thank you."

"Don't expect me to hold your hand through the process," Cole added, his voice sharper than the words warranted. "You said you're good at telling stories. Prove it."

Something flickered in Sadie's eyes—not hurt, exactly, but acknowledgment of the barb. She lifted her chin slightly.

"Oh, trust me... I will."

Cole watched her walk back toward the main hall, Cash trotting alongside her like he'd known her for years instead of hours. Through the window, he could see her settling at the table he'd indicated, pulling out her laptop and a leather notebook.

He should get back to his own work. The afternoon scenic ride would start soon, and Hank would need help with startup procedures. There were maintenance logs to update, supply orders to review, and a dozen small tasks that required attention.

Instead, Cole found himself standing on the platform, staring at the mountains and trying to figure out what had just happened.

He'd planned to overwhelm her with complexity. To make her understand that the Express wasn't something she could market like a product, that changing anything meant destroying something irreplaceable.

But she hadn't pushed back against his passion. She'd listened to it, respected it, and somehow managed to articulate what his father's work meant in ways that suggested she actually understood.

Cole pulled out his pocket watch and flipped it open. Three fifteen.

He closed the watch with a snap and headed toward his office. Cash was already there, settling into his bed with a contented sigh. Through the open door, Cole could see Sadie bent over her laptop, her face illuminated by the screen's glow. Her fingers moved quickly over the keyboard, pausing occasionally while she referenced something in her notebook.

She was working. Actually working, not just pretending for his benefit.

Cole sank into his father's chair and pulled up the supply order form on his computer. But his gaze kept drifting toward the doorway, toward the woman who'd somehow managed to slip past his defenses without him noticing until it was too late.

Cash stretched out on his bed, one eye opening to look at Cole as if the dog knew exactly what he was thinking.

"Don't start," Cole muttered.

But as Cash settled back to sleep and the afternoon light shifted across the depot floor, Cole couldn't quite convince himself that the slight tremor in his carefully ordered world was nothing. He couldn't forget the way Sadie's eyes had filled with tears at the Legacy Wall, or how she'd touched the display case containing his father's tools like they were precious artifacts rather than old equipment.

He couldn't forget how she'd said, "The love is evident in every detail," with such genuine understanding that it had felt like she'd seen straight through to the grief he kept locked away.

And he definitely couldn't forget those eyes—hazel with flecks of gold that caught the light and seemed to shift with her mood, warm and expressive and far too observant for his comfort. The way they'd looked at him when she'd said she understood what the Express meant to him, with such sincerity that he'd almost believed—

Cole jerked his attention back to the supply order, his jaw tight. Sadie Baker was here on a trial basis for twelve weeks. The fact that she'd asked good questions and shown respect for his father's work didn't change anything; she was probably temporary, and the Express was forever.

He'd learned that lesson with Sarah. People who elaborated on fresh perspectives and new opportunities eventually left, and the ones who stayed behind were the ones who got hurt.

Cole forced himself to focus on the screen in front of him, on the familiar routine of managing inventory and maintaining standards. But even Cash seemed to sense that something had shifted, the dog's ears twitching occasionally as if listening for footsteps that might or might not come back through that door.

Cole tried very hard not to think about the woman with the hazel eyes sitting within his view.

He tried. But the tremor in his carefully ordered world kept growing, and Cole was beginning to suspect that working with Sadie Baker was not going to be easy.

Which was exactly why he needed to maintain his distance, finish this proposal as quickly as possible, and remember that temporary people didn't get to rearrange permanent things—no matter how perfect their eyes looked in the afternoon light.

Chapter 5

S adie pushed through the depot doors at exactly nine o'clock Tuesday morning, her messenger bag heavy with her laptop, three different notebooks, and the printed research she'd compiled until two AM. The adrenaline that had kept her working through the night still hummed in her veins, mixing with the multiple cups of coffee she'd consumed and the nervous energy that came from knowing this meeting would set the tone for everything that followed.

Cole was already there, standing by the ticketing counter with Cash at his feet. He held a steaming mug in one hand and wore the same expression he'd had when she'd left yesterday—guarded, watchful, like he was bracing for impact.

"Morning," she said, injecting brightness into her voice that she didn't quite feel. Her eyes felt gritty from lack of sleep, but she'd put on mascara to hide the evidence and chosen a sweater in forest green that she hoped projected confidence rather than desperation.

"Miss Baker." He nodded toward the table by the windows where she'd worked yesterday. "I set up over there. Figured you'd want the light."

The gesture surprised her—small but thoughtful in a way that didn't match his typical demeanor. Sadie walked to the table and found he'd not only cleared the space but had also placed a second chair at an angle so they could work side by side.

She set down her bag and pulled out her laptop, aware of Cole following with Cash. He settled into the chair he'd positioned, his long legs stretching out in a way that made the space feel smaller. Cash immediately flopped down between them with a contented sigh.

Sadie opened her laptop and pulled out the first of her notebooks—the one with tabs color-coded by event and sticky notes flagging key statistics. "I worked on some proposals yesterday. Three main events that I think could significantly increase tourism revenue while honoring the Express's history and traditions."

She glanced at him, waiting for him to mention his own contributions, to pull out notes, or at least to indicate he'd given their assignment any thought beyond showing up this morning.

Cole just looked at her, his expression neutral.

The disappointment hit harder than it should have. She'd half-expected this—he'd made his resistance clear from the start—but part of her had hoped that yesterday's tour, the way he'd opened up about his father's work, might have shifted something. That he might have spent his evening thinking about possibilities instead of digging his heels in deeper.

Sadie forced her professional smile back into place and squared her shoulders. Fine. She'd done enough work for both of them. She just needed him to listen with an open mind.

"The first event," she began, pulling up the file on her laptop, "is a Depot Tree Lighting Ceremony."

Cole's mug stopped halfway to his mouth. "The town already has a tree lighting the day after Thanksgiving. It's been a tradition for years, longer than either of us has been alive."

"I know. I researched it." Sadie turned her laptop so he could see the mock-up she'd created—a rendering of the depot's exterior lit with thousands of twinkling lights, a massive evergreen tree positioned near the platform entrance. "But think about it—the town square ceremony is wonderful, but it's not connected to the Express. What if we created a second event here at the depot that specifically celebrates the train and its role in the community's Christmas traditions?"

"Two tree lightings?" Cole's skepticism was palpable.

"Not competition—complement. The town ceremony happens Friday evening after Thanksgiving. What if we did ours the following Saturday? Give people a full week-end of holiday kickoff celebrations." She pulled up the next slide, which showed Christmas decorations. "We'd decorate the entire depot and museum, serve hot cocoa and cookies, maybe have carolers. Make it a true community event where people can tour the decorated train, visit the museum exhibits, and celebrate the Express specifically."

Cole set his mug down carefully. "The depot's never been used for something like that."

"Which is precisely why it would feel special." Sadie leaned forward, warming to her subject despite his resistance. "People love the Express, but most of them only experience it during a one-hour ride. This would let them engage with the space differently—see where the conductors work and maybe what they do, appreciate the restoration of the building itself, and understand the full scope of what's offered here."

She pulled up her next slide—a budget breakdown and attendance projections based on similar events in comparable communities. "I've researched other heritage railways that host depot events. The average attendance is significant, and the community engagement scores are exceptional. People want to feel connected to local traditions, especially during the holidays."

Cole studied the screen, his jaw tight. "And you would like to do this on November 27th? That's less than four weeks away."

"Which gives us time to plan, decorate, and promote it properly." Sadie opened her second notebook, where she'd already started drafting the promotional copy. "We'd need all the train staff in their official uniforms—historical authenticity is important. Maybe we could get someone to dress as Santa Claus, read a Christmas story with a train theme to the children, or do photos with Santa in the depot. Keep it simple but meaningful."

"You've thought this through."

Sadie couldn't tell if that was approval or accusation. "That's what you hired me to do."

"The town hired you. I just work here. Big difference."

The words stung more than they should have. Sadie closed that notebook and pulled out the next one, refusing to let his resistance derail her momentum. "The second event is a Santa Express-themed ride."

"We already have themed rides," Cole said immediately. "Traditional ones that have been running for years."

"I saw those in the historical records—the Christmas Carol Ride and the Holiday Heritage Tour. They're lovely." Sadie pulled up the next presentation file. "But they're daytime educational rides. What I'm proposing is different—something specifically designed for families with young children, with Santa and Mrs. Claus actually aboard the train."

She turned the laptop toward him again, showing the concept she'd mocked up: the Express decorated with even more garland and lights, families boarding in winter coats, children's faces lit with wonder.

"Friday, December 10th, and Saturday, December 11th. Two full days of rides, maybe three departures each day. Santa and Mrs. Claus board with the passengers, perhaps some volunteers dressed as elves serving hot chocolate and cookies. Photos with Santa and Mrs. Claus in the main passenger car. After each ride, families come into the depot where we've set up crafting stations—kids can decorate ornaments or create small craft projects with volunteers while their parents tour the museum."

Cole was quiet for a long moment, his fingers drumming against his mug. "That's a lot of logistics. Volunteers, costumes, supplies, coordinating schedules—"

"All manageable with proper planning." Sadie flipped to her logistics spreadsheet. "I've already started outlining volunteer needs and reaching out to local craft suppliers about donated materials. The key is creating an experience that families will remember—and tell their friends about. Word-of-mouth marketing is invaluable in communities like this."

"December 10th and 11th," Cole repeated slowly.

"Yes. Two days give us the capacity to serve more families, and it creates a sense of event rather than just another themed ride. And the bottom line is, it would bring in a significant amount of cash flow." She paused, reading his hesitation.

Cole's expression shifted slightly—still resistant, but maybe considering. "One day is more manageable. December 10th."

"But—"

"If it sells out immediately and we can handle the logistics, we'll add the Saturday rides. But let's not over-commit before we know what we're dealing with."

Sadie bit back her argument. She'd learned enough about negotiation to recognize when to take the win and push later. "Fine. December 10th for sure, with Saturday as a strong possibility. But I think Martha should have the final decision on that. I believe 2 full days would be best."

"Pending," Cole said.

"Actually," Sadie said, deciding to press slightly, "if we're doing a trial run, we should plan for success. Which means having Saturday's logistics worked out ahead of time so we can activate them quickly if needed. Otherwise, we'll lose momentum."

Cole studied her for a long moment, and she couldn't quite read his expression. Finally, he nodded. "December 10th and 11th. But we scale appropriately based on volunteer availability and operational capacity."

Victory fizzed through Sadie's chest, though she kept her expression neutral. Two out of two. "Thank you. I believe families will love this."

"What's the third event?"

Sadie took a breath and opened her final presentation file. This was the one she'd spent the most time on, the one she believed could truly transform how people thought about the Mistletoe Express. "All Aboard on Christmas Eve."

She turned the laptop fully toward Cole, showing him the mock-up brochure she'd designed. The header image showed the Express at night, steam rising into a starlit sky, the depot behind it blazing with lights and decorated with evergreen wreaths.

Cole leaned forward, his eyes scanning the text:

All Aboard on Christmas Eve

An Unforgettable Journey Through the Heart of Christmas

The Premiere Ride of a New Holiday Tradition

Step into the magic of Mistletoe Falls on the most enchanting night of the year. This Christmas Eve, the Mistletoe Express invites you to be part of something new—a magical journey designed to capture the wonder of the season and create memories you'll treasure for years to come.

Before You Board

Arrive at the twinkle-lit depot, where evergreen garlands, carolers in Victorian dress, and the scent of cocoa and cookies set the stage. Each guest will be welcomed with a warm drink and a sweet treat as lanterns guide the way to the platform.

Onboard the Mistletoe Express

• Ride through the snowy Smoky Mountain foothills aboard our lovingly restored 1880s steam locomotive
• Enjoy festive carols sung live in the Main Coach
• Visit the Storytelling Car, where classic Christmas tales come alive for all ages
• Sip cocoa, savor holiday cookies, and watch the winter wonderland drift past your window
• Look for surprises along the route: bridges strung with lanterns, candlelit cabins in the distance, and perhaps even a glimpse of Santa himself waving from the hills.
• Take home a commemorative ornament, marking the very first All Aboard on Christmas Eve ride

The Grand Finale

As the Mistletoe Express returns to the depot, the evening culminates in a spectacular celebration. Passengers step onto the platform to find the towering Christmas tree aglow, carolers leading a candlelit chorus, and fireworks bursting into the snowy night sky. It's a breathtaking sendoff, ringing in Christmas with joy, music, and light.

This is the beginning of a new tradition—and you're invited to be part of its very first chapter. Don't miss your chance to experience the magic that will become a cherished Christmas Eve ritual for generations to come.

Limited tickets are available. Reserve early for the inaugural 'All Aboard on Christmas Eve' experience.

Cole read through it twice, his expression unreadable. When he finally looked up, his eyes were skeptical. "Christmas Eve? You want people to spend Christmas Eve on a train ride?"

"Yes." Sadie pulled up her research file, ready for this exact objection. "Because not everyone has family nearby. Not everyone has somewhere to go on Christmas Eve. And even people who do have traditions often look for something special or different to include in their celebrations."

She turned to a new slide showing demographic data. "Single parents looking for magic to give their kids. Empty nesters whose children live far away. Couples who want to create their own traditions. Travelers who are in the area for the holidays. There's a gigantic market of people who would love an elegant, meaningful way to spend Christmas Eve—especially if it supports a historical landmark and local community."

"The pricing—"

"Would be premium. This isn't a standard scenic ride." Sadie pulled up her pricing analysis. "We're offering an experience—the decorated depot, the pre-boarding reception, live music, storytelling, commemorative ornaments, and fireworks. The ticket price reflects that value. And the research indicates that people are willing to pay more for Christmas Eve experiences specifically because the night carries emotional significance."

Cole was quiet, his fingers tapping against his mug again—a tell, Sadie was beginning to realize, that meant he was processing rather than automatically refusing.

"You've really thought all this through," he said finally.

"I told you I'm good at telling stories. This is a story—not just about a train ride, but about being part of something bigger, about creating memories, about belonging to a tradition." She met his eyes directly. "Your father understood that the Express wasn't just about transportation or even preservation. It was about connection. This event honors that."

Something flickered across Cole's face. He looked back at the laptop screen, reading through the brochure copy again.

"The fireworks would require permits," he said slowly. "And probably approval from the fire marshal. Plus coordination with whoever handles the display."

"I know. I've already started researching local companies and permit requirements." Sadie pulled up yet another file. "The timeline is tight but manageable if we start the process this week."

"And you really think people would come? On Christmas Eve?"

"I think they'd be honored to be part of the inaugural ride. I think they'd tell everyone they know about it. I think it would become the signature event that puts the Mistletoe Express on the map beyond just regional tourism." She paused, then added more quietly, "I think your father would love that you're creating something new while honoring everything he built."

Cole's jaw tightened, and for a moment Sadie thought she'd pushed too far, invoked his father's memory in a way that would make him shut down completely.

Instead, he closed her laptop carefully and leaned back in his chair. "These events—all three of them—they can't interfere with the traditional rides. The Christmas Carol Ride, the Holiday Heritage Tour, and the standard scenic tours—those stay on the schedule exactly as they've always been."

"Of course. These would be additions, not replacements."

"And I have the final say on any operational decisions. If something's not safe or feasible for the equipment, we don't do it."

"Absolutely. You're the expert on what the Express can handle."

"And nothing happens without proper volunteer support. I'm not running myself and the regular staff into the ground because you promised things we can't deliver."

"Agreed. Part of my job is coordinating volunteers and ensuring we have adequate support." Sadie held her breath, afraid to hope that his objections meant he was actually considering her proposals rather than just preparing to shut them down.

Cole reached down to scratch Cash behind the ears, and the dog made a contented sound without opening his eyes. Finally, Cole looked at her again.

"Your trial period is twelve weeks. Martha needs to see results."

"I know."

"These three events are a lot to execute in that time-frame."

"I know that too. But they're structured to build on each other—the Tree Lighting is first, establishing the depot as an event space. The Santa Express proves we can handle complex logistics. And the Christmas Eve ride becomes the capstone that demonstrates sustained impact on tourism and community engagement."

"You've been doing this job for less than forty-eight hours."

Sadie couldn't tell if that was criticism or reluctant admiration. "I researched Mistletoe Falls for weeks before I came here. This isn't improvisation—it's strategic planning based on the Express's strengths and the community's needs."

Cole stood abruptly, and Sadie's heart sank, certain she'd pushed too hard after all. But he just walked to the window, looking out toward where the Express sat gleaming in the morning light.

"My father spent years bringing that train back to life," he said without turning around. "Every decision he made was about honoring what came before while making it viable for the future. He never changed anything just for the sake of change."

"Neither am I," Sadie said quietly. "Every event I proposed connects directly to the Express's history and purpose. The Tree Lighting celebrates the depot restoration. The Santa Express serves families, which is who your father wanted to reach. And the Christmas Eve ride creates the kind of meaningful tradition that ensures people will care about preserving this train for another hundred years."

Cole turned to look at her, and his expression was complicated—still guarded, but maybe less certain of his opposition. "If we're doing this, we're doing it right. No half measures, no cutting corners because the timeline is tight."

"I wouldn't want it any other way."

"And you present everything to Martha. This was your initiative."

"Our initiative," Sadie corrected. "You're agreeing to it, which means it's our partnership."

"I'm agreeing to cooperate. There's a difference."

Sadie let that slide, recognizing the distinction mattered to him even if the practical outcome was the same. "Fair enough."

Cole returned to the table and picked up his mug, which had to be cold by now. Cash stirred enough to look up at him, then settled back to sleep. "When does Martha want the proposal? Tomorrow, right?"

"Tomorrow morning. I already scheduled the meeting with her for ten o'clock in her office." Sadie hesitated, then added, "I can put together the formal write-up today if you want to review it before we present."

"You've clearly done all the work already."

The words carried an edge that made Sadie's defenses rise. "Because someone had to, obviously. I assumed we were both supposed to be developing ideas, but apparently—"

"I was here until nine last night working through maintenance schedules and volunteer coordination requirements," Cole cut in, his voice tight. "Trying to figure out how we could execute new events without compromising the Express's regular operations. Just because I didn't show up with color-coded notebooks doesn't mean I wasn't working."

Sadie felt heat rise in her cheeks. "I'm sorry. I didn't—"

"Know that I was thinking about this instead of sleeping? That I was running capacity calculations and trying to figure out staffing rotations? Yeah. You didn't." He set his mug down with more force than necessary.

They stared at each other, and Sadie felt the weight of her assumption.

"I'm sorry," she said again, meaning it more deeply this time. "You're right. I made assumptions."

Cole's shoulders dropped slightly, tension easing. "We both did. You assumed I wasn't trying. I assumed you were just throwing ideas around without understanding the operational complexity."

"And we were both wrong?"

"Looks like it." Something that might have been the ghost of a smile tugged at his mouth, there and gone so fast Sadie almost missed it. "Your proposals are solid. Ambitious, but solid. If we can pull them off without compromising safety or regular operations; they might actually work."

The compliment, grudging as it was, sent warmth through Sadie's chest. "Thank you."

"Don't thank me yet. You still have to convince Martha, get budget approval, recruit volunteers, and execute three major events in less than two months." Cole ran a hand through his hair, making it stick up in an unfairly attractive way. "And I have to keep running regular operations and managing my actual job."

"We have to convince Martha," Sadie said. "We have to execute three major events in less than two months."

"Right." He looked at her for a long moment, something shifting in his expression. "How long did all this take you?"

"I was up until about two AM. Then I got four hours of sleep and started again at six thirty." She smiled ruefully. "Coffee is the only thing keeping me upright at this point."

"I've got a fresh pot in my office... a better-tasting blend than what's in the staff room. Hank brings it in—some fancy roast from a shop in Gatlinburg." Cole gestured toward his office door. "Want some? You almost pulled an all-nighter to make this proposal perfect; you might as well have decent caffeine."

The offer surprised her more than his agreement to her proposals had.

"I'd like that," Sadie said. "Thank you."

Cole headed toward his office, and Cash immediately stood to follow. Sadie gathered her laptop and note-books, acutely aware that something had shifted be-tween them—not dramatically, not enough to call it a breakthrough, but enough that the air felt different from what it had an hour ago.

She followed Cole into his office, taking in details she'd only glimpsed yesterday: the filing cabinets labeled in his precise handwriting, the photographs of the Express at various stages of restoration, and his father's desk that he obviously couldn't bring himself to change. This was his sanctuary, and he was letting her in.

Cole poured coffee from a pot that did indeed smell significantly better than standard office brew. He hand-ed her a Styrofoam to-go cup—plain white, no decora-tion, completely practical—and their fingers brushed as she took it.

"So," he said, leaning against the desk. "Tomorrow at ten. You'll present the proposals; I'll be there for opera-tional questions and budget details."

"And to show Martha we're actually working together," Sadie added. "That matters to her."

"Yeah. It does." Cole took a sip of his coffee, his eyes never leaving hers. "For what it's worth—you're not what I expected."

"What did you expect?"

"Someone who'd look at the Express and see a project to fix. A problem to solve with marketing campaigns and social media." He paused. "But you're not looking at it that way."

"No," Sadie agreed quietly. "I'm looking at it the way your father did—as a story that deserves to be told, a tradition that deserves to thrive. That's not fixing it. That's honoring."

Cole nodded slowly, and Sadie had the sense that she'd just passed some test she hadn't known she was taking. "Ten o'clock tomorrow. Don't be late."

"I'm never late."

"No, not so far," he said, and this time the smile definitely reached his eyes.

As she turned to leave, Cole spoke again.

"Sadie."

She turned back, surprised at the use of her first name.

"The brochure you designed—the Christmas Eve one. My father would have loved it." His voice roughened slightly. "Just thought you should know that."

The words hit her square in the chest, unexpected and precious. "Thank you, Cole. That was very kind of you to say."

She left his office with her heart doing complicated things behind her ribs, Cash's tail wagging behind her as the dog escorted her to the depot doors like she'd been coming here for years instead of days.

As she walked back toward Holly House in the November morning light, Sadie pulled out her phone and started a new document. Typing a few quick notes. The formal proposal would take some time to write, but now she had something she hadn't had when she'd arrived this morning: Cole Bennett's cooperation. Maybe not his enthusiasm yet, and certainly not his full trust, but cooperation was a foundation they could build on.

Her phone buzzed with a text from Martha:

How's the proposal development going?

Sadie typed back, *Better than expected. We'll be ready for tomorrow's meeting.*

What she didn't add was that "better than expected" included four hours of sleep, numerous cups of coffee, and the first crack in Cole Bennett's defensive walls. Or that somewhere between her Tree Lighting proposal and his offer of better coffee, the stakes of this trial period had shifted from professional to something she couldn't quite name yet. Something that made her pulse quicken when she thought about tomorrow's meeting.

She had less than twenty-four hours to create a proposal that would convince Martha Caldwell these events could work and to prove that she and Cole could actually collaborate despite their differences.

And somewhere in there, she'd figure out why Cole Bennett's grudging approval felt more valuable than any professional compliment she'd ever received.

Chapter 6

Cole saw her before she saw him.

Sadie walked down Icicle Lane toward the town hall with the same determined stride she'd had yesterday morning when she'd arrived at the depot armed with color-coded notebooks and enough caffeine to fuel a locomotive. This morning she wore dark slacks and a cream-colored blouse under her wool coat, her messenger bag slung across her body like armor. Professional. Prepared. Everything he'd expected and somehow still found unsettling.

He'd spent last night lying awake in his cabin, Cash sprawled across his feet, trying to figure out exactly why he'd agreed so easily to turn his father's pride and joy into a testing ground for someone else's ideas. The depot tour had been bad enough—watching Sadie's genuine interest chip away at his defenses, seeing her actually understand what the Express meant to him and to this town. Yesterday's planning session had been worse, because somewhere between her exhausted determination and his own sleep-deprived honestly, he'd stopped fighting and started cooperating.

And now here they were, about to walk into Martha's office and make it official.

Sadie looked up as she approached the town hall steps, and her face shifted when she spotted him—surprise giving way to something that might have been relief or nervousness or both. She adjusted the strap of her bag and offered a small smile.

"Good morning," she said as they met at the bottom of the stairs.

"Morning." Cole gestured toward the building. "Ready for this?"

"As ready as three hours of sleep and a lot of coffee can make me." She started up the steps, and Cole fell into pace beside her. "I reviewed the proposal six times last night. I think I have it memorized at this point."

"Martha's thorough. She'll ask questions you won't expect."

"I figured as much." Sadie paused at the top of the stairs, turning to face him. The morning light caught in her hazel eyes, making them look more green than brown. "Are we... are we good? With presenting this together?"

Cole reached past her to open the heavy wooden door, buying himself a moment before answering. "We made an agreement. I don't go back on my word."

It wasn't exactly the reassurance she'd been looking for—he could see that in the slight tightening around her eyes—but it was honest. That had to count for something.

The town hall lobby smelled of old wood and lemon polish, its marble floors echoing their footsteps as they crossed toward the stairs leading to the second floor. A few other employees nodded greetings as they passed, and Cole caught June Reynolds from the post office watching them with undisguised interest. Small towns. Everyone would know about this meeting before lunch.

Martha's office door stood open at the end of the hallway, and Cole could see her through the doorway, reading something at her desk. She looked up as they approached, her expression shifting from concentration to welcome.

"Right on time," Martha said, setting aside her papers and gesturing toward the chairs arranged in front of her desk. "Come in, both of you. Coffee's fresh if you want it."

"Thank you." Sadie moved to the small coffee station in the corner, and Cole noticed her hands were steady as she poured. Either she was better at hiding nerves than he'd given her credit for, or she actually felt confident about this presentation.

Cole declined the coffee—he'd already consumed enough this morning to make his pulse jump—and settled into one of the chairs. The office was familiar territory: bookshelves lined with tourism guides and historical references, framed photographs of Mistletoe Falls landmarks covering the walls, and Martha's meticulously organized desk that somehow still managed to look welcoming rather than intimidating.

Sadie returned to sit beside him, setting her messenger bag at her feet and pulling out her laptop and one of those color-coded notebooks. Martha settled back in her chair, hands folded on the desk in front of her, and gave them both an expectant look.

"All right," Martha said. "Show me what you two have been cooking up."

Sadie opened her laptop, angling it so Martha could see the screen, and launched into the presentation with the same confidence she'd shown yesterday morning. Cole had to admit—grudgingly—that she knew how to tell a story. She didn't just list facts and figures; she painted a picture of what these events could mean for Mistletoe Falls, for the Express, and for the families who would experience them.

"The Depot Tree Lighting Ceremony," Sadie began, pulling up her first slide, "would take place on Saturday, November 27th, the day after the town's traditional tree lighting in the square. Rather than competing with that beloved tradition, this would complement it—a weekend of holiday celebration that gives visitors a reason to stay longer, spend more in local businesses, and engage more deeply with the town's heritage."

Martha leaned forward slightly, her sharp eyes moving between the screen and Sadie's face. "Walk me through the logistics. The town ceremony draws thousands of people. What kind of attendance are you projecting?"

"Based on similar events at heritage railways in comparable communities, I'm projecting between two hundred and three hundred attendees for the first year." Sadie clicked to a slide showing attendance statistics from other locations. "The key is creating an experience distinct enough to stand on its own while honoring the depot's historical significance."

"And the budget?"

Sadie flipped to her budget spreadsheet, and Cole found himself impressed despite his determination not to be. She'd broken down every expense—decorations, refreshments, promotional materials, and volunteer coordination costs. Nothing extravagant, but nothing cheap either. Quality without excess.

"Total projected cost is approximately four thousand dollars," Sadie said. "That includes decorations that can be reused in subsequent years, reducing future costs. I've already reached out to several local businesses about sponsorships, and the initial response has been positive. With sponsorships, out-of-pocket costs could drop to around twenty-five hundred."

Martha made a note on the pad in front of her. "What about the depot itself? Cole, is the space equipped to handle that kind of foot traffic?"

This was the first direct question aimed at him, and Cole felt both women turn to look at him. He kept his voice level and professional. "The depot was designed to handle passenger volume. The platform can easily accommodate three hundred people, and the museum wing provides indoor space if weather's an issue. We'd need to coordinate with volunteers for crowd management, but structurally, we can handle it."

"Parking?"

"There's the main lot, plus street parking along Depot Road and Pinecone Pass. For larger events, we've used the overflow lot at the community center before—it's only two blocks away."

Martha nodded, seeming satisfied, and turned her attention back to Sadie. "Continue."

Sadie moved through the Santa Express proposal with the same thoroughness—dates, logistics, volunteer requirements, projected attendance, and budget breakdown. She'd clearly done her homework, researching similar programs and adapting them to the Express's specific capabilities and limitations.

"The Santa Express would run Friday, December 10th, and Saturday, December 11th," Sadie explained. "Three departures each day at ten AM, one PM, and three PM. Each ride would be approximately forty-five minutes, giving families time to interact with Santa and Mrs. Claus, enjoy hot chocolate and cookies, and experience the decorated train. After each ride, families would have access to the depot for photos, crafts, and museum tours."

"Six rides total," Martha calculated. "How many passengers per ride?"

Cole spoke before Sadie could answer. "Maximum capacity is one hundred twenty passengers, but for a family event, we'd want to cap it lower—maybe eighty to ninety per ride. Gives family's space to move around, making the Santa experience more intimate."

"So we're looking at potentially five hundred-plus families over two days." Martha tapped her pen against her notepad. "That's a significant volume. Sadie, have you coordinated this kind of event before?"

"Not at this scale," Sadie admitted, and Cole appreciated her honesty. "But I've worked on comparable community events during my journalism assignments. The key is detailed planning and strong volunteer coordination. I've already started identifying potential volunteers from the business community here, and I'm working with Caroline Bennett at The Cozy Cup about coordinating refreshment donations."

Martha's eyebrows rose slightly. "You've talked to Caroline already?"

"Yesterday afternoon. She was enthusiastic about the idea and offered to help recruit other business owners for support."

Cole hadn't known that. Sadie hadn't mentioned talking to his sister-in-law, though he supposed there was no reason she should have. It still felt strange, knowing she was already integrating herself into his family's network without him being aware of it.

Martha asked questions about Santa costume rentals, volunteer training, safety protocols, and liability insurance. Sadie had answers for everything, or at least reasonable plans for finding answers. Cole found himself relaxing slightly—not because he suddenly trusted this would all work out, but because Sadie clearly wasn't approaching this carelessly.

"And the Christmas Eve event?" Martha prompted.

"All Aboard on Christmas Eve," Sadie said, clicking to her final presentation section. "This would be the signature event, the one that becomes an annual tradition families plan their holidays around. A special evening ride departing at six PM, lasting approximately ninety minutes, featuring the fully decorated Express, holiday music, storytelling, and a special stop at Whispering Falls where passengers can disembark briefly for photos and carol singing."

Cole watched Martha's expression shift from businesslike interest to something warmer. The older woman had grown up in Mistletoe Falls, had been friends with his father, understood what the Express meant to this community. Sadie's vision for Christmas Eve wasn't about tourism numbers—it was about creating memories.

"The route to Whispering Falls," Martha said thoughtfully. "That's the most scenic section of the line."

"And the most meaningful," Sadie added. "According to the historical records, Michael Bennett's first successful test run after restoration ended at Whispering Falls. He stood on the platform there and told everyone who'd helped with the project that they'd brought something beautiful back to life. I think ending our Christmas season there would be a fitting tribute."

Cole's throat tightened. He didn't remember telling Sadie that detail at the museum on Monday, which meant she'd gone digging and had done research. She had read through archives and oral histories until she'd found that story. His father's story.

Martha was quiet for a moment, and when she spoke, her voice carried a note of emotion she usually kept carefully controlled. "Michael would have loved that."

"I kind of imagined he would. That's why I think it's an important feature for this event," Sadie said softly.

The office felt smaller suddenly, the weight of memory pressing against Cole's chest. He stared at the corner of Martha's desk, focusing on the wood grain, willing his breathing to stay even.

"Budget for Christmas Eve?" Martha asked, returning to business, and Cole was grateful for the shift.

Sadie walked through the numbers, the logistics, and the promotional timeline. Martha asked about ticket pricing, capacity limits, and how this would integrate with the traditional holiday rides already on the schedule. Sadie had an answer for every question, or a reasonable plan to develop one.

Finally, Martha sat back in her chair and looked at Cole directly. "You've been quiet through most of this. What's your honest assessment? Are you on board with these events?"

The question hung in the air, and Cole felt Sadie tense beside him. This was the moment that mattered—not Sadie's polished presentation or Martha's approval, but whether he was genuinely willing to commit to this or if he was just going through the motions because he'd been forced into cooperation.

Cole took his time answering, choosing his words carefully. "When Sadie first proposed these ideas, my instinct was to shut them down. They felt like change for change's sake, like someone coming in and trying to fix something that wasn't broken."

He saw Sadie's shoulders drop slightly and continued before she could spiral further.

"But after reviewing her research and understanding how she's structured these events—they're not replacing anything. They're building on the foundation my father established. Each event connects to the Express's history and purpose. The Tree Lighting celebrates the depot. The Santa Express serves families, which is exactly who my father wanted to reach. And the Christmas Eve ride..." He paused, making himself say it. "It honors my father's vision while creating something new."

Martha's expression softened. "So that's a yes?"

"That's a yes," Cole confirmed. "I believe each event will increase tourism and interest in the Mistletoe Express. Sadie's done thorough work. If she executes these events properly, they could become exactly the kind of traditions this town needs."

The surprise on both women's faces would have been amusing if Cole weren't already regretting being so honest. Sadie looked like she wanted to say something but wasn't sure what, while Martha's knowing smile suggested she was reading far more into his cooperation than he'd intended to reveal.

"Well then," Martha said, gathering the papers in front of her. "I'm approving all three events. Sadie, you'll work directly with Cole on all operational aspects. Cole, you'll have full authority on any decisions involving the Express's safety and capabilities. I want weekly progress reports from both of you, starting next Wednesday."

"Understood," Sadie said.

"Weekly reports," Cole echoed, already dreading the additional meetings that would require.

Martha pulled out her calendar. "Let's schedule a check-in meeting for November 19th, one week out from the tree lighting. That'll give us time to address any issues before the event." She made a note, then looked up at both of them. "I have confidence you two can pull this off. The question is whether you'll kill each other in the process."

"We'll try to keep casualties to a minimum," Sadie said, and there was enough humor in her voice that Cole almost smiled.

Almost.

"Sadie, you can head out," Martha said. "Cole, could you stay a few minutes? I'd like to discuss some operational details."

Sadie stood, gathering her laptop and notebook. "Of course. Thank you, Martha. For believing in these ideas."

"Thank you for bringing them to us." Martha's warmth was genuine. "You're going to do good work here, Sadie. I can already tell."

Sadie's smile was almost shy as she headed for the door. She paused in the doorway, turning back to look at Cole. "I'm still planning to ride along this afternoon on the school group tour. Two o'clock, right?"

Cole had completely forgotten about that. "Right. The school group."

"If it's not a good time—"

"No, it's fine." And because some part of him apparently couldn't help himself, he added, "If you want to come an hour early, around one, I can show you the prep work. Behind-the-scenes knowledge might help you get the full picture."

Sadie's expression brightened. "I'd like that. Thank you."

She left, and the office felt bigger without her presence. Cole turned his attention to Martha, who was watching him with an expression he couldn't quite read.

"How are you really doing with all this?" Martha asked, her voice gentle but direct. "These events, working with Sadie—that's a lot of change in a very short time."

Cole considered deflecting, giving her the easy answer she wanted to hear. But Martha had known him since he was a kid, had worked alongside his father, and had been there during the worst days after the funeral. She deserved honesty.

"I'll believe it when I see it," he said. "If Sadie can pull off these events, more kudos to her. But we're talking about a lot of moving parts, a lot of coordination, and plenty of things that could go wrong."

"That's why you're going to work closely with her," Martha said. "These events aren't just Sadie's job now, Cole. They're yours too. You need to make sure they're top-notch and successful. The Express's reputation depends on it."

"I know that."

"Do you?" Martha leaned forward, her expression shifting from gentle to firm. "Because I need you to understand something. Sadie is working on a twelve-week trial contract. She's trying to prove herself to this town, to me, and yes, to you. But she can't do this alone. She needs your expertise, your knowledge of the Express, your connections with the volunteers and community members who've been supporting this operation for years."

Cole's jaw tightened. "I said I'd cooperate."

"Cooperation isn't the same as partnership," Martha countered. "I need you to actually work with her, Cole. Not just tolerate her presence or grudgingly approve her ideas. Actually engage, contribute, and help her succeed. Because if these events fail, it's not just her trial period that suffers—it's the Express, it's the town's tourism revenue, and it's the legacy your father built."

The words hit harder than Cole wanted to admit.

"I know you've been through a lot," Martha continued, her voice softening. "Losing your father the way you did, taking on the responsibility of the entire operation of the Mistletoe Express, and giving up a lot of your personal time because of your devotion to it. That took courage and dedication, and everyone in this town respects what you've done. But Cole..." She paused, choosing her words carefully. "You used to be different. More open, more willing to take chances. More alive. Your father wouldn't want you to spend your life maintaining what he built. He'd want you to build on it. He'd want to see you happy and thriving... but Cole... I'm being honest... you're stuck in a rut, and you really need to start living again."

Cole stared at his hands, at the calluses and old scars from years of manual labor. Martha wasn't wrong. He knew she wasn't wrong. But knowing it and changing it were two different things.

"I'll work with Sadie," he said quietly. "I'll make sure these events succeed. You have my word."

"Good." Martha's smile returned, warm and slightly mischievous. "And who knows? You might even enjoy yourself."

Cole seriously doubted that, but he kept the thought to himself.

He left Martha's office a few minutes later, her words still echoing in his head. The hallway was empty, and his footsteps sounded too loud in the quiet, each one a reminder that he was walking toward something he couldn't quite name and wasn't sure he wanted.

Partnership.

That's what Martha had called it. Not just cooperation, but actual partnership with Sadie Baker—a woman who'd been in town less than a week and had already managed to shake something loose in him. A woman who looked at the Express and saw possibility instead of just preservation. A woman who'd somehow found a story about his father that Cole himself hadn't thought about in quite a while and had cared enough to build an entire event around it.

He pushed through the heavy wooden doors and stepped out into the November morning. The air was crisp, carrying the scent of incoming snow and the distant aroma of fresh bread from the bakery down the street.

Twelve weeks. That's how long Sadie's trial contract lasted. Twelve weeks of working closely with her, of daily planning sessions and collaborative decision-making, of watching her integrate herself into his carefully ordered world. Twelve weeks of forcing himself to engage instead of just endure.

He could do this. He'd agreed to work with her and to make these events succeed. That didn't mean he had to like it. That didn't mean he had to let her get close and didn't mean he had to let down the walls that had kept him safe for the past few years.

He'd keep his distance. Do what he had to do and nothing more. Professional. Cordial. Helpful enough to ensure success, but detached enough to protect himself from whatever it was about Sadie Baker that made him want to believe things could be different.

Because they couldn't be different. People left.

Chapter 7

Sadie stepped through the depot doors at one o'clock and stopped dead in her tracks.

Cole Bennett stood by the ticket counter in full conductor's uniform—navy wool jacket with brass buttons gleaming, vest underneath, and the peaked cap that somehow made his steel-blue eyes even more striking. He was reading something on a clipboard, his posture straight, his jaw set with the kind of focus she'd come to recognize as his default setting.

Handsome didn't begin to cover it.

"You all right?" Cole looked up, and Sadie realized she'd been standing there staring like some star-struck teenager instead of a professional woman who had work to do.

"Fine." She adjusted her messenger bag and forced herself to move forward, trying to ignore the heat creeping up her neck. "Just... wasn't expecting the full uniform."

"Every train ride deserves the full authentic experience." He set the clipboard on the counter. "Coffee? I made a fresh pot about twenty minutes ago."

"Please." Sadie followed him toward his office, trying not to notice how the uniform jacket emphasized his broad shoulders. This was a professional observation. Research to understand the full scope of the Express operation. Nothing more.

Cole poured two mugs of coffee and handed her one.

"Sugar and creamer are in the cabinet if you need them," he said.

"Black's fine." Sadie took a sip. "This coffee is so good."

"It is. You running on coffee fumes again today?" The corner of his mouth twitched—not quite a smile, but close enough to count as progress.

"Something like that," she said. "So tell me, what does prep work look like for a school group ride?"

Cole straightened, shifting immediately into what Sadie was starting to think of as his teaching mode—patient, thorough, and genuinely engaged when talking about the Express. "Come on. I'll show you."

They moved through the depot, Cole grabbing the clipboard he'd left on the ticket booth counter, and out onto the platform where the Mistletoe Express waited, her green paint gleaming in the afternoon light, brass fittings polished to perfection. Cole set his coffee mug on a nearby bench and pulled a checklist from his jacket pocket.

"Every ride starts with a complete safety inspection," he said, handing her the checklist as he moved toward the locomotive. "It doesn't matter whether we ran a ride two hours ago or two days ago. We check everything before passengers board."

Sadie pulled out her phone to take notes, then thought better of it and grabbed the small notebook from her bag instead.

"Boiler pressure first." Cole checked a gauge and made a note on his clipboard. "Steam engines operate under pressure. Too low, and we don't have power. Too high, and we have a safety issue. Has to be in the optimal range."

"What's optimal?"

"For the Express, between one hundred twenty and one hundred fifty PSI for passenger runs." He showed her the gauge, pointing to where the needle rested comfortably in the green zone. "We maintain higher pressure for freight or for steeper grades, but the route we'll take today and back is mostly level with gentle grades."

"How long does it take to build up pressure?"

"About forty-five minutes from a cold start. But we keep her warm on days when we have scheduled runs, so it's just a matter of maintaining pressure between rides." He moved along the locomotive, checking connections, testing valves, and running his hands over surfaces with the kind of familiarity that came from years of daily practice.

"Water level," he continued, checking another gauge. "Steam engines consume water. We need to ensure we have sufficient supply for the full run, plus reserve."

"What happens if you run out of water?"

"The boiler would overheat, and we'd risk serious damage to the engine. But that's why we check." He tapped the gauge. "This is called a water glass—it shows the exact water level in the boiler. We monitor it throughout every run."

Sadie watched him work, noting the care he took with each inspection point, the way he touched the Express like she was something precious.

"Brakes next." Cole moved to check the brake system, explaining how steam-powered brakes worked, how the conductor had to coordinate with the engineer, and how safety was always the first priority. "My father used to say that the Express wasn't ours to own—we were just caretakers for future generations. Every decision we make has to honor that responsibility."

"Is that why you're so protective of it?" The question slipped out before Sadie could stop it. "Not protective—I mean, of course you're protective. But why you are so careful about change?"

Cole was quiet for a moment, his hand resting on one of the brake wheels. "When my father died, the Express was all I had left of him. Everything he believed in, everything he worked for—it was all here. Maintaining it exactly as he left it felt like keeping him alive somehow."

Sadie's chest tightened. "Cole—"

"I know it's not rational," he continued, not looking at her. "Martha said as much this morning. My mom tells me the same thing all the time. But knowing something intellectually and feeling it emotionally are two different things."

"It's not irrational to want to honor someone you loved."

"Maybe not. But there's a difference between honoring and being stuck." He finally looked at her, and the vulnerability in his expression made her breath catch. "I'm trying. Not to be stuck. It's just... hard."

Sadie wanted to reach out, to offer some kind of comfort, but she wasn't sure it would be welcome. Instead, she said quietly, "For what it's worth, I think your father would be proud of you."

Cole held her gaze for a long moment, then he cleared his throat and returned to his clipboard.

"Passenger cars next," he said, his voice deliberately businesslike again. "Need to make sure the heating works, the seats are clean, and the windows are secure."

They moved through each car systematically, Cole explaining safety protocols, emergency procedures, and passenger capacity limits. Sadie asked questions and took notes, but she was also watching him—the way his shoulders relaxed when he spoke about the Express, the unconscious affection in how he touched the original woodwork, and the pride that crept into his voice despite his attempts to keep things purely factual.

"You really love this," she observed as they finished inspecting the last passenger car.

"The Express? Of course."

"No, I mean—" Sadie gestured around them. "This. The whole operation. Teaching people about it, sharing the history, and making sure every detail is perfect. You love it."

Cole looked uncomfortable under the observation. "It's my job."

"It's more than that." She met his eyes. "You're good at it, Cole. Really good. And you care—not just about maintaining your father's legacy, but about creating experiences that matter to people. That's rare."

He didn't respond, but something in his expression softened, and Sadie felt like she'd somehow said the right thing even if she wasn't entirely sure what the right thing was.

The sound of a school bus pulling into the depot parking lot broke the moment. Cole checked his pocket watch—a gesture Sadie had noticed he did constantly, like touching a talisman.

"They're early," he said. "Come on. You can observe from the platform, or ride along if you prefer. Up to you."

"I'm still up for riding along, if that's okay."

"It's fine. Just stay out of the way during boarding." He started toward the platform, then paused. "You've ridden trains before, right? You know what to expect?"

Sadie hesitated, suddenly feeling foolish. "Actually... no. I've never been on a train."

Cole turned to stare at her like she'd just confessed to never having seen the ocean or tasted chocolate. "Never?"

"Never. My father preferred flying everywhere, and I've spent most of my adult life driving between assignments." She shrugged, trying to make it sound less pathetic than it felt. "I know it's strange for someone in my position—"

"It's not strange. It's just..." He shook his head, something almost like wonder crossing his face. "You're about to have your first train ride on the Mistletoe Express. That's special."

"I guess it is."

"Then we'll make sure it's a good one." Cole's expression shifted. "Hank's conducting today. I'll ride in the passenger car to speak with the kids and answer questions. You can sit wherever you want."

The school group was spilling out of the bus now—a chaotic swirl of first-graders in matching field trip t-shirts, their teacher trying to maintain some semblance of order, and four parent volunteers bringing up the rear with the kind of patient exhaustion that came from wrangling six-year-olds.

Cole straightened his conductor's cap and moved to greet them, and Sadie watched his entire demeanor transform.

"Good afternoon!" His voice carried across the platform, warm and welcoming. "Welcome to the Mistletoe Express. I'm Cole Bennett, and we're so glad you're here today."

The children's chatter quieted as they caught sight of him in full uniform, their eyes wide with excitement. Cole stepped forward to meet the teacher—a woman in her forties with kind eyes and graying hair pulled back in a practical bun.

"Ms. Rodriguez," Cole said, shaking her hand. "Good to see you again."

"Mr. Bennett. Thank you for accommodating us on such short notice." The teacher's smile was genuine, clearly familiar with Cole and the Express. "The children have been talking about nothing else for days."

"We love having school groups." Cole turned his attention to the parent volunteers, shaking each of their hands and thanking them for chaperoning. Then he crouched down to the children's level, his stern expression softening completely.

"How many of you have ridden on a train before?" he asked.

A few hands shot up. The excitement was palpable.

"Well, you're in for something special today. This train—" He gestured toward the Express. "—is over one hundred years old. She was built in 1887, which is so long ago that your great-great-great-grandparents might have been children when she first started running. Can anyone tell me what makes this train different from cars or buses?"

"It runs on tracks!" one boy shouted.

"That's right. And what makes her move?"

"Steam!" a girl with pigtails called out.

"Exactly. Steam power—the same kind of power that people used over a hundred years ago before we had cars and airplanes." Cole's enthusiasm was infectious; his entire face animated in a way Sadie had never seen.

"When we get on the train, you're going to hear that steam whistle blow. You're going to feel the power of the engine as we move. And you're going to see the same beautiful mountains that people saw when they rode this train a hundred years ago."

The children were mesmerized, completely focused on every word. Even the most fidgety ones had stilled, caught up in Cole's storytelling.

"Now, here are the important rules," Cole continued, his voice remaining warm but taking on a note of gentle authority. "We stay seated while the train is moving. We keep our hands inside the windows. We listen to our teacher and parent volunteers. And we remember that this train is special—we treat her with respect because she's a piece of history that we get to take care of for the people who'll come after us. Can everyone do that?"

A chorus of "Yes!" erupted from the group.

"Then let's board the Mistletoe Express."

Sadie watched from the platform as Cole stood at the bottom of the passenger car steps, offering his hand to each child as they climbed aboard. He learned their names as they passed. "Hello, Emma," "Nice to meet you, Jackson," "Those are cool sneakers, Miguel"—treating each child like they mattered, like they were important guests rather than just another school group.

Something in Sadie's chest cracked wide open watching him.

An older man in a conductor's uniform emerged from the locomotive—Hank Lawson, Sadie realized, the senior conductor she'd read about in the Express files. His weathered face broke into a smile when he saw Cole with the children.

"Group all aboard?" Hank called.

"Almost there," Cole responded. He helped the last few children up the steps, then turned to Ms. Rodriguez and the parent volunteers. "After you."

Once everyone was safely aboard, Cole looked up at the platform where Sadie still stood. "Coming?"

She descended the steps and let him offer his hand—the same courtesy he'd shown the children. His palm was warm and calloused against hers, steady as she stepped up into the passenger car.

The children had scattered throughout the car, most pressing their noses to the windows, their excitement barely contained.

Cole moved to the center of the car where everyone could see him. "I'm going to be riding along with you today to answer questions and tell you about what we're seeing. Mr. Lawson is our engineer and conductor—he's the one driving the train. He's been working on the Express almost as long as the train has been restored, and he knows her better than anyone."

Hank appeared in the doorway between cars, tipping his cap to the children. "Ready for an adventure?"

"Yes!" the children chorused.

"Then let's get moving."

Hank disappeared back toward the locomotive, and a moment later, the Express's whistle blew—a sound both mournful and joyful, echoing across the depot and into the mountains beyond. The children erupted in excited chatter.

Sadie had found a seat near the back where she could observe without interfering and watched as the train began to move. The initial lurch was gentle, the kind of motion that felt both foreign and somehow right. Steam hissed, wheels turned, and the Mistletoe Express pulled away from the depot.

Cole remained standing, one hand on a seat back for balance, completely at ease with the train's rhythm. "If you look out the left-side windows," he said once they'd built up speed, "you can see Mistletoe Falls downtown area and get a quick glimpse of the town square."

The children craned to see, their faces pressed against the glass.

"And coming up on the right," Cole continued as the train curved, "is what we call the Old Forest section. Some of the trees are over two hundred years old. When the first settlers came to this valley, these trees were already here. They've seen a lot of history."

Sadie found herself just as captivated as the children, watching the scenery unfold like a living painting. The late autumn colors were breathtaking—gold and orange and deep crimson against the evergreen backdrop, mountains rising in the distance with their peaks touched by early snow.

But more than the scenery, she watched Cole. He moved through the car answering questions, pointing out landmarks, and telling stories about the Express's history in ways that made it come alive for his young audience. His entire bearing had changed—the walls were down, the guarded expression gone, replaced by genuine warmth and engagement.

"Mr. Bennett?" One small girl tugged at his sleeve. "Does the train have a name? Like, besides Mistletoe Express?"

Cole crouched down to her level. "The train's official name is Mistletoe Express, but my father used to call her 'Lady' when he was working on her. He said she was temperamental like a lady—you had to treat her right or she'd let you know she wasn't happy."

"What made her happy?" the girl asked seriously.

"Regular maintenance, good fuel, and people who cared about her." Cole's smile was soft. "Just like people, really. We all need to be taken care of and valued."

The girl nodded, satisfied with this answer.

The train wound through the countryside, past farms and forests, crossing a small bridge over Mistletoe Creek where the water tumbled over rocks in a miniature waterfall. Cole narrated the whole journey, but it never felt like a lecture—more like a friend sharing something he loved with people he wanted to love it too.

"And this," Cole announced as they rounded a bend, "is Whispering Falls."

The waterfall appeared like magic, cascading down a rock face in a silvery ribbon that caught the afternoon light. The Express slowed and then stopped at a small platform that had been built specifically for viewing.

"This is where we turn around to head back," Cole explained. "But first, everyone can get out and take a closer look at the falls. Stay with your teacher and parent volunteers, and watch your step on the platform."

The organized chaos of getting twenty-two first-graders safely off the train and onto the viewing platform would have been comical if it weren't so sweetly earnest. Cole supervised with the same patient attention he'd shown all afternoon, making sure everyone had a chance to see the falls up close, answering questions about how waterfalls formed and why this one was called Whispering Falls.

"Because if you listen carefully," he told one fascinated little boy, "you can hear the water whispering secrets to the rocks."

Sadie stood at the edge of the platform, watching Cole with the children, their faces upturned as he pointed out a family of deer on the far side of the creek, and she couldn't help but smile, enjoying this friendly, laid-back side of him.

The return journey passed in a blur of children's laughter and Cole's steady presence, the train rocking gently on the tracks as they wound their way back toward the depot. Sadie watched the landscape pass, memorizing the rhythm of the rails, the sound of the steam whistle, and the way the light filtered through the windows.

Her first train ride.

On the Mistletoe Express.

With Cole Bennett as her guide.

There was something poetic about that, even if she couldn't quite articulate what it meant.

The depot came back into view, and Hank brought the Express to a smooth stop at the platform. The children were reluctant to disembark, several begging to ride again immediately, but Ms. Rodriguez and the parent volunteers began the process of organizing the group for their return to school.

Cole stood at the car steps again, helping each child down, receiving enthusiastic thank-yous and the occasional hug from the more exuberant students. By the time the last child had bounded off toward the bus, his stern expression had returned, but something in his eyes remained softer than before.

Sadie descended last, declining his offered hand this time—she needed a moment to steady herself, and his touch wouldn't help.

"Thank you," she said once they were alone on the platform. "For letting me observe. For explaining everything. For..." She gestured vaguely. "All of it."

"It's part of the job."

"No, it's not. Not the way you do it." Sadie met his eyes. "You made that ride special for those kids. You made my first ride on the Express something I'll never forget. That matters, Cole."

He shifted, clearly uncomfortable with the praise. "They're just kids. They deserve to have good experiences."

"Everyone deserves that." She adjusted her messenger bag, preparing to leave before she said something she couldn't take back. "I'll be here bright and early tomorrow. Nine o'clock. So we can start working on the tree-lighting details."

"Nine o'clock," he confirmed.

She started to walk away, then turned back. "For what it's worth? I truly enjoyed watching you with those kids today. I saw a side of you I'd like to know better."

She didn't wait for his response—she couldn't, not with the look on his face making it difficult to breathe.

As she crossed the platform, the Express's whistle blew one final time. She wondered if Cole was still standing there, watching her go, or if he'd already buried himself back in maintenance checklists and operational procedures.

Either way, she smiled. Her step felt lighter than it had when she'd arrived. She had glimpsed the man beneath Cole Bennett's guarded exterior.

And now she couldn't unsee it.

Chapter 8

Sadie arrived at the depot at eight thirty Thursday morning with two notebooks, three colored pens, and a determination to prove that yesterday's moment of connection with Cole hadn't been a fluke.

She found him in the museum, directing Charlie Dawson—the teenage volunteer she'd heard about previously—as they rearranged display cases to make room for some new archival photographs. Cole wore his usual work clothes today, no conductor's uniform.

"Morning," she called from the doorway.

Both Cole and Charlie turned. The teenager grinned immediately. "Miss Baker... right? Mr. Bennett said you're gonna start planning the Tree Lighting Ceremony today. That's going to be so cool."

"I hope so." Sadie smiled at his enthusiasm. "And please, just Sadie is fine."

"Charlie's been volunteering here since he was four-teen," Cole said, setting down the display case he'd been holding. "He knows the depot better than most adults. Charlie, can you finish up here? I need to work with Sadie on the event planning."

"Sure thing, Mr. Bennett." Charlie grabbed the next case with the kind of casual strength that came from regular physical work.

Cole gestured for Sadie to follow him back to the main depot area.

"Charlie seems like a great kid," Sadie observed as they walked.

"He is. He's homeschooled, and his mom allows him to volunteer a lot as part of his education. Reminds me of myself at that age—obsessed with the Express, always finding excuses to be here." Cole's expression shifted, something wistful crossing his face. "He's talking about studying mechanical engineering in college. Wants to work on historic railway restoration."

"Wow, that's wonderful."

"He's got potential." Cole stopped at one of the depot's main windows, looking out at the platform. "So. Tree Lighting. You said nine o'clock, but you're early."

"Couldn't sleep. Too many ideas bouncing around." Sadie pulled out her first notebook. "Anyway... I've been thinking about logistics, and I wanted to walk through the space with you before we start making final deci-sions."

Something in Cole's posture relaxed. "Good. Logistics matter. Let's start with the obvious question—where will the Christmas tree go?"

They moved through the depot and out onto the platform, Sadie taking notes while Cole pointed out structural considerations, sight lines, and how the crowd would flow during the ceremony. He knew every inch of the space and understood exactly how people would move through it.

"Here," Cole said, stopping near the center of the platform. "The tree should go here. It's visible from inside the depot through the main windows but positioned so people can gather around it on the platform for the lighting ceremony. We'll need to secure it properly—the platform's solid, but a twelve-foot tree in November wind requires proper anchoring."

Sadie sketched the layout in her notebook. "Twelve feet?"

"Platform ceiling clearance is eighteen feet at this point. A twelve-footer will look good in this space." He gestured around them. "People should be able to see it from the parking lot when they arrive, but it shouldn't overwhelm the depot itself."

"Makes sense." Sadie looked around the platform, imagining it filled with people, lights, the scent of pine, hot cocoa, and fresh cookies filling the air. "What about the museum? Should we keep it open during the event, or would you rather not?"

Cole's eyes lit up—the same expression he'd had yesterday when talking to the children about the Express's history. "Absolutely. The museum tells the story of how the depot was restored. People should see everything that's been accomplished. It connects the past to the present."

"We could set up a self-guided tour route," Sadie suggested, warming to the idea. "Maybe print simple guides that highlight key artifacts, explain the restoration process—"

"And we could position volunteers at strategic points to answer questions." Cole was already moving toward the museum entrance, his focus shifting to planning mode. "Hank would be perfect for that. He worked alongside my father during the restoration. He can tell stories that aren't in any of the written materials."

They walked through the museum together, discussing volunteer placement, lighting considerations, and how to manage crowd flow without making people feel rushed. Sadie found herself caught up in Cole's enthusiasm, watching how his entire demeanor changed when he was solving problems instead of defending territory.

"The platform," Cole said suddenly. "We should string lights along the platform railing. Create a pathway that leads people's eyes from the tree inside to the Express outside."

"Yes." Sadie was already writing. "And maybe we could position the Express so she's visible through the main windows? People could see her lit up while they're inside as well."

"Sounds good. We'll need to coordinate with the town's electrical crew, too. They'll have the equipment and expertise we need to make sure we don't overload any circuits."

"I can reach out to them today." Sadie made another note. "What about the tree itself? Anywhere nearby that I could order a tree and keep delivery costs low?"

"Mistletoe Tree Farm, about fifteen miles outside town. Family operation—they've been supplying Christmas trees to local businesses for years." Cole moved to the window again, looking out at the platform as if visualizing the space transformed. "We should pick it out in person. Make sure we're getting the right height and the right fullness."

"I was planning to just have one delivered—"

"They deliver, but you lose control over the selection." Cole turned to face her. "We could go together and pick out exactly what we want. Make sure it's perfect."

Sadie stared at him momentarily surprised. The Cole she'd met on Monday would never have volunteered to spend extra time with her, especially not on something that could easily be delegated. But here he was, offering not just his truck but his time.

"Okay," she said carefully. "When were you thinking?"

"November 20th? That would give us a week for decorating it before the event." Cole seemed to be calculating mentally. "The farm doesn't open for the season until the day after Thanksgiving. I'll call Gabe and ask if he'd mind if we come out before he officially opens to the public; I'm sure he won't have a problem with it."

"So, November 20. A Saturday, right?"

"Unless that doesn't work for you."

"No, that's fine. That's perfect, actually. I'll be sure and have the decorations and lights ordered and delivered before then and speak with someone about electrical specifics."

They continued planning, moving outside onto the platform to discuss the Express's positioning, debating the merits of white lights versus colored, and working through the timing of the evening's events.

"The ceremony should start at seven," Cole said. "Gives family's time for dinner, and it'll be dark enough for the lights to have full impact."

"And we end by ten at the latest," Sadie added. "Before it gets too cold for the kids, and it keeps the event feeling special rather than dragging on."

"Cocoa and cookies inside the depot after the tree lighting—"

"Served by volunteers in festive aprons—"

"While carolers perform by the Christmas tree—"

"And the Express sits front and center on its tracks like a crown jewel, all lit up and beautiful."

They stopped, both realizing they'd been completing each other's thoughts, their planning flowing like a practiced dance. Cole's expression shifted.

"You're really good at this," he said quietly.

"So are you." Sadie met his eyes. "We make a good team."

The moment stretched between them, charged. Cole's gaze dropped to her mouth, then back to her eyes, and Sadie's breath caught.

Then he stepped back.

"We should finalize the budget," he said, his voice deliberately businesslike again. "Make sure we're accounting for all the supplies we'll need."

The warmth evaporated as quickly as it had appeared, leaving Sadie feeling off-balance. One moment they'd been genuinely connecting, and the next Cole had retreated so fast she almost had whiplash.

"Right. The budget." She flipped to a new page in her notebook, trying to ignore the disappointment settling in her chest. "I have preliminary numbers, but we should go through them together to make sure I'm not missing anything."

They returned to the depot's main hall, and Cole led her to a table near the windows. He pulled out a calculator and a ledger—because of course he kept a handwritten ledger—and they began working through the numbers.

But something had changed. Cole was still helpful, still thorough, but the ease between them had vanished. He kept a physical distance, maintained eye contact only when necessary, and responded to her questions with polite efficiency rather than the engaged warmth from earlier.

Sadie tried to recapture the collaborative energy they'd had, but it was like trying to catch smoke. Every time she thought they were connecting again, Cole would pull back, reminding her with his careful distance that whatever moment they'd shared was over.

Hank appeared around ten-thirty, greeting them both cheerfully and asking about their progress. Cole's demeanor shifted immediately—warm and open with Hank in a way he'd stopped being with Sadie.

"Looking good," Hank said, reviewing their plans. "Your daddy would've loved this, Cole. Using the depot for a community gathering—that's exactly what he always loved to do."

Cole's jaw tightened slightly.

"I like what you have planned so far, Sadie. I have a feeling you'll do great things for this town of ours," Hank said as he smiled at her.

"Thank you," Sadie said, grateful for his kindness.

After Hank left, the silence between them felt heavier. Sadie checked her watch—they'd been working for over two hours, and her initial list of planning items was nearly complete.

"I think we've covered the major points," she said, closing her notebook. "I'll start reaching out to vendors today and get quotes for the decorations and supplies we discussed."

"Fine." Cole gathered his papers, organizing them with the same meticulous care he applied to everything else. "Please let me know if you hit any issues with local suppliers. Most of them know me—I can help smooth things along if needed."

It was a generous offer wrapped in professional courtesy, and Sadie wasn't sure which frustrated her more—the generosity or the distance.

"I appreciate that." She stood, slinging her messenger bag over her shoulder.

Charlie reappeared then, announcing he'd finished the museum work and needed to head home and get his schoolwork done. Cole walked him out, their conversation easy and natural.

She should leave. She had vendor calls to make, supply lists to finalize, and promotional materials to start drafting. The practical part of her brain recited the tasks waiting back in her office.

But she couldn't deny that she didn't want to leave.

She wanted to stay in this space where Cole had laughed at her observation about how many people would inevitably ask where the bathroom was during the event. Where he'd gotten excited explaining the engineering behind the platform's construction. Where they'd finished each other's sentences and had been excited about the upcoming event.

She wanted to stay in the moment before something had made him pull away.

Cole returned from walking Charlie out and found her still standing by the table.

"Something else we need to cover?" he asked.

Yes, she wanted to say. Why do you keep pulling back every time we connect? Why does getting to know me seem to scare you? What are you so afraid of?

But she couldn't ask those questions.

"No," she said instead. "I think we're good."

She made herself walk toward the door, each step feeling heavier than it should. At the threshold, she glanced back.

Cole stood, his hands in his pockets, looking out the window at the mountains with an expression she couldn't quite read. He looked lonely; she realized. Isolated in a space he'd made beautiful but had filled with ghosts instead of people.

Sadie turned away before he could catch her staring and stepped out into the November morning.

Chapter 9

Cole should have known that walking into The Cozy Cup on a Friday morning would be like stepping into the town's unofficial intelligence headquarters.

"Cole Bennett." June planted herself directly in his path, her arms crossed over her postal service uniform. "Just the man I wanted to see."

Cole glanced past her toward the counter where Caroline was pulling espresso shots, her blond hair pulled back into a ponytail that was swinging as she worked. His sister-in-law caught his eye and gave him a look that clearly said, You're on your own.

"Morning, June." He tried to be polite but not encouraging. In his experience, June Reynolds could turn a simple greeting into a twenty-minute interrogation if you let her.

"Don't you 'morning' me." June's eyes narrowed, but her smile was warm. "I want to know about this Sadie Baker."

Cole felt his shoulders tense. Of course. In a town the size of Mistletoe Falls, news traveled faster than the Express at full steam.

"What about her?" He kept his voice neutral and side-stepped around June toward the counter.

June followed naturally. "Is she nice? Does she understand how special our town is? Is she one of those new-age people thinking everything has to be all digital and modern or one of those social media-crazed young people? Because the last thing we need is some outsider coming in and trying to turn our traditions into---."

"She's been here six days, June."

"Which is plenty of time to make a first impression." June settled onto one of the counter stools, clearly prepared to stay. "Martha says she's smart and professional, but Martha said the same thing about that consultant we hired two years ago who wanted to turn the Fall Festival into some kind of craft beer extravaganza."

Despite himself, Cole had to laugh. That particular disaster had become town legend—a cautionary tale about the dangers of bringing in outside expertise without proper vetting.

Caroline appeared in front of him, wiping her hands on her apron. "Large black coffee?"

"Please." Cole pulled out his wallet.

"On the house as usual, Cole." Caroline waved him off. "Consider it payment for whatever entertainment June's about to provide."

"I heard that," June said, without any real offense. "And I'm being perfectly reasonable. We all want to know what this new girl is like. Cole's been working with her. He has firsthand information."

"I've been working near her," Cole corrected. "There's a difference."

"That's not what Martha said. She told me you gave her the depot tour Monday afternoon, and that you were assigned to work with her closely." This came from Mrs. Phillips, who'd apparently been eavesdropping from her table by the window. "My grandson saw her on the Express... he was part of the school field trip group on Wednesday. Said she was taking notes like crazy."

Cole accepted his coffee from Caroline and took a long drink, buying time. The truth was, he didn't know what to say about Sadie Baker. She'd surprised him—with her genuine interest in the Express, her thoughtful questions, and her obvious respect for things that mattered. She'd worked many hours to plan out events, and she'd created a great proposal, and it showed. Not in sloppiness or shortcuts, but in the level of care she'd put into understanding what the Express meant before suggesting anything new.

But he wasn't about to share all that with the Cozy Cup's morning crowd.

"She seems competent," he said finally. "Professional."

"Competent." June repeated the word like it tasted bad. "That's what you say about someone who knows how to use a photocopier, not someone who's going to be handling our Christmas traditions and promoting our town."

"June." Caroline's voice carried a note of warning as she set a plate of fresh scones on the counter. "Give the woman a chance. She's barely unpacked."

"I'm just saying, we need to know if she gets it." June reached for a scone, adding butter with the kind of focus that suggested this conversation was far from over. "Does she understand that the Express isn't just some tourist attraction? That it's part of who we are?"

Cole thought about Sadie standing in his father's office Monday afternoon, reading through those old maintenance logs with the kind of attention most people reserved for bestselling novels. The way she'd asked about his father's restoration techniques, wanting to understand not just what had been done but why.

"She's trying to understand," he said, surprising himself with the defensive edge in his voice. "She's doing research. Asking questions."

June's eyebrows rose. "Well. That's something, I suppose."

"It's more than something." Cole set his coffee down harder than necessary. "She spent Monday and Tuesday night working until the wee hours in the morning on a proposal for a few events that will benefit all of us. She's read through the years of Express history to understand what it's all about. She's not some consultant who blew into town with a PowerPoint and an attitude. She's actually trying."

The cafe had gone quiet. Cole looked up to find Caroline watching him with barely concealed interest, while June's expression had shifted from skeptical to thoughtful.

"So you like her," June said.

"I didn't say that."

"You didn't have to." June bit into her scone, looking entirely too pleased with herself. "You're defending her. That's practically a declaration of love in my opinion."

"That's ridiculous."

"Is it?" Caroline leaned against the counter, her smile gentle. "When was the last time you defended anyone?"

Cole opened his mouth, then closed it again. She had a point. He generally operated on the principle that people could think whatever they wanted—it wasn't his job to manage anyone's opinion or defend anybody's reputation. He showed up, did his work, and let his actions speak for themselves.

So why was he standing here arguing about Sadie Baker's qualifications to a group of gossips who'd make up their minds regardless of what he said?

"I'm just stating facts," he muttered.

"Mm-hmm." Caroline's tone suggested she wasn't buying it for a second. "She's a pretty woman... that's for sure?"

"What does that have to do with anything?"

"Humor me."

Cole shifted his weight, feeling trapped. "I don't know. She's normal. Professional."

"Hair color?" Mrs. Phillips prompted.

"Brown. Light brown." He paused, remembering the way the afternoon sun had caught in Sadie's hair yesterday as they'd walked through the depot. "With some gold in it. And her eyes are hazel—more green than brown when the light hits them right."

The silence that followed felt loaded.

"So you haven't noticed anything about her, right? She's normal... professional... huh?" Caroline's grin was insufferable.

Before Cole could form a response, the cafe door opened with its characteristic chime, and Sadie Baker walked in.

Cole's coffee cup stopped halfway to his mouth.

She looked different from how she had at the depot. Less armored, somehow. She'd traded yesterday's professional coat for a cream-colored cable-knit sweater that looked soft and comfortable, paired with dark jeans and ankle boots. Her brown hair was down today instead of pulled back, falling past her shoulders in loose waves that caught the morning light exactly the way he'd been describing thirty seconds ago.

She hadn't seen him yet. She was scanning the cafe, clearly looking for someone, and when her gaze landed on Caroline, her face lit up with a warm smile.

"Good morning!" Sadie made her way to the counter, moving with the kind of easy confidence that suggested she belonged here. "I hope I'm not too early for our meeting."

"Right on time." Caroline came around the counter, wiping her hands on her apron. "I've got everything set up in the back room where we can talk through the beverage options for the tree lighting. But first—have you met everyone here?"

Sadie's expression shifted to something between polite and pleasantly overwhelmed as she took in the cafe's occupants, all of whom were now watching her with undisguised interest.

"I don't think I've had the pleasure," she said.

"Well, then." Caroline gestured around the room with the enthusiasm of someone who thoroughly enjoyed making introductions. "Sadie Baker, meet the heart and soul of Mistletoe Falls. This is June Reynolds—she runs the post office and knows everyone's business."

"Only because people tell me things," June said, standing to shake Sadie's hand. "Welcome to town, honey. I've heard good things."

"Thank you." Sadie's handshake was firm; her smile genuine. "I'm still getting my bearings, but everyone's been incredibly welcoming."

"That's Mrs. Phillips by the window," Caroline continued. "She's a retired second-grade teacher and makes the best apple pie you'll ever taste. And you've already met Cole." She turned toward him with a smile that made him instantly suspicious. "My darling, lovable brother-in-law, Cole."

"Good morning, Cole."

"Sadie." He managed a nod, his throat inexplicably tight.

"Cole was just telling us how impressed he is with your work," June said, and Cole made a mental note to have a serious conversation with the postmaster.

"Was he?" Sadie's eyebrows rose slightly. "That's kind of him."

"Just stating facts," Cole said, immediately regretting it when Caroline's grin widened.

"Well, I'm certainly trying my best." Sadie turned her attention back to June, and Cole found himself studying her profile—the gentle curve of her jaw, the way she tucked her hair behind her ear when she was listening. "I understand the Express means a great deal to this community. I want to honor that while finding ways to share it with more people."

"That's precisely what we need," Mrs. Phillips called from her table. "Someone who understands the balance. We don't want to lose what makes us special, but we can't stay frozen in time either."

"My thoughts exactly. The Express has such a rich history. Cole was generous enough to give me a thorough tour Monday afternoon, and I'm still processing everything I learned. The restoration work alone is remarkable—I had no idea how much went into preserving a locomotive that old."

June settled back onto her stool, her expression shifting from skeptical to interested. "Did Cole tell you about his father's restoration journals?"

"He showed them to me." Sadie's voice carried genuine reverence. "They're incredible. The level of detail, the commitment to historical accuracy—it's clear this was a labor of love."

Cole's chest went tight. He hadn't expected her to mention his father, and he definitely hadn't expected the obvious respect in her voice when she did.

"Michael Bennett was one of a kind," Mrs. Phillips said softly. "The whole town mourned when we lost him. But Cole's done right by his father's vision. Kept everything exactly as it should be."

Sadie was nodding thoughtfully. "From what I've seen, Cole's maintenance standards are exceptional. The Express is in pristine condition—better than pristine, really. She runs like she did a hundred years ago, from my understanding."

"That's the point," June said, but her tone was more curious than defensive now. "We're not interested in modernizing just for the sake of it."

"Neither am I." Sadie's response was immediate and sincere. "My job isn't to change what works. It's to help more people discover what already exists. To tell the story in a way that reaches audiences who might not know about Mistletoe Falls yet."

Caroline caught Cole's eye across the counter, her expression knowing.

"So what are your plans?" Mrs. Phillips had abandoned any pretense of not listening and had moved to join them at the counter. "What are you going to do with our Express?"

"Well, Caroline and I are meeting today to finalize beverage options for the tree lighting ceremony at the depot." Sadie pulled a small notebook from her bag—the same one Cole had seen her using yesterday, he noticed, already half-filled with observations and questions. "That event is happening in just a couple of weeks, so it's my immediate priority. Beyond that, Cole and I are working on a Santa Express-themed ride in December and an All Aboard on Christmas Eve event that will be something very special—a chance to create a new tradition that honors all the history while giving families a magical experience."

"Christmas Eve." June exchanged glances with Mrs. Phillips. "That's ambitious."

"It is," Sadie agreed. "Which is why I'm not moving forward with anything unless Cole agrees it's feasible and appropriate. He knows the Express better than anyone, and I'm not going to override his expertise or his judgment."

Cole found himself staring at her. She'd made it clear she wasn't here to bulldoze over his authority or dismiss his concerns. In Monday's meeting with Martha and the mayor, she'd done the same thing—presenting her ideas while making space for his objections.

It was disarming.

And deeply inconvenient.

She was good. Very smooth with her words.

"Sounds like you two are working well together," Caroline said, not even trying to hide her satisfaction.

"We're figuring it out," Sadie said diplomatically. "Cole has been very patient with all my questions."

"Patient." June snorted. "That's a new one. This boy hasn't had a patient day in his life."

"I'm standing right here," Cole pointed out.

"Which is why I'm comfortable insulting you to your face," she said with a smile. "But seriously, Sadie, you should know that Cole's protective of the Express. If he's working with you, it means you've earned his trust. That's not something he gives lightly."

Sadie's gaze found his again, holding it. "I appreciate that. And I'm trying to be worthy of it."

The sincerity in her voice did something strange to Cole's equilibrium. He set his coffee cup down, suddenly feeling like he needed to leave before this conversation went somewhere he wasn't prepared to follow.

"I should get back to the depot," he said.

"Running away?" Caroline's tone was innocent, but her eyes were laughing.

"Working. There's a difference."

"If you say so." She came around the counter to give him a quick hug. "Thanks for stopping by. Love you big, Cole."

"Love you too. See you Sunday," he said.

"Sunday," she confirmed. "Bring your appetite. Your mom's making pot roast."

Cole nodded and turned toward the door, very aware of Sadie watching him. He paused, some impulse he didn't fully understand making him look back at her.

"Good luck with your meeting," he said.

Her smile was surprised and genuine. "Thanks. And Cole? I really do appreciate all your help so far."

He nodded again, not trusting his voice, and pushed out into the November morning.

The cold air hit his face like a wake-up call. He'd walked three blocks before he realized he was still thinking about the way Sadie had looked in the cafe's warm light, the easy way she'd handled June's interrogation, and the respect in her voice.

When she'd arrived at the cafe, something in his chest had lifted—relief, maybe, or anticipation. He'd wanted to see how the community would react to her, wanted them to see what he'd already noticed: that she was genuinely interested in understanding Mistletoe Falls, that she asked thoughtful questions and actually listened to the answers, and that she wasn't here to impose her vision but to find ways to enhance what already existed.

He'd wanted them to like her.

Which was dangerous, because wanting things led to disappointment. Letting people in meant giving them the power to leave. And Sadie Baker was here on a twelve-week trial contract—and no one knew if she'd be offered a full-time position or not.

But as he walked back toward the depot, Cole couldn't shake the image of how easily Sadie had slid right into the dynamics of the people surrounding her back at the cafe and talked openly with people she didn't even know. She'd been genuinely engaged, naturally warm, and authentically curious.

And somewhere between defending her to June and watching the cafe regulars warm up to her one question at a time, Cole had started to forget why keeping his distance was so important in the first place.

He shoved his hands in his pockets and picked up his pace, determined to get his mind back on work, back on the familiar routines that had kept him steady for the past few years. But the truth followed him down Icicle Lane like a shadow he couldn't outrun. He'd stopped thinking of Sadie Baker as an outsider threatening everything his father had built, and he had no idea when that shift had happened or what he was supposed to do about it now.

Chapter 10

Sadie had expected Caroline's back room to be cramped and cluttered like most small business storage rooms, but the space Caroline led her into felt more like someone's cozy kitchen—complete with a scarred wooden table and mismatched chairs.

"Make yourself comfortable." Caroline gestured to the table, already covered with sample menus, pricing sheets, and what looked like hand-drawn sketches of different drink presentations. "Let me just tell Jenna to handle the front for a bit."

Caroline disappeared back into the cafe, leaving Sadie alone with her thoughts and the sudden, overwhelming awareness that Cole had just walked out that door. That he'd wished her luck on this meeting.

She pressed her fingers to her temples, trying to clear her head. This was a business meeting. She had a job to do, events to plan, and a trial period to survive. She couldn't afford to get distracted by the way Cole Bennett's voice had softened when he'd told her good luck or the memory of his steel-blue eyes holding hers.

"Okay!" Caroline bustled back in, her energy filling the small room. "We're all set. Jenna's got the counter, and I've got my notes ready." She settled into the chair across from Sadie with the kind of comfortable ease that suggested she did this often. "So, let's talk about making the tree-lighting ceremony flawless."

Sadie pulled out her notebook and flipped to a fresh page, grateful to focus on something concrete.

"I've been thinking about beverage options that feel festive but aren't too complicated to serve," Sadie began. "We're expecting a good crowd—locals plus visitors from surrounding towns if the weather holds."

"I love a good crowd." Caroline leaned forward, her brown eyes bright with enthusiasm. "And I've got some ideas that might work perfectly. First question—are we thinking pre-made and served from urns, or are we setting up a full-service station?"

"What would you recommend?"

"Urns for the main offerings—classic hot chocolate, maybe spiced apple cider, and coffee for the adults who need their fix. But—" Caroline pulled out one of her sketches. "—we could also set up a small specialty station. Hot chocolate bar with toppings like whipped cream, peppermint sticks, mini marshmallows, and crushed candy canes. Makes it interactive, gives people something to do while they're waiting for the tree lighting, and it's Instagram-worthy."

Sadie studied the sketch, already seeing how it would work. "That's perfect. Festive but manageable. How many people can you serve with that setup?"

"Honestly? As many as show up. I'll bring my three largest urns for the hot chocolate, cider, and coffee—each holds five gallons, so that's about forty servings per batch. I can have my assistant Jenna there to help serve and refill. The specialty toppings station basically runs itself once it's set up."

"What about pricing?"

Caroline waved a hand dismissively. "For something like this? Community event, good exposure for the cafe, and honestly just a joy to be part of? I'll do cost plus minimal markup. Coffee's free—my contribution to keeping the volunteer crew functional."

Sadie made notes, already calculating rough numbers in her head. "That's incredibly generous. Are you sure?"

"Absolutely. Mistletoe Falls has been good to me and Luke. This is how we give back." Caroline's smile was warm and genuine. "Plus, events like this? They're the best kind of advertising. People remember who showed up and helped make the magic happen."

"Then I'd love to move forward with that plan." Sadie added a star next to her notes. "What about the logistics? Setup time, electrical needs, cleanup?"

They spent the next twenty minutes working through details—Caroline would arrive two hours before the ceremony to set up; she'd need access to three electrical outlets for the urns; and she'd handle all breakdown and cleanup afterward. She suggested positioning the beverage station near the depot's side entrance, which would create natural foot traffic while keeping people from congregating right in front of the main ceremony area.

"You've really thought this through," Sadie said, impressed by Caroline's combination of creativity and practicality.

"I've done enough town events to know what works." Caroline grinned. "And I've learned to anticipate problems before they happen. Like making sure we have extra napkins, paper towels, and cleaning supplies, because there are always spills."

Sadie laughed, making another note. "Speaking of anticipating needs—I'm also going to need a large cookie order. Something festive and Christmas-themed that can be served during the event. Do you have any recommendations for bakeries that could handle that kind of volume and deliver?"

"Oh, absolutely." Caroline didn't even hesitate. "Claire Whitfield at the Sugarplum Bakery. It's right on the town square—Mistletoe Lane; you can't miss it. Claire does all our special-occasion cookies, and her Christmas designs are stunning. Sugar cookies with royal icing, gingerbread men, snowflakes, Christmas trees—whatever you want, she can do it. And she's reliable about delivery."

Sadie added the name to her list. "Perfect. I'll stop by there next."

"Tell her I sent you," Caroline suggested. "She'll take good care of you."

"I will. Thank you." Sadie closed her notebook, feeling satisfied with what they'd accomplished. The tree lighting was coming together—venue secured, decorations planned, beverages arranged, and cookies next on the list. For the first time since arriving in Mistletoe Falls, she felt like she might be able to take a deep breath and relax for a little bit this evening.

"So." Caroline's tone shifted. "How are you settling in? Are you enjoying the town so far?"

The question caught Sadie slightly off guard. She'd gotten used to Martha's professional check-ins and Cole's careful on-again, off-again distance, but Caroline's interest felt genuine and personal—like something a friend would ask.

"I am. It's different from anywhere else I've worked or lived. The people here actually care about preserving what they have instead of just chasing whatever's trendy."

"We do love our traditions." Caroline smiled. "Sometimes maybe a little too much, but that's what makes us special. Where were you working before this?"

"Different places. I've been freelancing as a journalist since I graduated college—travel writing, destination features, that kind of thing. This is my first real tourism development position."

"So you've been moving around a lot?"

Sadie nodded. "Too much, honestly. I'm tired of living out of suitcases and hotel rooms. Tired of documenting other people's sense of home without ever having my own."

"Is that why you took this position? The twelve-week trial?"

"Partly." Sadie traced the edge of her notebook with her finger. "I wanted a chance to prove to myself that I could build something lasting. That I could put down roots somewhere instead of just passing through. But also—" She hesitated, then decided to be honest. "—I'm hoping this trial period turns into permanent employment. That I can actually stay here, maybe buy a home... live a normal, simple, quiet life."

"You're working incredibly hard to make that happen, from what I hear."

"I have to." Sadie tried to keep her voice light but heard the edge of desperation creep in anyway. "I have a hard time dealing with failure. This is my chance to finally have the life I've been looking for."

Caroline studied her for a moment, her expression thoughtful. "May I ask you something? And you can tell me to mind my own business if I'm overstepping."

"Sure."

"Where are you from originally? Do you have family somewhere?"

Sadie felt her shoulders tense slightly. "Knoxville."

"And you don't want to go back there? Be close to family?"

The question was gentle, but Sadie still felt it land like a weight. "It's just me and my father, and we don't have the healthiest relationship. He's—" She paused, searching for words that wouldn't reveal too much. "—he's very focused on success and status. My career choices haven't exactly met his expectations."

"That must be hard."

"It's fine." Sadie forced a smile. "We talk occasionally. It is what it is."

Caroline didn't push, but Sadie could see the sympathy in her eyes. Instead of probing further, Caroline shifted the conversation smoothly. "Well, you've got people here who are rooting for you. I know June can be a lot, but she means well. And she wouldn't have grilled you this morning if she didn't already care."

"That's a strange kind of caring."

"Welcome to small-town life." Caroline's grin was infectious. "Everyone's invested in everyone else's business, but it comes from a good place. Usually."

Sadie laughed, feeling some of her tension ease. "How did you end up here? Becoming part of the Bennett family?"

"Oh, that's a good story." Caroline settled back in her chair, clearly happy to share. "I moved here three years ago to open the cafe. I wanted to get out of Knoxville myself, actually. Small-town life appealed to me after growing up in the city. Luke came into the shop about a week after I opened, ordered the worst possible coffee combination I'd ever heard, and proceeded to come back every single day and order the same terrible drink just to talk to me."

"What was the drink?"

"Extra hot latte with four shots of espresso and hazel-nut syrup." Caroline shuddered dramatically. "It was basically liquid anxiety in a cup. But he kept ordering it, and I kept making it, and eventually I asked him if he actually liked it or if he was just trying to get my attention."

"What did he say?"

"He said he hated it, but it was working, wasn't it?" Caroline's smile was soft with the memory. "We got married six months later. Best decision I ever made."

"That's sweet."

"Luke's a good man. Protective, a little stubborn sometimes, but good." Caroline paused, then added carefully, "Like his brother."

Sadie felt her face warm slightly. "Cole seems very dedicated to the Express."

"He is. Almost too dedicated, if you ask me." Caroline's tone was gentle but honest. "He's devoted his whole life to that train... even more so since his father died. It's admirable, but it's also—I don't know. Lonely."

Sadie didn't know what to say to that, so she focused on a different question. "Is Luke as involved with the Express as Cole?"

"In his own way. Luke's the town mechanic, and he actually has a contract with the city to work on the train's maintenance twice a month. Occasionally, Cole calls him out if something malfunctions and he needs an extra hand. Luke knows that train almost as well as Cole does—just from a different angle."

"So it really is a family operation."

"Always has been. Michael Bennett started the restoration project years ago. Eleanor, their mom, supported him through the whole thing. When he died—" Caroline's expression grew more somber. "—Cole stepped right into his father's shoes. Took over everything at the age of twenty-six."

"That's a lot of responsibility for someone so young."

"It was, and it still is." Caroline looked at her directly. "Which is why I think it's good that someone like you is working with him now. He needs more people in his life. He needs different things to focus on."

Before Sadie could figure out how to respond to that, Caroline's expression brightened with sudden inspiration.

"Actually, you know what? You should come to Sunday dinner at the Bennett farmhouse."

"Oh, I couldn't—"

"Yes, you could." Caroline was already reaching for a notepad, scribbling down an address. "Eleanor would love to meet you, and she's another great person to talk to if you would like to learn more about the family history and the Express. Plus, the food is always incredible, and you'd get to see where Cole and my husband grew up."

"I don't want to impose on a family dinner."

"You're not imposing. I'm inviting you." Caroline pushed the paper across the table. "Sunday around four. Eleanor Bennett home, that's the address. She lives in the original Bennett farmhouse—a beautiful old place with a wrap-around porch and the best kitchen you've ever seen."

Sadie looked at the address, her mind already racing. A family dinner. A chance to learn more about the

Express history for her promotional work. A chance to understand more about Cole and what drove him.

A chance to see him again in a setting that wasn't the depot or a planning meeting.

"Are you sure it's okay?" she asked, even as she folded the paper and tucked it into her notebook.

"Absolutely. Eleanor loves feeding people. Luke and I will be there, obviously. Cole always comes—" Caroline's smile turned knowing. "—so you'll have familiar faces."

"Then I'd be happy to come. Thank you."

"Perfect!" Caroline stood, clearly pleased with herself. "Now, let me walk you out. And remember—Sugarplum Bakery; just tell Claire I sent you."

They made their way back through the cafe, which had filled up even more since Sadie had arrived. Several people looked up as they passed, offering friendly nods and curious glances. Mrs. Phillips gave her a warm smile, and another woman she didn't know waved.

It felt strange and wonderful at the same time, being recognized and being acknowledged.

"Thanks again for everything," Sadie said as they reached the door. "I sincerely appreciate your flexibility and your suggestions."

"Anytime. I'm excited to be part of this." Caroline gave her a quick hug that Sadie wasn't quite prepared for but found herself returning. "And I'll see you Sunday at Eleanor's. Come hungry."

Sadie stepped out into the November morning, the cold air sharp against her face after the cafe's warmth. She pulled her coat tighter and started walking toward the town square, already thinking about what questions she needed to ask Claire about cookie designs and delivery schedules.

But underneath the practical planning, underneath the professional focus, something else hummed through her thoughts.

Sunday dinner at the Bennett farmhouse. A chance to see Cole again, to learn more about his family, and to understand the history that had shaped him into the man who looked at her with those steel-blue eyes.

She told herself it was about the work. About gathering information for promotional materials and building relationships with key community members. About proving she could integrate herself into Mistletoe Falls and earn the permanent position she desperately wanted.

But Sadie had to admit the truth to herself.

She wanted to see him again. Wanted to understand him better. Wanted to know what it would take to make those defensive walls come down long enough to see if the warmth she'd glimpsed was real or just wishful thinking on her part.

Chapter 11

The Bennett farmhouse looked like something out of a dream.

Sadie pulled her SUV onto the long gravel driveway a few minutes before four, her breath catching as she took in the sprawling two-story structure ahead of her. The historic farmhouse sat proudly on what had to be several acres of gently rolling land, its white clapboard siding gleaming in the November sun. A wraparound porch circled the entire first floor, complete with rocking chairs and hanging ferns that somehow still looked lush despite the season.

This was the kind of home Sadie had spent her childhood sketching in notebooks—the kind of place that whispered permanence and family and roots that went deep into the earth. Nothing like the sterile mansion in Knoxville where she'd grown up, all glass and angles and rooms that echoed with emptiness.

She turned off the engine and sat for a moment, taking it all in. Fall mums in deep reds and golds lined the walkway leading to the front porch steps. Ornamental grasses swayed in large planters flanking the porch, and a hand-carved wooden sign near the door read "Bennett Family Est. 1892."

Sadie gathered her purse and the bottle of wine she'd brought—carefully selected from the small selection at the grocery store, hoping it was appropriate—and made her way up the brick walkway. The landscaping was immaculate but unpretentious, the kind of care that came from genuine love rather than hired help.

As she climbed the porch steps, admiring the detailed woodwork on the railings, the front door swung open.

"Sadie!" Caroline appeared in the doorway, her face lit with genuine pleasure. "Come in, come in."

Sadie stepped into a wide foyer that somehow managed to feel both grand and welcoming. Dark hardwood floors gleamed beneath her feet, and a beautiful antique hall tree stood against one wall, already laden with coats and scarves. The scent of something delicious—roasted meat and herbs—filled the air, making her stomach rumble despite her nervousness.

"This home is beautiful," Sadie said, handing Caroline the wine.

Caroline set the wine on the hall table and pulled Sadie into a quick hug. "I'm so glad you came. Come on, Eleanor's in the kitchen dying to meet you."

A woman appeared from what must be the kitchen, wiping her hands on a dishtowel. Eleanor Bennett was exactly as Sadie had imagined and nothing like it at the same time. She had a natural grace that came with age and confidence, her silver-streaked chestnut hair pulled back in a loose ponytail, soft blue eyes warm with welcome. She wore dark slacks and a cream-colored cardigan over a simple blouse, with an apron tied around her waist.

"You must be Sadie." Eleanor's voice was warm as honey, and before Sadie could offer a handshake, she found herself enveloped in a hug. "I'm so glad you could join us."

"Thank you for having me, Mrs. Bennett." Sadie returned the embrace, surprised by how natural it felt. "Your home is absolutely stunning."

"Eleanor, please. And thank you, dear. This old place has been in the Bennett family for generations." She pulled back, studying Sadie with kind eyes. "Caroline mentioned you have an interest in the Express's history. I'd be happy to share what I know."

"I'd love that."

"Wonderful. Caroline, will you check on the roast while I show Sadie around?"

"Already on it." Caroline disappeared toward what Sadie assumed was the kitchen, leaving her alone with Cole's mother.

Caroline slipped off her coat and scarf and hung them on the hall tree. Eleanor led her through the first floor with obvious pride and genuine love for every detail. The living room was large and inviting, dominated by a stone fireplace with a heavy wooden mantel displaying family photographs spanning decades. The furniture was comfortable rather than formal—a mix of antiques and pieces that had clearly been chosen for livability rather than style.

"This fireplace is original to the house," Eleanor explained, running her hand along the mantel. "Michael's great-great-grandfather built it in 1892 when he established the farm. The Bennett family has always been here in Mistletoe Falls."

"That's incredible," Sadie breathed, studying the photographs. She recognized a younger version of Cole in several of them—his expression that of a happy child and his eyes held a lightness she hadn't seen in the man she knew.

"Michael's father came from a very successful farming family," Eleanor continued as they moved into the den—a smaller, cozier room with built-in bookshelves and another fireplace. "He was one of six children, all born and raised in this house. Can you imagine? Six children, two parents, one house. The walls must have been bursting with life."

Sadie tried to picture it—the noise, the chaos, the constant presence of family—and felt a pang of envy. Her childhood home had felt empty even when her father was there.

They moved through the formal dining room, where a long wooden table was already set for dinner, and Eleanor shared stories about holiday gatherings and birthday celebrations, her voice full of warm nostalgia. Then they reached the kitchen, and Sadie actually stopped in her tracks.

"This is incredible."

The kitchen was enormous, but it felt warm rather than cavernous. White cabinets with glass fronts displayed dishes and serving pieces that looked both antique and well-loved. The countertops were warm butcher block, scarred with years of use but beautifully maintained. A massive Wolf range stood against one wall, flanked by double ovens. The island in the center was large enough to work on from all sides, with bar stools tucked underneath.

But it was the details that really caught Sadie's attention—the copper pots hanging from a rack above the island, the herbs growing in small pots on the windowsill above the farmhouse sink, the collection of wooden spoons in a ceramic crock, and the vintage mixer in robin's egg blue sitting on the counter.

"This is my pride and joy," Eleanor admitted, her smile soft. "I've been developing recipes for years—used to do some work for magazines and websites. I've been easing into retirement lately, but this kitchen—" She gestured around them. "—this is where I'm happiest."

Caroline looked up from where she was basting a pot roast. "Eleanor's being modest. She's had recipes featured in Southern Living and Better Homes & Gardens. She's won awards for her Christmas cookie designs."

"That's amazing," Sadie said honestly. "I can barely manage breakfast most days."

"Cooking is just about practice and patience," Eleanor said warmly. "And finding joy in feeding people you love." She moved to check something in one of the ovens, and the scent of fresh bread filled the kitchen. "Now, Luke should be back any minute. I had him run and grab something I forgot at the grocery store, and Cole—"

The front door opened, and a male voice called out. "Mom? Whose SUV is in the driveway?"

Sadie's heart kicked against her ribs. She'd known Cole would be here, but she suddenly felt unprepared for seeing him in this context. In his mother's kitchen. In the home where he grew up.

Footsteps approached, and then Cole appeared in the kitchen doorway.

He froze.

For a long moment, they just stared at each other. Cole's steel-blue eyes went wide with surprise, his mouth opening slightly as if he might speak but couldn't quite find the words. He wore dark jeans and a navy blue henley that brought out his eyes, his hair slightly mussed as if he'd been running his hands through it. He looked younger somehow, less guarded—or maybe just shocked enough that his usual defenses hadn't kicked in yet.

"Sadie," he finally managed.

"Hi." It came out smaller than she'd intended, almost shy.

"I invited her," Caroline said cheerfully, completely unrepentant. "Thought she might enjoy learning more about the family history for her promotional work. Plus, your mom makes the best pot roast, and it seemed criminal not to share that."

"I—of course. That's—" Cole seemed to be struggling with basic sentence structure. "Welcome."

Eleanor moved past Sadie to hug her son, and Sadie watched the way Cole's expression softened immediately, his arms coming around his mother with obvious affection. "Hi, Mom."

"Hello, sweetheart." She pulled back, studying his face with a maternal scrutiny that seemed to see everything. "You look tired."

"Long morning at the depot."

"On a Sunday?"

"Just some maintenance that needed attention." He glanced at Sadie again, something unreadable in his expression. "I didn't know we were having company."

"That's because my wife begged me not to tell you," Luke's voice came from behind him, and Cole's younger brother appeared, grinning. "You should see your face right now."

"Luke." Eleanor's tone carried a warning, but her eyes were dancing with amusement.

Luke was taller than Cole by maybe an inch, with sandy blond hair and blue-gray eyes that sparkled with mischief. He had the same broad-shouldered build as his brother, but where Cole carried himself with careful control, Luke moved with easy confidence. He crossed the kitchen to kiss his mother's cheek and hug his wife and then turned to Sadie with a warm smile.

"Luke Bennett. The better-looking brother."

"Debatable," Cole muttered.

"The more charming brother," Luke corrected, shaking Sadie's hand. "Welcome to the chaos of our happy family. I hope Caroline warned you about what you were getting into."

"Oh hush, Luke," Caroline said, appearing at her husband's side with a smile.

The moment felt almost overwhelming—the warmth of the kitchen, the easy banter between siblings, the way Eleanor moved between them all with practiced grace, adjusting a collar here, squeezing a shoulder there. This was what a family looked like when it was healthy and whole. When people actually wanted to be together.

"Sadie, why don't you help me bring the serving dishes to the dining room?" Eleanor suggested gently, as if sensing Sadie needed a moment. "Boys, you can manage the drinks and bread."

For the next fifteen minutes, Sadie found herself part of the practiced choreography of a family preparing for Sunday dinner. She carried serving bowls and platters while Eleanor directed traffic with calm efficiency. Cole and Luke brought in a pitcher of sweet tea and a basket of fresh bread, their movements comfortable and familiar. Caroline appeared with the pot roast, triumphantly setting it in the center of the table.

Through it all, Sadie felt Cole's eyes on her. Not constantly, not obviously, but in those brief moments when he thought she wasn't looking. When she reached past him to set down the bowl of roasted vegetables. When she laughed at something Luke said. And when Eleanor asked her to take the seat across from Cole at the table.

Finally, they were all settled—Eleanor at one end of the table, an empty seat at the other end, Cole and Sadie across from each other, and Luke and Caroline side by side. Eleanor said a simple grace, her voice steady and warm, and then Luke was passing the pot roast, and conversation erupted naturally.

"So, Sadie," Luke said, loading his plate with generous portions, "Caroline tells me you're working with my stubborn brother on the Express. How's that going?"

"Luke," Eleanor chided gently.

"What? It's a legitimate question."

"We're figuring it out. It's been interesting... but fun," Sadie said, risking a glance at Cole. His jaw was tight, but there was color in his cheeks that might have been embarrassment. "Your brother has an impressive depth of knowledge about the Express."

"That's a polite way of saying he's obsessed," Luke said cheerfully.

"I'm not obsessed," Cole protested. "I'm dedicated."

"You named your dog after Johnny Cash because Cash was a train enthusiast," Luke pointed out. "That's dedication that borders on obsession."

Caroline laughed. "He has a point."

Cole's mouth twitched. "Cash is a good name."

"It's a great name," Sadie agreed, earning a surprised look from Cole. "And for what it's worth, I think dedication is admirable."

The conversation flowed from there easily and naturally. Eleanor asked about Sadie's background, and Sadie found herself sharing carefully edited versions of her freelance work and her decision to move into tourism development. She elaborated on the places she'd documented—the fall festivals in Vermont, the coastal celebrations in Maine, and the holiday markets she'd covered across the Midwest.

"But you never stayed anywhere?" Eleanor asked gently. "Never wanted to put down roots?"

The question hit closer than Sadie was ready for. "I never found anywhere that felt like home."

"Until now?" Caroline prompted hopefully.

"Until now," Sadie admitted. "I can see myself living here and building the life I've always dreamed of."

Cole had been quiet through most of the meal, but now he spoke up. "You're doing good work here. Your plans are solid. Martha's really impressed."

Sadie felt warmth bloom in her chest. "Thank you. That means a lot."

"The town's buzzing about it," Luke added. "Everyone's excited to see what you and Cole have put together."

"Really?" Sadie asked. "People are already talking about it? I don't know what to say... but Cole knows exactly what will work and what won't. I'm just helping with the promotional side and some of the easier logistics."

"She's being modest," Cole said.

Lively conversations continue—Luke's recent work on one of the town's fire engines, Caroline's plans for holiday specials at the cafe, and the upcoming quilting circle's charity auction that Eleanor was involved in. But underneath it all, Sadie was intensely aware of Cole's presence across from her, the way he listened when she spoke, and the small smile that appeared when she made his mother laugh.

After dinner, as had apparently been established tradition, the women moved to the kitchen to clean up while the men took their coffee out to the back porch. Sadie found herself at the sink washing dishes, Caroline rinsed, and Eleanor dried and put them away.

"So," Caroline said, her voice pitched low enough that Eleanor had to lean in to hear, "what do you think of our Cole?"

Sadie felt her face heat. "He's very dedicated to the Express."

"That's not what I meant." Caroline bumped her shoulder gently. "Come on. You can tell us."

"Caroline," Eleanor said, but her tone was more amused than reproving. "Don't make the poor girl uncomfortable."

"I'm not making her uncomfortable. I'm just asking what anyone who saw them at dinner would be wondering." Caroline grinned at Sadie. "He couldn't stop looking at you."

"He was probably making sure I wasn't going to suggest painting the Express pink," Sadie said, trying for humor.

"That's not the look of a man worried about paint colors," Eleanor said thoughtfully. "That's the look of a man who's interested but doesn't quite know what to do about it."

Sadie's hands stilled in the soapy water. "I don't think—I mean, we're just colleagues."

"For now," Caroline said knowingly.

"Caroline's usually right about these things," Eleanor added, setting a dry plate in the cabinet. "She called Luke's proposal weeks before he managed to ask."

"That's because Luke told me he was going to propose," Caroline laughed. "He needed help to pick the ring."

"Still counts."

They worked in silence for a few moments, and Sadie found herself thinking about Cole out on that porch, probably sipping coffee and talking about machinery with his brother. What must it be like to have this—this easy family dynamic, this unconditional belonging?

"May I ask you something?" Sadie said quietly.

"Of course, dear," Eleanor responded.

"What was Michael like? Cole's father?"

Eleanor's hands stilled on the dish towel, and for a moment Sadie worried she'd overstepped. But then Eleanor's expression softened with memory.

"Michael was a dreamer," she said finally. "He saw potential in everything—that old train rusting in a rail yard, this farmhouse when it needed major repairs, even me." She smiled at a private memory. "His family built this farm from nothing. They were successful, respected. But Michael wanted something different. He worked for the town in various capacities over the years, but his heart belonged to that train."

"Cole told me it took fifteen years to restore the Express."

"Fifteen years of long nights and longer weekends," Eleanor confirmed. "He'd work his town job during the day, then spend every evening at the depot. The boys, they practically grew up there. Michael taught them everything about engines and restoration, about patience and dedication."

"It must have been hard," Sadie said. "All those years of work."

"Hard but purposeful. Michael believed some things were worth the effort." Eleanor met Sadie's eyes directly. "He used to say that preserving the past wasn't about keeping things frozen in time—it was about honoring what came before while building something that could last into the future."

"Cole inherited his father's dedication," Caroline said, rinsing the last dish. "But I think he sometimes forgets the second part. About building for the future."

The back door opened, and Luke stuck his head in. "Mom, Cole's getting restless out here. I think he's worried you're talking about him."

"We absolutely are," Caroline called back cheerfully.

"That's what I told him." Luke grinned. "Are you coming out? It's actually nice out here. We've got the porch heaters going."

"I should probably get going. I don't want to intrude on any more family time," Sadie said, suddenly nervous.

"Nonsense," Eleanor said firmly. "You're staying for coffee on the porch. I won't hear otherwise."

"But—"

"No buts." Eleanor hung up her dishtowel with an air of finality. "Besides, I want to hear more about your ideas for the Express. Caroline mentioned something about a Christmas Eve event?"

There was no arguing with that tone, and Sadie found herself being gently herded toward the back door.

Chapter 12

The back porch of the Bennett farmhouse wrapped around the west side of the house. Sadie had settled into one of the cushioned chairs, cradling the coffee mug Eleanor had pressed into her hands. The warmth seeped through the ceramic into her palms.

Cole sat in the chair beside her.

Luke sprawled in another chair with the ease of someone completely at home, while Caroline perched on the porch railing, her legs swinging slightly. Eleanor claimed the rocker near the door, the picture of contentment.

"So the tree lighting is November 27th," Eleanor said, her voice warm with interest. "Are you both ready?"

"Getting there," Cole said. "We're picking out the tree soon."

"We?" Luke's eyebrows rose. "As in, you're both going?"

"He knows the tree farm owner. We'll go together and pick one on the Saturday before Thanksgiving. That should give us plenty of time to get it ready," Sadie said quickly.

"Mm-hmm." Luke's grin was insufferable.

"Luke," Eleanor said mildly, but her eyes were dancing.

Cole shot his brother a look that would have intimidated most people. Luke just grinned wider.

"What?" Luke spread his hands innocently. "I'm just saying, my brother doesn't usually volunteer to spend his Saturdays tree shopping. Last year, Mom had to practically drag him to pick out the farmhouse tree."

"That's because you were supposed to go, and you conveniently had an emergency call," Cole pointed out.

"I'm a mechanic. Emergencies happen."

"At nine AM on a Saturday... you work for the city, and you always have weekends off."

Caroline laughed. "He's got you there, honey."

"Whose side are you on?" Luke asked his wife.

"Truth's side. Always." Caroline turned to Sadie with a warm smile. "Fair warning—Sunday dinners here involve a lot of sibling bickering. It's very entertaining."

"I'm noticing that," Sadie said, unable to stop smiling. The easy affection between them all was like watching something she'd only read about in books. Her childhood dinners had been silent affairs, her father reading the newspaper while she pushed food around her plate.

Luke checked his watch and groaned. "I've got an early job tomorrow. One of the town's snowplows needs new hydraulics." Luke stood, stretching. "Mom, as always, incredible meal. Sadie, it was great meeting you. Don't let this one—" he jerked his thumb at Cole "—work you too hard."

"I'll try," Sadie said.

Caroline hugged Eleanor, then moved to hug Sadie too. "I'm so glad you came. And I meant what I said—don't be a stranger. Stop by the cafe anytime."

"I will. Thank you."

After Luke and Caroline left, their voices and laughter fading as they walked to Luke's truck, Eleanor stood and gathered the empty coffee mugs. "I'm going to take these things inside and finish cleaning up the kitchen."

"I can help," Sadie offered, starting to rise.

"Absolutely not." Eleanor's tone was gentle but firm. "Cole, why don't you show Sadie the sunset view from the back of the property? The light's perfect right now."

She disappeared inside before either of them could respond, and Sadie found herself alone on the porch with Cole.

Cole stood, running a hand through his hair. "You don't have to. If you want to head home, I understand."

"Do you want me to go home?"

Cole's gaze locked with hers. "No."

"Then I'd like to see the view," Sadie said.

Something shifted in Cole's expression—surprise, maybe, or relief. He offered his hand to help her up, and Sadie took it without thinking. His palm was warm and calloused against hers, and for a moment after she stood, neither of them let go.

Then Cole cleared his throat and released her hand, gesturing toward the porch steps. "This way."

They walked side by side across the lawn, and Sadie was intensely aware of Cole's presence beside her—the way he moved with that quiet confidence, the way he'd shoved his hands in his pockets like he didn't quite know what to do with them.

The land rolled gently away from the farmhouse, grass still green despite the season, bordered by split-rail fencing. In the distance, the Smoky Mountains rose against the sky, their peaks touched with the last light of day.

"Your family is wonderful," Sadie said, breaking the comfortable silence.

"They liked you. I can tell." Cole glanced at her. "Luke doesn't usually warm up to people that fast. He's protective."

"Of you?"

"Of all of us. But especially me, I think." Cole's mouth quirked slightly. "He worries I work too much."

"Do you?"

"Probably." He stopped walking, and Sadie stopped beside him. They'd reached a spot where the land opened up, the view unobstructed. "But it's not really work when you love what you're doing."

Sadie turned to look at the sunset. The sky had transformed into layers of gold and pink and deep purple; the clouds edged in fire. The mountains stood in silhouette, and the whole scene looked painted—too perfect to be real.

"This is beautiful," she said.

"I grew up running around this land," Cole said quietly. "Used to build forts in those woods, fish in the creek that runs along the north property line. Luke and I would spend entire summers outside, only coming home when Mom rang the dinner bell."

Sadie tried to imagine it—two boys with dirt on their knees and adventure in their hearts, growing up with space to roam and family surrounding them. Her childhood had been spent in a showcase mansion with a father who was never home and silence that echoed off marble floors.

"That sounds perfect," she said.

"It was."

They stood in silence, watching the light fade. Sadie felt the chill starting to creep in as the sun sank lower, but she didn't want to suggest going back. Not yet.

"May I ask you something?" Cole's voice was careful.

"Of course."

"Earlier during dinner, you said you didn't have family traditions growing up. What did you mean by that?"

Sadie's first instinct was to deflect, to give him the polished version she usually offered. But standing here in the golden light with Cole beside her, something made her choose honesty instead.

"My mother died when I was eight. After that, my father just... shut down. He threw himself into work, and I was raised by a rotating cast of housekeepers and nannies." She kept her eyes on the mountains, unable to look at Cole while she said it. "Holidays were quiet. Just me and whatever staff member was working that day. My father would usually be at the office."

"That sounds lonely."

"It was. I used to read books about families who had traditions—elaborate Christmas mornings, Thanksgiving dinners with dozens of relatives, and summer vacations where everyone piled into station wagons. I thought maybe those were just stories, things that didn't really exist."

Sadie finally turned to look at him. He was watching her with an expression that made her chest tight—not pity, but understanding. Like he saw exactly what she'd been missing, and it mattered to him.

"That's why this job means so much to me," she said. "Not just the career aspect. But the chance to be part of something. To help create experiences for families, to be in a place where traditions matter and people actually show up for each other. Last year was my first experience here in Mistletoe Falls. I came for a freelance job and fell in love with the town. I couldn't stop thinking about the people here, and... it's hard to explain, but I just felt such a sense of peace and belonging when I was here the first time. When I came across the ad for the job opening... I jumped at the chance to come back, and well... here I am."

Cole held her gaze. "You fit in here."

"Do I?"

"I think you do. You fit today. With my family." He paused. "With me."

Sadie's heart did something complicated behind her ribs. This was Cole Bennett—the man who'd barely tolerated her presence days ago—telling her she fit. With him.

"Cole—"

"I wanted to be an astronaut at one point when I was a teenager," he said abruptly, and Sadie blinked at the subject change.

"What?"

"An astronaut." His mouth quirked. "Everyone thought I'd want to work on the train because of my dad, but I was obsessed with space. Had posters all over my bedroom, books about the Apollo missions, the whole thing."

Sadie couldn't help smiling. "Why space?"

"It seemed simpler than people." He shrugged. "Predictable physics. Clear objectives. You train for a specific mission, and you execute it. No emotions or complications or—" He stopped.

"Or what?"

"Or people leaving," he said quietly. "You can't lose what you never let yourself have. When I was a freshman in high school, my best friend died from cancer, and it really affected me as a child. I learned at an early age that life wasn't perfect and that people can leave in an instant and forever change your path in life."

The vulnerability in his voice made Sadie's throat tight. She understood that logic intimately—the fear that drove you to choose loneliness over the risk of loss.

"But you didn't become an astronaut," she said gently.

"No. Turns out I loved the train more than I loved the idea of escape." Cole's smile was small but genuine. "And now I'm here, dealing with people and emotions and complications every single day. Life's funny."

"So you're saying I'm more complicated than space travel?" Sadie couldn't resist teasing.

Cole's eyes met hers, and something shifted in his expression. "I'm saying you're definitely more unpredictable."

"Is that a bad thing?"

He took a step closer, close enough that Sadie had to tilt her head to maintain eye contact. "I'm not sure yet."

The air between them changed—charged, waiting. Sadie's pulse hammered in her throat as Cole's gaze dropped to her mouth, then back to her eyes.

"Sadie—" His voice had gone lower, rougher.

"Cole? Sadie?" Eleanor's voice drifted from the porch, distant but clear. "I'm putting on a fresh pot of coffee!"

The moment shattered. Cole stepped back, running a hand through his hair, and Sadie tried to remember how to breathe normally.

"We should—" Cole gestured vaguely toward the house.

"Yeah. Coffee sounds good."

But neither of them moved immediately. They stood in the fading light, the air still humming with what had almost happened.

"Sadie." Cole's voice was quieter now. "Would you want to have dinner sometime? Just us. Not work planning or family gatherings. Just... dinner."

Sadie's heart soared. "Are you asking me on a date?"

"I'm asking if you'd like to have dinner with me." He looked uncertain, vulnerable in a way she'd never seen him. "If that's something you'd be interested in."

"I'd be very interested," Sadie said, and watched relief flood his features.

"Good. That's—good." A small smile tugged at his mouth, transforming his face.

They walked back to the house side by side, their arms occasionally brushing. The contact sent awareness sparking through Sadie each time, and she wondered if Cole felt it too.

On the porch, Eleanor had indeed made fresh coffee, and they sat together in the gathering dusk while she asked about Sadie's apartment and whether she'd found everything she needed in town. The conversation flowed easily, Eleanor's warmth making Sadie feel included and valued in a way that made her throat tight.

"Come spend Thanksgiving with us, Sadie," Eleanor said as they finished their coffee.

Sadie hesitated. "I don't want to intrude on family time—"

"You're not intruding. I'm inviting you." Eleanor's smile was gentle but firm. "There's a difference. I won't have you spending the day alone."

Sadie glanced at Cole, who was watching her with an expression she couldn't quite read.

"You should come," he said.

"Then I'd love to. Thank you."

When Sadie finally gathered her things to leave, Eleanor hugged her tightly at the door. "It was wonderful having you here, dear. See you on Thanksgiving. Drive carefully."

"I will. Thank you so much for everything."

Cole walked her to her SUV, his hands in his pockets again. The driveway was dark now, the farmhouse windows glowing warm behind them.

At her car, Sadie turned to face him. "Thank you for today. For sharing your family with me."

"They're pretty great," Cole said. "Even when Luke's being annoying."

"Especially then." Sadie smiled.

"Listen, would you... text me when you get home? Just so I know, you made it safely."

The request surprised her. "You want me to text you?"

"Yeah. I do."

Sadie pulled out her phone. "What's your number?"

He recited it, and she added him to her contacts.

"I'll text you," she promised.

"Good." He stood there, hands still in his pockets, looking like he wanted to say something else but couldn't quite find the words.

"Goodnight, Cole."

"Goodnight, Sadie. Drive safe."

She climbed into her SUV and started the engine, and Cole stepped back but didn't leave. As she pulled away, she could see him in her rearview mirror, standing in the driveway watching her taillights disappear down the lane.

Chapter 13

"A little more to the left—no, your other left!" Sadie called up to the city worker balanced on the ladder, clipboard pressed against her chest as she squinted against the mid-morning sun.

The man adjusted the massive evergreen wreath, and Sadie tilted her head, considering. The wreath now hung perfectly centered above the depot's main entrance, its burgundy velvet bow catching the light exactly as she'd envisioned.

"Perfect! That's it—secure it there."

Wednesday morning at the Mistletoe Falls Train Depot had transformed into controlled chaos. City employees swarmed the property like industrious elves, their orange safety vests bright against the historic brick building. Two workers strung lights along the platform's iron railings while another team positioned large decorated banners along the lampposts that lined the wide sidewalks leading from the parking lot. The metallic sound of extending ladders mixed with the hum of conversation and the occasional burst of laughter.

Sadie moved through it all with her clipboard and color-coded checklist, delegating tasks and making adjustment calls on the fly.

"Miss Baker?" One of the younger workers approached, hard hat slightly askew. "We've got the garland up on the lampposts in the parking area. You want to approve it before we move to the platform posts?"

"Absolutely. Lead the way."

She followed him across the platform and down the steps, reviewing the garland work that spiraled up each lamppost, interspersed with clusters of burgundy and gold ribbons. The effect was elegant without being overwrought—exactly the balance she'd been aiming for.

"This is beautiful," she said, making a note on her clipboard. "Go ahead and replicate this on the platform posts. Same spacing, same ribbon placement."

"You've got it."

The distant sound of the Express's whistle cut through the morning air, and Sadie's pulse quickened.

She moved back toward the platform, positioning herself where she could oversee the work while watching the train's approach. The Express came into view around the bend, steam billowing white against the blue sky, her dark green paint gleaming in the sunlight.

The locomotive slowed, Hank at the controls, and Sadie could see Cole through the passenger car windows, his conductor's cap visible as he moved through the car. The train came to a smooth stop, and the doors opened.

Passengers began disembarking, buzzing with excitement, and Sadie watched Cole offering his hand to assist anyone who needed it.

"Did you see that waterfall, Mommy?" One of the children—a girl of about six—bounced on her toes. "I want to go again. Can we take another ride?"

"I saw it, sweetheart. One ride is enough for today; we'll come back again." The mother smiled at Cole. "Thank you so much. We truly enjoyed ourselves."

"Glad to hear it," Cole said, and even from several yards away, Sadie could see the warmth in his expression. "Come back and see us again."

The last passengers wandered toward the parking lot, and Cole began walking toward her. His eyes moved across the building—the wreaths, the garland, the banners, and the lights being strung along every available surface. Workers were positioning large snowflake decorations to hang from the platform's overhang, and potted poinsettias were being placed around the building.

"Sadie," he said. "This is—"

He stopped, seeming to struggle for words, and Sadie's stomach tightened. Was it too much? Too different from what she'd originally imagined?

"It's wonderful," he said finally, meeting her eyes. "Everything... the colors, the placement. Wow. Makes the whole building feel..."

"Magical?" Sadie supplied, holding her breath.

"Yeah, magical." Cole's gaze swept the depot again. "This is perfect."

Relief flooded through Sadie's chest, warm and sweet. "You really think so?"

"I really think so." Cole looked back at her. "I can't believe how fast this is all coming together."

"The city crew has been spectacular. Everyone knows exactly what they're doing, and they're actually ahead of schedule. No major disasters so far. Nobody's fallen off a ladder yet, so I'm calling it a win."

Cole's mouth quirked. "Setting the bar high, I see."

"I aim for excellence." Sadie grinned at him and felt her heart kick when he smiled back.

Before either could say more, a distinct voice carried from nearby.

"Well, this is quite the transformation!"

Sadie turned to see Martha Caldwell approaching, Mayor Hayes beside her, both bundled against the November chill in wool coats.

"Martha. Mayor Hayes." Cole straightened slightly, his professional demeanor sliding into place. "We weren't expecting you."

"Surprise inspection," Martha said, but her eyes were warm as they took in the surrounding activity. "I received Sadie's email this morning with the marketing updates and ticket sales numbers, and Roger and I decided we needed to see the progress in person."

"And I'm delighted we did." Mayor Hayes surveyed the depot with obvious approval. "This is impressive. Really impressive."

Martha moved closer to examine the garland work on the nearest lamppost, running her fingers over the ribbon. "The attention to detail is exceptional. Sadie, this is beyond what I expected."

"Thank you." Sadie tried to keep her voice steady despite the flutter in her chest. "I wanted everything to feel cohesive—like it all belongs together rather than just decorations thrown up randomly."

"You've succeeded." Martha turned to Cole. "And you've been working together on all of this?"

"She's done the bulk of the work," Cole said, and Sadie felt warmth flood her face. "I've helped where I could, but this vision is all Sadie's."

"The partnership is working, then." Martha's knowing look moved between them. "I'm pleased to see it."

Mayor Hayes pulled out his phone, snapping photos of the decorated depot. "The marketing numbers in your email were equally impressive, Sadie. Ticket sales for the Santa Express-themed rides and the All Aboard on Christmas Eve event are ahead of projections. I was shocked to see that the Santa Express is nearly sold out already for Friday."

Cole blinked. "It is?"

"It is," Martha confirmed.

"Cole, I'll catch you up to speed on where we are with ticket sales when we have time… But things are going way better than I expected," Sadie said.

Cole looked at her and grinned. "I'm impressed."

"Keep doing what you're doing," Martha said. "Both of you. Sadie, I've lined up a reporter to interview you on the upcoming events you've planned. He wants to do a front-page feature article for this Sunday's edition. He'll meet you here tomorrow at 11 AM. Cole, have the Express shined up and ready; the reporter is bringing a photographer with him."

"Not a problem at all," he replied.

"A feature? Martha... that's wonderful!" Sadie said.

"Well, dear... it helps to know the right people. I pulled in a favor and made it happen," Martha said with a grin.

They stayed a few more minutes, Martha asking specific questions about budgets, the mayor taking more photos for the town's social media. By the time they left, Sadie's heart was racing with a mixture of pride and anxiety.

Cole checked his watch. "I need to grab lunch and check on Cash. I've got another tour at one-thirty."

"Of course."

Cole started to turn away, then paused. "All this really looks amazing, Sadie." He gestured toward the decorated depot.

"Thanks."

He nodded and turned to walk toward the depot

"Cole, wait!"

He stopped, turning back toward her, and Sadie's courage almost failed.

"There's this pizza place in town," she said, walking toward him. "Angelo's? I've been wanting to try it, and I was thinking—well, I was planning to go there tonight for dinner. Around five. And I thought, if you're free, maybe you'd want to—I mean, you probably know if it's any good, and I could use a recommendation, or not a recommendation, just—"

She was rambling. Her carefully planned invitation dissolved into nervous word salad, but Cole was looking at her with an expression she couldn't quite read, and it was making her brain short-circuit.

"Are you asking me to dinner?"

"Yes. Maybe. If you want to. I understand if you have plans, or you're busy, or—"

"Five o'clock?"

"Five. Yes."

"I don't have plans." Cole took a step closer, and Sadie's breath caught.

"So you'll come? To dinner?"

"Yeah." A small smile tugged at Cole's mouth, transforming his face. "I'll come to dinner."

Relief and nervous excitement flooded through Sadie in equal measure. "Okay. Good. That's—great."

"Great," Cole echoed, and the way he was looking at her made her forget about the surrounding workers, the clipboard in her hands, and the dozen tasks still waiting for her attention.

"I should let you go," Sadie managed. "You said you need to check on Cash."

"Right. Cash." But Cole didn't move immediately. "Five o'clock. Angelo's."

"I'll be there."

"So will I."

He turned and walked away, and Sadie watched him go, her heart hammering against her ribs and a smile she couldn't control spreading across her face.

Chapter 14

Cole arrived at Angelo's well before five o'clock. He'd been ready since four and had spent the last twenty minutes at his cabin trying to convince himself that arriving early made him look too eager.

He'd lost that argument.

Angelo's had been here for thirty years, family-owned and operated, the kind of place where the tomato sauce recipe was guarded like a state secret and the mozzarella was made in-house each morning, hand-stretched in the back kitchen just the way Angelo's father taught him.

Pushing through the door, Cole was immediately enveloped by warmth: the rich scent of garlic and baking bread, the hum of easy conversation, and the soft Italian music drifting from hidden speakers. Red-checked tablecloths brightened every table, while the walls displayed vintage photographs of Italy and handwritten menus in ornate frames.

Behind the small hostess stand stood Angelo himself, gray hair swept neatly back, apron marked with what could only be marinara. He looked up as Cole entered, his weathered face breaking into a friendly smile.

"Cole Bennett. It's been a while since I've seen you here for dinner."

"Hi, Angelo." Cole shoved his hands in his pockets. "Table for two?"

"Two?" Angelo's eyebrows rose. "Well, well. Special occasion?"

"You could say that."

"Mm-hmm. Very good then. Let's get you seated, my friend." Angelo grabbed two menus and gestured for Cole to follow.

He led Cole to a booth in the back corner.

"Your server will be with you shortly," Angelo said, setting down the menus with a flourish. "Enjoy your dinner with us."

Cole stared at the menu. His palms were slightly damp. When was the last time his palms had been damp? He couldn't remember.

He glanced at his watch. Four fifty-three.

Cole looked up to see Sadie through the front window. She stood on the sidewalk just outside, and he watched as she checked her reflection in the glass, tucking a strand of hair behind her ear. She took a visible breath, squared her shoulders, and pushed through the door.

She'd changed since this afternoon and now had on dark jeans and a cream-colored sweater that looked perfect on her. Her hair was down, falling past her shoulders in loose waves, and she'd put on just enough makeup that he noticed without being able to say exactly what was different.

She was beautiful.

Cole stood as she approached.

"Hi." Her smile was slightly nervous.

"Hi. You look nice."

"Thanks. So do you." Her gaze flicked over him—the button-down shirt he'd changed into three times, the jeans he'd made sure were clean—and something warm flickered in her hazel eyes.

They stood there for a beat too long, and then both moved at once. Cole gestured to the booth just as Sadie stepped forward, and they nearly collided. He touched her arm briefly to steady her, and even through the sweater he could feel the warmth of her skin.

"Sorry," she said.

"My fault." Cole stepped back, waited for her to slide into the booth, then sat across from her.

A server appeared with water and a basket of bread, rattling off the specials before disappearing again. Cole and Sadie both reached for a menu at the same time, and Cole caught himself studying the words without actually reading them.

"So," Sadie said after a moment. "The newspaper interview is tomorrow morning. Are you ready for it?"

Cole looked up. "Do you want to talk about work?"

"No." She set down her menu, looking relieved. "Honestly, I really don't. I need a break from thinking about events and schedules and—" She caught herself. "Sorry. That probably sounded rude."

"No, I get it." Cole set down his menu. "It's just safe territory... you know?"

"Safe territory?"

"Yeah." He met her eyes. "I haven't done this in a while. Dating..."

Sadie's expression shifted—surprise, then relief. "Me either. I haven't been on an actual date in over a year?"

"Four years for me."

"Well," Sadie said, her smile turning genuine. "Score a point for us... we both might be a little out of practice with this dating thing."

"That's one way to look at it."

The server returned, and they ordered—a large pepperoni pizza to share, salads, and two Cokes—and once the menus were gone, Cole found himself with nothing to hide behind. Just him and Sadie and whatever conversation they could build between them.

"So," Sadie said, tearing off a piece of bread. "Tell me something about yourself that has nothing to do with trains."

Cole considered the question. "I'm a decent cook, but when it's just me, I tend toward quick, easy meals. Nothing fancy."

"What counts as quick and easy?"

"Grilled chicken. Pasta with jarred sauce. Scrambled eggs." He shrugged. "My mom keeps trying to teach me her recipes, but most of them require more patience than I have after a twelve-hour workday."

"I stress-bake," Sadie offered. "Cookies, brownies, anything sweet, actually. My apartment smells like a bakery half the time."

"That doesn't sound like a bad thing."

"It's not, except I end up eating everything myself." She smiled. "What else? What do you do when you're not working?"

"Hike with Cash. Read." He felt his face warm slightly. "Railroad history, mostly. I know that sounds boring."

"It doesn't sound boring. It sounds like you're passionate about what you do."

Cole studied her across the table, the way the low lighting caught the gold flecks in her eyes. "What about you? How do you spend your spare time?"

"I used to explore whatever city I was in. Try new restaurants, find the local bookshops, and take photos of interesting architecture." She paused. "Right now, my entire focus has been on work; I haven't had much spare time at all. In fact, dinner at your mom's house was a welcome relief."

Their salads arrived, and the conversation shifted. They discovered they both preferred fall and winter over summer, that neither of them had ever been skiing despite living in the mountains, and that they had completely opposite opinions on whether pineapple belonged on pizza.

"It's fruit," Cole said, trying not to smile at her mock outrage. "Fruit doesn't go on pizza."

"Tomato is a fruit."

"Tomato sauce is a vegetable in spirit."

"That's not how botany works."

"It's how my pizza philosophy works."

Sadie laughed, and Cole felt something warm settle in his chest. He liked making her laugh. He liked the way her eyes crinkled at the corners and the way she leaned forward slightly when she was engaged in conversation.

The pizza arrived, and they both reached for the parmesan at the same time. Their hands brushed, and both paused. The contact lasted only a second, but Cole felt it like static electricity, aware of every point where her skin touched his.

"Sorry," Sadie said, pulling back.

"No, go ahead." Cole gestured to the shaker, and she took it, their eyes meeting briefly before both looked away.

Cole took a bite of his slice, the cheese stretching perfectly, the crust crispy at the edges the way he liked it. Across from him, Sadie closed her eyes briefly after her first bite.

"Okay," she said. "This might actually be the best pizza I've ever had."

"Angelo knows what he's doing."

"I'm never leaving this town. This pizza seals the deal."

"Promise?"

Sadie smiled as she set down her slice. "Can I ask you something?"

"Sure."

"It's been four years since you've dated. That's a long time."

Cole's chest tightened slightly. He'd known this topic would come up, eventually.

"Yeah, it is. I had a relationship that ended badly."

"Do you want to talk about it?"

The question caught him off guard—not because she asked, but because she was giving him the choice. Not pushing, not assuming, just offering space if he wanted to fill it.

"Her name was Sarah. She'd moved here for a teaching position at the elementary school. We dated for about a year and a half."

Sadie only nodded, her attention steady on him.

"Things were good at first. We got along great. But after a while, she started talking about leaving—better opportunities, city life, all the things Mistletoe Falls couldn't offer." He turned his glass slowly in his hands. "She asked me to go with her."

"But you couldn't."

"I didn't want to," Cole corrected. "My life is here. The Express, my family, this town—I can't imagine living anywhere else. She couldn't understand that. Couldn't understand why I'd stay when there was a whole world out there."

"So she left."

"Yeah. And about a year later, my father died." He swallowed hard. "Heart attack at the depot. I was out on a ride when it happened."

Sadie's hand moved across the table, stopping just short of his. "I'm sorry. That must have been incredibly hard. Both things so close together."

"It was. Still, is sometimes." He glanced at her, struck by the compassion in her eyes. "But I don't regret staying here. This is where I belong."

For a moment, they sat quietly. Cole braced himself for the words he'd heard before—that he was wasting his life in a small town, that he should have left while he had the chance. That was Sarah's refrain in those last months.

"I understand that. Needing to be somewhere specific. It's not about whether one place is better than another—it's about where you can breathe. About what feels right... what feels like home."

He nodded, grateful. "What about you?" he asked, shifting the spotlight before the conversation grew too heavy. "You haven't gone on a date in over a year."

"I've been busy." Sadie smiled slightly. "Traveling and moving constantly doesn't exactly lend itself to relationships. And honestly, I was using the traveling and moving around as an excuse not to get close to anyone."

"Why?"

She considered the question, her fingers tracing patterns on the condensation of her glass. "If you don't get attached, you can't be disappointed when it ends. It's a pretty effective defense mechanism... and one I think you understand as well. That's why taking this job felt like such a risk, but at the same time... this job and this town just felt right. I knew when I found that ad for the job here that it was meant to be."

"For what it's worth," Cole said, "I'm glad you took the risk."

Sadie's smile was warm and genuine. "Me too."

Their server cleared their plates and brought the check, and Cole realized with surprise that nearly two hours had passed. It had felt like twenty minutes.

"So," Sadie said, reaching for her wallet. "How should we split this?"

Cole was already pulling out his wallet. "I've got it."

"Cole—"

"I asked you out." He paused. "Wait. You asked me out." He handed his card and the bill to the passing server before Sadie could argue further. "Next time you can pay."

"Next time?"

"If you want there to be a next time."

Sadie's smile could have lit up the entire restaurant. "I definitely want there to be a next time."

They walked out into the November evening. The temperature had dropped significantly, cold enough that their breath fogged in the air. The street was quiet, most shops already closed for the evening, and the gas lamps along Mistletoe Lane glowed warm against the darkness.

They walked slowly toward the parking area behind the restaurant where Sadie had left her SUV, neither rushing to end the evening.

"I had a good time tonight," Sadie said when they reached her vehicle.

"Me too." Cole found himself stepping closer. "Better than I expected, actually."

"Better than expected?" She raised her eyebrows, but her eyes were dancing. "What were you expecting?"

"I don't know. More awkwardness? Running out of things to say?" He paused. "Instead, I keep wanting to know more."

"We should do this again."

"Tomorrow? After the newspaper interview? Lunch?"

"I'd like that."

Cole felt something warm bloom in his chest. "Really?"

Sadie stepped closer, close enough that he could smell her perfume—something light and sweet. "Really."

They stood there in the cold parking lot, close enough that Cole could see the way the lamplight caught in her hair, and he could count the gold flecks in her hazel eyes. He wanted to kiss her. The urge was sudden and overwhelming, and for a moment he almost gave in to it.

Instead, he reached out and took her hand, his fingers lacing through hers. Her palm was warm against his, and he felt her breath catch.

"You're really something special, Sadie," he said quietly. "Good night, and drive carefully."

"Goodnight, Cole."

He opened her car door for her, waited while she started the engine, then stepped back as she pulled out of the parking space. He stood there watching her taillights disappear, his hand still warm from where it had held hers.

It had been so long since he'd let himself feel anything like this—this wanting, this hoping. With Sarah, even at the beginning, there had been a part of him that held back. Some instinct had warned him that something just wasn't quite right, that it wouldn't last.

With Sadie, he didn't feel that warning. He felt antici-pation. Possibility.

Chapter 15

"You're stalling," Cole said, watching Sadie poke at the kung pao chicken with her chopsticks like it might spontaneously combust.

"I'm not stalling." She picked up a piece, turned it this way and that, then set it back down. "I'm exercising reasonable caution."

"It's chicken and vegetables, not a bomb."

"Spicy chicken and vegetables." Sadie reached for the lo mein container instead, scooping a generous portion onto her plate. "See? I'm eating. Just choosing the option that won't require medical attention."

Cole shook his head and took another bite of the kung pao, savoring the heat. "Drama queen."

"Your eyes are literally watering right now."

He blinked, realizing she was right. "Okay, fine. Maybe it's got a little kick to it."

"A little kick?" Sadie's laugh burst out bright and un-guarded, filling his office with warmth. "Cole Bennett, admitting he miscalculated something. I should get this notarized."

"I didn't miscalculate. I'm simply acknowledging that individual spice tolerance varies."

"That's just defeat wearing a fancy hat." She reached for her water, still grinning. "But seriously, thanks for ordering lunch. This was really nice, especially after spending so much time with the reporter and smiling for that photographer."

Cole leaned back in his chair, the old wood creaking under his weight. "The interview went well, though, don't you think?"

"I do. The reporter actually seemed interested instead of just asking surface-level questions. Though I'm pretty sure the photographer took about a hundred pictures of you standing next to the Express."

"He took just as many of you."

"Only because you kept deflecting every time he asked you a question." She met his eyes across the desk, her smile softening into something that made his pulse skip. "I noticed, by the way."

Heat crept up Cole's neck. "You did most of the work on these events. Makes sense you'd get the credit."

"We're a team." Sadie's voice went quiet. "None of this would be coming together so smoothly if we weren't working together."

Cole wanted to say something—wanted to acknowl-edge that she was right, that somewhere in the past couple of weeks they'd stopped being reluctant colleagues and become something else entirely—but Cash chose that exact moment to heave himself up from his bed in the corner.

The dog padded over to the desk and positioned himself directly beside Sadie's chair, sitting with the kind of deliberate patience that suggested he'd been practicing this move. His tail swept across the floor in slow, hopeful arcs.

"Cash, no begging." Cole tried for stern and landed somewhere closer to amused.

"He's not begging," Sadie said, scratching behind the dog's ears. "He's just keeping me company. Aren't you handsome, boy?"

Cash's tail accelerated, thumping against the desk leg, and he leaned into her touch like she was the best thing that had happened to him all week.

"Traitor," Cole muttered.

"I think he just has excellent judgment." Sadie's fingers worked through the fur at Cash's neck, and the dog's eyes half-closed in bliss.

They settled into eating again, the office quiet except for the soft click of chopsticks and Cash's occasional contented sighs. Afternoon sunlight streamed through the window behind Cole's desk, warming the space and turning the air lazy and golden. Cole relaxed in a way he rarely did during work hours—shoulders dropping, jaw unclenching, and that constant hum of tension he carried fading to background noise.

His office had always felt exactly right before. Small but organized. Functional. A place where everything had its spot and nothing surprised him.

But with Sadie here, it felt different.

Better.

"So." Sadie pulled out her phone and tapped the screen, scrolling through what looked like a very long list. "Tree lighting logistics update. The electrical crew confirmed we're good to go—no breakers should blow with the extra load from the big tree. Claire from Sugarplum Bakery confirmed that one of her staff will deliver all the cookies at least two hours before the event starts. And Caroline finalized the cocoa bar setup yesterday."

"What about the carolers?"

"Confirmed. The church choir's providing eight singers. They'll perform before and after the actual tree lighting." She made a quick note. "Oh, and Mrs. Davis from the historical society volunteered to help lead museum tours."

"You've really thought of everything, haven't you?"

"I've tried." Sadie set her phone down and picked up her chopsticks again, but her hands weren't quite steady. "Although I keep having this nightmare where the tree falls over mid-ceremony and takes out half the platform like some kind of evergreen missile."

"That's not gonna happen."

"You can't know that for sure."

"Actually, I can." Cole leaned back, crossing his arms. "The platform's designed to handle passenger loads well over a hundred people at a time. One twelve-foot tree with proper anchoring? Not even close to a concern."

"Engineering facts are surprisingly reassuring."

"Want more? I've got plenty."

Sadie laughed again, and Cole decided right then that making her laugh might be his new favorite hobby. "I'll keep that in mind for the next time I'm spiraling."

"The Express's boiler can maintain steam pressure for up to three hours without refueling," he offered, warming to the subject. "And the whistle's pitch is exactly E-flat, which is supposedly one of the most pleasing tones to the human ear."

"Are you showing off right now?"

"Maybe." He couldn't quite suppress his grin. "Is it working?"

"Unfortunately, yes." Her eyes sparkled with amusement. "Keep going. Hit me with more train facts."

"The drive wheels are forty-two inches in diameter—that's the optimal size for passenger locomotives from this era. The brass fittings are all original; we've just cleaned and polished them over the years. And that specific shade of green on the Express? It's called Pullman Green, named after the Pullman Palace Car Company."

"Pullman Green," Sadie repeated, a smile playing at the corners of her mouth. "You know, most people don't get this excited about paint nomenclature."

"Most people don't appreciate the finer points of historic preservation."

"True." She set down her chopsticks and held his gaze, something shifting in her expression. "But you're not just rattling off trivia, are you? You genuinely care about every bolt, every piece of brass, and every layer of paint. Like they all matter."

"They do matter." The words came out more defensively than he'd meant them to.

"I know they do." Her voice softened, went gentle. "That's what makes you so good at this. All that dedication, all that knowledge you carry around—" She paused, her cheeks coloring slightly. "It's attractive, Cole."

The office shrank. Or maybe it was just that all the air had suddenly evacuated the room, leaving nothing but the two of them and the afternoon light. The weight of what she'd just said hung between them like something he could almost reach out and touch.

He opened his mouth—to say what; he had no idea—but Sadie's phone buzzed against the desk before he could figure it out.

She glanced at the screen, and her expression shifted from open to apologetic. "Oh. Martha needs to meet earlier than we planned—she's gotta leave work early today. She wants me at city hall as soon as I can get there."

Cole checked his watch, feeling the moment slip through his fingers like water. "Right now?"

"Apparently. I'm sorry. I hate to cut lunch short."

"Don't apologize. My lunch hour's almost over anyway—the next tour starts in an hour, and I've got work to do before then."

"Lunch is on me next time," she said, slinging her bag over her shoulder.

Then she was gone, her footsteps fading down the depot's main hall, and Cole sat alone in his office with Cash and a collection of empty takeout containers.

He should clean up. Should head out and help Hank run through the pre-ride inspection. Should do any number of productive things that would keep the depot running smoothly and the Express on schedule.

Instead, he sank deeper into his chair, breathing in the lingering trace of Sadie's perfume and the warmth she'd left behind like a physical presence.

His office had always been his sanctuary. Organized, controlled, exactly the way he needed it to be. A place where he could work without interruption, think without distraction, and maintain the careful order that kept everything running smoothly and kept his head clear.

But sitting here now, in the space Sadie had just occupied, Cole realized something.

His office didn't feel like a sanctuary anymore.

It felt empty.

He looked at Cash, who'd returned to his bed but was watching Cole with eyes that seemed to hold far too much understanding for a dog.

"Don't look at me like that."

Cash's tail thumped once against the floor.

"I like her," Cole said aloud, the words feeling both strange and inevitable in his mouth. "There. Happy?"

Another thump, more pointed this time, like Cash was saying, Finally, you idiot.

Cole ran both hands through his hair, remembering the way Sadie had laughed at his train facts. The way she'd listened, like they actually mattered, like his enthusiasm wasn't something to be tolerated or humored but something worth engaging with. The way she'd called his knowledge attractive and then blushed.

The depot had been his refuge for years—the one place that felt safe and predictable and his. But it felt less lonely when she was here. The work felt more purposeful when he could share it with someone who understood what it meant. The days felt less like something to endure and more like something worth experiencing.

His phone buzzed in his pocket. He pulled it out to find a text from Hank:

Where are you?

Right. Work. The thing he was supposed to be focused on instead of sitting in his office mooning over a woman who'd just called him attractive and then left him there to spiral about it.

He stood, grabbed his conductor's cap from its hook by the door, and Cash lifted his head with immediate interest.

"Come on," Cole said. "You can ride along this afternoon."

Cash bounded to his feet, tail wagging like this was the best news he'd heard all day, and followed Cole out of the office.

But as Cole stepped out into the November afternoon, settling his cap on his head and feeling the familiar weight of responsibility settle back onto his shoulders, he couldn't quite shake the feeling that his world was changing.

He'd spent four years building a life that was safe. Controlled. Predictable. A life where the biggest risk he took was trying a new maintenance technique and where the closest relationships he had were with his family, his colleagues, and Cash.

And then Sadie Baker had shown up with her color-coded lists and her genuine smile and her questions that made him remember why he'd fallen in love with the Express in the first place—not because it was his duty, but because it was beautiful and worth protecting and worth sharing.

She'd slipped past his defenses so gradually he hadn't even noticed. Or maybe he had noticed and just hadn't cared enough to stop it.

Either way, she was in now. In his office, in his days, and in his thoughts more often than was probably wise for a man who was supposed to be keeping his distance.

The scariest part wasn't that she was there.

The scariest part was that he wanted her there.

Cash bumped against his leg, and Cole reached down to scratch the dog's ears as they walked toward where Hank stood by the Express.

"There you are," Hank called. "Thought maybe you'd gotten lost."

"Not lost at all, just got sidetracked."

Hank's eyebrow rose, but all he said was, "Uh-huh. Well, come on then. Got a full house for this afternoon's ride."

Cole followed him to the Express, letting the familiar routine settle over him like a well-worn coat. Pre-ride inspection. Checking pressure gauges and brake lines. Making sure everything was exactly as it should be.

But even as he went through the motions, even as his hands moved with practiced efficiency over controls and connections he could navigate blind, part of his mind was still back in that office.

Still feeling the way Sadie's eyes had held his when she'd called his knowledge attractive.

Still wanting to know what might have happened if her phone hadn't buzzed.

Still wondering when he'd stopped being careful and started hoping instead.

Chapter 16

"What about that one?" Sadie pointed to a Fraser fir, its branches heavy with fresh snow.

Cole didn't even slow down. "Too big."

"You said we needed twelve feet, right?"

"Twelve feet is the target. That's pushing sixteen." He kept walking, boots crunching through the snow that had fallen overnight and transformed Mistletoe Tree Farm into something out of a storybook. "We'd need a crane to get it upright."

Cash bounded ahead of them down the row, his golden-brown coat dusted with white. He'd been in heaven since they'd arrived, rolling around in the snow as if it was the best thing he'd ever experienced. Now he stopped to investigate something at the base of a spruce, his nose working overtime.

"Don't eat that," Cole called.

Cash looked back, tongue lolling, completely unrepentant.

"He's fine," Sadie said. "Let him have fun."

"Last time I let him 'have fun' in the woods, he rolled in something dead, and I had to give him three baths." But Cole's voice held no real heat, and when Cash trotted back to them with snow clinging to his muzzle, he reached down to ruffle the dog's ears.

They'd been walking through the rows for a while now, the morning sun filtering through the evergreen branches and catching on snow crystals until everything sparkled. The farm stretched across gently rolling hills, row after row of trees of various sizes, all of them dusted white from last night's snowstorm. The air smelled of pine and winter cold, sharp enough to make Sadie's nose tingle.

"I can't believe I've never done this before," she said, tilting her head back to look at the trees towering overhead.

Cole slowed, glancing back at her. "Never?"

"Nope. First time at an actual Christmas tree farm." She brushed snow off a low-hanging branch, watching it cascade to the ground. "This is way better than I imagined."

"That's—" He paused, something crossing his face. "That's kind of sad."

"Maybe." She grinned at him. "But I'm doing it now, aren't I?"

"Yeah. You are."

They stood there for a moment, snow falling gently around them, and Sadie felt that flutter in her chest again—the one that had been showing up more and more often when Cole looked at her like that.

Cash barked, breaking the moment, and took off down the row at full speed.

"Cash, get back here!" Cole called, but the dog ignored him completely.

They rounded the corner where the row intersected with another, and Sadie stopped so fast Cole nearly ran into her back.

"That's it," she breathed.

The tree stood slightly apart from the others, maybe eleven feet tall, its branches full and perfectly shaped. Snow clung to every needle, making it look like something from a Christmas card, and the afternoon light hit it just right, making the whole thing seem to glow.

"That's the one."

Cole moved to stand beside her.

"It's perfect."

"The shape's solid, the branches are full, no obvious gaps—" He glanced at her and must have seen something in her face because he stopped cataloging features and just smiled. "Yeah. It's perfect."

Sadie grinned at him. "We found our tree."

"We did." Cole pulled out his phone. "Let me text Gabe that we're ready and send him the coordinates of where we are."

While he typed, Sadie walked closer to the tree, reaching out to touch the branches. The needles were soft under her fingers, and a little shower of snow fell when she brushed against them. Cash sat at the tree's base, looking up at her with what could only be described as approval.

"Gabe says give him about fifteen minutes to get the equipment ready," Cole said, pocketing his phone. "They'll cut it down for us and get it loaded on their delivery truck."

"I already texted the city crew. They'll meet us at the depot to help set it up." Sadie stepped back to admire the tree from another angle. "This is going to look incredible all decorated with lights."

"It will." Cole moved to stand beside her.

Sadie bent down and scooped up a handful of snow, packing it between her gloved hands. The cold bit through the knit fabric, but she didn't care. She was forming it into a perfect sphere, testing the weight, and trying very hard not to smile.

"What are you doing?" Cole asked.

"Nothing." She turned slightly, hiding the snowball behind her back. "Just enjoying the snow."

"Sadie—"

She threw it.

The snowball caught him square in the shoulder, exploding in a white burst across his dark jacket. Cole stood there, shock written all over his face, while Sadie dissolved into laughter.

He looked from his snow-covered shoulder to her, and she saw the exact moment his expression shifted from surprise to intent.

Sadie took off running down the row, her boots slipping slightly in the snow, but somehow she kept upright.

She heard Cole behind her, his footsteps pounding, and she shrieked when a snowball hit her back. She risked a glance over her shoulder and saw him bending down for another handful of snow, grinning in a way she'd never seen before—all playfulness and mischief and about ten years younger.

Cash had joined the chase, barking and bounding through the snow like this was the best game ever invented.

Sadie cut between two rows of trees, trying to lose Cole in the maze of evergreens, but he was faster than she'd expected. She could hear him gaining on her, could hear him laughing, and then his arm came around her waist from behind.

"Got you," he said, breathless.

She tried to twist away, still laughing, but her boot hit a patch of ice hidden under the snow. Her feet went out from under her, and Cole—still holding onto her—couldn't catch his balance. They went down together in a tangle of limbs and winter coats, hitting the snow with a soft whump.

For a second, they just lay there, stunned. Then Sadie started laughing, and Cole joined in, and Cash arrived to dance around them, barking excitedly and trying to lick both their faces at once.

"Get off," Cole said, half-laughing, pushing the dog away. "Cash, give us a second."

Cash bounded back, tail wagging furiously, then flopped onto his back, wiggling around in the snow himself.

Sadie pushed herself up on her hands.

He was flat on his back beneath her, one arm still loosely around her waist from when he'd caught her. Snow clung to his dark hair and his eyelashes, and his cheeks were flushed from the cold and running. He was breathing hard, and so was she, their breath fogging in the space between them.

His free hand came up, brushing snow from her cheek.

"Hi," she said.

"Hi." His voice had gone rough.

She closed the distance and pressed her lips to his. His hand tightened at her waist, and he was kissing her back, his other hand coming up to cup the back of her head, and everything else—the snow, the trees, Cash's excited barking—faded into background noise.

The kiss was sweet and innocent and over far too quickly.

When she drew back and opened her eyes, Cole was looking at her like she'd just rearranged his entire world.

"I've been wanting to do that for a while now," she said.

Cole's thumb brushed against her cheek, wiping away snow or maybe just touching her because he could. "Yeah?"

"Yeah."

His mouth curved into a smile that made her want to kiss him again.

Instead, they lay there in the snow, looking at each other, and Sadie thought about how ridiculous they must look—sprawled on the ground, covered in white, while a dog pranced around them like they were his favorite entertainment. She started laughing again, and Cole joined in. Cash took that as an invitation to pounce on them both again.

"Okay, okay," Cole said, finally sitting up and hauling Sadie with him. "We're getting up. See? We're moving."

They stood, brushing snow off their coats.

Cole reached up and brushed snow from her hair.

"We should probably head back to the tree before Gabe sends out a search party."

"Probably." But neither of them moved for another heartbeat, just standing there looking at each other in the middle of a Christmas tree farm with snow falling around them. Cash wagged his tail hard enough to shake his whole body.

They walked back toward their tree, and Sadie's hand found Cole's somewhere along the way. Their gloved fingers tangled together, and neither of them let go.

When they rounded the corner back to where their tree stood, Gabe was already there with another worker, a chainsaw in hand and safety gear laid out.

"There you two are," Gabe called. "Thought maybe you got lost."

"Just exploring," Cole said, and Sadie bit her lip to keep from laughing.

"Uh-huh." Gabe's eyes flicked from their joined hands to their snow-covered coats to Cash, who was still dusted completely white.

"We picked our tree," Sadie said, feeling heat rise in her cheeks despite the cold.

"So you did." Gabe moved toward the Fraser fir they'd chosen, circling it with a professional eye. "Good choice. She's a beauty. Are you ready to watch her come down?"

"Absolutely," Sadie said.

Gabe and his helper got to work. The chainsaw roared to life, and the sharp scent of fresh-cut pine filled the air. The tree swayed, tilted, and came down, landing in the snow with a soft whoosh.

"Perfect," Gabe pronounced. "We'll get this loaded up and delivered to the depot for you. Should take us maybe thirty, forty minutes to get there."

"That works," Cole said. "We'll head back now and make sure everything's ready."

While Gabe and his helper began preparing the tree for transport, Cole and Sadie walked back toward the parking area. Cash trotted beside them, finally calming down after all the excitement, his tongue lolling out the side of his mouth.

Cole opened the passenger door for Sadie, waiting until she climbed in before closing it and walking around to the driver's side. Cash hopped into the back seat, circled twice, and flopped down with a contented sigh.

The engine started with a rumble, and warm air began blasting from the vents. Cole backed out of the parking spot and turned onto the narrow road that would take them back toward town.

Sadie pulled off her gloves and held her hands up to the vent, trying to warm her frozen fingers. She could feel Cole glancing at her, then back at the road, then at her again.

"So," he said finally.

"So," she echoed.

"That happened."

"It did." Sadie turned to look at him, watching the way his jaw worked like he was trying to figure out what to say next. "Are you freaking out?"

"Maybe a little." He shot her a quick look, and she saw the corner of his mouth twitch. "Are you?"

"Maybe a little."

"Good. I'd hate to be the only one."

Sadie laughed. Cole reached across the console, and his hand found hers again, fingers threading together naturally.

They drove through the snow-covered countryside, past farms and fields and forests, the morning sun turning everything golden. The radio played a country tune, and Cash snored softly in the back seat.

Chapter 17

The flatbed truck's backup alarm pierced the air, its insistent beeping announcing the arrival of the depot's newest centerpiece.

"Left! Go left!" One of the city workers—Marcus, according to his name tag—waved his arms like he was directing a 747 into a gate.

Cole stood beside Sadie on the depot platform, and Cash sat alert between them. The Fraser fir they'd chosen filled the entire flatbed, its branches wrapped in netting that made it look like a giant green burrito.

"Think they've got this?" Sadie asked.

"Eventually." He glanced at her, catching the way the morning sun turned her hair to warm honey. "Though Marcus might have an aneurysm first."

"I heard that, Bennett!" Marcus called.

"You were meant to."

The truck finally aligned with the platform, and Gabe killed the engine. He and his helper—a younger man Cole didn't recognize—climbed out and moved to inspect their positioning.

"Perfect," Gabe announced, slapping the side of the truck. "Let's get this beauty unloaded."

The next twenty minutes involved more coordination than Cole had used in his last three train operations combined. The tree stand waited exactly where they'd positioned it earlier—a heavy-duty commercial model bolted into the platform with reinforcing brackets that could handle hurricane-force winds, never mind one twelve-foot Fraser fir.

"On three," Gabe said, positioned at the base of the trunk while Cole, Marcus, and the other city worker—Jerome—grabbed strategic points along the netting. "One, two—wait, nobody move. Sadie, can you grab that rope that's about to slip?"

Sadie darted forward, catching the securing rope before it could slide off the back of the flatbed. "Got it!"

"Okay, now. One, two, three—"

They lifted, and the tree came off the truck like they'd practiced it a hundred times. Cole felt the weight of the tree pull on his muscles, his boots finding purchase on the platform as they shuffled toward the stand.

"Little to the left," Jerome grunted.

"My left or Marcus's left?" Gabe asked.

"Your left!"

Cash, apparently deciding this was all very exciting, barked once and received a chorus of "not now, boy" from every man simultaneously.

Sadie stood near the stand, hands hovering like she wanted to help but wasn't sure how. "Should I—do you need—"

"Just tell us if we're lined up," Cole said, his arms burning as they maneuvered the twelve-foot tree into position.

She stepped back, tilting her head. "Little more to the right. No, too much. Back left. There! Right there!"

The trunk slid into the stand with a satisfying thunk, and everyone let go at once, stepping back quickly in case the laws of physics decided to stage a rebellion. The tree stood tall and straight, its netted branches still compressed but clearly perfect.

"Nobody breathe," Marcus said.

They all froze. The tree didn't move.

"I think we're good," Gabe said finally, moving forward to secure the base bolts. "Cole, do you want to cut the netting while I get this locked down?"

Cole grabbed the utility knife from his tool belt and started at the bottom, slicing through the heavy twine that had compressed the branches during transport. The fir seemed to sigh as the netting fell away, its branches spreading wide and full, exactly as beautiful as it had been at the tree farm.

"Oh," Sadie breathed. "It's even better here.."

Cole had to agree. The tree dominated the platform space without overwhelming it, its perfect shape and full branches creating exactly the focal point the tree lighting ceremony needed. A few needles had fallen during the move, but otherwise, it looked like something from a magazine spread.

"Now for the fun part," Gabe said, pulling out a ladder. "We've got to secure the top to the building so this thing doesn't take a dive if the wind picks up."

It took another fifteen minutes to drill anchor points into the depot's exterior brick and run steel cables from the tree's trunk to the building. Cole climbed the ladder three times to adjust positioning while Gabe and Jerome held things steady below. Marcus provided running commentary that was more entertaining than helpful, and Sadie documented everything with her phone, murmuring about promotional materials and social media content.

By the time Gabe pronounced the installation complete, Cole's shoulders ached and his hands smelled like pine sap.

"She's not going anywhere," Gabe said, testing the cables one final time. "Could probably withstand a tornado at this point."

"Let's not test that theory," Cole said.

Gabe and his helper packed up their equipment while Cole signed off on the delivery receipt. Marcus and Jerome stood back, admiring their work.

"You folks want help decorating?" Marcus asked. "Jerome and I are free for another hour if you need extra hands."

Sadie glanced at the boxes of decorations stacked just inside the depot's main doors—lights, ornaments, tinsel, all carefully organized and labeled because that's how Sadie did everything.

"No, we've got it," Sadie said, grinning. "But thank you."

Cole looked at her. She looked back, her hazel eyes bright with something that might have been challenge or mischief or both.

Marcus raised his eyebrows. "You sure? That's a lot of tree."

"We're sure." Sadie's smile didn't waver. "Cole and I can handle it."

"If you say so." Marcus shrugged, clearly not believing them but not willing to argue. "You've got our number if you change your mind."

After Gabe's truck pulled away and the city workers headed off to their other jobs, Cole and Sadie stood alone on the platform. Just them, one giant tree, and Cash, who'd already claimed a sunny spot near the depot entrance for his morning nap.

"You know that's going to take us hours, right?" Cole said.

"I know." Sadie turned to face him. "But I want it to be just us. Is that weird?"

"No. It's not weird."

Her smile softened into something that made his chest feel too small for his lungs. "Good. Because I've been planning this tree in my head for weeks, and I want to actually enjoy decorating it. Not just coordinate it."

"Then let's enjoy it." Cole gestured toward the depot. "Lights first?"

"Lights first."

They hauled the boxes out onto the platform, and Cole opened the first one to find six massive coils of white lights, each strand carefully wound and labeled with small tags that read "Section 1," "Section 2," and so on.

"You organized the lights," he said.

"I organized everything." Sadie pulled out her phone and showed him a photo of a hand-drawn diagram with the tree marked in sections, each section numbered and color-coded. "I may have gotten a little carried away."

Cole stared at the diagram, at the precise measurements and the notes about spacing and coverage, and felt something warm bloom in his chest. This was her process—the way she took chaos and turned it into order, the way she cared enough to plan every detail.

"This is incredible," he said.

"It's obsessive."

"It's both." He met her eyes. "And I like it."

Her cheeks colored slightly, and she tucked the phone back into her pocket. "Well. Then let's see if my obsessive planning actually works."

It did. The sections made sense once they started, creating a clear path from bottom to top that kept them from tangling strands or missing gaps. Cole worked the lower sections while Sadie climbed the ladder for the higher parts of the tree.

"How's it look from down there?" Sadie called, stretching to reach a branch near the top.

Cole stepped back, tilting his head. The white lights created a soft glow against the dark green needles, even in full daylight. "Perfect. Good coverage."

She climbed down, and Cole offered his hand to steady her on the last step. Her palm was warm against his, and she didn't let go immediately. "Your turn. I'll hold the ladder."

They switched places, and Cole finished the topmost section while Sadie provided encouragement and direction from below. Cash woke up long enough to investigate the light coils, determined one wasn't a toy, and returned to his nap.

"Last strand," Cole announced, winding it around the peak. "How's it look?"

"Like a Christmas card." Sadie's voice held satisfaction. "Come down and see."

Cole descended and stepped back beside her. The tree glowed with hundreds of tiny white lights, each bulb positioned to highlight the natural beauty of the branches. It wasn't garish or overwhelming—just warm and inviting and exactly right.

"We did good," Sadie said.

"We really did."

She turned to face him, close enough that it would take almost nothing to lean down and kiss her.

"Ornaments next?" she asked, her voice slightly breathless.

"Ornaments next."

The ornament boxes revealed treasures that made Cole's hands still as he lifted each one out. Large glass bulbs in deep burgundy, hunter green, cream, and gold—colors that matched the depot's aesthetic perfectly. Vintage-style ornaments with a mercury glass finish that caught the light like captured moonlight. And then, nestled in their own box with careful tissue paper wrapping, a collection of train-themed ornaments that made his throat tight.

"Sadie."

She looked up from organizing the tinsel. "Do you like them? I found them at a specialty shop online that does custom historical ornaments. There's a little Express replica, and that one's a Victorian-era station, and the locomotive ornament is from the same decade as our train—"

"They're perfect." He lifted the miniature Express carefully, marveling at the detail. Someone had hand-painted the dark green and brass and had captured the exact curve of the smokestack and the wheels. "This is amazing."

"I thought they should honor the real star of the show." She came to stand beside him, looking at the ornament in his palm. "The Express is what makes all of this possible. Everything else is just window dressing."

Cole looked at her. He was falling hard for her.

"You get it. You get me," he said quietly.

"I'm trying to." Her hand found his arm and squeezed gently. "Come on. Let's get these on the tree before I start getting emotional about ornaments."

They hung them together, Sadie directing placement while Cole handled the higher branches. She had a vision—the train ornaments positioned where they'd catch the most light, the glass bulbs creating pops of color without overwhelming the white lights.

"What about this one?" Cole held up a particularly large burgundy bulb.

"Middle section, left side. There's a gap that needs filling."

He found the spot and hung it, stepping back to check the effect. "You're good at this."

"I've had practice." She handed him another ornament, this one gold. "I used to help the nannies decorate our house when I was a little girl. Before my mom died, it was this huge production—every room had a tree, every doorway had a garland. After she was gone, my father stopped caring about all of it. But the staff still put up decorations, and I'd help whoever would let me."

Cole hung the ornament and turned to look at her. There was something in her voice—not sadness, exactly, but a distance that suggested she'd tucked those memories away somewhere safe.

"You've mentioned your mom a few times," he said carefully. "And that your childhood was lonely. But every time you talk about it, you don't seem as sad as what you're describing actually sounds like."

Sadie reached for another ornament, turning it in her hands and watching the light refract through the glass. "Is that a question?"

"More like an observation. And maybe curiosity." Cole moved closer, close enough to see the way her fingers worried the ornament's hook. "You're one of the most alive, energetic, genuinely joyful people I've met. And I keep trying to reconcile that with this picture you're painting of growing up with a father who was never there."

"You want to know how I turned out okay." It wasn't a question.

"I want to know you," Cole said. "The whole picture. Not just the parts you show everyone."

Sadie set down the ornament and looked up at him. "That's a bigger conversation than ornament-hanging really allows for."

"Then we'll take a break from ornaments."

"Cole—"

"I'm serious." He reached for her hand, threading his fingers through hers. "If you want to talk, I intend to listen. And if you would rather not talk, that's okay too. But don't think you have to keep decorating just to avoid the conversation."

She studied him for a long moment, and he could see her deciding—weighing whether to deflect with humor or lean into the vulnerability she'd been dancing around. Then she squeezed his hand.

"Can we sit?" she asked. "This is the kind of thing that needs sitting."

"Yeah. Of course."

He led her to one of the wooden benches positioned along the platform's edge, the ones that overlooked the mountains in the distance. The morning had warmed slightly; the sun climbing higher and chasing away the early chill. Cash lifted his head from his nap spot, watched them settle onto the bench, then rose and padded over to lie at their feet.

Sadie didn't sit beside Cole. She stood in front of him, and when he raised his eyebrows in question, she took a breath and lowered herself onto his lap.

Cole's hands went to her waist automatically, steadying her. "Sadie—"

"Is this okay?" She was sitting sideways across his thighs, one arm draped around his shoulders, her face level with his. "I just—I think I need to be close for this. For what I want to tell you."

"This is more than okay." His voice came out rough but honest. Having her in his lap, warm and solid and choosing to be there, felt right in a way that made everything else fade to background noise. "Take your time."

She nodded, then settled more comfortably against him, her head resting just below his shoulder. One of his arms wrapped around her back, the other rested on her knee, and they sat like that for a moment—just breathing together, just being.

"I wasn't lying when I said I had a lonely childhood," Sadie began, her voice quiet but steady. "But I also wasn't telling you the whole truth. Because the truth is complicated, and it's hard for some people to understand why I am the way I am about my father."

Cole's hand moved in slow circles on her back, encouraging without pushing.

"My mom died when I was eight," she continued. "Ovarian cancer. It was fast—six months from diagnosis to funeral. One day she was this vibrant, laughing woman who baked cookies and sang off-key and made our enormous house feel like a home. And then one day she was gone, and my father was gone with her."

"Gone how?"

"Not literally. He's still alive, still living in Knoxville, still running his company. But the man I knew as my father—the one who used to twirl my mom around the kitchen and read me bedtime stories and taught me how to catch fireflies—that man died with her." Sadie's fingers played with the collar of Cole's shirt, a nervous gesture that made him want to pull her closer. "What was left was this shell. This person who looked like my father but didn't act like him. He sold our house—the one I'd grown up in, the one that still smelled like my mother's perfume—and built a new mansion. Bigger. More modern. Completely sterile."

"That must have been hard."

"It was. But I didn't understand what was happening at first. I was eight. I thought maybe he was just sad, that eventually, he'd come back. But he never did." She shifted slightly, getting more comfortable. "He threw himself into work. Eighteen-hour days, seven days a week. I was raised by nannies, housekeepers, and tutors. Good people, mostly. Kind people who did their best to fill the gap."

Cole thought about his own childhood—dinner around the family table every night, his parents at every school play and baseball game, his father teaching him about the train while his mother made sure homework got done. The thought of Sadie rattling around a mansion with paid staff instead of family made his chest ache.

"I'm guessing he didn't come to school events," Cole said.

"Never. Not one. Graduation, science fairs, the school musical where I had exactly two lines—none of it." Sadie's voice held no bitterness, just a statement of fact. "He'd send expensive gifts instead. A new bike. A laptop. Once, a car for my sixteenth birthday, delivered by his assistant with a card that said 'Happy Birthday' and nothing else."

"Sadie."

"I know how it sounds. Poor little rich girl, right?" She lifted her head to look at him, and her eyes were clear—no tears, no self-pity. "But that's not how I see it anymore. It took years of therapy after college to get here, but I finally understand that my father is who he is. He lost the love of his life, and he couldn't handle it, and he coped by shutting down completely. That's his choice. His path. And it's not one I have to walk with him."

Cole's hand cupped her face, his thumb brushing across her cheekbone. "That's a very mature way to look at it."

"Maturity or self-preservation?" She smiled slightly. "I used to be angry. Hurt. I'd call him and beg him to come visit, to have dinner, to just acknowledge I existed beyond the trust fund he was building for me. But he never did. And at some point, I realized I was hurting myself more than he was hurting me. So I stopped."

"Stopped calling?"

"Stopped expecting. Stopped hoping for something that wasn't going to happen." She settled back against him, her head on his shoulder again. "We talk maybe once a month now. Stilted, awkward conversations where he asks if I need money and I say no and he tells me I'm wasting my potential and I change the subject. It's not a relationship. It's barely a connection. But it's all we have, and I've made peace with that."

Cole was quiet for a moment, processing. His own father had been everything—teacher, mentor, friend. The idea of having a parent who was alive but completely absent felt almost worse than loss. At least with death, there was no choice involved. No ongoing rejection.

"You said your father has money," Cole said carefully. "How much are we talking about?"

Sadie laughed softly. "Does it matter?"

"No. But I'm curious."

"He's a billionaire." She said it casually, like she was mentioning the weather. "Baker Real Estate Development. Commercial properties, high-rises, and mixed-use developments across the Southeast. He's incredibly successful by any measure that matters to him."

Cole felt his eyebrows rise. A billionaire. Sadie's father was a billionaire, and she was here in Mistletoe Falls working a trial contract position for a salary that was probably pocket change compared to what she'd grown up with.

"And he wants you to take over the company," Cole guessed.

"He's been trying to convince me since I graduated college. Keeps offering me positions—VP of Marketing, VP of Development, heir apparent to the throne." Sadie's voice held wry amusement. "He thinks I'm throwing my life away on journalism and now tourism development. That I'll never make 'real money' or amount to anything significant."

"But you don't want it."

"I don't want any of it." She lifted her head to look at him again, and her expression was fierce. "I don't want his money. I don't want his company. I don't want the life he's offering me. Because I grew up in that world, Cole. I lived in a mansion where every room was designed by professionals, every meal was prepared by a chef, and every surface was so perfect you were afraid to touch anything. And I was miserable."

Cole's hand tightened on her waist. "What do you want?"

"A home." The word came out firm, certain. "Not a mansion. Not a showplace. A home where there are scuff marks on the floor and photos on the walls and dishes in the sink because someone actually uses the kitchen. I want to marry someone who chooses me not because I'm Richard Baker's daughter but because I'm me. I want a big family—four or five kids, maybe more. I want to be a stay-at-home mom who raises my children knowing they're loved every single day. I want Sunday dinners like your mom makes. I want neighbors who know my name. I want to belong somewhere."

She stopped, her cheeks flushing. "Sorry. That probably sounds ridiculous."

"It doesn't sound ridiculous." Cole's voice was rough with emotion. "It sounds perfect."

"Really?"

"Really." He leaned forward, pressing his forehead to hers. "Everything you just described—that's what family should be. What life should be. And the fact that you want it despite growing up without it? That takes courage."

"Or stubbornness."

"Both, maybe." He smiled. "But mostly courage."

They sat like that, foreheads touching, breathing the same air. Cole could feel her heartbeat against his chest and could smell the faint scent of her shampoo—something light and sweet like vanilla. Having her this close, having her trust him with pieces of herself she clearly didn't share often, felt like a gift he hadn't known he was hoping for.

"Can I ask you something?" Sadie said after a moment.

"Anything."

"Do you think less of me? For cutting my father out of my life?"

"No." Cole pulled back enough to look at her properly. "I think you're protecting yourself. That's not something to be ashamed of."

"Some people don't understand. They think family is family, and you owe them loyalty no matter what."

"Family is supposed to show up," Cole said firmly. "Family is supposed to care. Your father stopped doing both of those things a long time ago. You don't owe him anything just because you share DNA."

Sadie's eyes went bright, and for a second, Cole thought she might cry. Instead, she laughed—a watery, relieved sound that made him want to hold her tighter.

"Thank you," she said. "For understanding and not judging."

"Nothing to judge." He tucked a strand of hair behind her ear. "You're one of the strongest people I've ever met, Sadie Baker. You took all that pain and loneliness and turned it into something good. That's not easy."

"I had help. The nannies who raised me—Mrs. Clark and Gabriela especially—they loved me when my father couldn't. They taught me what family should look like, even if I didn't have one of my own. I owe them everything."

"Then they did one heck of a job. They deserve praise."

She smiled at that, and some of the tension drained from her shoulders. "I don't talk about this much. Most people don't need to know. But I wanted you to know."

"Why?"

"Because you matter." She said it simply, like it was obvious. "Because this—" she gestured between them "—matters. And I don't want there to be big secrets between us. I don't want you wondering why I am the way I am."

Cole's chest felt too full, emotions crowding against his ribs. "You matter to me too. More than I probably should admit this early."

"How early are we talking?" Her smile turned mischievous. "Because I kissed you just a few hours ago, and I've been thinking about doing it again pretty much constantly since then."

"Have you now?"

"Have you?"

"Maybe." He was definitely smiling now. "Possibly."

"Liar." But she was grinning, and the heaviness of the previous conversation had lifted, replaced by something lighter and warmer. "You've been thinking about it constantly too."

"Fine. Constantly." He leaned in, close enough that their lips almost touched. "Happy?"

"Very." She closed the distance.

The kiss was soft and sweet and tasted like the promise of more. Cole's hand came up to cradle her face while his other arm pulled her closer, and Sadie's fingers tangled in his hair. They kissed until Cash whined from his spot at their feet, probably objecting to being ignored, and they broke apart laughing.

"We should finish the tree," Sadie said, though she made no move to get up from his lap.

"We should," Cole agreed, also not moving.

"The tinsel isn't going to hang itself."

"Most likely not."

"And we still have the tree topper to put on."

"Very important."

They grinned at each other like fools, and Cole thought about what she'd said—about wanting a home filled with love and laughter and scuff marks on the floor. About wanting to belong somewhere.

He wanted to tell her she already belonged. That Mistletoe Falls had claimed her the moment she'd arrived, that his family had adopted her after one dinner, that he'd fallen for her somewhere between her first nervous presentation and her methodical organization system for Christmas lights.

But it was too soon to say things like that out loud, too soon to make promises about futures that might not materialize.

Except it didn't feel too soon. It felt exactly right.

"Come on," Sadie said, finally sliding off his lap and pulling him to his feet. "Let's finish this tree before I lose all motivation to move."

They returned to the decorating with renewed energy, hanging the rest of the ornaments while Cash supervised from his sunny spot. Sadie told him about her college roommate, who'd been her first real friend, and Cole shared stories about the Express's most memorable passengers. They debated the merits of tinsel—Sadie loved it, Cole remained skeptical—and compromised on elegant draping rather than the explosive coverage she'd initially envisioned.

By the time they stepped back to admire their work, the afternoon sun was starting its descent toward the mountains, painting everything in gold.

The tree was magnificent. White lights glowed against dark green needles, ornaments caught the slanting sunlight and threw it back in burgundy and gold, and the silver tinsel added just enough shimmer without overwhelming the whole effect. The train ornaments hung prominently, little reminders of what this was all really about.

"It's gorgeous," Sadie breathed.

"It really is." Cole's arm came around her shoulders, pulling her against his side. "We make a good team."

"We do." She leaned into him, and they stood like that for a long moment—just looking at what they'd created together.

Cash chose that moment to stand, stretch, and trot over to investigate the tree more closely. He sniffed the lower branches, gave one ornament an experimental lick, and, apparently deciding it wasn't food, lay down directly in front of the tree like he was claiming it.

"I think he approves," Sadie said.

"High praise from Cash."

The depot door opened, and Hank appeared on the platform, stopping short when he saw the tree.

"Well, would you look at that?" He said, moving closer. "That's about the finest Christmas tree I've ever seen. You two did this all by yourselves?"

"We did," Sadie said, unable to hide her pride.

Hank's eyes crinkled with humor. "Tree's not the only thing that's looking good around here, if you take my meaning."

Cole felt heat creep up his neck. "Hank."

"What?" Hank grinned.

After he left, Cole and Sadie returned to putting away the empty boxes and cleaning up the scattered pine needles that had fallen during installation. The work was companionable and easy, the kind of task that didn't require conversation but felt better done together.

"What time is it?" Sadie asked, carrying the last box toward the depot entrance.

Cole checked his watch. "Almost four."

"Do you have any other work to do today?"

"Not until tomorrow. We're done for the day."

"Good." She set down the box and turned to face him, and the late afternoon light turned her hair to honey again and made her eyes look more green. "Because I'm starving, and I think you should take me to dinner."

"Should I now?"

"You should." She walked toward him in that confident stride that made his heart kick. "Unless you have other plans?"

"No other plans." He caught her hand, threading their fingers together. "Where did you want to go?"

"Anywhere with you sounds perfect."

Cole pulled her closer, and she came willingly, fitting against him like they'd been doing this for years instead of days. He kissed her again—longer this time, deeper, until they were both breathless and Cash was whining his objection to being ignored.

When they finally pulled apart, Sadie's cheeks were flushed and her eyes were bright.

"Dinner first," she said firmly. "Then more of that."

"Deal."

They gathered their things, called Cash, and headed toward Cole's truck. The tree stood behind them on the platform, lights glowing softly in the gathering dusk, ready for Saturday's ceremony. Ready to welcome the community and celebrate everything that made Mistletoe Falls special.

But as Cole opened the passenger door for Sadie and watched her climb in with that smile that made him forget his own name, he thought the tree might not be the most important thing they'd built today.

They'd built trust. Understanding. A foundation that felt solid enough to hold whatever came next.

And for the first time in four years, Cole wasn't afraid of what came next.

He was looking forward to it.

Chapter 18

Sadie's hands trembled as she locked her SUV, and it had nothing to do with the November cold seeping through her wool coat. She had spent most of the afternoon finalizing things at the train depot for the tree lighting ceremony, then had driven to her apartment to quickly get ready.

The depot parking lot was already half full, and more cars were turning in from Pinecone Pass in a steady stream. Families bundled in winter coats walked toward the platform, children skipping ahead while parents called for them to slow down. The sun had started its descent behind the mountains, painting everything in shades of gold and amber, and the first snowflakes were beginning to fall—gentle, perfect, like someone had ordered them specifically for tonight.

She smoothed down the front of her dress, the deep burgundy fabric soft under her palms. She'd changed outfits four times before settling on this one—knee-length, fitted but not tight, elegant without being too formal. The neckline was modest, the sleeves three-quarter length, and paired with her good boots and the wool coat, she looked professional and festive and hopefully like someone who belonged at an event she'd spent weeks planning.

Her hair fell in loose waves past her shoulders, and she'd hurried to apply makeup that was supposed to look natural.

Sadie took a deep breath, watching her exhale fog in the cold air, and made herself walk toward the depot.

The scene that greeted her made her chest tighten with pride and panic.

Evergreen garland wrapped around every lamppost, secured with burgundy and gold ribbons that fluttered in the light breeze. The tree stood magnificently on the platform, its unlit branches already drawing eyes and creating anticipation. White lights lined the platform railings, waiting to be switched on. Large snowflake decorations hung from the overhang, spinning slowly. The whole building glowed with warm light from within, welcoming and festive.

But it was the people that made Sadie's breath catch.

Hundreds of them, streaming toward the depot from every direction. More than she'd dared hope for. Families with children, elderly couples walking arm in arm, teenagers in groups, business owners she recognized from town. The crowd kept growing, voices rising in excited chatter, laughter floating on the cold air.

Near the side entrance, Caroline's beverage station was already operational. Three large urns sat on a table draped in festive cloth, steam rising from them and carrying the scent of cinnamon and chocolate. Caroline herself was arranging cups while Eleanor Bennett stood beside her, elegant in a cream cardigan and burgundy scarf, organizing the toppings bar with the efficiency of someone who'd hosted hundreds of gatherings. Luke appeared with another box of supplies, saying something that made both women laugh.

Claire from Sugarplum Bakery had set up her cookie display nearby, and even from this distance, Sadie could see the artistry. Gingerbread men with perfect icing details, snowflakes that looked like lace, Christmas trees decorated with tiny candies, and train-shaped cookies that made her smile. Claire and a young woman who must be her assistant were arranging platters with careful precision.

The carolers had gathered near a small raised area that served as their performance space. Eight of them, dressed in full Victorian costume—women in long velvet dresses with capes, men in period coats and top hats. They were running through warm-ups, their harmonies drifting across the platform and adding to the magical atmosphere.

A small stage had been erected for the mayor's speech, complete with a podium and microphone. Sound equipment hummed softly, Christmas music playing at just the right volume to enhance rather than overwhelm.

Sadie saw Martha Caldwell standing near the stage, clipboard in hand, surveying everything with the sharp eye of someone who missed nothing. The mayor was already working the crowd, his booming laugh recognizable even from here. She spotted Mrs. Phillips from the cafe, June Reynolds from the post office, and dozens of other faces she'd come.

A camera crew from the local television station was setting up near the tree, the reporter checking her microphone while the cameraman adjusted his equipment. The newspaper photographer who'd interviewed them was already snapping photos of the arriving crowd.

This was real. This was happening. This was everything she'd worked for, and suddenly it felt enormous.

"There you are."

Sadie spun to find Cole walking toward her, and her heart did that thing it had been doing lately—that skip and jump that made breathing complicated.

He wore his full conductor's uniform, and the sight of it made something warm bloom in her chest. The navy wool jacket with its brass buttons gleaming, the vest underneath, the peaked cap that somehow made his steel-blue eyes even more striking. He looked official and handsome and so perfectly Cole that she had to resist the urge to just stare at him.

Cash trotted beside him, and Sadie couldn't help but smile. The dog wore a festive Christmas bowtie in red and green plaid, attached to his collar and making him look absurdly dapper. His tail wagged as he spotted her, and he bounded forward to greet her with his usual enthusiasm.

"Hey, handsome," she said, crouching down to scratch behind his ears. "Don't you look fancy tonight?"

Cash leaned into her touch, his whole body wiggling with pleasure.

"He's been preening ever since I put his bowtie on him," Cole said, stopping in front of her. "I think he knows he looks good."

Sadie straightened and found Cole looking at her with an expression that made heat rise in her cheeks.

"You look breathtaking," he said quietly.

"I changed four times."

"Worth it." His eyes moved over her face, warm and appreciative without being inappropriate. "The dress is perfect. You're perfect."

"I'm terrified," she admitted, the words tumbling out before she could stop them. "Look at all these people, Cole. What if it's not good enough? What if they're disappointed? What if—"

He stepped closer, close enough that she could smell his cologne—something clean and woodsy that she'd come to associate with comfort. His hand found hers, threading their fingers together.

"Look at what you created," he said, his voice steady and sure. "All of this—the decorations, the organization, the community coming together—this is because of you."

"We created it together," she corrected, squeezing his hand.

"You did the hard work. I just helped where I could." He tilted his head toward the growing crowd. "These people came because you gave them something worth coming for. You should be proud, Sadie."

She wanted to argue, to deflect, to list all the ways this could still go wrong. But the way he was looking at her—with pride and affection and absolute confidence—made it challenging to hold onto the anxiety.

"I'm still nervous," she said.

"That's okay. I'm right here." He leaned forward and pressed a kiss to her forehead, soft and brief and somehow more grounding than any words could be. "We've got this."

Movement in her peripheral vision made Sadie glance to the side. A family walking past had noticed the gesture, the mother smiling at them with warm approval. Two teenage girls giggled and whispered to each other. Mrs. Davis, who was hurrying toward the carolers with last-minute instructions, gave them a knowing look.

"Come on," Cole said, tugging her hand gently. "Let's make sure everything's ready before the official start time."

They moved through the crowd together, and Sadie felt the shift in how people looked at them. Not just at her—the new tourism coordinator doing her job—but at them as a unit. A couple. Cole's hand stayed in hers as they navigated between clusters of people, and he greeted locals with easy familiarity while introducing Sadie to visitors she hadn't met yet.

"Beautiful event," one older man said, shaking Sadie's free hand. "My grandchildren are beside themselves with excitement."

"Thank you so much for coming," Sadie replied.

They checked in with Caroline at the beverage station, where Eleanor immediately pulled Sadie into a warm hug.

"You look beautiful, dear," Eleanor said, holding Sadie at arm's length to admire her dress. "And this event—" She gestured around them, her eyes bright. "—you've done something wonderful here."

"I had a lot of help. I sincerely appreciate you and Luke and Caroline helping earlier today as well," Sadie managed, emotion threatening to close her throat.

"We were happy to give it." Eleanor's smile held such maternal warmth that Sadie had to blink against sudden tears. "My son hasn't smiled this much in years. Thank you for that."

Luke appeared with another box of cups, grinning when he saw them. "There's the woman of the hour. And my brother, looking unusually cheerful."

"Zip it, Luke," Cole said, but he was smiling.

"The tree looks incredible... really this whole event does," Luke continued, setting down the box. "Caroline's been taking pictures like crazy. Pretty sure she's already posted a dozen to social media."

"Guilty," Caroline called from behind the table. "But people are eating it up. We're getting comments like crazy, and some are even asking about the Santa Express rides."

"Speaking of which," Luke said, his tone turning more serious as he looked at Sadie, "I know we've only really talked in passing, but I want you to know—what you're doing for this town, for the Express, for my family—" He paused, seeming to gather his thoughts. "It matters. You matter. I'm glad you're here."

Sadie felt her vision blur. "Thank you, Luke. I appreciate you saying that."

"Good. Now go be brilliant at your event. We've got the beverage station handled." He winked at Cole. "Try not to mess this up, big brother."

Cole shook his head, but his smile didn't fade as they moved on to check Claire's cookie station. The baker was effusive in her praise of the turnout, already talking about how this exposure would help her business and how she'd love to work with Sadie on future events.

Everywhere they went, Sadie felt it—acceptance. Belonging. People who'd been strangers weeks ago now greeted her by name, thanked her for her work, and included her in their conversations like she'd always been part of the community fabric.

Mrs. Davis appeared in a rush, dividing her attention between the carolers and the museum tours she'd organized inside the depot. "The museum is getting steady traffic," she told Sadie breathlessly. "Families are loving the exhibits. Several have asked about the Express's history. This is undoubtedly what we needed to remind people why this train matters."

The carolers began their first set, their voices rising in perfect harmony on "God Rest Ye Merry Gentlemen," and the crowd quieted to listen. Children stopped running to stand with their parents, couples swayed together, and the snow fell steadily, catching in hair and on coat shoulders and creating the kind of moment that felt almost too perfect to be real.

Sadie stood beside Cole, watching the faces in the crowd, and felt peace and calmness spread over her. This was working. Not just the logistics or the decorations or the activities—but the heart of it. The community coming together, the families creating memories, the sense of magic and tradition and connection that made Mistletoe Falls special.

She'd helped create this. She belonged to this.

"Miss Baker?" A voice pulled her attention, and Sadie turned to find the television reporter approaching with her cameraman. "We'd love to get a quick interview with you and Mr. Bennett before the ceremony starts. Would you have a few minutes?"

Sadie glanced at Cole, who nodded. "Of course."

The reporter—a woman in her thirties with a professional smile and warm demeanor—positioned them near the tree. The cameraman adjusted his equipment, tested the lighting, and gave a thumbs-up.

"We're rolling," he said.

"I'm here at the Mistletoe Falls Train Depot," the reporter began, speaking to the camera, "where the community is gathering for the inaugural Tree Lighting Ceremony at the Mistletoe Express Train Depot. With me are Sadie Baker, the town's new Tourism Development Coordinator, and Cole Bennett, Lead Conductor of the historic Mistletoe Express. Thank you both for speaking with us."

"Thank you for covering the event," Sadie said, falling into her professional mode even as her heart hammered.

The reporter asked about the planning process, the significance of the depot location, the community response. Sadie answered smoothly, highlighting the collaboration and the importance of honoring tradition while creating new experiences. Cole added details about the Express's history and the depot's restoration, his passion for the train evident in every word.

"One more question," the reporter said, and something in her tone made Sadie tense slightly. "The two of you have been working very closely on this project. Will you be working together on more events involving the Mistletoe Express?"

"Yes," Cole said simply, looking at the reporter and then at Sadie. "We will be. Sadie has two more large events in the works, and I'll be assisting her."

"We have Santa Express themed train rides coming in just a couple of weeks," Sadie said. "And we'll have a grand event on Christmas Eve, which we are calling 'All Aboard on Christmas Eve.' All the information for these events is on the city's website."

The reporter's expression turned delighted. "Well, that's wonderful. I wish you both the best of luck with these events."

After the interview wrapped, they barely had time to breathe before Martha found them. She looked pleased, her usual critical expression softened by satisfaction.

"Excellent turnout," she said without preamble. "Better than projected. The council is very pleased." She paused, looking directly at Sadie. "We should discuss making your position permanent. After the holidays, of course. But between us—" Her smile turned knowing. "—you've more than proven yourself. You're a shoo-in for this position and have my vote."

Sadie couldn't speak. She'd worked toward this, hoped for this, but hearing it said so directly made it real in a way that stole her breath.

"Thank you," she managed. "Thank you so much."

"You've earned it." Martha's gaze flicked to their joined hands, and her smile deepened.

After Martha moved on to coordinate something else, Sadie turned to Cole. "Did she just—"

"Basically offer you the permanent position?" Cole's grin was enormous. "Yeah, she did."

"I might actually get this job."

"You will get this job," he corrected, pulling her closer despite the surrounding crowd.

She wanted to kiss him. Wanted to throw her arms around him and celebrate this moment properly. But the crowd was growing, the ceremony would start soon, and there were still details to coordinate.

The next twenty minutes passed in a blur of last-minute checks and coordination. The crowd swelled to well over three hundred people, filling the platform and spilling into the surrounding areas. Hank appeared briefly to tell Cole something about the Express's positioning. "Your daddy would be bursting with pride," he told Cole.

Several families from the school groups Cole had conducted stopped to thank them both. June Reynolds from the post office made a point of telling Sadie she'd "known from the start" that Sadie would be perfect for Mistletoe Falls.

Through it all, Cole stayed close. Not hovering, not smothering, but present. His hand at her back as they navigated the crowd. His quiet reassurance when she second-guessed a detail. His pride was evident every time someone complimented the event.

Mayor Hayes found them as the ceremony start time approached. "Ready?" he asked, his jovial face even more cheerful than usual. "The crowd's getting excited. Time to give them what they came for."

Sadie's stomach flipped. "Ready as we'll ever be."

The mayor made his way to the stage, and someone adjusted the sound system. The Christmas music faded, the carolers finished their set, and the crowd began to quiet in anticipation. Families gathered closer, children positioned for optimal tree-viewing, and the general murmur of conversation dropped to expectant whispers.

Cole's hand found Sadie's again, and she held on tight.

Mayor Hayes's voice boomed through the speakers, warm and welcoming. "Good evening, Mistletoe Falls! And welcome to all our visitors joining us tonight!"

The crowd cheered, children's voices rising above the rest.

"We're gathered here for something special," the mayor continued. "A new tradition for our town, but one rooted in the history and heart that make Mistletoe Falls the magical place it is. Tonight, we celebrate the lighting of our depot Christmas tree—a symbol of community, tradition, and the enduring spirit that brings us together each holiday season."

Sadie felt the significance of what she'd created. This wasn't just a tree lighting. It was a statement about what mattered, about preserving history while embracing the future, and about community coming together to celebrate shared values.

"This event wouldn't be possible without many dedicated people," Mayor Hayes said. "Our volunteers, our sponsors, the businesses that contributed—but especially two individuals who envisioned this celebration and brought it to life."

"Sadie Baker, our Tourism Development Coordinator, brought fresh eyes and creative vision to our town. And Cole Bennett, who carries on his father's legacy with the Mistletoe Express, provided the expertise and dedication that made this possible. Would you both please join me on stage?"

The crowd applauded, and Sadie felt frozen for half a second before Cole tugged her hand gently. They walked to the stage together, climbing the few steps, and suddenly they were standing in front of hundreds of people who were all looking at them.

The applause continued, enthusiastic and genuine. Sadie saw faces she knew now—June and Mrs. Phillips near the front, beaming. Claire and her assistant were clapping enthusiastically. The Bennett family clustered together, Eleanor with tears on her cheeks, Luke whistling, and Caroline bouncing with excitement. Hank was standing with his hand over his heart. Charlie was waving wildly. Martha nodded approval.

Children she'd met during the school tour. Business owners she'd worked closely with. Volunteers who'd helped with setup. All of them applauding for her. For what she'd built.

Sadie felt tears threatening and fought them back. Not now. Not in front of everyone.

"Thank you both," the mayor said, gesturing for the applause to quiet. "Your partnership has given us something to be proud of. Now—" He gestured toward the tree. "—Shall we light it up?"

The crowd cheered again, children's voices rising in excitement.

"Sadie and Cole will do the honors," Mayor Hayes announced. "On the count of ten, we'll all count down together. Ready?"

Sadie and Cole positioned themselves at the control switch—a simple lever that would activate the tree's lights. Sadie's hand trembled as she placed it on the switch. Cole's hand covered hers, warm and steady.

"Ten!" the mayor's voice boomed.

"Nine!" the crowd joined in.

"Eight!"

Sadie looked at the tree, dark and waiting. Looked at the crowd, faces upturned with anticipation. She looked at Cole, whose eyes were already on her.

"Seven! Six!"

"You've got this," he murmured, just for her.

"Five! Four!"

"We've got this," she corrected.

"Three! Two!"

Their eyes held. The moment stretched. The world narrowed to just them.

"ONE!"

They flipped the switch.

Light exploded across the tree. Hundreds of white bulbs blazed to life, cascading down from the top in perfect waves, illuminating every branch and needle. The tree glowed against the dark sky and falling snow, the lights reflecting off the white flakes and creating a shimmering, magical effect that stole breath.

The crowd gasped in unison. Children's voices rose in awed "Oooohs!" Spontaneous applause erupted, growing louder as people took in the full effect.

The carolers immediately launched into "O Christmas Tree," their voices soaring over the crowd, and people began to sing along. Phones emerged, capturing the moment. Couples pulled each other closer. Children pointed and exclaimed. Parents smiled with that particular expression that meant they were storing this memory for keeping.

Sadie stared at the tree—their tree, the one she and Cole had decorated together—and felt emotion swell in her chest until she could barely breathe. It was perfect. Everything was perfect. The lights, the snow, the crowd, the music, the feeling of belonging that wrapped around her like a warm embrace.

She turned to Cole.

"We did it," she whispered, tears finally spilling over.

"You did it," he said, and then he was kissing her.

Right there on the stage. In front of hundreds of people. In front of his family and their colleagues and the mayor and the television cameras.

When they broke apart, both smiling, the crowd's energy had shifted. Approving sounds rippled through—knowing laughter, a few whistles, and someone definitely shouting "I KNEW IT!" in June Reynolds' distinctive voice.

The mayor was grinning. "Well then. I'd say this Tree Lighting Ceremony is officially a success on multiple fronts."

The crowd laughed again, the sound warm and accepting, and Sadie felt Cole's arm come around her waist. She leaned into him, not caring who saw, not caring about professional boundaries or appropriate public behavior. This was real, and this was hers to own.

The ceremony transitioned into celebration. The mayor concluded his remarks, the carolers continued performing, and the crowd dispersed into the various activities—hot chocolate and cookies, photographs with the tree, tours of the museum, general mingling and enjoying. The snow kept falling, the lights kept glowing, and the whole scene looked like something from a movie.

Sadie and Cole descended from the stage and were immediately surrounded. People thanked them for creating such a beautiful event. Parents expressed gratitude for a family-friendly celebration. Business owners praised the exposure for the town. Children showed them cookies shaped like trains and babbled excited words about Santa coming soon.

Eleanor fought her way through the crowd and pulled Sadie into a fierce hug. When she released her, the older woman's eyes were wet. "You did good, honey."

"Thank you," Sadie managed, her own eyes streaming.

"Sweetheart, you're a gift. To this town, to the Express, and to my son." She glanced at Cole, who was being enthusiastically hugged by Luke. "He hasn't been this happy in years."

Caroline appeared next, squealing and hugging Sadie with girlfriend enthusiasm. "That kiss! Oh my gosh.... That was way better than anything I've ever seen in my life. Who knew... my brother-in-law... the romantic! It was perfect! And you look so beautiful, and the tree is gorgeous, and oh my gosh, Sadie, you did it!"

Luke clasped Cole's shoulder, said something that made his brother smile, then turned to Sadie. "Ya did good, Sadie. I guess this means you really do like my brother."

"You could say that," Sadie said, with a grin.

Hank materialized from the crowd, his weathered face creased with emotion. He shook Cole's hand with the kind of grip that said more than words, then turned to Sadie.

"Michael would have loved this," he said simply. "All of it. The event, the community coming together, his boy being happy." He paused, his eyes bright. "You're a treasure, Miss Sadie. And I'm so glad you came to our humble little town."

She hugged him and said, "You don't know how much those words mean to me. Thank you."

Hank's smile was rare and precious.

As his words settled over her like a blessing, Sadie had to excuse herself briefly to find a quiet corner and get her emotions under control. She ended up beside the tree, pressing her hands to her face and trying to remember how to breathe past the overwhelming joy.

"Sadie?"

She turned to find Cole approaching, concern etched on his face. "I'm fine," she said quickly. "I'm just—it's a lot. Good overwhelming, not bad overwhelming. Just taking a minute to regroup."

He pulled her close, and she went willingly, pressing her face against his chest and feeling his arms come around her. They stood like that for a moment, the celebration continuing around them but feeling distant and muted.

"Everyone's so welcoming and loving here," she said into his jacket. "Your family, the town, everyone. I needed this... all of it. I never imagined it could be like this"

"Like what?"

"Like belonging actually feels good. Like it's not something you have to earn or prove or constantly fight to maintain." She pulled back enough to look at him. "I've spent my whole life feeling like I had to justify my presence everywhere I went. But here—" Her voice broke. "—here it just feels natural."

Cole's hand cupped her face, his thumb brushing away tears. "That's because you do belong."

"I'm falling for you, Cole Bennett," she said. "Hard and fast and completely."

Something blazed in his eyes. "I've already fallen."

Cole rested his forehead against hers.

"I have something for you," he said.

"What is it?"

He reached into his jacket pocket and produced a small wrapped box. "I've been carrying this around all evening, waiting for the right moment."

Sadie took the box with trembling hands. It was light, wrapped in simple paper with a small bow. She looked at Cole, questioning, and he nodded encouragement.

Inside the paper was a small box. Inside that, nestled in tissue paper, was an ornament.

Sadie's breath caught.

The ornament was exquisite—hand-painted with obvious care and skill. It depicted the Mistletoe Express in perfect detail, every line and curve of the locomotive captured faithfully. The dark green paint, the brass fittings, even the small windows of the passenger cars—everything was there, miniature and beautiful.

But it was the inscription along the bottom that made tears spring to her eyes again:

Sadie's First Christmas in Mistletoe Falls - 2025

"Cole," she whispered.

"An artist in town made it," he said, watching her face. "I wanted you to have something special that marked this moment. Your first Christmas here."

She stared at the ornament. Her collection—all those ornaments from places she'd documented but never belonged to, from communities she'd passed through without claiming. This one was different. This one represented home and belonging.

"How did you know this is exactly what I needed?" she asked.

"Just a lucky guess." His smile was soft.

"First Christmas," she repeated, her voice thick.

They stood beside the tree, holding each other, while the celebration continued around them. The carolers had moved on to "Joy to the World," and children's laughter mixed with adult conversation and the general hum of community happiness. Snow fell steadily now, accumulating on coat shoulders and hat brims and turning the whole scene into something from a storybook.

Eventually, they had to rejoin the crowd. There were more congratulations on a job well done, more thanks to give, and more coordination required. The evening progressed with the kind of natural flow that marked a successful event. The media completed their coverage, the reporter giving Sadie her card and suggesting a follow-up story about the Santa Express.

The Bennett family helped with cleanup, Luke and Caroline working with the beverage station while Eleanor made sure the cocoa bar was properly packed away. Volunteers collected trash and folded tables with the easy cooperation of people who'd done this many times before. Mrs. Davis emerged from the depot looking satisfied with the museum tour turnout.

Through it all, Sadie worked alongside Cole, the two of them moving with the kind of synchronized rhythm that came from genuine partnership. He carried the heavy items, and she coordinated the volunteers. She thanked people for coming; he ensured equipment was properly stored. They traded smiles and brief touches and the kind of comfortable silence that said more than words.

By nine o'clock, the crowd had thinned to just the core group—the Bennett family, Martha, and the mayor saying their final goodbyes; Hank doing a last check of the property; and a few dedicated volunteers finishing the final cleanup tasks.

Eleanor insisted on a group photo in front of the lit tree. She gathered everyone together—Cole and Sadie in the center, Luke and Caroline beside them, Hank and Martha and a handful of others filling out the group. Cash positioned himself right in front, tongue lolling, looking pleased with himself.

"Everyone say 'Mistletoe Falls!'" Eleanor called, her phone raised.

"Mistletoe Falls!" they chorused, and the flash went off.

The final volunteers departed with waves and promises to see them at the Santa Express preparation. Martha gave Sadie a meaningful look before leaving, her approval clear. Mayor Hayes pumped both their hands enthusiastically and declared the event an "unqualified success." Hank gripped Cole's shoulder one more time and shook his hand before heading home.

Finally, it was just the Bennett family and Sadie standing in front of the glowing tree.

"You two did something special tonight," Eleanor said, looking between Cole and Sadie with open affection. "Your father would be so proud, Cole. Of all of this."

"Thanks, Mom."

Eleanor hugged Sadie one more time, then herded Luke and Caroline toward their vehicles with the kind of maternal efficiency that brooked no argument. "These two need some time alone. Come on, let's go home."

"But I want to hear about—" Caroline started.

"Tomorrow," Eleanor said firmly. "Sunday dinner. You can interrogate them then."

After they left, Sadie and Cole did a final walk-through of the depot, making sure everything was secure. The tree lights were on an automatic timer, casting their glow over the empty platform. Inside, the museum was dark and locked. The beverage station had been completely packed away, the cookie display was gone, and the carolers' performance space was empty.

Everything was done. Everything was perfect.

They walked to the parking lot together, Cash between them and looking tired but content.

At her vehicle, Sadie turned to face Cole.

"Thank you," she said. "For tonight. For the ornament. For everything."

"Thank you," he countered. "For being you."

She reached up to cup his face, feeling the slight stubble on his jaw, the warmth of his skin despite the cold. "This night has been magical. I wish I could bottle it up and savor it forever.."

She kissed him until Cash whined his objection to being ignored.

When they broke apart, Sadie was shaking—from cold, from emotion, from the overwhelming rightness of everything.

They smiled at each other, and Sadie felt her heart swell.

"Tomorrow," she said finally. "Your mom's house?"

"Four o'clock."

"Perfect." Sadie stepped back reluctantly. "I'll see you then."

"Drive carefully. Text me when you get home?"

"I will."

She climbed into her SUV, starting the engine and cranking the heat. The ornament sat carefully in the passenger seat, wrapped in its tissue paper and box. Cole stepped back, and Cash sat beside him, both watching her.

She backed out of the parking space slowly, not wanting to leave but knowing she had to. Before leaving the parking lot, she glanced over at the train depot and noticed Cole and Cash were heading toward the woods beside the depot. She'd never asked where he lived, had assumed he must live somewhere in town, but watching him disappear into the tree line made her curious.

Where was he going? Did he live back there somewhere? How far was it?

She made a mental note to ask him. There was still so much to learn about him, still so many discoveries ahead. The thought made her smile instead of making her anxious. She liked that there were still mysteries, still surprises waiting.

Chapter 19

"Sadie! Come in, come in." Eleanor said as she greeted Sadie with a hug. "I hope you're hungry. I may have made too much food again."

"I'm always hungry for good food," Sadie said honestly, following Eleanor inside.

Caroline appeared from the kitchen, her blonde hair pulled back in a messy bun, her smile bright and knowing. "There's the woman of the hour! Everyone in town is talking about last night."

"Good things, I hope," Sadie said.

"Excellent things. June Reynolds told everyone at church this morning that it was the most romantic thing she'd seen in forty years." Caroline's eyes sparkled with mischief. "Her exact words were 'that Bennett boy finally got his head on straight. She had me laughing so hard when she said that."

Eleanor shook her head with fond exasperation. "June does have a way with words."

"Where is everyone?" Sadie asked, noticing the quiet.

"Luke's in the den watching a game, and Cole should be here any minute. He texted, saying he was running late—he had to check on something at the depot." Eleanor gestured toward the kitchen. "Come join us."

Sadie followed Eleanor into the massive kitchen, the space filled with the rich aroma of ham and fresh bread.

"Can I do anything?" Sadie asked.

"You can keep us company," Eleanor said warmly. "And tell us how you're feeling after last night. That was quite an evening."

Sadie felt heat rise to her cheeks. "It was amazing. Better than I could have imagined."

"The kiss was pretty amazing too," Caroline added with a grin. "Cole isn't one for public displays of affection. You must be special."

"Caroline," Eleanor chided gently, but her eyes were amused.

"What? It's true. My brother-in-law is usually Mr. Private-and-Professional. But last night..." Caroline made an exaggerated swooning gesture. "Romance novel moment."

Sadie laughed despite her embarrassment. "It was kind of perfect, wasn't it?"

"It was," Eleanor agreed, her expression softening. "And seeing Cole happy..." Her voice caught slightly. "That meant everything to me."

The front door opened, and Sadie's heart did that flip again, the one that seemed to happen every time Cole was near.

"Speak of the devil," Caroline said.

Cole appeared a moment later, and Sadie's breath caught the way it always did when she saw him. He wore dark jeans and a forest green henley, his hair slightly mussed from the wind. When his gaze found hers across the kitchen, he smiled.

"Hey," he said, crossing to her.

"Hey yourself."

He kissed her—brief and sweet.

"Isn't that sweet?" Luke called from the doorway, his tone teasing.

"Luke Bennett," Eleanor said firmly, but she was smiling.

"What?" Luke grinned at Sadie. "Good to see you again, Sadie. Glad Cole didn't scare you off."

"It takes more than your brother's sometimes grumpy face to scare me," Sadie replied.

"I'm not grumpy," Cole protested.

"You absolutely are," Luke and Caroline said in unison, then laughed.

Eleanor clapped her hands. "All right, all right. Less teasing, more eating. Everything's ready. Let's move to the dining room."

The next few minutes passed in the comfortable chaos of a family meal being arranged on the table. Dishes were passed, stories were shared, and gentle teasing flew back and forth as they ate. Sadie laughed more than she had in months, enjoying the easy affection between them all.

Cole sat beside her, his knee brushing hers under the table, his hand finding hers. Eleanor asked about the Santa Express preparations, and Sadie and Cole fell into easy conversation about logistics and timelines.

After dinner, as everyone helped clear the table, Eleanor paused in the kitchen doorway. "I have a new cookie recipe I've been dying to try. Cranberry-white chocolate shortbread. Would you girls want to help me test it?"

"Absolutely," Caroline said immediately.

"I'd love to," Sadie added.

"Great." Eleanor turned to Cole and Luke. "You two are excused. Go do whatever it is you do when you're banished from my kitchen."

"Take a walk?" Luke suggested to Cole. "It's a nice evening. We could check on that fence section Dad always worried about."

Cole glanced at Sadie, something unreadable crossing his face. She smiled at him, nodding. "Go. I'm fine. I'll be here when you get back."

"Okay." He squeezed her hand once, then followed Luke toward the back door.

Sadie watched them go.

"They're close," Eleanor said softly beside her. "Always have been. Luke's the only one who can really get through to Cole when he's working something out."

"Is he working something out?" Sadie asked.

Eleanor's smile was gentle. "Aren't we all?"

Caroline pulled flour from the pantry while Eleanor gathered butter and sugar, and Sadie found herself at the massive island, measuring out ingredients under Eleanor's patient instruction. The kitchen was filled with the sound of mixing ingredients and conversation.

"This kitchen is amazing," Sadie said, watching Eleanor's practiced hands cream butter and sugar together. "Do you still develop recipes often?"

"Occasionally," Eleanor said. "Mostly for fun now. I used to take it more seriously and earned a good income from it—had pieces published in magazines and won a few awards. But after Michael died..." She paused, her hands stilling briefly. "It took me a while to find joy in it again. Cooking had always been something we shared. He'd taste-test everything and give me honest feedback. Without him..."

"I'm sorry," Sadie said quietly.

"Thank you, dear." Eleanor's smile returned, though it carried a hint of sadness. "But I'm finding my way back to it. And having people to cook for helps. Family meals, occasions like last night—those are what make it meaningful."

Caroline added flour to the bowl, her movements careful. "Eleanor taught me a lot about baking. When Luke and I first got married, boxed brownie mix was my favorite friend."

"That's hard to believe," Sadie said. "Your cafe seems to do well."

"Lots of practice and a very patient teacher. In the beginning, when I started the cafe, the specialty beverages were my domain, and my employees did most of the baking." Caroline bumped Eleanor's shoulder affectionately. "Plus, Luke was very motivated while Eleanor taught me a few things. He ate everything I made, even the disasters, just to encourage me."

Eleanor laughed. "That boy would eat anything. Still would."

They worked in comfortable rhythm for a few minutes, shaping dough into rounds and placing them on baking sheets. Through the kitchen window, Sadie could see Cole and Luke walking across the property, their figures dark against the sunset-painted sky. They were too far away to hear, but she could see them talking, Luke's hands moving as he spoke, Cole's posture tense.

"They're fine... boys will be boys," Eleanor said, following her gaze.

Sadie turned back to the counter, but curiosity needled at her. "Is everything okay? Cole seemed... I don't know. Quiet during dinner."

Eleanor and Caroline exchanged a look that Sadie couldn't quite interpret.

"Cole's always been one to process things internally," Eleanor said carefully, sliding the first tray of cookies into the oven. "He feels deeply but doesn't always know how to express it. It can make him seem distant when really he's just trying to work through his thoughts."

"He was hurt before," Caroline added, her tone gentle. "About four years ago. A woman he'd been dating—Sarah. She wanted him to leave Mistletoe Falls with her, and when he wouldn't, she left anyway."

Sadie's stomach tightened. "He mentioned her. At dinner a few weeks ago."

"Then you probably understand it hit him hard." Eleanor washed her hands, her movements deliberate. "He closed himself off after that. He threw himself into work. We worried about him—still do, honestly. Then Michael passed. Cole's been so focused on duty and obligation that he forgot how to just... live."

"Until you showed up," Caroline said with a soft smile. "We've seen more of the real Cole in the past few weeks than we have in quite some time. That's because of you."

Sadie felt emotion rise in her throat. "I don't know if I can take credit for that."

"You can," Eleanor said firmly. "You've reminded him that there's more to life than work." She paused, studying Sadie with a maternal intensity that seemed to see everything. "You're planning to stay, aren't you? After your trial period?"

Sadie set down the spoon she'd been holding.

"I want to," she said honestly. "More than anything. I'm planning to stay in Mistletoe Falls regardless of what happens with the job."

Eleanor's eyebrows rose slightly. "Regardless?"

"If the position doesn't work out, I can go back to freelancing. Travel journalism, lifestyle pieces—I've built up enough connections over the years that I could make it work." Sadie heard the defensiveness in her voice and tried to soften it. "But honestly, I don't want to go back to that life. I want to put down roots and have job security here."

"But freelancing would mean traveling again, wouldn't it?" Caroline asked.

"It would. Which is why I'm really hoping the job becomes permanent." Sadie managed a smile. "Martha seemed confident last night. She told me I'd 'more than proven myself' and that the council was impressed. So, I'm trying to stay optimistic."

"That's wonderful," Eleanor said warmly. "Martha doesn't give praise lightly. If she's confident, you should be too."

"I am. Mostly. Things have moved so fast with Cole these past few weeks. We haven't really talked about what happens if the job doesn't work out. And honestly, why would we? The relationship is still so new. But eventually, if it comes to that, we'll need to figure it out together."

Caroline leaned against the counter, her expression gentle. "Have you thought about what other work you might do here? If you wanted to stay, but the coordinator position didn't pan out?"

"Not really. I've been so focused on making the trial period successful that I haven't let myself consider backup plans." Sadie shaped dough between her palms; the repetitive motion was soothing. "I know that probably sounds naive. But after spending my whole adult life having backup plans for my backup plans, I wanted to just... commit to this. Believe it would work out."

"That's not naïve," Eleanor said. "That's faith. And there's nothing wrong with having faith in yourself."

"But..." Sadie heard the hesitation in Eleanor's voice.

"But Cole has been hurt before," Eleanor finished gently. "And while I can see that you're nothing like Sarah—that your reasons for being here are entirely different from hers—he might not see that as clearly... or he may dwell on things. He's a deep thinker. If he turns inward or becomes quiet, don't worry... encourage him to talk."

Sadie's hands stilled.

"My son has learned to protect his heart by keeping people at a certain distance. And I think you've gotten past those defenses in a way no one has since his father died." Eleanor's smile was sad and knowing. "That's wonderful. But it also means he's vulnerable in a way he hasn't been in years. And vulnerability can be terrifying."

"Especially when the future is uncertain," Caroline added. "Not that I'm saying it is! Martha's practically guaranteed you the job, from the sounds of it. But Cole might be worried about the 'what ifs.' Men can be strange creatures sometimes... especially when they've been hurt deeply in the past."

Sadie absorbed this, turning it over in her mind. She thought about Cole's expression at dinner—the way he'd been quiet, thoughtful, his eyes tracking her movements like he was trying to memorize something. She thought about how tightly he'd held her last night after the tree lighting, the intensity in his voice when he'd said, I've already fallen.

"I never really considered what he might be thinking or what could be rolling around in his mind. I should probably talk to him," Sadie said. "About my plans, about what I'd do if the job doesn't work out. He should know I'm not going anywhere."

"He should," Eleanor agreed. "Communication is key to any relationship."

The timer chimed, and Eleanor pulled the first batch of cookies from the oven. The scent of cranberry and white chocolate filled the kitchen, rich and inviting.

Through the window, Sadie watched Cole and Luke. They'd stopped walking now, standing near the tree line. Luke was gesturing, emphatic about something. Cole's hands were shoved in his pockets, his shoulders tense. Then Luke said something that made Cole look away, toward the mountains, his profile stark against the fading light.

Whatever they were discussing, it looked serious.

***

Cole's boots crunched through the dried grass as he and Luke walked the fence line. The sun was setting behind the mountains, painting the sky in streaks of orange and purple, the air crisp enough to make his breath fog.

"So," Luke said after they'd walked in silence for a minute. "Last night was something."

"Yeah."

"You kissed her in front of the entire town."

"I'm aware."

"On stage. While the mayor was watching."

Cole shot his brother a look. "Is there a point to this?"

"Just making sure you realize what you did." Luke's grin was insufferable. "Because the brother I know doesn't do public displays of affection."

"Things change."

"They sure do." Luke's expression shifted, becoming more serious. "You're in love with her."

It wasn't a question, but Cole felt the words land like a challenge, anyway. He kept walking, his gaze fixed on the horizon.

"Cole..."

"It's complicated."

"How is it complicated? You like her. You make each other happy. Seems pretty straightforward to me."

Cole stopped walking, turning to face his brother. "Her trial period ends January 24."

Luke's eyebrows rose. "So?"

"So what if the city doesn't make her a permanent employee? What if she has to leave?"

"What if she doesn't? Are you going to waste the next two months worrying instead of being happy?" Luke crossed his arms. "That doesn't sound like living, man. That sounds like surviving. There's a difference, and you need to break that cycle."

Cole's jaw tightened.

"You're thinking about Sarah."

Cole nodded.

"That was four years ago," Luke said.

"I know when it was."

"And Sadie's not Sarah."

"She's got a twelve-week trial. What if this town isn't enough for her either? What if—"

"Stop." Luke held up a hand. "You're comparing two entirely different women. Sarah never wanted to be here; the school system transferred her here. This town was always temporary for her. But Sadie?" He shook his head. "Sadie chose to come here. I don't get the feeling she wants to leave... I get more of a vibe that she's trying to build something for herself."

"Building something temporary," Cole countered. "A trial position. No guarantees."

"Come on, Cole. She's not looking for an exit. She's looking for a home."

Cole wanted to believe that. But the memory of Sarah's goodbye—the way she'd looked at him with pity and disappointment, like he was wasting his life by staying—still lived under his skin.

Luke was quiet for a long moment, studying his brother. Then he sighed and sat down on a fallen log, gesturing for Cole to join him.

"Do you remember when Caroline and I started dating?" Luke asked.

"Yeah."

"We knew each other for six months before we got married. Six months. Everyone thought we were crazy." Luke smiled at the memory. "Mom kept hinting that maybe we should wait. Get to know each other better. Make sure it was real and not just infatuation."

"I remember."

"And do you remember what you told me?"

Cole frowned, trying to recall. "I told you to be careful."

"You did. But then you said something else." Luke turned to look at him directly. "You said, 'When you know, you know. Don't let fear make you miss out on something real.'"

The words hit Cole square in the chest. He had said that. He'd said the words his father had told him at the age of eighteen when they had had a father-son talk. He had asked his father when he'd know if he really loved a woman. He'd asked his father how he'd know he'd found that one special person meant for him.

Cole also remembered watching Luke and Caroline together when they had been dating, and he had seen something undeniable—a rightness that transcended logic or timelines. He'd been happy for his brother and had stood up as best man at a wedding that happened faster than anyone expected.

"That's different," Cole said, but the protest sounded weak even to his own ears.

"How? Because it's you instead of me?" Luke shook his head. "You gave me good advice four years ago. Maybe it's time you took it yourself."

"Sarah—"

"Sarah didn't want the life you have. Sarah wanted you to be someone different, to want different things. That's not love, Cole. That's trying to change someone into what you need instead of accepting them as they are." Luke's voice was firm but not unkind. "I think Sadie likes who you are. She respects what you do. That's the difference."

Cole absorbed this, turning it over in his mind. Everything Luke was saying made sense. Logically, he knew Sadie was nothing like Sarah. But logic didn't erase fear.

"What if she realizes she can do better than a small-town conductor with no ambition beyond maintaining a train?"

"Is that really what you think?" Luke's tone sharpened. "Or is that what Sarah made you think?"

Cole didn't answer.

"Because here's what I see," Luke continued. "I see a woman who lights up when she talks about the Express. I see someone who spent hours decorating a Christmas tree with you just because she wanted to. I see a woman who fits into our family as if she's always been part of it. I see someone who kisses you in front of hundreds of people because she's not ashamed or embarrassed—she's proud." He paused. "That's not a woman who thinks you're not enough. That's a woman who thinks you're everything."

Something in Cole's chest loosened slightly, like a fist unclenching.

"I haven't let myself feel this much since Dad died. And now Sadie's here, and she's amazing, and I can see a future with her so clearly it terrifies me. Because what if it doesn't work out? What if I lose her too?"

"You might," Luke said simply. "That's the risk. Love doesn't come with guarantees. But you know what? Neither does hiding. You could pull back, protect yourself, and keep her at arm's length—and you'd still lose her. Just slower. More painfully. Because she'll see you retreating, and eventually, she'll stop trying to reach you."

Cole closed his eyes, the truth of those words settling heavy in his gut.

"But if you're brave," Luke continued, his voice gentler now, "if you show her what she means to you, maybe you get something incredible. Maybe you'll get the life Dad always wanted for you. The one where the Express isn't your whole world, just part of it. The one where you're not just surviving, you're living. You'll have exactly what Mom and Dad had."

Luke stood, offering his hand to pull Cole up. "And for what it's worth? I think Sadie's worth any risk. I think she's the best thing that's happened to you in years. Don't let Sarah's ghost ruin that."

Cole stood, his brother's hand firm in his. They looked at each other, and Cole saw concern and affection and unwavering support in his brother's eyes.

"When did you get so wise, goofball?" Cole asked, managing a smile.

"I've always been wise. You just don't usually listen." Luke grinned. "Come on. We should get back before Mom sends out a search party."

They walked back toward the farmhouse; the sky deepening to purple above them. As they approached, light spilled from the kitchen windows, warm and inviting. Through the glass, Cole could see the women gathered around the island—his mother demonstrating something with her hands, Caroline laughing, and Sadie...

Sadie looked completely at home. Flour dusted her burgundy sweater, her hair falling forward as she leaned over the counter, her smile genuine and unguarded. Eleanor's hand rested on her shoulder, maternal and affectionate. Caroline said something that made Sadie throw her head back with laughter.

Cole stopped walking, his chest tight.

"When you know, you know, big brother," Luke said quietly beside him.

Chapter 20

C ole stared at the volunteer schedule without actually seeing it.

The names blurred together on the screen—familiar faces who'd signed up weeks ago to help with the Santa Express rides. He'd been sitting at his desk for the better part of an hour, reviewing logistics for the event that was now just days away, but his mind kept drifting back to the conversation with Luke.

You're going to waste the next two months worrying instead of being happy?

His brother's words had hit hard because they were true. Cole wanted to trust his gut instinct about Sadie. He wanted to believe she was different from Sarah.

He did believe it. Mostly.

But believing and trusting were two different things when your last relationship had ended with someone looking at you like your dreams were too small, your life too limited, and your choices a waste of potential.

Cole pulled out his father's pocket watch and flipped it open. One fifteen. The steady tick was a reminder that time kept moving whether he was ready or not.

Time moves forward.

The depot's main door opened with its characteristic creak, and Cash lifted his head from his bed in the corner. The dog's tail started wagging before Sadie appeared in his office doorway.

"Hey," she said, her smile bright and warm. "I brought lunch."

She held up a paper bag from The Cozy Cup, and the scent of fresh bread reached him across the office. Cash abandoned his bed entirely, trotting over to greet her with enthusiastic nudges.

"Caroline packed extra peanut butter cookies for Cash," Sadie added, reaching down to scratch behind the dog's ears. "She said he's been looking thin lately, which I'm pretty sure is a lie because this guy is solid muscle."

Cole stood, something in his chest loosening at the sight of her. She wore jeans and a cream-colored sweater, her dark hair pulled back in a ponytail.

"Caroline's been trying to fatten him up since I adopted him," Cole said, moving around the desk. "She thinks every living thing needs more food."

"To be fair, her food is incredible." Sadie set the bag on his desk and pulled out wrapped sandwiches and a small container of cookies. "Turkey and cranberry for you. And she sent her apologies for not having time to chat this morning. Apparently, Mondays after big town events are always busy at the cafe."

"Everyone wants to rehash what happened," Cole agreed. "June Reynolds probably held court for an hour."

"I'm sure we were a hot topic." Sadie's eyes sparkled with amusement as she handed him a sandwich. "The kiss seen 'round Mistletoe Falls."

Cole felt heat rise in his face, but he didn't look away. "Any regrets?"

"About kissing you in front of half the town?" Sadie moved closer, close enough that he could smell her perfume—something light and sweet that he'd started associating with her presence in his life. "Not even a little."

She reached up and touched his face, her palm warm against his jaw, and kissed him. Brief and sweet, but real enough to settle some of the restless worry that had been building in his chest since yesterday.

When she pulled back, her smile had softened into something more genuine. "Now, can we eat? I'm starving, and we have a lot to go over for Santa Express."

They settled into chairs beside the desks. Sadie spread out her ever-present notebooks alongside their lunch, flipping to pages covered in her neat handwriting and color-coded sticky notes.

"So, I've been thinking about the flow for Friday," she began, unwrapping her sandwich. "Three departures, ten AM, one PM, and three PM. Each ride is forty-five minutes, which gives us time between for boarding, photos with Santa, and turnover."

Cole nodded, taking a bite of his sandwich. Caroline had nailed it—the cranberry sauce was homemade, the turkey was perfectly seasoned, and the bread was still warm.

"I confirmed with Santa and Mrs. Claus this morning," Sadie continued. "Tom and Betty Hicks are perfect for the roles. Betty even offered to bring her own costume, but I told her we had one." She paused, her pen hovering over her notes. "Though apparently the city's Mrs. Claus costume needs some repairs. The seam is splitting in the back, and the hem is coming undone."

"Can it be fixed?"

"I think so. I just need someone who can sew." Sadie bit her lip, then said carefully, "I was thinking maybe your mom? If she has time. I don't want to impose, but Caroline mentioned she's really good with that kind of thing, and—"

"Mom would love to help. She enjoys anything that involves sewing."

"Are you sure? I can try to find someone else if—"

"Sadie." He waited until she looked up at him. "Mom would be happy to help. She likes you. She likes being included."

The smile that crossed Sadie's face was genuine relief.

"Okay," Sadie said softly. "Great. I'll call her this afternoon."

They ate in silence for a few minutes, Cash positioning himself strategically between them in case any food happened to fall. Cole watched Sadie make notes in the margins of her planning sheets, her brow furrowed in concentration, and tried to identify what felt different about her today.

She was here. She was engaged. She'd kissed him hello and talked about their upcoming events with obvious enthusiasm. But there was something in the way she held herself—a carefulness that hadn't been there before the Tree Lighting. Like she was conscious of taking up space in his office, in his life.

Or maybe he was imagining it, creating problems that didn't exist.

"I heard back from the last two volunteers this morning," Sadie said, flipping to a new page. "The Martinez family had to back out—their daughter has a dance recital that weekend. And Jeff Thompson has to go out of town for work. So we're down two people for station coverage."

Cole's jaw tightened. "That's going to make the craft stations tight."

"I know. I'm working on finding replacements. Abby at the B&B said she'll reach out to a few people she knows that might help. And I thought about asking Charlie if any of his friends might be interested in volunteering."

"Charlie would recruit half his class if you asked him; he's part of a large homeschooling network."

"Good to know." Sadie's smile was quick and bright. "The kid is enthusiastic about everything Express-related."

She continued talking through the logistics—backup plans for the backup plans, contingencies for weather issues, and supply lists that had been checked and rechecked. Cole found himself relaxing slightly as he listened to her problem-solve. This was what Sadie did best—see potential obstacles and address them before they became real problems. She was good at this work. She cared about getting it right.

She was going to be amazing at this job.

The thought brought immediate tension back to his shoulders. She was going to be amazing at this job. The permanent position would be hers if she wanted it. Martha had essentially promised as much on Saturday night. But wanting the job and wanting to stay in Mistletoe Falls weren't necessarily the same thing.

Sarah had liked her teaching position here. Had been good at it, even. But the job hadn't been enough to make her want to stay.

"Cole?"

He blinked, realizing Sadie was looking at him with concern.

"Sorry, what?"

"I asked what you thought about having hot chocolate and coffee available during the pre-boarding wait time. Nothing elaborate, just something warm for families while they're getting settled." She tilted her head, studying his face. "Are you okay? You seem distracted."

"I'm fine. Just thinking through the schedule." The lie came easily, and he hated himself for it. "Hot chocolate and coffee during boarding is a good idea. We can set up a station by the ticket counter."

Sadie nodded slowly, but her eyes stayed on him for a beat longer than necessary. Like she was trying to read what he wasn't saying. Then she went back to her notes, and Cole felt the moment slip away.

They worked through the rest of the lunch, finalizing details and troubleshooting potential issues. Sadie talked about promotional materials and last-minute ticket sales. Cole explained the locomotive's maintenance schedule and the safety protocols for running multiple trips in one day. They were a good team—that much was undeniable. Their planning sessions had developed a natural rhythm over the past month, each of them knowing when to take the lead and when to defer to the other's expertise.

But underneath the productive surface, Cole felt something unsaid sitting heavy in the quiet between words.

He wanted to ask her what she'd thought about when she'd driven home from his mom's house yesterday. Whether the reality of his family—loud and teasing and deeply rooted in this small town—had made her feel more at home or more aware of everything she'd left behind in her previous life.

He wanted to ask her to stay.

But the words stuck in his throat.

"The weather forecast is still showing a potential system Thursday or Friday," Sadie said, pulling up something on her phone. "Nothing definite yet, but if we do get snow, we'll need to make sure the depot is extra safe for families. Maybe put down salt on the platform the night before?"

"I'll handle it." Cole finished his coffee and stood to throw away their lunch trash. "If the forecast gets worse, we might need to send out an email warning to ticket holders. Let them know conditions could delay the ride."

"Good idea." Sadie made another note. "I'll draft something we can send out if needed."

The depot door opened again, and Hank's voice carried through the main hall. "Cole? You here?"

"In the office," Cole called back.

Hank appeared a moment later, his conductor's cap in his hands and his expression serious. "Got a question about the firebox maintenance before next weekend. We're running six trips over two days—that's a lot in two days."

Cole glanced at Sadie, who immediately started gathering her notebooks. "I should get going, anyway. Let you two talk shop."

"You don't have to leave," Cole said, but she was already standing.

"I have phone calls to make and a meeting with the mayor in two hours." She smiled at Hank. "Good to see you, Hank. Thanks for all your help with Santa Express prep."

"Not a problem at all, Miss Sadie," Hank said warmly.

Cole watched Sadie's face light up—genuine pleasure that made something in his chest ache. She gathered her things quickly, gave Cash a final pat, and moved toward the door.

"I'll call your mom about the costume this afternoon," she said to Cole. "And I'll text you if I find replacement volunteers."

"Sounds good."

She paused in the doorway, and for a moment Cole thought she was going to say something else. Her mouth opened, and her eyes met his with an intensity that felt like she was gathering courage for something important.

Then, Hank shifted his weight, the floorboards creaking, and the moment fractured.

"I'll see you tomorrow?" Sadie said.

"Tomorrow," Cole confirmed.

She left, and the office felt bigger without her. Cole heard her footsteps crossing the main hall, heard the depot door open and close, and heard the silence that followed.

Hank cleared his throat. "Didn't mean to interrupt."

"You didn't." Cole forced himself to focus. "What's the question about the firebox?"

They spent the next twenty minutes going over maintenance schedules and safety protocols. Hank had legitimate concerns about running the Express six times in two days—concerns that required Cole's full attention and careful planning to address. By the time they finished, Cole's mind was firmly back on operational logistics, on the familiar territory of mechanical problems that had clear solutions.

"You doing all right?" Hank asked as they walked toward the main hall together. "You seem wound pretty tight lately."

Cole almost deflected. Almost gave the standard "I'm fine" that usually satisfied people. But this was Hank—the man who'd worked beside his father for years and who'd been there through the worst days after the funeral.

"I'm working on it," Cole said instead.

Hank studied him for a long moment, then nodded. "That girl's good for you... you know that, right?"

"Yeah."

"But?"

"But nothing." Cole shoved his hands in his pockets. "Just trying to figure out how not to screw it up."

"By not screwing it up, you mean by not getting in your own way?" Hank's tone was gentle but direct. "Because from where I'm standing, the only thing that could mess this up is you deciding it's not worth the risk of getting hurt again."

Cole didn't answer, and Hank clapped him on the shoulder.

"I know you, son. I call it like I see it. Your dad told me once that the scariest thing about love is that it asks you to trust someone else with the most fragile parts of yourself." Hank's voice was quiet. "But he also said that the alternative—keeping those parts locked away where no one can hurt them—isn't really living. It's just surviving. He shared those words with me when I was nervous about proposing to my Livvie."

***

Cole spent the rest of the afternoon on depot maintenance—checking the Express's brake lines, reviewing the passenger car's heating system, and ensuring everything was ready for the increased usage next weekend would bring, even though he'd have to repeat each of these maintenance checks again next Thursday. The work was familiar and soothing, requiring his hands and focus but leaving his mind free to wander.

He kept coming back to that moment in his office when Sadie had almost said something. When she'd looked at him, like there was something important she needed to tell him.

What had she been about to say? Was it about the job? About staying? About them?

Or was he reading meaning into nothing because he wanted so badly to hear that she was planning to stay?

By six o'clock, the depot seemed empty and hollow, and all he wanted to do was go home. Cole locked up his office, set the security system, and headed toward the cabin with Cash trotting beside him. The walk followed its usual path through the woods. The late November afternoon was already fading toward evening.

Inside, he started a fire in the stone fireplace and made himself dinner—nothing fancy, just a grilled chicken sandwich and some french fries that he ate while staring at the flames. Cash sprawled on the couch, content after his long day at the depot, and the cabin settled into its familiar evening quiet.

Cole pulled out his phone and stared at Sadie's name in his contacts. He could call her. Should call her, maybe. They'd texted back and forth earlier about volunteer updates, but that was logistics, not real conversation.

He wanted to ask her what she'd almost said this afternoon. He wanted to tell her that if she was planning to leave, he'd rather know now than spend the next two months falling deeper in love with her.

But that meant showing her the parts of himself that were still raw and wounded. Meant trusting that she wouldn't look at his vulnerability and decide he was too much to deal with.

His phone buzzed with a text, and his heart jumped before he even looked at the screen.

Sadie: *Found two replacement volunteers! Abby came through with her book club friends. Both are experienced with kids and excited to help. Crisis averted.*

Sadie: *Also, your mom was wonderful. She's picking up the costume tomorrow and said she can have it ready by Thursday. She invited me to dinner Friday night, which I think was actually just an excuse to feed me again. Your family is very invested in making sure I eat.*

Sadie: *Anyway. Thanks for lunch (even though I brought it). See you tomorrow?*

Cole read the messages twice, hearing her voice in the words and seeing her smile in the casual tone. She was checking in. Sharing her day. Making plans.

Cole: *Great work on the volunteers. And yes, Mom's feeding people is her love language. Friday dinner sounds good. I assume at least I'm invited as well?*

Cole: *See you tomorrow.*

Sadie: *P.S.—I declined your mom's offer for dinner Friday; I told her I already have plans.*

Cole: *Plans?*

Sadie: *With you. You're making my dinner at your house.*

Cole: *Wait a minute... did I forget something? Dinner at my house? I don't remember us talking about this?*

Sadie: *We didn't. I want to have dinner with you. Not at a restaurant. If you don't want me to visit your home... if it's like the worst bachelor pad ever... I'll let you off the hook this time, and you can come to my place????*

Cole: *No, it's all good. Friday. My house for dinner.*

Sadie: *Excellent. Night, Cole.*

Cole: *Goodnight, Sadie.*

He set the phone down and smiled as he stared at the fire. Tomorrow he'd see her again. On Friday they'd have dinner together and privacy to talk about anything and everything.

And maybe that was okay. Maybe trust wasn't built in one big conversation but in a hundred small moments of showing up.

His father's pocket watch sat on the coffee table, catching the firelight. Time moves forward.

Cole picked it up, felt its familiar weight, and made himself a promise: He would stop waiting for disaster. Would stop assuming loss was inevitable. Would start trusting that maybe—just maybe—some things were worth the risk of hope.

But even as he made the promise, a small voice in the back of his mind whispered the question he couldn't quite silence:

What if she leaves anyway?

He didn't have an answer. All he could do was show up tomorrow, and the day after that, and keep choosing to trust until either his faith was rewarded or his fears proved true.

The fire crackled. Cash snored softly. And Cole sat in his cabin in the woods, surrounded by the life he'd built from duty and grief, and tried to imagine what it might look like if he built it from love instead.

Chapter 21

Cole's keys rattled as he locked the depot's main door, the sound echoing across the empty platform. Friday evening had settled over Mistletoe Falls with the kind of crisp clarity that made every breath feel sharp and clean. He'd already set the security system, double-checked the Express's overnight covers, and left Cash's water bowl filled for tomorrow morning.

His hand paused on the key in the lock. Sadie was coming to his cabin tonight. She'd see where he lived, how he lived. The thought made something flutter nervously in his chest—anticipation mixed with nervousness in equal measure.

"Cole!"

He turned to see Sadie rounding the corner of the depot building, a canvas grocery bag slung over one shoulder and that smile on her face that always made his breath catch. She wore jeans and a burgundy sweater under her open coat, and her dark hair was loose around her shoulders.

Cash, who'd been sitting patiently at Cole's feet, abandoned all pretense of loyalty and bounded toward her with enthusiastic barks.

"Traitor," Cole muttered, but he was grinning as he watched Sadie crouch down to greet the dog.

"Hi, Cash! Yes, I'm happy to see you too." She laughed as Cash wiggled and wagged, then looked up at Cole with sparkling eyes. "I brought reinforcements. Caroline sent extra treats for him."

"Of course she did." Cole walked over, and when Sadie stood, he didn't hesitate. He pulled her close and kissed her hello. "Ready for the grand tour?"

"I've been ready all day." She held up the grocery bag. "I stopped at the market and grabbed a few things to add to our dinner plans. I hope that's okay?"

"More than okay. What'd you bring?"

"That's a surprise." Her smile turned mischievous. "You'll find out when we get to your place."

They started walking, Cash immediately taking the lead. Cole was hyperaware of Sadie's presence beside him—the scent of her perfume, the sound of her footsteps crunching through dried leaves, and the warmth of her hand when it found his.

The late November evening cast everything in shades of gold and shadow, the bare branches overhead creating patterns against the darkening sky. It was beautiful in the stark way winter could be, all clean lines and honest spaces.

"This is amazing," Sadie said after a few minutes. "I can't believe you get to walk through this every day."

"It's peaceful. Gives me time to think between work and home."

"That's important." She squeezed his hand. "Having that transition space. I never really had that when I was traveling—it was just hotel to assignment to hotel. No in-between."

Cole glanced at her. "Do you miss it? The traveling?"

"Sometimes I miss the novelty. Waking up in a new city, discovering new places." She paused, then added more quietly, "But I don't miss the loneliness. The constant feeling that I was just passing through everywhere I went."

He wanted to tell her she didn't have to pass through anymore. That she could stay. But the words caught in his throat, so instead he just held her hand tighter and kept walking.

"So how long have you had this place?" Sadie asked.

"Built it about six years ago. The property came up for sale, and I jumped on it. Ten acres total."

"Ten acres?" Her eyebrows rose. "That's a lot."

"I wanted privacy. Wanted my own space." He felt his face warm slightly, embarrassed by the admission. "I'd been living with my parents, and I was ready for something of my own. Something separate from the family home."

"That makes sense. Every adult needs their own space eventually."

"Yeah. And then after—" He stopped himself, but Sadie caught it.

"After your dad died?"

Cole nodded. "After he died, I was really glad I already had this place. Somewhere I could go to process everything without having to act like everything was okay."

Sadie's hand tightened in his. "I'm glad you had somewhere safe."

They walked in comfortable silence for a few more minutes, the path winding through the trees, Cash occasionally stopping to investigate interesting smells before pulling them forward again.

"Why here?" Sadie asked as they rounded a bend. "Why so far from everything?"

Cole slowed his pace, considering the question. It was the kind of thing he'd normally deflect—too personal, too revealing. But this was Sadie, and she'd just asked to come to his home. She deserved honesty.

"I wanted to be close enough to the depot that I could walk there," he said slowly. "But I also wanted to be far enough away that I wasn't surrounded by people all the time. That I had quiet."

"Privacy," Sadie said, understanding in her voice.

"Yeah. I love this town. Love the community. But sometimes—" He struggled to find words that didn't make him sound like a hermit. "Sometimes I need to not be Cole Bennett, the train conductor. Sometimes I just need to be Cole, sitting on my porch with my dog and not having to talk to anyone."

"That doesn't make you antisocial," Sadie said gently. "That makes you human. Everyone needs space to breathe."

"Yeah. Exactly."

"I get it more than you know. Growing up, my house was enormous. Rooms and rooms of perfect furniture and expensive art. But it was never quiet in the way you mean. It was just empty. Cold."

The cabin came into view a few minutes later, appearing through the trees like something from a storybook.

Sadie stopped walking, her breath catching. "Cole. This is beautiful."

He tried to see it through her eyes—the two-story structure with its wood and stone exterior, the large windows reflecting the last of the evening light, and the rocking chairs on the porch where he sat most mornings with his coffee. It was simple, practical, exactly what he'd wanted when he'd designed it.

But seeing Sadie's face light up made him see it differently. Made him see it as more than just function—as a home.

"It's not fancy," he said, suddenly nervous again.

"It's perfect." She turned to him, her hazel eyes warm. "It's so completely you. Solid and thoughtful and peaceful."

Cole felt heat rise in his face. "Come on. Let me show you inside before you freeze."

He unlocked the front door and ushered her in, Cash immediately bounding ahead to grab his favorite toy—a well-chewed tennis ball that he dropped at Sadie's feet with an expectant look.

"Oh, you want me to throw this for you?" Sadie laughed, setting down her grocery bag to scratch behind Cash's ears. "Maybe after dinner, buddy."

Cole watched them together, something warm settling in his chest. Cash had taken to Sadie from day one, and seeing his dog so comfortable with her felt significant in a way he couldn't quite name.

"Let me take your coat," he said, and Sadie shrugged out of it, handing it to him along with her scarf. He hung them on the hooks by the door, hyperaware of how domestic the gesture felt.

When he turned back, Sadie was looking around the cabin with obvious interest, taking in everything—the stone fireplace with its crackling fire that he had come out earlier to start, the leather couch with his grandmother's quilt draped across the back, the bookshelves lined with railroad history books and family photos.

"Cole, this is amazing," she said, moving further into the space. "Can I look around?"

"Of course."

He stayed by the door, letting her explore at her own pace. She ran her fingers along the mantel, studying the framed photograph of him and his father beside the Mistletoe Express. Paused at the bookshelf, reading titles and smiling at what she found. She walked to the windows overlooking the woods, where cardinals sometimes perched on the feeder he'd hung last spring.

"Your kitchen is gorgeous," she called from the open-plan space. "Forest green cabinets? I love that."

"My mom helped me pick the color." Cole finally moved, joining her in the kitchen area. "I wanted something simple but not boring."

"It's perfect. Very you." She looked up, noticing the loft visible from below. "What's up there?"

"Storage mostly. And a workspace—I keep train maintenance records and schedules up there. My dad's old typewriter." Cole shrugged. "I haven't done much with it yet. Keep meaning to finish it properly, but there's always something else that needs attention."

"It's a great space. Lots of potential."

They stood there for a moment, listening to the soft pops of the fire. Cash had sprawled in front of the fireplace, already content.

"I can't believe you built this," Sadie said quietly. "It must have taken so much planning, so much work."

"I hired a builder for most of it. But I designed the layout myself. Knew exactly what I wanted." He looked around, seeing it again through her eyes. "I wanted something that felt like home. Not just a house."

"You succeeded." Sadie turned to face him fully.

"I'm glad you're here," he said, because it was true and because he wanted her to know it.

"Me too." Her smile was soft and genuine. "Now, are you going to feed me? Because I'm starving."

"Homemade pizza still okay?"

"Yep, sounds good to me!" Sadie grabbed her grocery bag and started unpacking. "I brought fancy cheeses.

Fresh mozzarella, goat cheese, and this amazing herb blend I found. Plus some prosciutto and arugula in case we want to get creative."

Cole grinned, moving to pull out his pizza dough ingredients. "You brought the good stuff."

"I don't mess around when it comes to food."

They fell into an easy rhythm—Cole mixing dough while Sadie prepped toppings, both of them moving around the kitchen with surprisingly little awkwardness for a first time cooking together. Cash positioned himself strategically between them, clearly hoping something would fall.

"Music?" Cole asked, reaching for his phone.

"Sure."

He pulled up his usual playlist, and soon Johnny Cash's voice filled the cabin, rich and steady.

"I should have guessed," Sadie said with a grin. "You named your dog after him, after all."

"Best dog name ever chosen."

"I'm not arguing."

They worked together easily, Sadie chopping vegetables while Cole rolled out dough. When flour dusted his shirt, Sadie laughed and brushed it off. When they disagreed about the ratio of sauce to cheese, they compromised by making two small pizzas instead of one large one.

"This is fun," Sadie said as they assembled their creations. "I haven't cooked with someone like this in a long time."

"Me neither." Cole drizzled olive oil over his pizza. "Usually it's just me and whatever's fastest."

"Well, tonight we're doing it right."

They slid the pizzas into the oven and cleaned up while they waited. The cabin filled with the smell of baking bread and melting cheese, mixing with the scent from the fireplace.

When the pizzas came out, they were perfect—crispy crusts, bubbling cheese, and toppings caramelized just right. They ate at Cole's small table, Cash lying hopefully at their feet, and talked about everything and nothing. Sadie told him about a story she'd covered in Vermont about a maple syrup farm. Cole shared a story about a summer when he and Luke had tried to build a tree-house and ended up creating a barely standing platform that their father had diplomatically called "structurally creative."

"I would have loved to see that," Sadie said, laughing.

"It was pretty terrible. Dad made us take it down after a week when it started listing to one side."

"At least you tried."

"That's what he said. He told us that trying and failing was better than never trying at all."

Sadie's expression softened. "Your dad sounds like he was a really good man."

"He was the best."

They finished dinner and moved to the kitchen, Sadie washing and Cole drying their dinner dishes.

"Cole? Can we talk about something?"

The serious tone in her voice made his stomach tighten, but he nodded. "Of course."

"I've been thinking about something your mom and Caroline said to me."

Cole's hands stilled on the dishtowel. "What did they say?"

"That you've been hurt before. That you might be worried about my leaving." She turned off the water and dried her hands, then turned to face him fully. "And I realized they were right. Not that they told me anything I shouldn't know—they were just helping me understand a few things. But they made me realize that I've been assuming a lot of things."

Cole set down the plate he'd been drying. "Sadie—"

"Let me finish. Please." She reached for his hand, threading her fingers through his. "I need to tell you something. Something important."

His heart was pounding, but he nodded.

"Martha basically promised me the permanent position," Sadie said, her voice steady despite the emotion in her eyes. "After the tree lighting, she told me I'd more than proven myself. That the council is impressed. She pretty much in not so many words said, the position is mine."

"Right... I got the same impression."

"Cole, I need you to understand something else." She squeezed his hand. "Even if that job doesn't come through—though I really believe it will—I'm staying in Mistletoe Falls."

He blinked and nodded.

"I'm staying. No matter what happens with the coordinator position. I can freelance if I have to, find other work, or figure something out. But I'm not leaving this town."

"Sadie—"

"I've spent seven years running... trying to find my place in this world," she continued, the words coming faster now, like she'd been holding them in and finally letting them free. "New cities, new assignments, never staying anywhere long enough to care. Because caring meant risk. Caring meant I might get attached to something, and then losing it would hurt. So I just kept moving, kept documenting other people's lives instead of building my own."

Cole's throat was tight. He recognized that pattern because he'd lived a version of it himself—just in one place instead of many.

"But I'm done running. I'm done being afraid of putting down roots. I want a home. I want a community. I want traditions and neighbors and the kind of life where people know my coffee order and ask how I'm doing because they actually care about me."

"You want Mistletoe Falls," Cole said quietly.

"I want Mistletoe Falls. I want this town, this life, these people who welcomed me when I was a stranger and made me feel like I belonged before I'd even proven myself." She paused, her eyes searching his face. "And I want you, Cole. I want to build something real with you. Something that doesn't have an expiration date."

His breath caught.

"I know you're scared," Sadie continued, more gently now. "I understand why. You lost your best friend when you were in high school. Sarah left, and your dad passed away—loss is what you know. But Cole, I'm not Sarah. I didn't come here because I was assigned here or because it was convenient. I chose Mistletoe Falls. I'm choosing this life."

She stepped closer, close enough that he could see the determination in her eyes mixed with vulnerability.

"I'm choosing you."

Cole couldn't speak. Every word he might have said felt inadequate compared to what she'd just given him—complete honesty, total vulnerability, and a promise he hadn't dared ask for.

"Say something," Sadie whispered, and he could hear the fear creeping into her voice. "Please."

He pulled her into his arms instead, holding her tight enough that he could feel her heartbeat against his chest. "Luke called me out when we were at Mom's house for dinner," he said quietly, his words muffled against her hair. "Told me I was going to waste the next two months worrying instead of being happy. That I needed to stop comparing you to Sarah."

"He was right."

"He was." Cole pulled back just enough to see her face. "Sarah wanted me to be someone different, somewhere else. She looked at my life and saw it as small, limited, and a waste of my potential. When she left, she looked at me as if I were disappointing her just by being myself."

"Cole—"

"But you're not her. I know that." He cupped her face with both hands, making sure she could see the truth in his eyes. "You look at the Express and see my father's legacy, not a tourist attraction to be modernized. You look at this cabin and see a home, not isolation. You look at me and see—" His voice cracked slightly. "You see me... someone worth staying for."

"You are worth staying for."

"I'm falling in love with you," Cole said, the words coming out raw and honest. "Maybe I've already fallen. I don't know. But I know that thinking about you leaving makes it difficult to breathe. And knowing you're choosing to stay—" He had to stop, emotions clogging his throat.

"I love you," Sadie said, clear and certain. "I'm in love with you. And I'm not going anywhere."

Cole rested his forehead against hers and wrapped his arms around her.

"I'm choosing to trust this," he said quietly. "Choosing to trust you. Choosing us, even though it's..."

"Scary? Life's full of uncertainties... all we can do is roll with it and see where it takes us." Sadie's hands cupped his face. "But we're doing it together. That makes all the difference."

They held each other for a long moment, the cabin quiet around them except for Cash's soft snoring from the couch. Outside, full darkness had fallen, but inside everything felt warm and bright and right.

"I should probably get you home before it gets too late," Cole said reluctantly. "But I don't want you to go."

"Then let's take the long way." Sadie pulled back, smiling. "Walk me home? I want to see how to get here from the main road. And I could use some exercise after all that pizza."

"You sure? It's cold out there."

"I'm sure."

They bundled up in coats and scarves, clipped Cash's leash on, and headed out into the November night. The full moon was bright enough that they barely needed the flashlight Cole had grabbed, casting everything in shades of silver and shadow.

The walk started in comfortable silence, both of them processing what they'd just shared, hands clasped tightly together. Cash pulled ahead, excited about this unexpected evening adventure, his breath fogging in the cold air.

"This is beautiful," Sadie said as they followed the winding driveway through Cole's property. "I can't believe you own all of this."

"When the property came up for sale... I bought it without second-guessing. I knew this was where I wanted to build a home."

"It's perfect for you." She squeezed his hand.

The driveway wound through trees and open spaces, gradually sloping downward. Cole pointed out landmarks as they walked—the creek that ran along the western boundary, the ridge where he sometimes hiked in the mornings, and the old oak tree that was at least two hundred years old.

They reached the end of his property and emerged onto Pinecone Pass, the paved road immediately familiar. Sadie looked around, orienting herself.

"Oh! I know exactly where we are now. We're just off the main road into town."

"Yep. Just a few minutes' walk to the town square from here."

"This is perfect. I can totally drive here next time."

"Next time," Cole repeated, liking the sound of it more than he should.

They walked hand in hand down Pinecone Pass, the town gradually coming into view ahead of them. Mistletoe Falls was alive with Friday night energy—shops open late, lights blazing, and people strolling the sidewalks despite the cold.

As they entered the downtown area, Sadie's face lit up. "It's like a Christmas village."

She wasn't wrong. Every storefront glowed with warm light and holiday decorations. The Cozy Cup was still open, Caroline visible through the window serving a customer. The bookstore next door had created an elaborate display of winter-themed books. The boutique across the street had dressed its mannequins in festive sweaters and scarves.

White lights were strung everywhere—wrapped around lamp posts, draped across storefronts, and hanging in swoops between buildings. Families walked together, children bundled in puffy coats and pointing at decorations. Couples strolled arm in arm, stopping to window shop or duck into stores.

They passed other shops—the candy store with its display of homemade fudge and chocolate truffles, the toy store with a train set running in the window, and the gift shop that sold handmade ornaments and local crafts.

Street musicians were set up on one corner, playing acoustic guitars and singing holiday songs. A small crowd had gathered to listen, parents swaying with children in their arms, couples standing close together for warmth.

"This is magical," Sadie said softly.

"It's Friday night in Mistletoe Falls."

"No, it's more than that." She stopped walking, turning to look at him. "When I was here last year covering that story about the town's Christmas traditions, I wrote about all of this as if it were some kind of fairy tale. The lights, the decorations, the way everyone seemed happy. But I was wrong about what made it special."

"What do you mean?"

"I wrote about it like it was magic—like there was something enchanted about this place that made it different from everywhere else." She gestured to the surrounding scene. "But it's not magic. It's something even better. It's real. It's people choosing to celebrate together, to create beauty and joy. It's community in the truest sense."

Cole felt his throat tighten. She got it. She understood what made Mistletoe Falls special in a way that went beyond tourism marketing or surface appeal.

"And I want to be part of that," Sadie continued, her eyes bright with emotion. "I want to help hang the lights and plan the events and know everyone's names. I want to walk through town on a Friday night and wave at people who actually know me, who care about me. I want traditions and routines and the kind of life that's built on connections rather than just passing through."

"You are already part of it," Cole said.

"Because of you. Because you welcomed me into the Express and into your family."

"You belong here, Sadie. You've belonged since the day you arrived."

She kissed his cheek, soft and sweet. "Thank you for believing that."

They continued walking, reaching the town square, where the gazebo stood illuminated with hundreds of white lights. Santa sat in a chair set up inside the gazebo, and children lined up to visit with him. Parents took photos, children bounced with excitement, and older kids tried to act too cool while still secretly wanting a turn.

Carolers moved through the square in matching scarves, their harmony drifting across the cold air. "Silent Night" was sung in a four-part harmony that was achingly beautiful.

Cole and Sadie stood at the edge of the square, watching it all. Just two more people in the crowd, but together. Cash sat at their feet, tail wagging slowly, content to people-watch.

Sadie looked up at Cole, and he was already watching her. He'd been watching her all evening—cataloging the joy on her face, the way she looked at his town with such genuine appreciation, and the easy way she fit into his life.

"This," she said softly. "This is what I want. Not just the pretty lights or the festivities. But the feeling underneath it all. The sense of belonging. The knowledge that I'm building a life instead of just documenting other people's lives."

She paused, her hand finding his.

"I found my story here, Cole. Not a story to write and walk away from, but a story to live. And you're the heart of it."

Cole couldn't speak past the emotion in his throat, so he did the only thing that made sense. He kissed her there in the town square, surrounded by carolers and Christmas lights and families celebrating together.

When he pulled back, he saw his own emotions reflected in her eyes.

"You have me," he said, the words coming easier now. "You've had me since the day you cried at the Legacy Wall in the museum back at the depot."

Sadie laughed, the sound breaking through the emotion. "I didn't cry."

"You had tears in your eyes."

"Fine. I had tears." She wrapped her arms around his waist, resting her head against his chest. "But can you blame me? Your father's story is beautiful."

"It is." Cole held her close, looking around at the square, at the town his father had loved and worked to preserve. "He would have liked you."

"I wish I could have met him."

"Me too."

They stood like that for a long moment, holding each other while the world moved around them. The carolers finished "Silent Night" and started "Joy to the World." A child squealed with delight after visiting Santa. Someone laughed, the sound carrying across the square.

Mistletoe Falls was alive with celebration.

And for the first time since his father had died, Cole felt like he was doing more than just maintaining that beauty. He was adding to it. Building on it. Creating new traditions alongside the old ones.

With Sadie beside him, he was finally moving forward instead of just standing still.

"We should probably get you back to Holly House," he said reluctantly. "It's getting late."

"I suppose you're right."

They walked slowly toward Holly House, taking the long way through residential streets decorated with lights and wreaths. Cash trotted between them, occasionally stopping to sniff at something interesting before being gently tugged along.

When they reached the B&B, Sadie turned to face him on the porch, backlit by the warm glow from the windows behind her.

"Thank you for tonight," she said. "For letting me see your home, for cooking with me, and for that conversation we needed to have."

"Thank you for choosing to stay."

"Always."

They kissed goodbye—sweet and lingering, full of promise for all the tomorrows ahead. When Sadie finally went inside, Cole stood on the porch for a moment longer, Cash sitting patiently beside him.

Through the window, he could see Sadie talking to Abby, both women laughing about something. She looked happy. At home.

Cole started the walk back to his cabin, Cash trotting beside him, and found himself smiling. Tomorrow they'd continue preparing for the Santa Express rides next weekend. On Sunday they'd go to his mom's house for dinner. Next Friday she'd probably come back to the cabin, and the time after that, and the time after that, until it became routine.

Until she became part of his daily life in a way that went beyond work or planning or careful distance.

He pulled out his father's pocket watch as he walked, the metal cold against his palm. Time moves forward.

Chapter 22

The little girl's squeal of delight pierced through the general din of excited chatter filling the main passenger car, and Sadie felt her smile widen impossibly further. She stood near the entrance to the dining car, clipboard forgotten in her hands, watching as Santa—volunteer Tom Hicks in his element—lifted the child onto his knee while Mrs. Claus adjusted the girl's crooked reindeer antlers.

"And what would you like for Christmas, sweetheart?" Santa's voice carried a perfect blend of jolly warmth and theatrical grandeur.

"A puppy! And a dollhouse! And for it to snow on Christmas morning!" The girl's enthusiasm was infectious, spreading through the car like ripples on water.

Around them, the Mistletoe Express hummed with life. Families packed the plaid-cushioned benches, children pressed against frost-kissed windows to watch the snowy landscape glide past, and the scent of hot chocolate and sugar cookies mingled with pine from the fresh garland draped along every available surface. Twinkle lights strung overhead cast a warm glow that made everything feel softer, more magical, as though they'd all stepped inside a living snow globe.

The Santa Express one o'clock ride. Saturday afternoon. Everything was working exactly as planned.

Better than planned, actually.

Charlie appeared beside her, his elf costume slightly askew, carrying a tray of steaming mugs. "Third refill for the Millers," he announced, grinning. "Their kids can't get enough of the peppermint cocoa."

"Good thing Caroline made extra." Sadie made a note on her clipboard, though at this point the notes felt unnecessary. The volunteers had the routine down perfectly—hot chocolate service in the main car, cookie distribution in the observation car, Santa photos here, and craft activities waiting at the depot for after the ride. Every piece fit together seamlessly.

She'd spent weeks planning this event, coordinating volunteers, ordering supplies, and arranging schedules. But standing here watching it unfold, seeing families create memories that would last lifetimes, made every sleepless night worth it.

The express whistle blew—two short blasts that meant they were approaching Whispering Falls. Right on schedule.

Cole's voice carried from the front of the car, warm and steady as he addressed the passengers. "If you'll look to your right, folks, you'll see Whispering Falls coming into view. In winter, the falls partially freeze, creating ice formations that catch the sunlight like natural chandeliers. It's one of the most photographed spots in the Smoky Mountains."

Sadie didn't need to see him to picture the scene perfectly—Cole in his conductor's uniform, pocket watch in hand, with that subtle pride in his voice when he talked about the Express and its route. She'd watched him conduct dozens of rides over the past weeks, but something about today felt different. Lighter. He was thoroughly enjoying himself, and he was happy.

The realization made her chest warm.

A mother near the window called her children over for photos as the falls came into view, and the car erupted in oohs and ahhs. Phones and cameras appeared, capturing the moment, and Sadie made a mental note to ask if anyone would share photos for the town's social media pages.

"Miss Baker?" Betty Hicks—Mrs. Claus—beckoned her over, her round face flushed with happiness beneath her white wig. "We're running low on candy canes. Do we have more in reserve?"

"I'm on it." Sadie pulled her walkie-talkie from her belt. "Mark, this is Sadie. Can you grab the backup candy cane box from the depot storage? We'll need it for the three o'clock ride."

Mark's gravelly voice crackled back immediately. "Copy that. I'll have it ready on the platform."

Everything was working. Every single piece.

The ride continued its loop through the mountain foothills; the Express chugging steadily along tracks that had carried passengers for over a century. Sadie made her way through the car, pausing to chat with families, answering questions about the depot's history, and watching children's faces light up when Santa called them by name—a trick Tom and Betty had mastered through careful study of the reservation list.

Volunteers dressed as elves distributed cookies shaped like trains and Christmas trees, each one meticulously decorated by Claire from Sugarplum Bakery. The car's large windows provided unobstructed views of the winter wonderland outside, and several couples had claimed the corner benches, nestled close together with cocoa mugs warming their hands.

This was what she'd envisioned when she'd first proposed the Santa Express. Not just a train ride, but an experience—something that would bring families together, create traditions, and give children memories they'd carry into adulthood. The kind of magic that made small towns like Mistletoe Falls special.

The kind of magic she'd never had growing up.

She pushed the thought away. This wasn't about her childhood. This was about all these children, these families, and this community coming together to celebrate something good.

The Express began its return journey to the depot; the whistle announcing its approach. Through the windows, Sadie could see the platform coming into view, already set up for the post-ride activities. Tables laden with craft supplies waited under the covered area, volunteers in festive aprons ready to help children decorate ornaments and create holiday cards. The depot itself glowed with Christmas lights, the massive tree they'd installed for the tree lighting ceremony still standing proudly near the entrance.

Her tree. Their tree. The one she and Cole had decorated together.

The train pulled into the station, steam hissing as Hank brought it to a smooth stop. Cole appeared at the front of the main car, calling out in his conductor's voice. "Mistletoe Falls Station! Thank you for riding the Santa Express, folks. We hope you'll join us at the depot for crafts, cocoa, and more holiday fun. And remember—Santa and Mrs. Claus will be available for photos on the platform for the next thirty minutes."

The families began gathering their belongings, children still buzzing with excitement, and parents herding them toward the doors. Sadie positioned herself at the exit, smiling and thanking each family as they disembarked, handing out candy canes and information cards about the upcoming Christmas Eve event.

"This was wonderful," one mother told her, balancing a toddler on her hip while two older children tugged at her coat. "We'll definitely be back next year."

"We're so glad you enjoyed it." Sadie pressed information cards into the woman's free hand. "The Christmas Eve event will be even more special. We'd love to have you."

The woman's eyes lit up. "Christmas Eve? Oh, we'll be there."

Passenger after passenger expressed similar sentiments—gratitude, delight, and promises to return. By the time the last family descended onto the platform, Sadie's face hurt from smiling, but the ache felt good. Earned.

She stepped down onto the platform herself, breathing in the crisp December air. Around her, the depot hummed with activity. Children clustered around craft tables; volunteers helped them glue glitter onto paper ornaments; Caroline and Luke manned the beverage station, serving hot cider and cocoa; and Santa held court near the Christmas tree for an endless stream of photo opportunities.

Perfect. Everything was absolutely perfect.

Cole appeared at her elbow, his conductor's cap slightly askew, his cheeks flushed from the warmth of the train car. "Another ride down, one more to go."

"How'd it look from the front?" She asked, though she already knew. She'd been watching him.

"Flawless." He reached out, his gloved hand finding hers and squeezing briefly. "You did this, Sadie. This whole thing—it's incredible."

"We did this," she corrected, squeezing back before releasing his hand. They were on duty, after all. Professional. "I just coordinated. You and Hank and all the volunteers made it actually happen."

"Take the compliment."

She laughed. "Fine. We're both amazing. How's that?"

"Better." He glanced at his pocket watch. "We've got about forty-five minutes before boarding for the three o'clock. I need to check in with Hank about the fire-box—make sure we're good for the final run."

"And I need to make sure we have enough sup-plies." Sadie consulted her clipboard, running through her checklist. Candy canes—handled. Cookies—plenty. Craft supplies—should be fine, but she'd double-check. Hot chocolate—might have to prep another batch.

They stood together for a moment, watching the or-ganized chaos of happy families. A little boy ran past chasing his sister, both of them giggling. An elderly cou-ple sat on one of the benches, holding hands and watch-ing the activity with soft smiles. Charlie emerged from the depot carrying a fresh box of craft supplies, nearly dropping it when another child darted in front of him.

Cole's walkie-talkie crackled. "Cole, are you there?" Hank's voice.

"Yeah, Hank. What's up?"

"Need you to take a look at the pressure gauge when you get a chance. Nothing urgent, just want your eyes on it before the next run."

"On my way." Cole turned to Sadie. "Duty calls."

"Go. I'll handle things here."

He started to walk away, then paused and looked back. The expression on his face made her breath catch—open affection, contentment, something that looked a lot like joy. "Hey, Sadie?"

"Yeah?"

"You and me, babe... we got this."

Before she could respond, he was striding toward the Express, calling out to Hank. But his words settled around her shoulders like a warm hug and boosted her confidence.

Sadie threw herself into preparations for the final ride, checking supplies, thanking volunteers, and ensuring everything was positioned correctly for the three o'clock boarding. The craft stations were going through materials faster than she'd anticipated, but they had enough. The cookie supply was holding steady. The beverage station—

Her phone rang.

She almost ignored it—too busy, too much to coordinate—but the caller ID made her pause.

Martha Caldwell.

Sadie stepped away from the bustle of the platform, moving toward the quieter side of the depot building. "Hi, Martha. Is everything okay?"

"Sadie." Martha's voice carried an unusual urgency. "I need you at Town Hall. Now."

"Now?" Sadie glanced at her watch. Two fifteen. "Martha, we have the final ride at three. I really should be here—"

"I understand, but this can't wait. It's about the Express. About your position. I need you here as soon as possible."

Sadie's stomach tightened. "Is something wrong? I thought—"

"Nothing's wrong." Martha's tone softened slightly. "Just the opposite, actually. But I can't explain it over the phone. Can you come?"

The trial period. Her position. The words echoed in Sadie's head. January twenty-fourth was still weeks away. What could Martha possibly need to discuss that couldn't wait?

Unless it was bad news. Unless they'd decided to end the trial early. Unless—

"Sadie?" Martha's voice pulled her back. "I know the timing is terrible, but this really can't wait. It's important. Very important."

Sadie looked back toward the platform. Cole was visible near the Express, speaking with Hank, both of them examining something on the locomotive. Charlie was organizing the line for the craft tables. Volunteers were handling the beverage station smoothly. Everything was under control.

She didn't actually need to be here for the final ride. Everything was set up. The volunteers knew what to do. Cole could manage the train operations, and the post-ride activities would run themselves at this point.

But she wanted to be here. This was her event. She should see it through to completion.

"Okay," Sadie heard herself say. "I'll be there in ten minutes."

"Thank you. We'll be waiting in my office."

"Martha, what's—"

But Martha had already hung up.

Sadie stood for a moment, phone still pressed to her ear, staring at the scene before her. The depot glowed with Christmas lights. Families laughed and talked. Children ran between craft tables. The Mistletoe Express sat on its tracks like a faithful old friend, steam rising gently into the winter air.

Everything she'd worked for. Everything she'd built.

And Martha needed her at Town Hall. Now. About her position.

She found Cole still near the Express, now alone as Hank had disappeared into the depot. He looked up as she approached, his expression shifting from concentration to concern when he saw her face.

"What's wrong?"

"Nothing. I hope." She tried to give a reassuring smile. "Martha just called. She needs me at Town Hall. Something about my position, about the Express."

Cole's brow furrowed. "Right now? We have the three o'clock ride—"

"I know. But Martha said it's important. Very important." Sadie gestured toward the platform. "Everything's set up here. You and the volunteers can handle the final ride, right? I should be back for cleanup."

"Of course we can handle it." He stepped closer, lowering his voice. "But what's this about? Your position? The trial doesn't end until January."

"I don't know. She wouldn't explain over the phone." The worry must have shown on her face because Cole's expression softened.

"Hey." He touched her arm briefly. "It's probably good news. Maybe they want to make your position permanent early. You've exceeded every expectation."

"Possibly." But something in Martha's voice had seemed too urgent for simple good news. Too carefully neutral.

"Go," Cole said. "Find out what's happening. We've got everything covered here."

Sadie looked at him—really looked at him. At the man who'd gone from reluctant colleague to partner to the person she loved more than she'd thought possible. Standing there in his conductor's uniform, surrounded by the train his father had restored, doing work he'd devoted his life to.

"I'll be back as soon as I can," she promised.

"I know. Drive carefully."

She hurried to her SUV in the parking lot, her mind racing through possibilities. Early permanent position offer. Budget discussions. Changes to her responsibilities. Maybe an expanded role given the success of the events.

Or maybe something was wrong. Maybe someone had complained. Maybe the council had concerns. Maybe—

Stop, she told herself firmly. Speculation wouldn't help.

The drive to Town Hall took less than five minutes, but it felt like hours. Sadie parked and made her way to the rear entrance. The building was quiet—most offices closed on Saturday afternoon. Her footsteps echoed in the hallway as she climbed to the second floor.

Martha's office door stood open, light spilling into the dim hallway.

Sadie paused just outside, smoothing her sweater, trying to calm her racing heart. Through the doorway, she could see Martha standing behind her desk, as she spoke to someone Sadie couldn't see.

Then Martha turned and spotted her.

"Sadie. Thank you for coming." Martha's expression was carefully controlled, but something sparkled in her eyes. Excitement? Nervousness?

Sadie stepped into the office.

And stopped.

Mayor Hayes sat in one of the visitor chairs, his usual jovial expression replaced with something more serious.

And beside him sat two people Sadie had never seen before—a woman in a sleek charcoal suit, her dark hair pulled back in a neat bun, and a man in a sports coat and tie, both holding leather portfolios embossed with an official-looking seal.

Everyone turned to look at her.

"Sadie," Martha said, her voice warm but formal. "Please sit down. We have a lot to discuss."

The woman in the charcoal suit smiled and extended her hand. "Ms. Baker. I'm Jennifer Palmer, and this is my colleague Sean Abrams. We're with the Tennessee State Tourism Development Office."

State Tourism Development.

Sadie's mind went blank.

Then started racing.

"Please," Jennifer Palmer said, gesturing to the empty chair beside the mayor. "Sit. We have something we'd like to discuss with you."

Sadie sat.

And even as she did, even as Jennifer Palmer began opening her portfolio and Martha moved to sit behind her desk, Sadie's thoughts flew back to the depot.

To Cole, preparing for the final ride.

To the Express, sitting proudly on its tracks.

Something told her that whatever happened in the next few minutes was going to change everything.

She just didn't know whether that change would be good or bad.

Jennifer pulled out a bound document and placed it on the desk where Sadie could see it.

The cover read: Tennessee Historic Heritage Railways Initiative - Mistletoe Falls Partnership Proposal.

"Ms. Baker," Jennifer began, her voice professional but warm, "we've been very impressed with your work here in Mistletoe Falls. The events you've coordinated, the way you've increased visibility for the Mistletoe Express, your ability to honor tradition while embracing innovation—it's exactly the kind of vision we need for this project."

Project. What project?

"We've been working with Mayor Hayes and Ms. Caldwell for several weeks now," Sean Abrams added, his voice carrying a slight Southern accent. "And we believe Mistletoe Falls—specifically the Mistletoe Express—is the perfect flagship for our statewide heritage railway program."

Several weeks.

The words landed like stones.

They'd been planning something for weeks. Without telling her. Without telling Cole.

Jennifer flipped open the proposal, revealing pages of text, charts, architectural drawings, and budget projections.

"What we're proposing," she said, "is a comprehensive expansion and enhancement program that would position the Mistletoe Express as the premier heritage railway destination in Tennessee."

Expansion.

Enhancement.

Sadie stared at the documents, her mind struggling to process what she was seeing.

And somewhere in the back of her thoughts, one question echoed:

Does Cole know about this?

Chapter 23

The office felt smaller than it should have.

The document sat in the center of Martha's desk like a declaration of war.

Tennessee Historic Heritage Railways Initiative - Mistletoe Falls Partnership Proposal.

"Ms. Baker," Jennifer said, her voice warm but businesslike, "I know this may be a lot to take in. Why don't I walk you through the specifics?"

Sadie nodded, not trusting her voice yet.

Jennifer leaned forward, her manicured hands gesturing to the bound proposal. "The State Tourism Development office has been working with Mayor Hayes and Ms. Caldwell for approximately six weeks now—"

Six weeks.

The words hit Sadie like a physical blow. Six weeks. That meant they'd started planning whatever this was before she'd even arrived in Mistletoe Falls. Before her trial position had officially begun.

"—and we believe Mistletoe Falls, specifically the Mistletoe Express, represents a unique opportunity for Tennessee's heritage tourism program."

Sean Abrams picked up the thread smoothly. "What we're proposing is a comprehensive partnership that would position the Express as the flagship operation for our statewide Historic Railways Initiative."

Flagship. The word sounded impressive. Important. Permanent.

It also sounded big. Corporate. Nothing like the intimate operation she'd spent the past weeks learning to love.

"Let me show you the scope." Jennifer turned the proposal so Sadie could see the architectural renderings on the next page.

Sadie's breath caught.

The depot had been transformed in these drawings. The building she knew remained, but it had grown. An entirely new wing extended from the eastern side, doubling the current footprint. The platform had been expanded to accommodate multiple boarding areas. A modern glass-and-steel structure labeled "Visitor Center & Gift Shop" sat where the parking lot currently ended.

"The grant we're offering," Jennifer continued, "is two-point-five million dollars over three years."

Two point five million.

"What would that money fund?" Her voice came out steadier than she felt.

"Excellent question." Sean flipped to another page; this one was covered in budget breakdowns and timelines. "Depot expansion first—the new wing would house a professional museum with guided tours, interactive exhibits, and a proper archive center for preserving railway history. The ground floor would include a year-round gift shop, ticketing center, and climate-controlled waiting area."

"Climate-controlled," Mayor Hayes added with a chuckle, "so families aren't freezing during winter waits."

"The Express itself would see operational expansion," Jennifer said. "We're proposing multiple daily tours year-round, seven days a week. Spring wildflower tours, summer sunset rides, fall foliage specials, and winter wonderland experiences."

Multiple daily operations. The Express running constantly.

Sadie's chest tightened.

"Marketing is crucial," Sean said. "State funding would provide a professional campaign—regional initially, with potential for national reach. We're talking partnership with Travel Tennessee, features in Southern Living, and potential PBS documentary coverage. The Mistletoe Express becomes synonymous with Tennessee heritage tourism."

"And local businesses?" Sadie asked, finding her voice. "What happens to them when you bring in state-sponsored operations? Will local businesses get pushed out by corporate chains?"

"Local businesses are integral to authenticity," Jennifer said firmly. "The entire point of this program is showcasing real Tennessee heritage, not creating a sanitized theme park experience. We'd actually be working to strengthen local partnerships—coordinating with shops, restaurants, and artisans to create an integrated tourism experience. More visitors means more business for everyone."

"The gift shop would prioritize local crafts," Sean added, "with a percentage of sales going directly to local artisans. Think of it as a showcase for Mistletoe Falls businesses, not competition."

It sounded good. Almost too good.

"Who controls creative decisions?" Sadie pressed. "If the state is funding this, don't you get the final say on aesthetic choices? On what events we run? On how we present the history?"

"Creative control remains local," Martha interjected. "That's nonnegotiable in the partnership agreement. The state provides resources and infrastructure support, but programming decisions, aesthetic choices, and operational philosophy stay with Mistletoe Falls leadership."

"Which brings us to staffing," Jennifer said, and something in her tone made Sadie's pulse quicken. "Current employees would not only retain their positions but would likely see promotions and salary increases as operations expand. We'd be hiring additional conductors, tour guides, maintenance staff, and administrative support—creating jobs, not eliminating them."

"What about Cole Bennett?" The question burst out before Sadie could stop it.

The two officials exchanged glances.

"Mr. Bennett," Mayor Hayes said carefully, "would be offered the position of Operations Director. He'd oversee all Express operations, depot management, facility expansion implementation, staff training, and hiring. Essentially, he'd be promoted from lead conductor to directing the entire operation."

"He'd still conduct when he wanted," Martha said gently, watching Sadie's face. "But he'd also have authority over the bigger picture—expanding his father's legacy in ways Michael Bennett probably dreamed about but never had the resources to achieve."

It sounded perfect. Like someone had designed a dream scenario specifically for Cole.

So why did Sadie's stomach feel like she'd swallowed stones?

"And me?" she asked quietly.

Jennifer smiled. "That's why you're here. We'd like to offer you the position of Director of Historic Railway Tourism."

The title hung in the air—official, and permanent and terrifying.

"You'd report to both the town and state tourism boards," Sean explained. "Your focus would be exclusively on the Express, depot, and museum operations. Your salary would be seventy-eight thousand annually with full benefits and a three-year guaranteed contract."

Three years. Not twelve weeks. Not a trial position with termination hanging over her head like a sword. Three years of security.

"You'd have an office at the depot," Martha added. "Marketing budget, administrative support, the resources to implement your vision properly. Everything you've done so far with shoestring budgets and volunteer coordination—imagine doing it with proper funding and staff."

Sadie's mind raced. The tree lighting ceremony with professional lighting designers. The Santa Express with hired entertainers instead of relying on volunteer availability. The Christmas Eve premiere with orchestra music and catered refreshments and marketing that reached beyond regional newspapers to national media outlets.

Resources to do everything right.

Everything she'd dreamed of when she'd imagined herself in a permanent position, building something meaningful, creating experiences that mattered.

But.

"This is a lot of growth very fast," Sadie said slowly. "The depot expansion alone would take how long?"

"Construction timeline is approximately eighteen months," Sean said. "We'd break ground in spring and complete phase one by next winter season. The expansion wouldn't interrupt current operations—we'd work around your schedule."

"And the state branding requirements?" Sadie pressed. "If we're the flagship for Tennessee Historic Railways, what does that mean for how we present ourselves? Do we lose the small-town authenticity that makes Mistletoe Falls special?"

"Authenticity is exactly what makes this marketable," Jennifer said firmly. "We're not interested in creating a corporate tourism experience. We want to preserve and showcase what already exists—the genuine heritage, the community involvement, and the family-friendly atmosphere. That's what draws visitors and creates memorable experiences."

Everything they said made sense. The partnership sounded thoughtful, well-planned, and designed to enhance rather than overwhelm what already existed.

But Sadie couldn't shake the feeling that something fundamental would change. That daily operations meant losing the seasonal rhythm that made each event special. That professional marketing campaigns meant losing the grassroots community involvement that made every visitor feel welcomed rather than processed. That state funding meant answering to bureaucrats and grant requirements and quarterly reports instead of the simple question: what would make families happy?

And underneath all of it, the question that mattered most: what would Cole think?

Cole, who'd spent four years protecting his father's legacy from any change that might diminish it. Cole, who'd initially resisted even her modest event proposals because they felt too new, too different, too much like abandoning tradition. Cole, who'd finally started trusting her specifically because she'd proven she understood the difference between honoring the past and exploiting it.

How would he react to a two-point-five-million-dollar state takeover—because that's what this felt like, even if everyone insisted it was a partnership?

"When does this happen?" Sadie asked. "What's the timeline?"

Mayor Hayes cleared his throat. "The town council voted Thursday evening. Two days ago."

The world tilted slightly.

"You already decided?" Sadie's voice came out flat. "Without Cole? Without the staff? Without anyone who actually works at the Express?"

"The grant funding cycle ends December thirty-first," Sean explained. "If we don't have a signed commitment by year-end, the funding goes to our backup project. We had to move quickly to secure this opportunity for Mistletoe Falls."

"The decision needed to be made at the municipal level first," Martha added. "Once the council approved the partnership in principle, we could begin discussing specific positions and staffing. That's why we're here to-day—to offer you the directorship and begin planning for implementation."

"Does Cole know?" The question came out sharper than Sadie intended. "Does he know any of this?"

The silence that followed answered her question.

"We wanted to brief you first," Mayor Hayes said carefully. "Your position is crucial to the program's success. We needed to know if you were interested before bring-ing others into the conversation."

"He deserves to know." Sadie's hands tightened in her lap.

"I agree," Martha said quietly. "Which is why I called him as well when you were on your way here. I asked him to come to City Hall as soon as the final Santa Express ride wrapped up. He should be arriving any moment."

The air left Sadie's lungs.

Cole was coming. Right now. To this office, to this meeting, to learn that everything he'd protected had been decided without his input or consent.

And Sadie was sitting here, having already heard the proposal, having already been offered the job that represented all this change, and having already spent time imagining what she could do with state resources and guaranteed funding.

She'd be the one to watch him learn. To see his face when they told him. To witness the moment when he realized the Express—his father's Express, his life's work—had been signed away to bureaucrats and grant proposals and expansion timelines.

Would he see her as part of this? As someone who'd known before he did? As someone who might actually want this opportunity even though it meant everything he feared?

"Ms. Baker." Jennifer's voice was gentle. "I know this is overwhelming. The position offer stands regardless—you have until December eighteenth to give us your answer. That gives you a week to consider."

"Wow. This is all moving so fast," Sadie said.

Sean and Jennifer began gathering their materials, closing portfolios, and straightening papers with the efficient movements of people accustomed to high-stakes meetings. They stood, offered handshakes and business cards, and promised to be available for any questions.

"We're very excited about this partnership," Jennifer said warmly. "And we truly hope you'll join the team, Ms. Baker. Your work these past weeks has been exceptional."

Then they were gone, the office door closing behind them with a soft click that sounded unnaturally loud in the sudden quiet.

Sadie remained in her chair, Martha and Mayor Hayes settling back into their seats. The proposal document still sat on Martha's desk, its presence impossible to ignore.

"That was a lot," Mayor Hayes said, his jovial tone forced. "Would you like water? Coffee?"

"I'm fine." Sadie wasn't fine. Her mind was racing, her heart hammering against her ribs, and her hands were cold despite the office's warmth.

Martha studied her with those sharp eyes that missed nothing. "What are you thinking, dear?"

What was she thinking?

That seventy-eight thousand dollars would mean financial security for the first time in her adult life. That a three-year contract meant she could finally stop living like everything was temporary. That an office at the depot meant she'd see Cole every day and work alongside him.

That resources and staff support meant she could create experiences that truly honored what the Express represented while making it sustainable for generations to come.

But also—

That daily operations meant Cole working himself to exhaustion. That expansion meant construction disruption and change and the loss of the intimate atmosphere that made every ride special. That state oversight meant quarterly reports and performance metrics and grant compliance instead of simple community service.

That this opportunity—this incredible, life-changing, professionally validating opportunity—might cost her the man she loved.

"I'm thinking," Sadie said slowly, "that this is everything I wanted when I applied for this job. Security, resources, and the chance to build something meaningful."

"But?" Martha prompted.

"But I'm also thinking about what Cole said when he first gave me the depot tour. About how his father spent years restoring the Express because he believed some things were worth the effort. About how preserving the past wasn't about keeping things frozen in time but about honoring what came before while building something that could last into the future."

Sadie looked directly at Martha. "Does this honor what Michael Bennett built? Or does it turn his dream into something he wouldn't recognize?"

"That's a question only Cole can answer," Martha said quietly. "And you'll have to trust that he's capable of seeing opportunity alongside change."

Mayor Hayes checked his watch. "He should be here in the next few minutes. The final ride ended at three-thirty, and it's nearly four now."

Four o'clock on a Saturday afternoon. Outside, Mistletoe Falls was probably bustling with families who'd just experienced the Santa Express magic. Children still clutching candy canes, parents taking photos in front of the decorated depot, and volunteers cleaning up craft supplies and hot chocolate stations.

Cole would have seen every passenger safely off the train.

He'd be driving here thinking Martha needed to discuss scheduling or budgets or some administrative detail that couldn't wait until Monday.

He had no idea his entire life was about to change.

Sadie's throat tightened.

"Martha," she said, her voice barely above a whisper, "what if he says no?"

"To the promotion?"

"To all of it. The expansion, the partnership, the changes." Sadie twisted her hands together. "What if he looks at this proposal and sees betrayal instead of opportunity? What if he thinks we've destroyed what his father built?"

Martha's expression softened. "Then we'll have a difficult conversation about whether personal comfort matters more than institutional sustainability. The Express is just breaking even, Sadie. You've seen the numbers. Without this partnership, without significant investment and operational changes, the Express might not survive another five years."

The words hit hard because they were true. Sadie had seen the budget reports and had watched Cole juggle maintenance costs, operational expenses, and payroll with money that barely stretched far enough. The events she'd created were helping, but they were temporary solutions to a permanent problem.

"So this is happening whether Cole agrees or not," Sadie said.

"The partnership is happening," Mayor Hayes confirmed. "The council has committed. But how it happens—and who leads it—that's still being decided. Cole can be part of shaping this future, or he can watch someone else shape it for him."

Heavy boots echoed in the hallway outside. Steady, familiar footfalls that Sadie would recognize anywhere.

Her heart lurched.

Martha and Mayor Hayes both looked toward the door. Sadie couldn't move, couldn't breathe, couldn't do anything except sit frozen in her chair while those footsteps grew louder.

Closer.

Right outside the door.

The footsteps stopped.

Then a knock.

"Come in," Martha called.

The door opened.

Cole filled the doorway, still wearing his conductor's uniform from the ride, his cap tucked under one arm. His steel-blue eyes swept the office.

His expression shifted instantly from professional courtesy to concern. "Sadie? What's wrong?"

She couldn't answer.

"Cole," Martha said, her voice gentle but firm. "Thank you for coming. Please sit down. We have something important to discuss."

Cole's gaze held Sadie's for one more heartbeat—questioning, worried, searching her face for clues about what was happening.

Then he stepped into the office and closed the door.

And Sadie knew that whatever happened in the next few minutes would change everything.

Chapter 24

"Cole," Martha said, gesturing to the empty chair beside Sadie. "Please have a seat."

He moved into the room on autopilot, his boots heavy on the carpet, and lowered himself into the chair. The leather creaked under his weight.

"What's going on?" he asked, looking between Martha and the Mayor.

"Cole, we have some news about the Mistletoe Express. Significant news. And we wanted to make sure you heard it from us directly." Mayor Hayes said.

"What kind of news?"

Martha leaned forward. "For the past six weeks, Mayor Hayes and I have been in discussions with the Tennessee State Tourism Development Office about a partnership opportunity for Mistletoe Falls."

Six weeks.

The number hit him like a fist to the gut.

"Six weeks," he repeated slowly. "You've been planning something for six weeks?"

"We've been negotiating," Martha corrected gently. "Working through details, reviewing proposals, and ensuring this was the right fit for our community and specifically for the Express."

"Without involving me."

Mayor Hayes shifted in his chair. "The initial conversations were exploratory. We didn't want to get anyone's hopes up—or concerns raised—until we knew if this was viable."

Cole's jaw tightened. Exploratory conversations. That was bureaucrat-speak for "we made decisions without you."

"What partnership?" he asked, forcing his voice to stay level.

Martha turned the document on her desk so he could see it. Bold text across the top read: Tennessee Historic Heritage Railways Initiative—Mistletoe Falls Partnership Proposal.

"The state is launching a heritage railway program," Martha explained, "designed to preserve and promote historic rail operations across Tennessee. They want the Mistletoe Express to serve as the flagship operation."

Flagship. The word sounded important. Official. Nothing like the family operation his father had spent years building.

"The state has approved a grant," Mayor Hayes continued, "of two-point-five million dollars over three years to fund expansion and enhancement of the Express operations."

Two and a half million dollars.

Cole stared at the number in the document, trying to make his brain process what that meant.

Two-point-five million was more money than his father had ever dreamed of having.

"What would that fund?" Cole heard himself ask.

"Depot expansion," Martha said, flipping to a page showing architectural renderings. "A new wing that would double your current space. A professional museum with guided tours and interactive exhibits. Archive center for preserving railway history. Year-round climate-controlled visitor center and gift shop."

Cole studied the drawings. The depot—his father's depot, the building they'd restored board by board—had been transformed into something that looked more like a tourist complex than a historic station.

"The Express itself would have expanded operations," Mayor Hayes added. "Multiple daily rides year-round. Spring wildflower tours, summer sunset rides, fall foliage specials, and winter wonderland experiences."

Daily rides. Every single day. No off-season for maintenance, no breathing room, no quiet days when he could focus on repairs and upkeep without the constant pressure of passenger schedules.

"Professional marketing campaign," Martha continued. "Statewide initially, with potential for regional and national reach. Partnership with Travel Tennessee, features in tourism publications, and documentary coverage. The Mistletoe Express becomes synonymous with Tennessee heritage tourism."

Cole's hands tightened on the arms of his chair. "And the town council?"

"Voted Thursday evening," Mayor Hayes said. "Approved the partnership in principle. The state needs a signed commitment by December thirty-first to secure the grant funding."

December thirty-first.

"You voted without talking to me," Cole said, his voice flat. "Without asking what I thought. Without giving me any say in whether my father's legacy should be turned into a state tourism flagship."

"The decision needed to be made at the municipal level first," Martha said carefully. "Once the council approved the partnership, we could begin discussing specific positions and implementation. That's why you're here now."

"Now," Cole repeated. "After it's already decided. After you've already committed. This isn't a conversation, Martha. This is a notification."

Mayor Hayes leaned forward. "Cole, son, I understand this feels sudden—"

"Sudden?" The word came out sharper than Cole intended. "You've been planning this for six weeks. The only thing that's sudden is finding out I had no voice in it."

He looked at Sadie, who'd been silent through the entire exchange, her face pale and her eyes fixed on her hands. "How long have you known?"

She finally looked at him, and he saw misery in her eyes. "I just found out."

"And what do you think?" he asked.

Sadie drew in a shaky breath. "I think it's overwhelming. I think it's happening too fast." She paused, seeming to gather courage. "I think the money and resources could be amazing for sustainability. I think I'm scared we'll lose what makes the Express special. I think I wish you'd been part of the conversation from the beginning."

"But?" Cole heard the word hanging unspoken.

"But they offered me a job I want. And I'm terrified to take it."

There it was.

They'd offered her something. Of course they had.

"What job?" Cole asked, though part of him already knew.

"Director of Historic Railway Tourism," Martha said. "Sadie would oversee all Express operations, programming, and marketing. A three-year contract and an office at the depot. She'd have the resources and staff support to implement her vision properly."

Three-year contract. Everything Sadie needed—security, validation, and resources to do a job she wanted.

"Cole," Mayor Hayes tried again, "think about what this means for the Express's future. Your father spent fifteen years restoring that locomotive because he believed it was worth preserving. This partnership ensures it survives not just for another fifteen years but for another century."

"My father," Cole said, his voice tight, "would have wanted a say in how his legacy was preserved."

"Cole... we're offering you the position of operations director," Martha said gently.

Cole's attention snapped back to her. "What?"

"Operations Director," Martha repeated. "You'd oversee all Express operations, depot management, facility expansion implementation, and staff hiring and training. Essentially, you'd be promoted from lead conductor to running everything operational. This position includes a significant raise in salary."

"So basically, here's a fancy title and a big salary so you won't cause a fuss over all this," Cole said flatly.

"It's recognition of your expertise and leadership," Mayor Hayes countered. "You'd still conduct when you wanted—the hands-on work you love. But you'd also have authority over the bigger picture."

"The bigger picture," Cole echoed. "Daily rides year-round—that's not sustainable for the equipment. Steam locomotives need maintenance windows, rest periods, and time for proper overhauls. You can't run her constantly and expect her to last."

"We'd hire additional maintenance staff," Martha said. "Professional mechanics, engineers who specialize in historic locomotives."

"Wait... back up a second. The Express would become a logo for Tennessee tourism instead of a family legacy? A gift shop... selling what, exactly? Mass-produced trinkets made overseas with 'Mistletoe Express' stamped on them?" Cole asked.

"Local artisan partnerships," Martha said firmly. "Authentic crafts, not corporate merchandise. That's written into the proposal."

"Written by people who don't understand what makes this place special." Cole stood abruptly. "Does anyone actually care what I think, or is this just a courtesy notification before you do it, anyway?"

Martha's expression softened. "Cole, we care very much about what you think. That's why you're here. That's why we're offering you this position. We need your leadership to make this successful."

"You need my cooperation so you can say you have buy-in from the Bennett family." He heard the bitterness in his own voice and hated it, but he couldn't stop the words. "So when people ask if Michael Bennett's son approved of turning his life's work into a state tourism flagship, you can say yes."

"That's not fair," Mayor Hayes said.

"Fair?" Cole's laugh was hollow. "You negotiated for six weeks behind my back, voted without including me, designed an entire expansion without asking if I wanted it, and now you're offering me money and a title to make it palatable. Don't talk to me about fair."

Silence fell over the office. Martha's eyes held sympathy but also determination. Mayor Hayes looked uncomfortable but unmoved. Sadie sat frozen in her chair, her face pale and her hands still clasped in her lap.

Cole forced himself to breathe, to think, to not say something he'd regret.

"I need time," he said finally. "To think. Not here, with everyone watching, being sold something that's already been decided."

"We understand," Martha said. "But we do need your answer by December eighteenth. The state needs time to process paperwork."

"December eighteenth," Cole repeated. "Fine."

He looked at Sadie. "Are you coming?"

She looked up, and he saw the conflict written across her face. Torn between him and this office, between what he needed and what they were offering her.

"I should stay," she said quietly. "Finish this conversation."

The words hit harder than they should have. She was choosing to stay here, with them, discussing plans for a future he wasn't sure he wanted any part of.

She was choosing them.

"Right," Cole said, his voice flat. "Of course."

He turned to Martha and Mayor Hayes. "I'm really disappointed in you both. I'll let you know my answer soon."

Then he was moving, crossing the office, reaching for the door handle. Behind him, he heard Sadie say his name, but he couldn't turn around. Couldn't look at her face and see whatever expression she wore, whether it was regret or relief or something else entirely.

He pulled the door open and stepped into the hallway.

The walk to his truck felt like moving through water. Every step required conscious effort, his mind simultaneously racing and completely blank. He climbed into his truck, started the engine, and headed home.

The cabin appeared through the trees, and Cole parked beside it, turning off the engine and sitting in silence. He could see Cash's face appear in the window of his home, the dog's tail already wagging with excitement.

At least someone was happy to see him.

Cole climbed out and made his way to the front door. Cash met him with enthusiastic jumps and licks, his entire body wiggling with joy. Cole scratched behind the dog's ears, feeling some of the tension in his chest ease slightly.

"Yeah, buddy," he muttered. "I missed you too."

He should make dinner. Should do something productive with the evening, catch up on paperwork or maintenance logs, or the dozens of small tasks that always needed attention. He should head back to the depot and oversee the cleanup after the day's Santa Express tours.

Instead, he turned and sank into one of the rocking chairs on the front porch, Cash settling at his feet. The December cold bit through his jacket, but Cole didn't move. He just sat there staring at the woods, at the darkening sky, at nothing and everything.

They'd turned the Mistletoe Express into a corporate project.

The thought circled his mind like a vulture. Two-point-five million dollars, expansion plans, state branding, daily operations, professional marketing. Everything designed to transform the Express from a small operation into something bigger, broader, and more profitable.

More sustainable, Martha had said. His father would want sustainability.

Or would he? Would Michael Bennett have looked at these plans and said, 'No, this isn't what I built; this isn't what I spent years of my life restoring?'

Cole pulled his father's pocket watch from his vest pocket, the metal cold against his palm. Flipped it open, read the inscription he'd memorized years ago: *Time moves forward—M.B. to C.B.*

Time moves forward. Don't get stuck in the past. Build on what came before, but don't be afraid to grow.

But did he mean this kind of growth? This kind of forward?

Cole closed the watch; the soft click was loud in the quiet evening.

Sadie wanted the job. He'd seen it in her eyes, heard it in her voice when she'd admitted she was terrified to take it. She wanted it because it was everything she'd worked for—security, resources, and validation that she belonged here and could build something meaningful.

Of course, she wanted it. She'd be a fool not to.

And he'd be a fool to ask her to turn it down.

But taking it meant she'd be the one implementing these changes. Planning the expansion, coordinating with state officials, and marketing the Express as Tennessee's flagship heritage railway. Every day she'd come to work excited about transformation while he tried to preserve what already existed.

Could he love her through that? Could he watch her be enthusiastic about changing his father's vision and not resent her for it?

More importantly, could he say no?

If he refused the operations director position, they'd do the expansion anyway. Hire someone else to run it. The partnership was approved; the council had voted, and the grant was secured. His participation was requested but not required.

If he said yes, he'd be complicit in transforming something he'd promised himself he'd protect. He'd be the one approving changes, implementing state requirements, and turning his father's dream into whatever this new version would become.

Either way, he lost.

Either way, the Express he'd known was gone.

And Sadie would be there, at the center of it all, making it happen.

Cash shifted at his feet, pressing against Cole's legs in the way dogs did when they sensed distress. Cole reached down to scratch his head, grateful for the simple, uncomplicated affection.

The sky had gone fully dark now, stars beginning to appear between the bare tree branches. Somewhere in town, families were probably settling in for Saturday evening—dinners around kitchen tables, children excited about Christmas coming in less than two weeks, and couples making plans for the holiday week ahead.

Sadie was most likely still at Town Hall. Still in Martha's office, discussing timelines and logistics and all the details of how this expansion would work. Still chose to stay there instead of coming with him.

Cole opened the pocket watch again, reading the inscription one more time.

Time moves forward.

His father had chosen those specific words to encourage growth, to remind Cole that preserving the past meant building on it, not freezing it in amber.

But Michael Bennett had also believed some things were worth protecting exactly as they were. Worth fighting for. Worth saying no to opportunities that looked good on paper but fundamentally changed what made something special.

Cole just didn't know which belief applied here.

The watch's steady tick-tick-tick filled the silence, marking seconds that became minutes that became the long wait until he had to decide.

December eighteenth.

The watch kept ticking.

Time moved forward whether he was ready or not.

Chapter 25

Cole's thumb hovered over the send button.

I can't make it to dinner today. Need some space.

He deleted it. Tried again.

Not coming to dinner. Sorry.

Too abrupt. His mom would worry.

He stared at his phone, sitting on his cabin's front porch with Cash at his feet. Through the trees, he could see the late afternoon sun filtering through bare branches, painting everything in shades of gold and amber. In two hours, he was supposed to be at the farmhouse for Sunday dinner. The thought of sitting at that table, pretending everything was fine while Luke joked and Caroline asked questions and his mother watched him with those knowing eyes—

He didn't want to deal with it.

His fingers moved across the screen:

Hey Mom. Not going to make it to dinner today. Not feeling up to it.

The response came within a minute.

Are you sick?

Cole exhaled slowly. How did he answer that? He wasn't sick. He was drowning. He was being crushed under the weight of a decision that felt impossible. He was so angry and confused he couldn't think straight.

But he couldn't say that. Couldn't worry her. He couldn't drag her into this mess when he didn't even understand it himself.

No. Just need some space to think. Not in the mood to be around people right now.

The three dots appeared. Disappeared. Appeared again, and then;

Okay, I'm here if you need to talk. I love you.
Love you too.

He set the phone down on the arm of the chair and leaned back, closing his eyes against the afternoon light.

Yesterday's meeting replayed in his mind for the hundredth time since he'd walked out of City Hall. The state officials, with their leather portfolios and official seals. Martha's careful neutrality. Mayor Hayes's borderline enthusiasm. The bound proposal with its architectural renderings and budget projections and timeline that would change everything.

Two-point-five million dollars. Daily operations. Professional staff. State oversight.

The Mistletoe Express transformed into Tennessee's flagship heritage railway program.

And Sadie.

He'd asked her to come with him. She'd stayed.

That moment kept circling back, sharp-edged and unavoidable. *I should stay. Finish this conversation.* As if the conversation was more important than walking out with him. As if her professional future mattered more than—

Cole stopped himself. That wasn't fair. She had a job to do. Responsibilities. He couldn't expect her to just walk away from a meeting because he was upset.

But the hurt remained anyway, lodged somewhere behind his ribs.

Cash shifted at his feet, pressing closer against his legs. The dog always knew when something was wrong.

Cole opened his eyes and stared out at the woods. Bare branches stark against the winter sky. The kind of late afternoon stillness that usually brought him peace. Today, it just felt empty.

His phone buzzed. He glanced at the screen.

Sadie: *Hey. I know yesterday was a lot. Can we talk?*

His jaw tightened. He'd ignored her messages this morning. Three texts and a missed call while he'd been sitting on this porch, watching the sun climb through the trees and trying to make sense of the mess in his head.

What was there to say? The expansion was happening whether he participated or not. The council had voted. All that remained was for Cole to accept the operations director position or watch someone else take it.

Either way, he lost.

He set the phone face down on the chair arm without responding.

A walk would help. Movement always helped when his thoughts got too loud.

"Come on, boy." Cole stood, his muscles stiff from sitting too long in the cold. Cash jumped up immediately, tail wagging, ready for whatever came next.

They took the trail that wound through his acreage. The ground was hard beneath his boots, frost still clinging to the shaded spots where sunlight never quite reached. His breath fogged in the December air.

The rhythm of walking usually cleared his mind. Today his thoughts just churned in the same circles, picking at the same questions like worrying a loose tooth.

If I say yes, I'm accepting that everything changes.

Daily operations meant constant work and no breathing room. The Express running seven days a week, basically nonstop. More staff, more oversight, and more bureaucracy. State requirements and quarterly reports and performance metrics.

And expansion. Construction starting in spring. The depot doubled in size. A visitor center. Professional museum. Gift shop selling who-knew-what to tourists who'd never heard of Michael Bennett or understood what fifteen years of restoration meant.

If I say no, someone else runs it, and I lose it anyway.

That option felt worse. Walking away from the Express meant abandoning everything. Letting strangers make decisions about operations and maintenance. Watching from the sidelines while his father's dream became something unrecognizable.

At least if he took the job, he'd be in the room. Have some say in how things changed.

But having a say wasn't the same as having control. Operations Director sounded impressive until you realized it meant implementing someone else's vision. Following state guidelines. Answering to bureaucrats who cared about tourism numbers and economic impact, not the soul of a restored steam locomotive.

There's no way of winning this.

Cole stopped walking, breathing hard despite the easy pace. Cash nosed at his hand, whining softly.

"I know," Cole muttered, scratching behind the dog's ears. "I don't know what to do either."

The admission felt like weakness. His father had always known what to do. When the Express's boiler failed during restoration, Michael had figured it out. When funding dried up halfway through the project, he'd found a way forward. When everyone said it couldn't be done, he'd done it anyway.

Michael Bennett had been decisive. Confident. Clear about his purpose.

Cole felt none of those things right now.

He pulled out his phone and checked the time. Nearly three o'clock. The farmhouse would be filled with the smell of his mother's cooking by now. Luke and Caroline were probably already there, drinking coffee in the kitchen while his mom bustled around making everything perfect.

Another text from Sadie:

I understand if you need space. But I'm here when you're ready. I love you.

Cole's chest constricted. She loved him. He believed that. Had felt it in every kiss, every conversation, every moment they'd spent building something together over the past weeks.

But love didn't change the facts. She'd been offered a job with a three-year contract, everything she needed to build the life she wanted in Mistletoe Falls. Of course she'd take it. She'd be a fool not to.

And that job meant implementing the expansion. Marketing the Express as Tennessee's flagship heritage railway. Creating programming and events that served the state's tourism goals, not the intimate community experience they had now.

Could he watch her be excited about changes that felt like loss? Could he love her through that?

The question sat heavy in his mind, unanswered.

Cash barked, pulling his attention to a squirrel darting up a nearby oak. The dog lunged forward, stopped by Cole's firm hand on his collar.

"Leave it."

Cash whined but obeyed, settling back at Cole's side.

They walked back toward the cabin. The December cold bit through Cole's jacket, but he didn't rush. Didn't want to return to the empty cabin and the questions waiting there.

Why did accepting this job feel like a betrayal? Why did the thought of the Express changing make him feel like he was drowning? Why couldn't he just say yes and move on like a rational person?

He didn't have answers. Just the crushing weight of a decision that felt impossible regardless of which way he turned.

The cabin appeared through the trees. The one place that felt completely his in a world that kept demanding he change.

Cole climbed the porch steps and sank back into the chair. Cash settled at his feet with a contented sigh.

The woods were quiet around him. His phone sat silent on the chair arm, with no new messages. The December cold seeped through his jacket, but he didn't move.

Tomorrow he'd have to face Sadie. Tomorrow he'd have to work at the depot. Tomorrow he'd have to keep functioning while everything inside him screamed that he was about to lose something irreplaceable.

But for now, he just sat in the cold afternoon light and let himself hurt.

He picked up his phone one more time and stared at Eleanor's last message. *I'm here if you need to talk. I love you.*

And Sadie's: *I'm here when you're ready. I love you.*

Everyone loved him. Everyone wanted to help. But no one could make this decision for him.

Cole set the phone down and closed his eyes.

The question he couldn't answer sat in his chest like a stone: Why does this feel like I'm being asked to let go of something I can never get back?

Chapter 26

Cole looked up as Sadie pulled into his driveway. Surprise flickered across his face.

Sadie grabbed the pizza box and got out of the car. The December cold bit through her coat, but she barely noticed.

"Hey," she said softly, climbing the steps.

"Hey." His voice was hoarse, rough around the edges. "What are you doing here?"

"Your mom called. She's worried about you." Sadie held up the pizza box. "And I figured you probably haven't eaten all day, so I stopped at Angelo's. Can I join you? Or should I leave?"

For a long moment, Cole just looked at her.

"Stay," he said quietly. "Please."

Sadie settled into the chair beside him and opened the pizza box, setting it on the small table between them.

The smell of pepperoni and melted cheese filled the cold air.

"Angelo's," Cole said, almost a smile touching his mouth. "Our first date."

She pulled out a slice and handed it to him. "Eat."

He took it, and after a moment, bit into it. He chewed mechanically, but at least he was eating.

They sat in silence for a few minutes, just eating pizza on his front porch while the sun continued its slow descent toward the mountains. Cash moved between them, hopeful for dropped cheese.

Sadie finished her slice and wiped her hands on a napkin, gathering her courage. She hadn't driven here to sit in silence. She'd come because Cole was hurting.

"Talk to me," she said gently. "Please."

Cole set down what remained of his pizza and leaned back in his chair, his eyes fixed on the woods beyond his property. "I don't know what to say. I don't even know what I'm feeling right now."

"Then tell me what you do know."

He was quiet for so long she thought he might not answer. When he finally spoke, his voice was tight with frustration. "I know that expansion is happening whether I want it or not. I know the council voted without asking me. I know the state approved two-point-five million dollars to transform the Express into something I won't recognize. And I know I have to decide whether to take a job I never asked for or walk away from a job I love."

"It feels like an impossible choice," Sadie said.

"Exactly." Cole's hands gripped the arms of his chair. "If I say yes, I'm accepting massive changes I don't want. If I say no, someone else runs it, and I lose everything anyway. There's no way to win."

"So what's really stopping you from saying yes?"

"What do you mean?"

Sadie shifted in her chair to face him more fully. "I mean, you just said it yourself—if you don't take the job, you lose the Express to someone else. At least if you accept the position, you're in the room making decisions. You have influence over how things change. So why does saying yes feel impossible?"

Cole's jaw tightened. "Because it feels like betrayal."

"Of what?"

"Of everything my father built. Everything he spent his life restoring." His voice roughened. "He wanted the Express to be intimate. A community operation, not a state tourism flagship. He wanted families to feel connected to history, not processed through some professional visitor experience. If I accept this expansion, I'm letting all of that go."

"Are you?" Sadie asked quietly. "Or are you making sure it grows in a way that honors what he built?"

Cole shook his head. "You don't understand. Daily operations, state oversight, and professional staff—that changes the fundamental nature of what this is. It stops being his dream and becomes something else entirely."

"Cole." Sadie waited until he looked at her. "I think you're right that I don't fully understand. But I think there's something else going on here. Something deeper than logistics or operational concerns."

"What?"

Her heart hammered against her ribs. This was the moment. The truth she'd seen yesterday in Town Hall when Cole's face had gone pale at the architectural renderings. The fear she'd recognized because she understood what it meant to hold on to things when you were terrified of losing them.

"I think you're afraid," she said gently, "that if the Express changes, you'll lose your connection to your father."

Cole went still.

Sadie pressed on, keeping her voice soft. "The Express is the last thing you had together. The last place where you can still feel close to him. Every time you conduct, every time you maintain her, every time you walk through that depot—you're walking where he walked. Doing what he taught you to do. And if it changes, if it becomes something different from what you built together, you're afraid that connection will break. That you'll lose him all over again."

"Sadie—"

"Am I wrong?"

Silence stretched between them, broken only by Cash's soft breathing and the distant call of a crow somewhere in the woods.

Cole's hands had gone white-knuckled on the chair arms. His jaw worked as if he were trying to speak but couldn't find the words. When he finally looked at her, his eyes were bright with something that might have been tears or might have been anger or might have been both.

"I see you, Cole," Sadie said simply. "I understand what it's like to hold on to things so tightly because they're all you have left of someone you love."

Cole looked away, his throat working. "The Express is—it's the only thing I have that's real. That I can touch. Memories fade. Objects break. But the train—I can maintain it. I can keep it exactly as he left it. And that means he's still here somehow. Still with me?"

"Oh, Cole." Sadie's own throat tightened with emotion. "Your father isn't in the train. He's in you."

"That's not—"

"Listen to me." She leaned forward. "He's in every value he taught you. In your care for this community. In the way you look at that locomotive, not as a machine but as something worth preserving. In your integrity and dedication and the love you show for this work. That's his legacy. Not the metal and steam."

Cole's shoulders hunched forward.

"Your father is still with you. Not because the train stays the same, but because he shaped who you are. And that doesn't change regardless of what happens to the Express."

"I feel like I'm losing him all over again," Cole said roughly. "I'm letting go of the last piece of him I can still touch."

Sadie's heart broke for him. She wanted to fix this, to take away his pain, to make the decision easier somehow. But she couldn't. All she could do was tell him the truth.

"I think your father would want you to build on what he started," she said quietly. "Not freeze it in time. He spent years bringing that locomotive back to life so that it could serve families and create memories. He didn't restore it to make it a museum piece. He restored it so it could live."

"I know that. I do. But knowing it and feeling it are different things."

"I know." Sadie reached across the space between their chairs, found his hand, and laced their fingers together. "And I'm not trying to tell you what to feel. I'm just trying to help you see what you're really afraid of. Because once you name it, maybe you can figure out what to do about it."

Cole's grip tightened on her hand. "And what about you? What do you want from all this?"

Here it was. The question she'd known was coming. The moment when she had to be honest about her desires, even knowing it might hurt him.

"I want to take the director position," Sadie said steadily. "I intend to stay in Mistletoe Falls and build a life here. And I want a future with you."

"But you want the expansion."

"I want the Express to be sustainable. I want more people to learn about the incredible work your father did. I want to preserve the historical integrity while creating opportunities for growth." She squeezed his hand. "Cole, I'm not excited about changing what he built. I'm excited about honoring it by making sure it lasts for generations. There's a difference."

"Is there?" His voice held a note of bitterness. "Because from where I'm sitting, it looks like you're ready to turn his dream into a state tourism program and call it progress."

The words stung, but Sadie forced herself not to pull away. "That's not fair, and you know it."

"I know. I'm sorry." Cole scrubbed his free hand over his face. "I'm just—I'm worried and frustrated, Sadie. And I don't know how not to be scared about the future."

"Then we figure it out together." Sadie shifted closer, both hands holding his now. "But Cole, I need you to understand something. I'm taking this job. Whether you accept the Operations Director position or not, I'm saying yes to the state. Because it's the right opportunity for me, and because I believe this expansion—done right—is good for the Express."

His eyes met hers, searching. "Even if I can't do it? Even if I walk away?"

"Even then." Her voice caught. "But I need to know something too. If you can't accept this expansion, if you can't be part of it—can we make this work? Can you handle my being excited about something you resent? Can we build something together when we're on opposite sides of this?"

"I don't know." The honesty in his voice hurt worse than a lie would have. "I want to say yes. I love you, Sadie, but I don't know if I can watch you implement changes. I don't know if I'm strong enough for that."

Sadie blinked hard against the tears threatening to fall. "I'm not giving up on you, Cole. I'm not walking away just because this is hard. I'm here. I'm fighting for us. I just need to know you're fighting too."

Cole pulled her hand to his chest and pressed it there over his heart. "I don't want to lose you."

"Then don't. Choose us. Choose forward."

"I'm trying. I swear I'm trying."

"I know you are." Sadie leaned forward until their foreheads touched, both of them holding on like they were each other's lifeline. "And I'll be here while you figure it out. But Cole, you have to decide. Because this expansion is happening. The council voted. The state approved it. The only question left is whether you're part of building it or whether you watch from the sidelines."

They sat like that for a long moment, foreheads pressed together, hands clasped between them, breathing the same cold air while everything hung in balance.

Finally, Cole pulled back just enough to look at her. "I need time."

"I know. I get it."

"I'm not saying no. I'm just—I need to think."

Sadie squeezed his hands one more time, then let go. She stood suddenly exhausted. The emotional weight of the conversation pressed down on her shoulders, making her feel like she'd run a marathon.

"You're leaving?" Cole looked up at her, something like panic crossing his face.

"You said you need time to think. I'm giving you that." Sadie managed a small smile. "But I'm not giving up on you."

She turned to leave, made it two steps before Cole's voice stopped her.

"Sadie."

She looked back.

"Thank you," he said quietly.

"Always."

She walked to her car, climbed in, and started the engine. She didn't let herself cry until the cabin was disappearing in her rearview mirror.

Chapter 27

Cole's keys rattled against the depot's lock, his fingers stiff from the cold morning air. The metal mechanism resisted for a moment before yielding with a familiar click that usually brought him comfort. This morning, it just felt heavy.

He pushed through the main entrance and let the door close behind him with a soft thud. The depot settled around him in its early morning silence—the kind of quiet that typically felt peaceful but today pressed against his chest like a weight.

His boots echoed as he crossed to the thermostat and adjusted the heat. The ancient radiators clanked to life, their familiar sound filling the space.

He should start his usual opening routine.

Instead, he walked toward the museum entrance.

The door swung open soundlessly, and Cole stepped into the converted warehouse space his father had transformed over a decade ago. The exposed brick walls held carefully curated displays—photographs, artifacts, tools, and stories preserved behind glass and mounted on plaques.

His father's story. The town's story. The Express's story.

Cole moved slowly through the familiar space, his hands shoved deep in his jacket pockets. He stopped at the first display—the timeline of the depot's construction in 1892, its destruction by fire in 1904, and its resurrection in 1905. Black and white photographs showed men in suspenders and caps standing beside the newly completed brick building, their faces solemn with the weight of their accomplishment.

They'd built something meant to last. Something that served a purpose beyond itself.

His chest tightened as he continued through the exhibits. Logging operations had sustained the town for decades. Passenger service that had brought tourists to experience the mountain air. The slow decline as diesel replaced steam and highways replaced rails. The years of abandonment when the depot sat empty and forgotten, windows broken and roof sagging under the weight of neglect.

Then his father's work. The restoration had consumed Michael Bennett's life.

Cole stopped in front of the center display—the one that drew the most visitors, the one that always made his throat tight. Photographs chronicled the Express's resurrection. His father as a young man standing beside the locomotive in that rail yard, the engine looking more corpse than machine. Detailed shots of rust-eaten metal and missing parts. Drawings showing restoration plans. Images documenting every stage of the painstaking work that had followed.

And there, in the place of honor above it all, the photograph that mattered most: Michael Bennett on the day of the Express's first restored run, his hand on the engine, his smile enormous, his eyes bright with the kind of joy that came from creating something that would outlast him.

Cole's jaw clenched. He'd stood in front of this photograph thousands of times. Given the tour hundreds of times. He'd told the story until it was burned into his bones.

But standing here this morning, with Saturday's meeting still raw in his mind and Sadie's words from last night echoing in his ears—Choose us. Choose forward—he found himself looking at the image differently.

Time moves forward.

The inscription on the pocket watch felt like it was burning against Cole's chest. His father had selected those specific words. Not preserve the past or protect what was. Forward. Movement. Progress.

Cole turned away from the display and walked to the Legacy Wall at the back of the museum. More photographs covered the surface—the Express's first passengers after restoration, the depot's grand reopening, community celebrations, and school groups touring the museum. His father appeared in many of them, always with the same expression: pride mixed with purpose.

And there, tucked among the larger images, was a smaller photograph. His father and Hank were standing beside the Express maybe eight months before Michael died. His father's hand rested on the locomotive as if he were touching an old friend, and Hank stood beside him with his arms crossed and a slight smile on his face.

Cole's phone buzzed in his pocket. He pulled it out, half-expecting another message from his mother checking on him or maybe Luke asking if he was okay.

It was a text from Sadie.

Sadie: *Good morning. I hope you got some sleep. I'm here if you need me.*

He stared at the message for a long moment, his thumb hovering over the keyboard. What was he supposed to say? That he'd spent half the night lying awake trying to figure out how to feel about Saturday's bombshell? That her words kept circling through his mind? That he still didn't have answers, but at least the paralysis was starting to crack?

The depot's main door opened and closed with its characteristic creak, and heavy footsteps echoed across the wooden floor.

"Cole? You here?" Hank's gravelly voice carried through the building.

Cole pocketed his phone without responding to Sadie's text and walked back through the museum toward the main hall. Hank stood near the ticketing counter, pulling off his wool coat.

"Morning," Cole said.

Hank turned, and his expression shifted immediately from a neutral greeting to sharp attention. "You look awful, son."

"Thanks."

"I'm serious." Hank hung his coat on the rack and crossed his arms, studying Cole with the kind of scrutiny that came from decades of knowing someone. "What's going on?"

Cole opened his mouth to deflect with something about not sleeping well or having a lot on his mind—the kind of vague non-answer that usually worked. But standing there under Hank's knowing gaze, the deflection died in his throat.

"Can we talk?" Cole asked instead.

"Sure." Hank gestured toward the small office area. "Coffee first?"

"Yeah. Coffee would be good."

They moved to the office, and Hank started the coffee machine, while Cole sank into one of the chairs.

After the coffeepot finished, Hank handed him a steaming mug and settled into the chair opposite. He didn't say anything, just waited with the patience of someone who understood that some conversations needed space to begin.

Cole wrapped his hands around the mug, feeling the warmth seep into his cold fingers. Where did he even start?

"Saturday afternoon," he began, "Martha called me to Town Hall. She said she needed to discuss something about the Express and it couldn't wait."

Hank's eyebrows rose slightly. "Go on."

"When I got there, Sadie was already in Martha's office. And the mayor was there. And two people from the state Tourism Development office." Cole took a sip of coffee, using the moment to organize his thoughts. "They've been planning something for six weeks. Since before Sadie even started her trial period."

"Planning what?"

"A partnership. Tennessee Historic Heritage Railways Initiative." The words tasted strange in his mouth—formal, official, nothing like the organic way the Express had always operated. "The state wants to make the Mistletoe Express its flagship operation for heritage tourism."

Hank went very still. "Flagship."

"Two-point-five million dollar grant over three years. Depot expansion—double the current size, new wing for a professional museum, visitor center, and gift shop. The Express running daily rides year-round. Multiple departures every day." Cole set his mug down, his hands suddenly too restless to hold it. "Professional marketing campaign. Statewide reach. Documentary coverage. Partnership with Travel Tennessee."

He forced himself to continue, to get all of it out there where he could examine it in the light. "They offered me a promotion. Operations Director. Substantial pay

increase, a leadership role overseeing all Express operations, and the expanded depot facilities."

"And Sadie?"

"Director of Tourism Development. Permanent position, salaried with benefits. She'd run all the programming, events, and marketing." Cole's jaw tightened. "The
council already voted. Thursday night, two days before
they told us. They approved the partnership in principle.
The state needs a signed commitment by December
thirty-first to secure the funding."

Hank absorbed this information with the same methodical consideration he applied to mechanical problems. His weathered hands wrapped around his coffee
mug, his sharp blue eyes fixed on Cole's face.

"They decided without talking to you," Hank said finally.

"Without asking. Without including me in any part of
the planning." The bitterness Cole had been trying to
contain leaked into his voice. "Six weeks of negotiations
and conversations and decisions, and the only reason I
found out was because they needed my answer for the
operations director position."

"What does Sadie think?"

"She just found out too. They briefed her before I
arrived." Cole stood, too agitated to sit still. He moved
to the window, staring out at the Express. "I asked her to
leave with me after they told me everything. She stayed
to finish the conversation."

"And that hurt."

It wasn't a question, but Cole answered anyway. "Yeah. It hurt."

"But you understand why she stayed."

Cole's hands tightened on the window frame. "She has a job to do. Responsibilities. I can't expect her to just walk away from a meeting because I'm upset."

"But it still hurt," Hank repeated gently.

"It still hurt," Cole admitted.

They were quiet for a moment, the only sound being the soft hiss of the radiators.

"Last night," Cole said, "Sadie came to my cabin. We talked. She told me she's taking the director position whether I accept the operations director job or not."

"And?"

"And she's right to take it. It's a good opportunity. Security, resources, and the chance to build something permanent here." Cole turned from the window to face Hank. "But I don't know if I can watch this happen. An expansion that turns this place into something my father wouldn't recognize."

"You think the expansion would dishonor him in some way."

"I think it would erase him and what he built." The words came out sharper than Cole intended. "I think two-point-five million dollars and professional marketing campaigns and visitor centers and gift shops selling who knows what turn the Express into a commodity."

Hank set his coffee mug down carefully. "Can I tell you something about your father?"

"Always."

"A few months before he died, we had a conversation. It was late evening, both of us here at the depot after a long day. The Express was running well, and the museum was bringing in steady visitors. Things were good." Hank leaned forward, his elbows on his knees. "Michael said to me, 'Hank, we've done good work here. Now I want to figure out how to make sure this lasts beyond us. How do we make all this last beyond our lifetime?'"

Cole's chest tightened. "He said that?"

"He was already thinking ahead, Cole. He knew the Express couldn't stay exactly as it was forever—not if he wanted it to survive." Hank's voice was gentle but firm. "Your father loved this train more than almost anything. But he loved it enough to know it needed to evolve."

"But daily operations—"

"Would mean more families experiencing what he preserved. Right now, you serve hundreds of families a year. With this expansion? You could serve thousands." Hank stood and moved to stand beside Cole at the window. "How many kids never get to experience what your father restored because there's not enough capacity? How many families want to visit but can't because tickets sell out or the days and times we currently offer don't fit their needs?"

Cole hadn't thought about it that way. He'd been so focused on what would be lost that he hadn't considered what could be gained.

"Michael wanted the Express to serve people," Hank continued. "That was always the point. Not just to preserve it, but to share it. To let families make memories, to teach kids about history, to give people something beautiful and meaningful." He turned to look at Cole directly. "If you refuse this expansion because you're scared of change, you're not honoring your father or his legacy at all. You're betraying it."

The words hit like a physical blow. "That's not fair."

"Isn't it?" Hank's expression was compassionate but unyielding. "You've spent four years maintaining his dream, son. But you haven't been building your own life. You've been stuck... frozen in time, if you will. And I think part of you knows that turning down this opportunity isn't about protecting your father's work—it's about protecting yourself from having to move forward."

Cole wanted to argue. Wanted to defend his position, to explain all the legitimate concerns about losing what made the Express special. But the words wouldn't come because somewhere deep down, he knew Hank was right.

He'd been frozen. Ever since his father died. Ever since Sarah left. He'd been going through the motions, maintaining, preserving, protecting—but not living. Not building. Not moving forward.

"I'm a fool," Cole said finally, the admission quiet but honest. "I'm scared that accepting this means letting Dad go."

"Your daddy's fingerprints are all over this place, Cole. In every board he replaced, every piece of brass he polished, and every mechanical system he restored. That doesn't disappear because you add a visitor center or run more tours. If anything, it means more people get to experience what he poured his life into."

Cole turned back to the window, his vision blurring slightly as emotion rose in his throat.

"Your father wouldn't want you to live like this," Hank said quietly. "Frozen at thirty years old, refusing to let yourself be happy because you think happiness means forgetting him. He'd want you to grab onto life and love. He'd want you to take risks and build something new. He'd want you to move forward."

Cole turned to look at him.

"Cole... you start moving forward by saying yes." Hank placed a hand on Cole's shoulder. "You accept the operations director position. You work with Sadie to shape what this expansion becomes. You make sure the things that matter most stay protected even as everything else grows around them."

Cole let out a shaky breath.

"You'll figure it out as you go. That's what your father did. He didn't have a master plan when he started restoring the Express. He just started, and he figured out each problem as it came." Hank squeezed his shoulder once before letting go. "Besides, you won't be doing it alone. You'll have Sadie. And you'll have me as long as you need me."

"You'd stay? Even with daily operations and state oversight and all the changes?"

"Someone needs to make sure you don't run the Express into the ground trying to do everything yourself."

Maybe forward was the only way to truly honor what came before.

"I need to think about specifics," Cole said slowly. "There are things I'd want in place. Contingencies. Non-negotiables about how this expansion happens."

"Like what?"

"Final say on historical accuracy for the museum exhibits. Hiring authority for mechanics and conductors—I pick my team, people who understand the Express isn't just a tourist attraction. Maintenance standards that can't be compromised for operational demands." The words came faster now as his mind started working through the practical details. "Community involvement stays integral. Local volunteers, local artisans for the gift shop. And my father's name stays prominent. Not just a plaque. His story needs to be central to everything."

Hank nodded. "Sounds reasonable. Important, even."

"You think the state would agree to conditions?"

"I think the state needs you more than you need them. You're Michael Bennett's son. If they want this partnership to work—really work, not just look good on paper—they need you leading it." Hank moved back toward his chair and settled into it. "But you have to be willing to negotiate from a position of strength, not fear. You have to go into that conversation knowing what you're worth and what you're bringing to the table."

Cole turned that over in his mind. Position of strength. Not fear.

"I need to talk to Sadie," Cole said.

"I figured." Hank stood and retrieved his coat from the rack. "I'll go check on the Express and give you some privacy. Take your time."

"Hank?" Cole waited until the older man turned back. "Thank you. For everything you said and for setting me straight."

Hank's weathered face creased into a smile. "That's what family does, son. And you've been family to me since you were a kid handing me wrenches while we worked on the Express."

He headed out toward the platform, leaving Cole alone in the office, a decision crystallizing in his mind.

Cole pulled out his phone and stared at Sadie's message. I'm here if you need me.

His thumbs moved across the screen.

Cole: *Can we talk? In person. I've been thinking.*

The response came within seconds, like she'd been waiting for his message.

Sadie: *Yes. When and where?*

Cole: *Now? I can come to you, or you can meet me at the depot.*

Three dots appeared immediately, then disappeared, then appeared again. Cole found himself holding his breath, waiting.

Sadie: *I'll come there. Twenty minutes.*

Relief flooded through him, warm and steadying.

Cole: *Thank you. For everything.*
Sadie: *Always.*

Chapter 28

Cole's hands rested on the folder in front of him, despite the adrenaline humming through his veins. The conference room at Town Hall felt smaller than he remembered—maybe because of the large monitor mounted on the wall displaying Jennifer Palmer and Sean Abrams from the Tennessee Tourism Development office, both looking professional and expectant in their Nashville suits.

Or maybe because everything riding on the next hour made the walls feel like they were closing in.

Martha sat to his right, her reading glasses perched on her nose and a leather portfolio open in front of her. Mayor Hayes occupied the chair beside her, his usually jovial expression replaced with careful attention. The camera positioned at the center of the conference table captured all four of them for the state officials—Cole,

Sadie, Martha, and the mayor—framed together like they were already a team.

Sadie sat beside Cole, her folder of notes aligned perfectly with the table's edge. She looked calm and professional in dark slacks and a burgundy sweater. But Cole saw the slight tension in her shoulders.

They'd spent all of Monday afternoon at the depot working through contingencies, discovering that what each of them wanted complemented rather than conflicted with the other's vision. Last night they'd refined their proposals separately, then met early this morning over coffee at The Cozy Cup to align their approach.

This meeting had felt necessary yesterday.

Now, sitting across from Martha and the mayor with the state officials watching from the screen, it felt like standing at the edge of a cliff, ready to jump.

This is it, Cole thought. No going back now.

"Thank you all for gathering on such short notice," Martha said. "Cole, Sadie—you requested this meeting to discuss the partnership terms. Jennifer, Sean, the floor is yours."

Jennifer leaned forward on the screen, her smile warm but businesslike. "Thank you, Martha. Cole, Sadie—we're hopeful you're here to accept the positions we discussed Saturday."

"We have the contracts ready pending your final commitment," Sean added, holding up a bound document visible through the camera. "Pending your signatures, we can move forward immediately."

Cole noticed how they were presenting it—a done deal, just waiting for signatures, as if the only question was when rather than whether. The presumption might have irritated him yesterday. Now it just strengthened his resolve.

He glanced at Sadie. She met his eyes and gave the smallest nod.

Position of strength, Hank's voice echoed in his memory. *Not fear.*

Cole pulled his folder closer and opened it to reveal the typed list he'd spent Monday evening perfecting. "Thank you for the opportunity to discuss this. Sadie and I appreciate the confidence you're showing in us. But before we can accept these positions, we need to discuss some essential conditions."

Martha and Mayor Hayes exchanged glances—this clearly wasn't what they'd expected. On the screen, Jennifer's eyebrows rose slightly, though her expression remained professionally neutral.

"Conditions," Jennifer repeated carefully.

"Yes." Cole kept his voice calm but firm. "I'll need certain authorities and protections written into the contract before I can accept the operations director position."

"We're listening," Sean said, pulling a notepad closer.

Cole took a breath and began. "First, operational authority and historical integrity. I'll need final authority over all mechanical operations, maintenance standards, and safety protocols. The Express is a steam locomotive built in 1887. She requires specialized knowledge and can't be treated like a modern diesel engine."

He watched Jennifer and Sean's faces on the screen, looking for resistance or dismissal. Instead, both were taking notes, their expressions attentive.

"Any staff involved in her operation—engineers, firemen, conductors—need my approval," Cole continued. "I'll hire people who understand historic preservation, not just tourism operations. These positions require specific expertise, and I need authority over who touches this locomotive."

"That's reasonable," Jennifer said. "Continue."

The acknowledgment steadied Cole's nerves. "For the museum expansion, I want the final say on historical accuracy for exhibits. My father spent years researching this train's history. I do not want the history simplified or sensationalized for tourist appeal."

"That's exactly the kind of expertise we're hoping you'll bring," Jennifer said. She looked at Sean, who nodded in agreement. "We want authenticity, not theme park attractions. Your father's restoration is what makes this program valuable."

Cole felt something in his chest loosen slightly. They were listening. Really listening.

"Daily operations can't compromise long-term preservation," he said, pressing forward. "If the Express requires maintenance, operations pause. Non-negotiable. I want it written into the contract that preservation takes priority over revenue schedules."

Mayor Hayes shifted in his seat. "Cole, the revenue projections are based on a certain operational capacity—"

"Then we adjust the projections," Cole said, his voice firm but respectful. "If this partnership is about long-term sustainability, we can't run the Express into the ground chasing quarterly numbers. She's 138 years old. She needs proper care, and that means sometimes saying no to additional rides."

Martha spoke up, her voice carrying quiet authority. "Cole knows this locomotive better than anyone in Tennessee. If we want her running safely for the next fifty years, we need his expertise guiding every operational decision."

"Agreed," Jennifer said without hesitation. "Preservation priority will be written into the contract. What else?"

Cole glanced at his list, feeling more confident with each point they accepted. "Hiring authority. I pick my operations team. I need people who respect this train, who understand what she means to this community."

"Specifically?" Sean prompted.

"Hank Lawson stays on as Senior Operations Manager. He worked with my father for years. His knowledge is irreplaceable." Cole's voice took on an edge of non-negotiation. "Any new hires in mechanical or conductor roles go through me. I won't have the state placing people who see this as just another job."

"Cole, we'll need to follow state employment guidelines—" Mayor Hayes began.

"Then write it into the partnership agreement that operations hiring requires my approval," Cole said, not backing down. "I'm not asking to ignore employment law. I'm asking for authority over who operates a 138-year-old steam locomotive. There's a difference."

Silence filled the conference room for a beat. On the screen, Jennifer and Sean were conferring quietly, their microphones muted. Cole felt his heart rate pick up. Had he pushed too hard? Demanded too much?

Then Jennifer unmuted. "Mr. Bennett, you're absolutely right. We'll include language giving you final hiring authority for all operations positions, with the understanding that standard employment practices and anti-discrimination laws still apply."

"That's all I'm asking."

"What else?" Jennifer's tone was genuinely curious now, almost impressed.

"Community integration. Local volunteer involvement continues—the Express has always been supported by this community, and they deserve to remain part of her story. And when this expansion creates new jobs—visitor center staff, museum guides, gift shop employees—local residents get first consideration. We hire from Mistletoe Falls before we look outside."

"Smart," Sean murmured, making a note. "Local hiring strengthens community buy-in."

"Gift shop inventory: local artisans only," Cole continued. "No mass-produced merchandise. If we're selling items with the Express's name on them, they represent Mistletoe Falls quality and craftsmanship."

"That's actually perfect," Jennifer said, her professional mask slipping into genuine enthusiasm. "Authenticity is our selling point. Mass-produced souvenirs would undermine everything we're trying to accomplish."

"And community events like the ones Sadie created," Cole said, glancing at her. "The Tree Lighting, the Santa Express—those continue. We're not just a tourist attraction. We serve our town first."

Mayor Hayes was nodding now. Martha had a slight smile playing on her lips.

Cole turned to his final point, and his voice got quieter but somehow more intense. "My father's story needs to be central to everything. Not a footnote. Not 'restoration funded by a preservation society.' His name, his work, his vision—that's the heart of why the Express exists."

The room had gone completely still. Even through the screen, Cole could see Jennifer and Sean's expressions shift.

"The Legacy Wall at the museum expands with the new wing. Prominent placement. His tools, his photographs, and his story told in his own words from the journals he kept during the restoration."

He paused, gathering himself. Sadie's hand found his under the table, her fingers lacing through his in quiet support.

"And I want a dedicated scholarship fund in his name," Cole continued. "Part of the annual operating budget goes to funding railway preservation education for young people interested in historic restoration. The Michael Bennett Heritage Scholarship."

The silence stretched for several heartbeats. Cole saw Mayor Hayes blink rapidly, his eyes suspiciously bright. Martha had pressed her hand to her mouth.

On the screen, Jennifer's professional composure had cracked into something genuine and moving. "Mr. Bennett," she said quietly, "I never had the pleasure of meeting your father, but I can only imagine how proud of you he would be if he were here with us today."

"We'll write the Michael Bennett Heritage Scholarship into the grant budget," Jennifer continued. "Annual funding administered through the Express with your oversight. Does that work?"

Cole couldn't speak past the emotion in his throat, so he just nodded.

Martha found her voice first. "Cole, this is perfect. Your father deserves this kind of recognition."

Cole squeezed Sadie's hand once, then let go and sat back in his chair. He'd said everything he needed to say. Protected what mattered. Honored his father. Set terms that would let him accept this position with integrity.

Now it was Sadie's turn.

She pulled her folder closer, and Cole saw her shoulders straighten, her professional confidence settling over her like armor.

"I appreciate Cole's focus on operational integrity," Sadie said, addressing the screen directly. "Now I'd like to discuss the tourism development side and what I need to be successful in this role."

Jennifer and Sean both leaned forward attentively.

"First, programming philosophy," Sadie began. "The events I create need to prioritize experience over volume. I'm not interested in cramming as many people through as possible to maximize revenue."

"Can you elaborate?" Sean asked.

"Quality experiences that create lasting memories—that's our brand," Sadie said. "If that means we run fewer tours, but each one is exceptional, that's the right choice. I need the authority to make those calls without having to justify why quality matters more than quantity."

"And what about partnerships?" Jennifer prompted.

"I need the authority to decline sponsors or partnerships that don't align with our values," Sadie said without hesitation. "If a company wants to sponsor an event but requires us to stock their mass-produced merchandise in our gift shop, I need the power to say no without seeking approval up the chain. Local artisans built this community. They deserve our loyalty."

"Marketing authenticity," Sadie continued, moving to her next point. "Professional marketing campaigns can't sanitize what makes us special. No stock photos of generic trains. No scripted testimonials. Real families, real experiences, real Mistletoe Falls."

"You want content control," Sean said, understanding immediately.

"Final approval over social media presence, website content, and promotional materials," Sadie confirmed. "The state can provide resources and guidance, but final content approval stays with me. Our story includes struggles—Cole's father restoring this train over a large portion of his lifetime, the community rallying to save the depot, families volunteering because they believe in preservation. That's our authentic narrative. I won't let marketing consultants turn it into bland tourism copy."

"Ms. Baker," Jennifer said warmly, "we are interested in hiring you specifically because you understand authentic storytelling. We trust your judgment."

Sadie's expression didn't soften. "Then put it in writing."

A beat of surprised silence, then Jennifer laughed—genuine and appreciative. "Fair enough. Content approval stays with you. What else?"

"Seasonal rhythm and staff well-being," Sadie said, flipping to her next page. "Daily operations year-round sounds impressive on paper, but it's not sustainable for staff or quality. I want permission to build in slower periods."

Mayor Hayes frowned. "The grant budget assumes certain revenue projections—"

"Then revise the projections," Sadie said, her voice firm but not confrontational. "I won't sacrifice staff well-being or quality for unrealistic revenue targets. If this partnership is about long-term sustainability, that includes the people who make it work. Spring and fall can be lighter schedules. Give staff recovery time, allow for deeper maintenance, and prevent burnout."

Cole watched Martha's face carefully. She was smiling now, with a look of satisfaction on her face.

"Sustainable operations matter more than maximizing every possible revenue day," Sadie added. "That needs to be acknowledged in my contract."

"Noted," Sean said, typing rapidly. "We'll work with you on realistic revenue projections that allow for seasonal adjustments."

"Event development freedom," Sadie continued. "I need creative freedom to develop new events and discontinue ones that don't work. Tourism evolves. What families want changes. I'll provide quarterly reports on event success, attendance, and feedback. But I need trust to experiment, to try new things, to let some ideas fail so we can find what really works."

Martha spoke up again. "Sadie's proven she can innovate while honoring tradition. The Tree Lighting and Santa Express were her ideas, and they've exceeded every expectation."

"Quarterly reports and the freedom to innovate," Jennifer said. "Granted. What else, Ms. Baker?"

"Community collaboration," Sadie said. "I want a formal Community Advisory Board. Local business owners, volunteers, and longtime residents—people who can provide feedback on how events impact the town. We're not an island. The Express's success needs to benefit Mistletoe Falls, not just bring in outside tourism dollars that bypass the local economy."

"That's excellent thinking," Sean said, with genuine approval in his voice. "Community buy-in is what makes these programs successful long-term."

"Part of my role should include coordinating with local businesses," Sadie added. "Local businesses come first. A rising tide lifts all boats. If tourists come for the Express, they should discover everything else Mistletoe Falls offers."

"And finally," Sadie continued, her voice taking on a more personal note, "my current trial contract runs through January 24th. I need acknowledgment that this permanent position begins January 25th, with salary and benefits starting then."

"Of course," Jennifer said.

"And one more thing." Sadie's expression grew more serious. "My permanent residence is Mistletoe Falls. This isn't a position where I'm expected to relocate to Nashville or report regularly to state offices. I live here. I work here. That's non-negotiable."

Cole felt his heart skip a beat. She was claiming this. Claiming home.

"The director position is based in Mistletoe Falls," Sean confirmed. "We want you embedded in the community. That's the whole point."

Sadie set down her pen and folded her hands on top of her folder. "Then those are my conditions."

She glanced at Cole, and in that look he saw everything—partnership, trust, and the shared understanding that they'd just done something important together. As equals. As a team.

The conference room was quiet for a moment; the only sound was the distant tick of the wall clock. On the screen, Jennifer and Sean were conferring again, their microphones muted, their heads bent together in discussion.

Cole's pulse thundered in his ears. They'd put everything on the table—every condition, every non-negotiable, every protection they needed to accept these positions with integrity. Now they just had to wait and see if the state would meet them where they stood.

Or if they'd just negotiated themselves out of jobs.

Jennifer unmuted the microphone, and both she and Sean were smiling.

"Mr. Bennett, Ms. Baker," Jennifer said, her voice warm with genuine respect. "This is exactly the kind of leadership we hoped for when we identified Mistletoe Falls as our flagship program."

Cole felt Sadie's hand find his again under the table.

"Cole," Jennifer continued, addressing him directly through the screen, "your conditions protect the Express's integrity while ensuring operational excellence. We'll write operational authority into your contract, including preservation priority over revenue schedules. Hiring authority for operations roles—approved, with Hank Lawson formalized as Senior Operations Manager. Final say on museum historical accuracy—granted. The Michael Bennett Heritage Scholarship will be allocated annually from the grant budget, with you overseeing its administration."

She turned her attention to Sadie. "Ms. Baker, your conditions actually strengthen the program rather than limiting it. Programming authority with a focus on quality over volume—we're aligned on that philosophy. Content approval for all marketing materials stays with you. Seasonal pacing with sustainable operations—we'll revise revenue projections to reflect realistic scheduling. Creative freedom with quarterly accountability—exactly what we want from our directors. The Community Advisory Board is an excellent addition. We'll budget for immediately. And your position begins January 25th, based permanently in Mistletoe Falls."

Sean picked up the thread. "Local hiring preference for new positions created by the expansion—we'll write that into our vendor and employment contracts. Local artisans for gift shop inventory—that's our preference as well."

Mayor Hayes was beaming now, his earlier concern replaced with obvious satisfaction. Martha had taken off her glasses and was watching Cole and Sadie with an expression that looked almost maternal in its pride.

"We'll have revised contracts drawn up reflecting these terms," Jennifer said. "You'll have them by tomorrow morning for review with the understanding that both parties can request clarifications on specific language."

"December 18th still works as our final signing deadline?" Sean asked.

Cole looked at Sadie. Her eyes were bright; her smile was barely contained.

"We'll need to review the written contracts," Cole said, finding his voice steady despite the emotion threatening to overwhelm him. "But yes. If the terms match what we discussed today, we're ready to commit."

"Agreed," Sadie added.

Jennifer's smile widened into something radiant. "Then I think we have a partnership. Welcome to the Tennessee Historic Heritage Railways Initiative. We're honored to have you leading this program."

Sean raised a coffee mug visible on screen in a mock toast. "To the Mistletoe Express and the team that's going to make her a model for heritage tourism across the state."

"To the Express," Mayor Hayes echoed, his voice thick with emotion.

Martha just nodded, but her eyes said everything words couldn't.

The meeting continued for another twenty minutes—logistics about contract delivery, timelines for construction beginning in spring, and preliminary budget discussions. But Cole barely registered the details. His mind was still catching up with what had just happened.

They'd done it. They'd negotiated terms that protected everything that mattered. They'd been heard, respected, and valued.

And more than that, they'd done it together. Not as adversaries trying to reconcile different visions, but as partners working toward the same goal.

Finally, Jennifer and Sean signed off with promises to send contracts first thing tomorrow morning. The screen went dark, leaving just the four of them in the conference room.

Martha closed her laptop with a soft click. "I'm proud of you both," she said quietly. "That was professional, thoughtful, and exactly what this program and town needed."

She stood and gathered her portfolio, then paused. "Cole, I'm proud of you."

Cole felt his throat tighten. "Thank you."

Martha turned to Sadie. "And you've proven why I hired you. You fought for quality and sustainability, not just the flashy opportunity." She smiled. "You're going to do remarkable things here."

Mayor Hayes stood as well, shaking both their hands with his characteristic enthusiasm. "This will transform Mistletoe Falls in the best possible way. You've given us a roadmap that honors who we are while building something sustainable for the next generation."

Then Martha and the mayor were leaving, their voices fading as they walked down the hallway, leaving Cole and Sadie alone in the suddenly quiet conference room.

Cole stared at his folder of notes; his typed list of contingencies that had felt so important an hour ago now felt like just papers. Evidence of careful planning, but not the thing itself.

The thing itself was sitting beside him, close enough to touch, her own folder closed and her hands resting on top of it.

"Did that really just happen?" Sadie asked, her voice barely above a whisper.

Cole turned to look at her. "I think we just accepted jobs running a two-point-five-million-dollar state tourism program."

"With conditions."

"Significant conditions."

They stared at each other for a beat, and then the tension broke into relieved laughter—the kind that came from surviving something intense and coming out the other side intact.

"We did it," Sadie said, still laughing. "We actually did it."

"We did." Cole reached across the small space between their chairs and took her hand, threading his fingers through hers. "Together."

"Thank you," Cole continued. "For not giving up on me."

Sadie's eyes filled with emotion. "Thank you for being brave enough to choose forward."

They sat like that for a long moment, hands clasped, the December sunlight slanting through the conference room windows and painting everything in vivid shades of gold. Outside, Mistletoe Falls was going about its Tuesday afternoon—shops open, people walking the streets, and life continuing in the steady rhythm of a small town that didn't know yet how much was about to change.

Or maybe how much it was about to grow while staying exactly what it had always been.

"We should tell people," Sadie said eventually. "Your family. Hank. Everyone's been waiting to hear what we decided."

"Dinner at Mom's tonight?" Cole suggested. "Celebrate properly?"

"She'd never forgive us if we didn't."

They stood together, gathering their folders and papers, putting the conference room back in order.

"Sadie?"

She turned toward him, her expression open and questioning.

"I love you."

Sadie's eyes brimmed with tears that didn't fall. She closed the distance between them and reached up to cup his face with both hands, her touch gentle and sure.

"I love you too," she whispered.

Cole kissed her—sweet and tender and full of every promise he didn't have words for yet. Future promises. Forever promises. The kind that felt both terrifying and inevitable, like standing at the edge of something vast and beautiful and choosing to step forward into it.

When they finally pulled apart, Sadie smiled up at him with a look that held joy and relief and hope all tangled together.

"Come on," she said, taking his hand and pulling him toward the door. "Let's go tell everyone that the Mistletoe Express just got a whole lot more interesting."

Chapter 29

The last family descended the steps from the platform, the father carried a sleeping toddler while his wife herded two older children toward their car in the parking lot. Their voices drifted back through the December night, excited whispers about Santa and presents and the magical train ride they'd just experienced.

Sadie watched them go, her breath fogging in the cold air, her feet aching in a way that felt like victory. The Christmas Eve event—the last piece of the three-event puzzle she'd proposed back in early November—was nearly over. Nearly two hundred passengers had boarded the Mistletoe Express, riding through the snowy countryside to Whispering Falls and back while carolers sang and hot cocoa warmed chilly hands. The magic of Christmas wrapped around everything like the gentlest blessing.

The depot glowed behind her, every window blazing with warm golden light, evergreen garlands draped along the eaves and railings, and thousands of white lights twinkling like captured stars. The massive tree they'd decorated for the Tree Lighting ceremony still stood proud near the main entrance, and the Express herself sat gleaming on her tracks, steam rising lazily from her stack into the night sky.

They'd done it. All three events. And judging by the smiles on every departing face, the laughter of children, and the grateful thanks from parents, they'd done it well.

Cole appeared at her elbow, his conductor's cap slightly askew, his cheeks flushed from hours of keeping passengers safe and entertained. "That's most of them. Just a few stragglers left inside grabbing last-minute cocoa."

"We really pulled it off." Sadie turned to look at him, this man who'd been so resistant to change eight weeks ago, who'd seen her as a threat to everything he loved. Now he stood beside her transformed—still protective of the Express and his father's legacy, but open to the future in ways she'd never imagined possible back in early November.

"You pulled it off," Cole corrected, his voice warm. "This was your vision. I just made sure the train didn't break down."

"We pulled it off together."

His hand found hers, fingers threading through hers with familiar warmth despite the cold. "Together. Yeah, I like the sound of that."

Around them, the depot hadn't fully emptied yet. Volunteers moved through the main hall, visible through the windows, beginning the cleanup process that would restore everything to its usual pristine condition. Eleanor directed the dessert table breakdown with her usual efficient grace, while Caroline and Luke gathered empty cocoa cups and stacked them in plastic bins. Charlie swept cookie crumbs from the floor with more enthusiasm than precision, and somewhere in all that organized chaos, Cash was probably napping in Cole's office after an evening of greeting passengers with enthusiastic tail wags.

A few local families lingered on the platform despite the late hour, reluctant to let the magic end. The Phillips family stood near the Express, taking one last photo in front of the decorated locomotive. Martha spoke with Mayor Hayes near the ticket office entrance, both of them looking satisfied in the particular way town officials got when an event exceeded expectations.

"I should probably help with cleanup," Sadie said, though she didn't move. Exhaustion had settled into her bones, the good kind that came from meaningful work well done.

"In a minute." Cole squeezed her hand gently. "Let's just enjoy this for a second. It's Christmas Eve, after all."

Snow had begun falling while they'd been managing the final boarding, light flakes that caught the glow of the Christmas lights and turned the whole scene into something out of a snow globe. The kind of perfect December night that made you believe in magic, even as an adult who knew better.

Sadie leaned into Cole's shoulder, breathing in the cold mountain air mixed with the lingering scent of cocoa and evergreen. Through the depot windows, she could see Hank emerge from the museum wing, say something to Eleanor that made her laugh, then head toward the ticket office with that purposeful stride of his.

A moment later, music suddenly filled the night air.

Not just any music, but an unmistakable harmonica opening that could only be one song, 'Orange Blossom Special' by Johnny Cash, that fast-paced train anthem that had been making people grin and tap their feet for decades. The outdoor speakers sent the sound echoing across the platform and into the parking lot, the harmonica mimicking a train whistle with playful precision.

Everyone stopped what they were doing. Heads turned. The Phillips family paused mid-photo. Caroline looked up from her bin of cocoa cups. Even Charlie stopped sweeping.

Cole's entire body went still beside Sadie, and when she glanced at his face, she saw emotion flash across his features—surprise, recognition, and something deeper that made her throat tighten.

Hank emerged from the depot, stepping out onto the platform with a smile that held both mischief and meaning. His weathered face creased with warmth as he looked directly at Cole.

"Your daddy played this song every single day while we worked on the Express, Cole," Hank called over the music, his voice carrying across the platform. "Every. Single. Day. Seemed fitting we end tonight with it."

Cole's hand tightened on Sadie's, and for a heartbeat she thought he might be overwhelmed, might retreat into a protective shell. But instead, his face broke into a grin—genuine and wide and full of light.

"Dad's song," he said, almost to himself. Then louder, to Hank: "He'd crank it up every time we hit a milestone on the restoration."

"And we hit a milestone tonight for sure," Hank said.

The mood shifted instantly. What had been tired satisfaction transformed into something electric and joyful. Luke let out a whoop and grabbed Caroline's hand, spinning her in an impromptu twirl that made her shriek with laughter. Charlie abandoned his broom entirely and started dancing with exaggerated moves that looked like a combination of every dance trend from the past decade mashed into one enthusiastic performance.

Eleanor's eyes glistened as she swayed to the music, her hand pressed briefly to her heart before Martha caught her hands and pulled her into a spirited two-step. Mayor Hayes clapped along from the sidelines. The Phillips family joined in, the parents dancing with their kids in that unselfconscious way that only happened at community celebrations when everyone remembered why small towns were special.

The platform and parking lot became an impromptu dance floor, people laughing and moving to Johnny Cash's famous train song, celebrating not just the successful event or even Christmas Eve, but something bigger—life and community and the kind of connections that made a place feel like home.

Sadie felt the music pulse through her, felt the joy radiating from everyone around them, and suddenly she understood. This wasn't just a song. This was Cole's father present with them tonight, celebrated not through sadness or solemn remembrance, but through exactly the kind of vibrant, living joy he would have wanted.

Cole turned to face her fully, his grin still in place, his eyes bright in the Christmas lights. He extended his hand with exaggerated formality despite the chaos of dancing around them. "Dance with me?"

Sadie laughed, glancing at the energetic celebration happening all around them. "It's kind of a fast song for someone who's been on her feet all evening."

"Then we'll go slow."

She placed her hand in his. "I'd love to."

Cole pulled her close, one hand settling at the small of her back, the other holding hers with gentle firmness. Around them, people spun and laughed and moved with the quick tempo of "Orange Blossom Special," but Cole and Sadie created their own rhythm. They swayed together slowly, their movements deliberate and unhurried, as if they'd found a different song playing underneath the one everyone else heard.

The world narrowed to just the two of them despite the celebration continuing in every direction. Sadie looked up at Cole and saw her entire future reflected in his eyes.

"Thank you," she said.

"For what?"

"For taking a chance on me. On us. For choosing to move forward."

Cole's expression softened, his hand tightening slightly at her back. "Thanks for not giving up on me, sweet Sadie."

They moved together as the harmonica wailed and the rhythm pounded, their slow dance a stark contrast to the energetic celebration surrounding them. Luke spun Caroline past them with a laugh. Charlie attempted some kind of breakdancing move that ended with him nearly colliding with Mayor Hayes. Eleanor and Martha were doing a version of the Charleston that had them both giggling like schoolgirls.

But Sadie had eyes only for Cole. For this man, who'd taught her that home wasn't something you had to earn through perfection—it was something you claimed through courage. That family could be chosen as much as inherited. That love didn't guarantee loss; it guaranteed living.

The music built toward its crescendo, Johnny Cash's voice rising with the harmonica in that final triumphant surge. Cole spun Sadie out with practiced ease, then pulled her back in smoothly. His eyes held hers with an intensity that made her breath catch.

"Ready?" he asked, his grin turning mischievous.

"For what?"

And then—with perfect timing and that crooked smile she'd come to love—Cole dipped her low.

Sadie laughed as the world tilted, her hands gripping his shoulders as he held her securely, his strength keeping her safe even as everything went beautifully off-balance. The Christmas lights blurred above her, snow fell gently onto her upturned face, and somewhere beyond her inverted view of the world, she could hear people cheering.

Cole's face hovered above hers, close enough that she could see the snowflakes catching in his dark hair and could count the laugh lines at the corners of his eyes. His expression held everything—love, and certainty and joy and promise.

"Merry Christmas, Sadie Baker. Welcome home."

Her heart swelled so full she thought it might burst.

Just as Cole started to bring her upright, a furry golden-brown blur bounded across the platform at full speed. Cash—apparently awakened by all the commotion—had emerged from the depot and immediately spotted what he could only interpret as his two favorite people playing the most exciting game ever.

The dog launched himself at them with enthusiastic abandon, front paws landing squarely on Cole's thigh while his wet nose bopped Sadie's arm. His entire body wiggled with pure canine joy, tail wagging so hard his whole back end swayed, and he let out a bark that seemed to say, "I want to play too!"

Cole laughed—a deep, genuine sound of complete happiness—as he carefully brought Sadie upright while simultaneously trying to maintain his balance against Cash's exuberant assault. Sadie laughed too, reaching down to scratch behind Cash's ears even as the dog continued his celebration dance around their feet.

"Cash, buddy, we were having a moment," Cole said, but his tone held only affection.

Cash responded with a spinning jump, clearly interpreting this as encouragement to continue the game.

Around them, the platform erupted in laughter. Luke was doubled over laughing, Caroline had tears streaming down her face from giggling, and even Hank was chuckling at the dog's perfect comedic timing. The music ended with a final harmonica flourish, and someone started clapping—maybe Eleanor, maybe Martha; it was impossible to tell—and then everyone joined in.

The applause filled the December night, echoing off the depot walls and rising into the snowy sky. People were clapping for the successful event, yes, but also for Cole and Sadie, for Cash's perfect photobomb, for the Express gleaming behind them, for community and connection. All the beautiful, messy, joyful chaos that made life in Mistletoe Falls exactly what it was.

Sadie stood in the center of it all, Cole's arm around her waist, Cash dancing circles around their feet, surrounded by people who'd become family to her in the span of eight weeks. The depot glowed with thousands of lights. The Express sat proudly on her tracks. Snow fell in soft, perfect flakes. And somehow, Sadie could almost feel Michael Bennett's presence—not as sadness or loss, but as approval and love and the certain knowledge that his son had finally learned to live again.

Leave A Review

If you enjoyed this book, please consider leaving an honest review on Amazon

Visit Our Website:

www.tarabaisden.com

Visit Our Amazon Author Page HERE

Find Us On Social Media:

Facebook

Facebook Author Page

Instagram

Also by Tara Baisden

<u>Laurel Ridge Series</u>

#1. Season of Hope

#2. Finding Grace

#3. His Perfect Plan

#4. Love Redeemed

#5 Snowbound Blessings

#6 Sheltered Hearts

#7 Restoring Faith

#8 Love Rekindled

#9 Where She Belongs

#10 Shelter in His Arms

#11 Where Love Stands

#12 The Pieces We Mend

#13 Where Love Grows

#14 Where Hearts Heal

#15 Harvest of the Heart

#16 Heart of the Season

About The Author

Tara Baisden writes the kind of sweet, wholesome romances that feel cozy, comforting, and full of heart. She's the author of the beloved *Laurel Ridge* and *Riverbend Valley* inspirational series, as well as the *Mistletoe Falls* series, where Christmas magic and small-town charm are always on the menu.

A proud West Virginian, Tara makes her home on a peaceful stretch of mountain land where deer wander past her windows, the garden never quite weeds itself, and her pets supervise her writing schedule with great dedication. When she's not dreaming up stories of love, faith, and second chances, you'll likely find her quilting, digging in the dirt (sometimes successfully), hiking in the mountains, or curled up with a good book.

Family means everything to Tara, and some of her favorite moments are spent on the porch with loved ones—sharing stories, laughter, and maybe a slice of pie (because every good gathering needs pie). She also loves exploring the rich history of her home state and can't resist stopping at any bookstore she comes across.

Tara's readers often say her characters feel like family and her fictional towns like places they'd love to visit. Through every story, she hopes to inspire faith, celebrate love, and remind readers of the beauty found in life's simple joys.

You can connect with Tara at www.tarabaisden.com or follow her on social media for new releases, behind-the-scenes peeks, and the occasional glimpse of country life.

About Mistletoe Falls

Welcome to the fictional town of Mistletoe Falls, Tennessee!

Where Christmas Magic Lives Year-Round

*H*igh in the Tennessee mountains, where winter lingers longer and Christmas spirit fills the air year-round, lies a town that feels almost too perfect to be real and looks like it stepped straight out of a holiday postcard.

The winding mountain road to Mistletoe Falls tells you this isn't just any destination. Scenic Route 265 climbs higher into the Smoky Mountains with each breathtaking curve, past ancient trees heavy with snow that arch over the road like nature's own cathedral. But it's the final approach that steals your breath—crossing the enchanting Snowbell Covered Bridge, draped in evergreen garland and twinkling lights, as it spans the crystal waters of Mistletoe Creek below.

Beyond the bridge, the Welcome Pavilion greets every arrival with a hand-carved wooden sign: *"Welcome to Mistletoe Falls—Home of the Christmas Spirit."* The cheerful red pavilion, complete with candy cane striping and an archway of year-round twinkle lights, promises that something wonderful awaits just around the bend.

Mistletoe Falls (population 6,200) nestles in a perfect valley where the musical sound of cascading waterfalls mingles with church bells and children's laughter. The town spreads gracefully along Mistletoe Creek, whose series of waterfalls create the melodic backdrop to daily life.

This is Tennessee's beloved Christmas Town—because Christmas simply lives here. From the gas lamp streetlights wrapped in evergreen garland to the horse-drawn carriages clip-clopping down brick streets, every detail whispers of simpler times and sweeter moments.

The town square draws everyone like a magnet, centered around a Victorian gazebo where carols drift through the air and community life unfolds. Ancient oak trees frame the square, their branches creating natural shelter for the wooden benches below—each dedicated to a beloved neighbor who helped shape this special place. Thousands of lights transform the square into pure magic.

Mistletoe Lane curves gently around the town square before branching into charming side streets lined with century-old brick buildings. Each storefront tells a story through hand-carved details and cheerful striped awnings in hunter green, burgundy, and cream. Wide brick sidewalks invite leisurely strolls, while cozy benches appear just when you need them most.

The architecture whispers of careful love—original stonework preserved alongside modern conveniences, ensuring comfort while honoring the past. Three-story buildings house everything from the town bakery to the bookshop, with apartments above where business owners live.

From November through February, Mistletoe Falls transforms into a living snow globe. The special mountain microclimate ensures gentle snowfall that blankets everything in pristine white, while temperatures hover between 15 and 45 degrees—perfect for outdoor adventures and cozy indoor moments.

The partially frozen waterfalls become nature's chandeliers, catching winter light like thousands of diamonds. Snow-covered trails wind through frosted forests where the only sounds are your footsteps and the distant laughter from the town below. Long winter evenings mean crackling fireplaces, hot cider, and the kind of conversations that matter.

The Mistletoe Lodge stands as the town's crown jewel—a century-old mountain lodge with wraparound porches and stone fireplaces where love stories begin over morning coffee and evening wine. Its guest rooms blend historic charm with modern comfort, creating the perfect retreat for visitors who never quite want to leave.

The Snowbell Covered Bridge serves as more than transportation; it's where proposals happen and first kisses are shared, sheltered from mountain weather while framing perfect views of the approaching town.

The Mistletoe Christmas Tree Farm spreads across rolling hills on the town's outskirts, where families create memories among rows of Fraser firs and the air smells like pine and possibility.

What makes Mistletoe Falls magical isn't just its picture-perfect setting—it's the people who call it home. Three generations often work side by side in family businesses, while newcomers quickly discover they're not visitors but neighbors-in-waiting.

Local business owners coordinate holiday decorations and community events with the kind of collaboration that creates the seamless magic visitors remember long after they've returned home. This isn't performed charm—it's the real thing, preserved and protected by people who understand what they have.

In Mistletoe Falls, Christmas isn't a season—it's a way of life. The town square's gazebo hosts summer concerts alongside winter caroling. Local shops maintain touches of holiday magic through every season, because visitors quickly learn that any time is the right time to discover this special place.

The waterfalls provide cooling mists in summer and ice sculptures in winter. Mountain trails offer wildflower walks in spring and dramatic vistas in fall. But somehow, every season here feels like it's building toward December's grand celebration.

www.ingramcontent.com/pod-product-compliance
Lightning Source LLC
Chambersburg PA
CBHW011845300726
48970CB00009B/2652